The Skin of the Sky

The Skin of the Sky

Elena Poniatowska

Translated from the Spanish by Deanna Heikkinen

Farrar, Straus and Giroux

New York

Farrar, Straus and Giroux
19 Union Square West, New York 10003

Copyright © 2001 by Elena Poniatowska
Translation copyright © 2004 by Farrar, Straus and Giroux, LLC
All rights reserved
Distributed in Canada by Douglas & McIntyre Ltd.
Originally published in 2001 by Ediciones Alfaguara, S.A., as *La piel del cielo*
Published in the United States by Farrar, Straus and Giroux
First American edition, 2004

Library of Congress Control Number: 2004109452

ISBN-13: 978-0-374-26575-5
ISBN-10: 0-374-26575-5

Designed by Jonathan D. Lippincott

www.fsgbooks.com

1   2   3   4   5   6   7   8   9   10

To Mane and Viviana, Felipe and Pepi,
Paula and Lorenzo, my children

The Skin of the Sky

"Mamá, does the world end over there?"

"No, it doesn't."

"Prove it to me."

"I'll take you farther from there than you can see with the naked eye."

Lorenzo listened to his mother as he watched the horizon at dusk. Florencia was his accomplice, his friend; they communicated merely by looking at each other. That was why she yielded to the urgency in her son's voice, and the very next day, as she held the little one's hand, she bought second-class tickets to Cuautla at the San Lázaro station in Mexico City.

Lorenzo was thrilled when the locomotive pulled out, and as he watched the landscape fly by in the opposite direction, bidding him farewell, he was filled with amazement. Why was it that the posts flew by so quickly, but the mountains didn't move at all? And what bothered him most was the line of the horizon. He was sure they would reach the end of the world and fall into the abyss, train and all. As they approached the peak of the mountain, Lorenzo kept getting up out of his seat, crying, "Here comes the cliff; it's going to end."

Florencia could see the fear in the boy's eyes. "No, Lorenzo, you'll see, it begins again. You're going to come to a valley and then another valley. There are other mountains after Popo and Iztá, another horizon. The Earth is round, and it spins; it doesn't have an end. It continues, continues, and continues. The sunset revolves and goes to other countries. It's never-ending."

That trip nourished Lorenzo for months. Before falling asleep, he would go over it again and again to see if he had missed something. But it raised more questions. "Mamá, is what I see just an insignificant part of the whole?" The alarming limitation of the senses was another cause for his sleeplessness. "Why can't eyes see farther away? Why can't they take in more space? Mamá, am I the one who can't grasp any more?"

"Pretty soon I won't have answers for you. You'll find them at school," she said.

Florencia knew all about the Earth and the sky, the multitude of living creatures in the air and in the water. "We have to cover up real well tonight because it's going to be cold. See, my son, how many stars there are and how they shine?" The children didn't need school. Florencia delighted in teaching all five of them. She hadn't counted on the fact that her eldest would question what was already established as fact. They only needed one book, the one about nature. "Okay, Emilia, draw me a circle here in the dirt," Florencia said. "Lorenzo, you draw another one on top of it."

Juan and Leticia were spectators.

"Juan, tell me what it is."

"It's two tomatoes on top of each other," Juan said.

"An eight!" shouted Lorenzo.

They laughed. The circles multiplied, as did the sticks, the dots over the *i*'s, and Florencia's stories about the age of the trees, the rings on the trunks that expanded with the years, the pollen in the center of flowers, the convex crystal that could light a bonfire with the sun's rays.

Florencia never stopped dazzling them. Her face would bead up with sweat as she played with her children. It was impossible to resist the magic of her body, her legs that danced in time to some internal music.

Lorenzo and Juan looked alike; they had the same build, the same inquisitive eyes, the same nervousness. And what grace Emilia and Leticia had. "Little angels," Florencia's friend Doña Trini called them. They walked on their tippy-toes and smiled at everyone they met. "Here come the little angels," the neighbors said.

Waking up in San Lucas was to open oneself to the first rays of the sun. Laughing, Florencia sat them down to breakfast. Hot golden bread out of a golden basket, along with jam and butter she had made herself. The large cups of café con leche, ay, marvelous!

"Let's see who can make the best milk mustache." She laughed as she watched her children, with Santiago, the youngest, on her knees. Lorenzo and Emilia, the oldest, consumed her with their eyes; the next in line, Leticia and Juan, couldn't live without her. After breakfast they ran to the garden to finish their chores. "Emilia and Lorenzo are the only ones allowed to get water from the well."

They were also the ones chosen to light the candles at night and to let La Blanquita, the cow, out to the pasture. Emilia even knew how to milk her. Lorenzo liked the sound of the milk squirting into the bucket, but nothing enticed him as much as visiting their horse, El Arete. The moment Lorenzo entered the barn, El Arete turned his head with the grandest gesture imaginable and fixed his twinkling eyes on the door. Watchful, ears perked up, he seemed to be asking a question. He was all liquidy gold, a gold with so much red in it that they had considered calling him Colorado. Florencia preferred El Arete—the earring—because he was delicate, fine, and shiny, like the earrings that swung from her earlobes.

The horse was seven years old, three years younger than Lorenzo. "That animal is more mysterious than the pyramids of Teotihuacán," Florencia said. "We'll never really know him. This horse is yours, Lorenzo, and the donkey is for Emilia."

"Yes, yes. Emilia can have the donkey," he said.

Florencia invested so much ritual in the morning tasks on the farm that it sanctified them. Nothing was more important than doing things properly to start the day out right. The animals had to be cared for, and the trees and plants as well. The order of the world depended on the work being done conscientiously.

Amado, "the de Tenas' worker," arrived at six. The children loved him. Nobody really knew where he came from or where he slept, but his total devotion to Doña Florencia was immediately apparent. He baled the hay, arranged the bales, cleaned the stable, and fixed what was beyond repair with a slow, sunny-warm knowledge while he spun yarns about his village in an unhurried voice.

The children were allowed to accompany him in the afternoons, to sell the leftover milk and walk through the tree-lined Coyoacán neighborhood, because he looked after them better than any woman would. He took special care of Santiago, the youngest.

Sitting atop Amado's shoulders was the perfect way for the child to experience the world. With this creature on his shoulders, Amado looked like Saint Christopher walking in the middle of the river.

Years earlier, he had carried Lorenzo the very same way as he told him stories about Roman gladiators.

In one story, Graco, the best of all the gladiators, the most skillful and impetuous of the slaves, asked permission of the emperor to fight against his master. Although surprised, because no one had ever requested this, the emperor conceded—if and only if the old man agreed.

The young Graco came upon his mentor, his hair white and his muscles tired, seated in the afternoon sun on a warm rock, his noble countenance in a meditative state.

"Teacher, I want to fight you."

"Why me, son? I have taught you everything you know."

"Because you are the only one I have not defeated."

The veteran gladiator eyed him at length. "All right, we'll fight."

The fighters entered the Coliseum amid all the bluster and expectation of the crowd. From his gold-and-silver royal box, the emperor gave the signal. The fight began. As it went on, the young man looked stronger and more agile, and the old man stumbled, breathless, under Graco's merciless blows. A female lament ran through the stadium each time the teacher hit the dirt. Lorenzo imagined the fighters, the short tunics and the strong legs shod with sandals like the ones in the book he leafed through at night with his mother.

Once, when his teacher fell, Graco dared to put his foot on him, and a sharp murmur ripped through the circle around the arena. The old man was bleeding, not a single place on his body uninjured. Then, to the bewilderment of the crowd, he knocked the young man down and seized his neck tightly, but without killing him. The emperor declared the old master victorious, the most outstanding of all the gladiators, and as they left together through the tunnel of the Coliseum, Graco protested. "Master, you never showed me that move."

"No, I didn't. It is called the traitor lock."

Lorenzo felt the same elation from that story as he did when Florencia showed him how to decipher letters—those little dancing black spiders that were so difficult to capture. "There are twenty-six of them. Remember that, twenty-six." Thanks to her, he excelled in his first year of school because he already knew how to read, add, and subtract. "I never finished elementary school, son," Florencia said. "I don't want the same thing to happen to all of you." She taught with every step they took around the small farm. She would draw a symbol in the dirt: "Guess what letter this is." In the kitchen, she had them watch for the exact moment the milk would rise, so they would understand pasteurization. Fascinated by the explosion of the bubbles and the rising steam, the older ones would argue about whose turn it was to take the pot off the stove in time. "Look, they dance and sing."

At night the mysteries became more incomprehensible, unfathomable. Florencia taught them to recognize Ursa Major and Minor and the Seven Sisters, and at home by candlelight she showed them how to hold their fingers to make a butterfly, a snail, or a wolf with shadow play on the wall. Then there was the magic of soap bubbles. "They float because they weigh less than the air," she'd tell them, and from there it was just a hop, skip, and jump to the story of the Wright brothers. Lorenzo took that leap easily, holding Florencia's hand.

The animals on the farm were part of their education. What a wonder it was to see the baby chick—that ugly and frail little thing with its ridiculous peeping—become a majestic rooster with a monarchic crest within just a few months. That rooster had much to flaunt, and his attitude impressed Lorenzo, especially his scornful treatment of females. He would mount a hen furiously, and the fool would submit, bending her beak and closing her eyes. The intense vibration of their feathers ignited the atmosphere as well as Lorenzo's thoughts. An enormous wave of life came from the corral whenever the rooster broke into song, which was answered by the other roosters in the Coyoacán neighborhood. "Kikirikí, I don't want any slackers around me," Florencia sang, clapping gaily. The rooster, his neck stretched out, exploded like a flamboyant tree. He was an animal in flower, a red-feathered flower that challenged the universe.

Sometimes the red member of Orion, their sheepdog, came out of his thicket of fur, which intrigued Lorenzo. With Santiago in her arms, tied tightly inside the rebozo ("He gets heavier every day." Florencia smiled), his mother put everything into perspective with a naturalness that Lorenzo would never find in another woman. "He wants to put it into some bitch." Seeing her son's rapt attention to the rooster and Orion, Florencia explained that all species—plants, animals, humans—procreated so as not to die. "It's their desire, son."

"What do you mean, desire?"

"Desire for life."

When the cow began to bellow, Doña Trini lent them a bull, but he mounted her so quickly that Lorenzo missed it. Or maybe Florencia just didn't encourage a view of the spectacle. She sent her son with Amado to pay Doña Trini. Nine months later, when La Blanquita was ready to have her calf, Florencia called the older ones. "I'll need you to bring me water."

La Blanquita began to pace back and forth in the stable, desperate, her hooves scraping the rocks. She went from the manger to the door, unable to get comfortable. Something in her belly shook her entire body, she had to get rid of the encumbrance, and every now and then a hoarse bellow escaped her throat. At a certain moment, as if being ordered, she went to the hay and spread her legs. Something inside her must have opened up, because she doubled over under the impact. "It's not coming out," said Florencia. She rolled her sleeve above her elbow and put her hand, and then her entire arm, into the cow's bloody insides. "It's coming just fine now; it's coming just fine," she said loudly, and she pulled. First the enormous head came out and then the body, the skinny legs, the delicate hooves pressed against the ribs.

As the drenched calf lay on the hay, Florencia's arm kept rummaging around inside La Blanquita, and with eyes half closed, the cow allowed it. Florencia was searching for something, and when she found it, she pulled hard and brought out a gelatinous red bag that to Lorenzo looked like a huge twisted tongue. The calf didn't move, and the cow had become distant and indifferent.

Florencia washed her arm in the bucket as her two eldest children looked on, frightened. And she said, "Throw that water out and bring more."

When they returned, the placenta (that's what their mother called it) was gone, as was the dribbling blood. She caressed La Blanquita, rubbed the star on her forehead. The children were quiet. Then Florencia spoke to the calf: "Now you, stand up. Come on."

She encircled its belly and back, supporting it against her chest. The calf got to its knees and then up on its feet, balancing. Turning to her children, Florencia said triumphantly, "You see that? What it takes humans a year and a half to accomplish, an animal can do at birth."

Lorenzo was spellbound. Oh, my mountain flower, oh my water flower, my Florencia!

The days that followed brought the pleasure of watching the cow nurse her calf as it stood under her great belly as if under a protective sky. La Blanquita, back to her old self, licked her offspring, nuzzled it with her forehead, then licked again. Her powerful hot stream of urine yellowed the dung-covered floor, and she filled her four stomachs, chewing slowly and constantly, her enormous udders resting on top of the newborn that sucked them impolitely.

That San Lucas farm was a celebration of life. The luminosity, whether from the sky or his mother, caused Lorenzo to squint. After the rain, the smell of fresh grass rose from the ground, and the trees dripped their greenness, filling him with feeling. Lorenzo would always associate the smell of wet dirt with his mother, not knowing that sometimes nature can take revenge, which Florencia could never do.

Only his father's visits darkened Lorenzo's days. The pleasure that their mother's presence afforded the children was inhibited by their progenitor. He descended from a taxicab, wearing gloves. Even his words wore gloves, and his blue gaze, very foreign, rested with indifference on the dirt-packed floor of the house.

"Children, come greet your father."

Florencia took a chair out to the patio. Don Joaquín de Tena did not make the least effort to help her. As he sat down, he lifted his pant leg so as not to wrinkle the crease. And Florencia looked at him with eyes like La Blanquita's, damp and sweet, sometimes imploringly. Lorenzo did not like one thing about that stiff man, with his silver-handled cane or his black umbrella, depending on the weather.

"Tell your father what you've been up to."

Emilia would become lively, communicative. The smaller ones interrupted, without getting close, to avoid getting him dirty. Lorenzo never said a word. Don Joaquín de Tena barely noticed them, his gaze faded, as if his eyes, sunken deep in their sockets, could achieve no color. Dead fish eyes, thought Lorenzo. It didn't matter to this man that his eldest son never spoke to him. He never even noticed. He regarded his children as a bunch, like grapes. He didn't distinguish among them.

"Say good-bye to your father." And Florencia sent them to bed.

Lorenzo never noticed when his father left. He did know that some of his clothes were in the closet. "Your father's shirts," said Florencia as she ironed them meticulously with her callused countrywoman's hands.

Don Joaquín de Tena lived in the Juarez section of the city with his sister, and on Sunday afternoons he traveled to Coyoacán in a cab. He made that trip in deference to Florencia.

For him, for his sister, Cayetana de Tena, for Mexican society as a whole, Joaquín was single. His social class nullified his union with Florencia, and therefore his children didn't exist. No de Tena would acknowledge an illegitimate child. On several occasions Cayetana quietly discussed the farm woman—Joaquín's mistake—with her trusted cousin Carito, as if she were an illness to be vaccinated against. At times two weeks would go by and Joaquín wouldn't come. Sometimes even three months, and Florencia would explain, in case they missed him, "Your father went to a reunion with his former classmates at Stonyhurst, in England," or, "Your father went to Vichy for the healing waters." Not even a postcard. How nice for Lorenzo. The less news, the better. That man came between them and their mother.

———

But Don Joaquín did something even worse. He denigrated her with his very presence, although maybe it was only Lorenzo who noticed. His mother may not have known about Piccadilly Circus, but she realized that the Earth was not the center of the universe, and she concluded therefore that man was not the center of the world. Believing that, she put everything into its rightful proportion. "Let's not make a mountain out of a molehill," she would say to Emilia, who tended to be overly dramatic. "Tonight it seems enormous to you. Tomorrow you'll realize its insignificance."

"It's just that father doesn't pay any attention to me; he doesn't see me," Emilia would shout, pulling her hair.

"So? He doesn't pay attention to me either, and it hasn't killed me," Lorenzo answered. What was the significance of the cry of an unloved little girl beneath the immensity of the celestial canopy?

If Florencia missed Don Joaquín, it wasn't apparent. She had her children, the animals, and the plants, so there was no opportunity to long for the past. When Santi—the one she always carried in her arms—slept wrapped up in his crib and she sewed or mended their clothing, one of the other children would lean up against her knees. "Mamá, tell me a story."

She had no time for thoughts that did not focus on the immediate present. After a prolonged absence by Don Joaquín, Lorenzo heard her tell Amado that the money was running out. Amado must have done something. Maybe he asked around the neighborhood. Who knows what he did, but ten days later Florencia was offered a job selling candy in the concession stand at the Eden movie theater, and she agreed to be there before the four-o'clock show and to bring her two eldest to help her. Lorenzo's and Emilia's lives were no longer confined to their garden paradise after that. They identified with the images projected on the screen, images that caused them both great uneasiness, hurling them into the unknown.

One night, at home, Lorenzo heard a pleading tone in his mother's voice that he had never heard before.

"How can you sell candy at a movie theater?" Don Joaquín demanded.

"Because I don't have enough money. You have to understand, Joaquín, there are a lot of mouths to feed. I can't manage any other way."

"I cannot allow my son to walk around carrying a box of candy at the Eden. What happens if someone recognizes him?"

"No one knows us. You've been careful to make sure of that. The only person who comes to the farm from time to time is Doña Trini, and it's always to help us out."

"Oh, yes, the one who's always wearing an apron."

"She may be in an apron, but she soothes my soul as lovingly as La Blanquita licks her calf."

"People in Coyoacán know who the children are, Florencia, and a lot of people go to the Eden movie theater."

"Not people from your neighborhood. The Eden is a community movie theater."

"I cannot allow it."

At that moment Lorenzo heard his mother sob. It was the first time ever. I'll kill that man, I'll kill him, he thought, shaking with rage. He would have gone into his mother's room and hit him if the door had not been locked.

2

Lorenzo became friends with Don Silvestre, the projectionist at the Eden, who allowed him to stay in the projection booth, candy box and all. At intermission he would run out quickly to sell. "Candy, gum, chocolates, candied peanuts," he'd yell up and down the aisles as he slipped between the rows of seats. When the lights went out, he returned to the booth, and the backstitching sound of the projector was his lullaby. Florencia stopped worrying about the content of the movies: Lorenzo had followed the story lines at first, but another interest soon caught his attention. When Don Silvestre rewound the film in the booth, the water went back into the jug, the storm returned to the sky, the rose became a bud, the arrow sprang back to the bow, and Lorenzo spent his time racking his brain trying to figure out if humans could go back to being children.

The neighborhood ragamuffins barely got into the lobby, tickets in hand, before they buzzed around the candy counter, enticed by the honey eyes of thirteen-year-old Emilia, her breath smelling of licorice, her lips redder than the chewy red candies, and her waist sylphlike. Florencia sent her back to the garden plot, saying, "The Eden isn't for you. You'd better stay at home and take care of your little brothers and sister." With Emilia's absence, some of the boys disappeared, but others weren't concerned. Lorenzo noticed that they also found his mother desirable. Oh, my sweet, my Florencia, with your body of blooming petals!

One of the parasites ventured to say, "Tell me what time you close, so I can walk you home."

Florencia answered sternly, "My son is the gentleman who accompanies me."

Lorenzo pestered Don Silvestre with questions: "What is light? What material is film made of? What are camera lenses like?"

These were mysteries that the good projectionist had never thought about, even in his wildest dreams. One afternoon the reel broke on Don Silvestre, and Lorenzo cut it, pasted it, and started it running again. "Who would know what time is?" he harassed the projectionist.

"I think your teacher at school must know," Don Silvestre answered.

Florencia was more explicit: "To me time is a measurement, a stopwatch. It's ungraspable; it moves; it doesn't belong to anyone."

"I want to know if it's air, if it's space. What the heck is it, Mamá?"

Her son's intensity scared her. She perceived his anguish and thought, My son will never be happy. She had to shake him, lighten him up, train him to be less serious.

> *"Pretty bubbles, so rich and fine*
> *Such seductive shades and kinds*
> *Bubbles, bubbles, bubbles of love*
> *Bubbles that burst with your touch*
> *That burst like an oh so fragile illusion!"*

Florencia spun her children around, singing:

> *"These dreams are seagulls*
> *That travel to the most remote beaches*
> *Sprinkling the fleecy waves*
> *With their feathers that widen the sea."*

Although all four of them whirled around her and danced with one another—with Santi sometimes in her arms and sometimes in Emilia's—those sessions were meant for Lorenzo. His arm around his mother's waist, he also danced his own sweet illusions of a love gone by: "Mamá, don't you love my father anymore?"

"Of course I do, silly one. Why wouldn't I love him?"

"Because of the pretty bubbles that burst."

"That's a song, son, not reality."

"Then what is reality, Mamá?"

"Ay, son, reality is everything we see and touch with our hands."

"And what we can't see but is still there, is that also reality?"

"Of course."

"But what about the invisible, what you and I only feel, is that reality?"

"Yes, that too."

"And what's in my heart is a reality?"

"Of course, Lorenzo, it's your reality, even though you don't share it with anyone."

One afternoon when he was very young, Lorenzo rushed into his mother's arms after Don Joaquín had scolded her. He wouldn't let go. He didn't want to sleep in his own bed. He slept next to her, his head on her pillow. "This child understands everything," Florencia told Doña Trini the next day. From that moment on, Florencia never attempted to return him to his place among his brothers and sisters.

Joaquín de Tena noticed the strong bond. "Listen, Flor, it's time for that little boy to let go of your apron strings."

If Florencia had realized how much she influenced her son's life, she would have limited her empire, but she was a fiery woman, certain that she would always have him by her side. They established not only a mother-son relationship but a complicity that she would never have with Joaquín.

At times Florencia became impatient. There was no way to satisfy her eldest son's questions. "Lorenzo, time is an illusion." Was it really?

Then the boy would ask, "What is an illusion?"

Florencia would respond, "It's a dream."

"What is a dream?"

"It's a phenomenon that happens in our brains while we sleep."

"Then I have already had an illusion."

"Yes, and you've also had nightmares and woken up crying, and now let's go to the yard; it's time to feed the chickens."

Lorenzo would have liked to be bigger, to embrace her and never let her out of his grasp.

Don Joaquín de Tena was not the head of the family, either at the small farm or at his sister's house, but there was nevertheless a dignity in his countenance, something calm between his brows and his sunken eye sockets. Don Joaquín would never hurt anyone; even Lorenzo perceived that. He would withdraw first. He was not involved in life. He would never throw himself into the struggle. He had nothing in common with the rooster in the yard, neither its ferocity nor its retort to the other roosters.

Florencia, on the other hand, was a fighting cock. And Lorenzo would be too; of course he would. He wanted nothing to do with that well-ironed dandy who showed up on Sundays.

The worst thing Florencia could have done to her five children was to die. One night a black butterfly flew into her bedroom, and within ten minutes Florencia was no longer breathing. That's what Doña Trini told Lorenzo. Without understanding, the children went in to see her lying on the bed, her hair loosely spread across the white pillow, her hands folded, and a sad black rosary in her fingers. They had never seen her pray. She appeared to be asleep, a smile on her lips. Stunned, Lorenzo begged her to wake up. They took him out of the room. No one cried. That night, Amado and Trini lit the candles, and a monotonous praying pierced the children's ears. At dawn, still not understanding, Lorenzo went out to pace back and forth between the stable and the vegetable garden. Doña Trini yelled through the trees, "Lorenzo, come have breakfast." The boy didn't come. "Lorenzo, come eat lunch." "Lorenzo come have a snack."

Amado went to look for him. Who knows what he saw in the boy's eyes, but he came back without him. "It's best to leave him alone," he told the neighbor. Finally Lorenzo showed up in the kitchen, and Doña Trini put a bowl of soup on the table without a word.

At eight o'clock on Monday morning, all five children traveled in a cab from Coyoacán to the heart of Mexico City. One suitcase held all their clothes.

They never saw Trini or Amado ever again.

Lorenzo heard Doña Cayetana order Tila, the cook, "Take the orphans up and show them their bedrooms—the two girls together,
the two little ones together, and the biggest one at the very top, in
the attic." From that day on, their aunt, Aunt Tana, would refer to
them as the orphans, as if they had no father either. In truth, they
didn't. They would greet Don Joaquín once a day, kissing his hand,
but he remained as distant as always.

"Get ready. You're going to school tomorrow," ordered Aunt
Tana. "Thanks to my cousin Carito Escandón, I was able to get the
Marist order to accept you."

The torture of it all wasn't the building, or the multitude of
children in the patio at recess, or the priests, or the supervisors, or
the old desks, or the dirty latrines; the hellish part was Aunt
Tana's, "Hurry up; run, run." She had instructed Tila to put four
glasses of milk on the windowsill that faced the street, each glass
covered with a sweet roll, and the children were supposed to eat on
the run, with one foot out the door. "Outside, go ahead, outside.
Run you'll be late." At the last minute she grabbed Santiago by the
collar. "Not you. You stay here." Astounded, Juan and Leticia left,
sweet rolls in their hands. By the third day, Lorenzo threw his into
a sewer. He would never be able to accept anything from that
woman.

Too proud, Lorenzo and Emilia never asked what had become of
the small farm, the animals, Amado, Doña Trini, Coyoacán. Once,
Emilia went up to Lorenzo's attic room to ask him timidly, "How do
you think my little donkey is?"

"I don't know anything about that donkey," Lorenzo answered
angrily.

Emilia cried all the tears she had not cried since her mother's
death. Then they heard Aunt Tana's sharp voice order the older orphans to come downstairs to recite the daily rosary, since they were
the only ones missing.

"Hail Mary, full of grace, the Lord is with thee; blessed art thou
among women, and blessed is the fruit of thy womb, Jeeeeeesus . . ."
Aunt Tana's singsong voice always ended on a questioning note so
that the small community at 177 calle Lucerna could respond.
There were Tila, two other servant girls, Don Joaquín and his five

orphans, and Don Manuel, Aunt Tana's tall and almost nonexistent husband, whom she dominated completely. Any guest invited for tea was immediately required to join in the rosary ritual. Even Mr. Buckley, a North American banker, was privy to this custom among good Mexican families, where the servants were the equals of their employers when they stood before the Virgin of Guadalupe and an ivory crucifix. Mr. Buckley's importance in the house on Lucerna was quite obvious as Doña Tana ordered the five children to greet him at the door and say in unison, "Welcome, welcome, Mr. Buckley." Such ceremony was humiliating to Lorenzo; nonetheless, he watched Mr. Buckley closely to determine what it was that made him so unique.

Doña Cayetana, her husband, and her brother spoke French at the table "*à cause des domestiques.*" Lorenzo and Emilia were the only ones who were privileged enough to sit with the adults. "I'll never learn French," Emilia screamed, covering her ears one noontime before she left the table. "French gags me. I prefer English."

"Little girl, don't make tacos out of your food."

"That's how my mother taught me."

"You're going to have to get rid of that nasty habit. Anyone who sits at my table must have good manners. Emilia, why don't you bow your head when the Host is raised?"

"Why should I hide my face if I want to know what's going on?"

"It's time for you all to start catechism classes. Your mother educated you like savages."

Emilia defied her: "Don't you mess with my mother, because I won't be responsible for what might happen." One time Emilia got into the lotus position on the living-room rug, remembering how she used to sit on the floor with her mother.

Tana yelled at her. "What's wrong with you? Do you think you're a dog? No decent young lady sits cross-legged on the floor!" Cayetana's perpetually arched eyebrow was a condemnation of her nieces' and nephews' manners.

"Give French a try," advised Tila in the kitchen. "You'll see how happy it'll make the señora."

The priests at school were French. The prefects came from France. Tana and Carito ran into the father superior, *Mon père* Laville, in Casa Armand, the most exclusive store, choosing brocade for his chasuble from a sumptuous spread of fabrics, because he distrusted the taste of the embroidery nuns. "I select it personally," he boasted.

Emilia's graceful figure would soon disappear from the house. A determined Doña Tana, with the help of a charity raffle among her friends at the order of San Vicente, was able to purchase her a one-way ticket to San Antonio, Texas, where Tana's cousin, Almudena de Tena, would oversee the girl's nursing studies. "Pull your hair up, Emilia. Only maids wear it down to go out in public." Emilia's hair was an impertinence, similar in color to El Arete, and on the streets it ignited stares. Pedestrians and drivers jeered and whistled, impressed by the smallness of her waist, her long legs, her breasts like two apples. "Hey there, cutie-pie!" Intolerable, a de Tena at the mercy of these brazen ragamuffins. So when Emilia expressed an interest in nursing, Doña Cayetana Escandón de Tena remembered Almudena, in Houston, who was married to a doctor.

Emilia left with a tiny suitcase, her hair loose and hanging to her waist. With the secret hope of succeeding in America, she was happy to leave the detested house but sad to abandon her brothers and sister. She determined at least to send for Santiago, who needed her the most. He could work in a bank like Mr. Buckley. "Sure, I'll be glad to help the little fellow out once he's over here," the banker had said on one occasion.

"Hail Mary, full of grace, the Lord is with thee; blessed art thou among women, and blessed is the fruit of thy womb, Jesus . . ."

But for the orphans, Florencia, with flowers growing from her head, was the one to revere—much more than the Virgin Mary.

"Brother, when you throw a rock into the air and it moves in a straight line in front of you, why does it fall to the ground?" asked Juan.

"It doesn't move in a straight line. It makes a parabola and then falls," answered Lorenzo.

"Why does it fall?"

"Because of gravity, everything falls."

"Gravity is the most important force on Earth? If we remove all the other forces, does gravity stay?"

"I suppose so."

"But how does the rock move in the air? Does it spin?"

"I haven't thought about it."

"When you do, will you tell me?"

"Sure, Juan."

"What is all this foolish talk?" interrupted Tana. "From what I've been told, Juan, you seem to care a lot about rocks—playing war in the streets with a band of hoodlums. Your time would be better spent teaching that little sister of yours something useful, since she watches you with those big eyes. Come on, let's get to those multiplication tables."

Both brothers knew them by heart, which infuriated Leticia, who covered her ears charmingly with her dimpled hands.

"When your daughters outgrow their dresses, give them to me for Leticia," Aunt Tana said to Carito Escandón on the telephone. "You see what a cute shape she has."

Leticia had grown as slender as Emilia, but was more independent, more self-assured, better adapted to the circumstances. Affable, she spun like a colorful top. She would affectionately hug the adults who would allow it. She was fair-skinned, with wavy hair and big green eyes. Cayetana would boast, "Thank God that one takes after us."

Lorenzo also fell under his younger sister's spell. The girl followed him everywhere. Crossing her arms like a sergeant, at mealtime she would inquire, "Have you washed your hands, Lorenzo? I know you only wash them when you first wake up." One morning Lorenzo heard someone whistling, and he felt as if a bird had flown right into his chest. He suddenly saw his mother in Leticia.

Tana's recrimination sprung out like a black cat: "Girls don't whistle!"

"Ay, Aunt, don't be mean. Get me a canary. We need a canary in the house, Auntie!" She sang. She made everyone laugh. She was the only one to throw her arms around her aunt's neck, and to everyone's astonishment, Tana would hug her back.

Within a week Tila brought in a canary along with the heads of lettuce and the veal roast. "They sold it to me real cheap at the market."

Juan, the second boy, had a mysterious life that Doña Cayetana distrusted. She didn't like him. One night, after she accused him of stealing three silver ashtrays, Juan dared to dance a frenetic dance in the semidarkness of the hallway. His moving body reflected on the walls like shadow play. He sang in response:

> *"Damned witch,*
> *whom all will decry;*
> *outrageous witch,*
> *soon you will putrefy."*

At times Lorenzo would ask himself who Juan really was, what he did. He got good grades at school, but he never expected any reward. Maybe he rewarded himself, but how? He went out into the streets alone. None of his brothers and sisters shared his solitude, and now that Emilia was gone, Lorenzo would run upstairs and shut himself in his room. "Don't bother him," his aunt would say. "He has to study." Outside, on the way to school, Lorenzo visualized Juan walking back and forth just as he did, in the same solitary trance, attempting to find his mother, who was also looking for him among one of the hurried figures on the street, and she would bend down right now and hug him. Sometimes, in his desperation, Lorenzo would even hide in wait for his father's silhouette, complete with cane and hat, and he'd imagine his voice saying, Come on, let's go home. But the elegant man would pass right by him, the reality was not broken, and the young de Tena would choose another possible father from among the pedestrians. No one ever spoke to him. Sometimes the dogs followed him for a while and then ran off to another destination. Did that happen to his brother? Do you feel alone, Juan? he wondered. What do you do when you're alone? Where do you go? Neither one was the same boy he'd been before, and each, remaining silent, attempted to prove his self-sufficiency to the other.

Lorenzo was concerned about Juan, but he never said anything. What would become of them? What did their future hold? The innocent little Santiago followed Don Joaquín like a lapdog and accompanied him right up to the door of the taxi when he left for the Ritz. At night, when he saw him return, Santiago would ask, "Father, do you want your slippers?"

The boy wouldn't leave his father's side. As Don Joaquín prepared his toilette, Santiago would hand him his shirt, the hand mirror, his suspenders, his cuff links, the small plate with half a lemon, which he used to smooth his gray hair. Then Santiago would inspect his head to make sure no minuscule piece of citrus had marred the alignment of each scrupulously arranged hair. Don Joaquín was going bald. "Here, here, Father! Wook! Wet me get it off!" The child would follow him downstairs and keep him company during breakfast. He even filled in for Tila, who was busy straightening the bedrooms.

Within a year Don Joaquín declared, "I have my own valet de chambre." The only thing he had taught the child was to count his handkerchiefs and his blue monogrammed shirts that had been embroidered by the nuns, and to read "J. de T.," with the *de* in lowercase letters and more legible than the *J* and the *T*. Santiago could also pronounce the brand name of the French shirt collars—Doucet, Jeune et Fils. In the evening, the boy recognized the sound of the car motor that brought his father back, and he would run to the door.

"Already wagging your tail?" Don Joaquín would ask, amused.

At night the boy would kiss his father's hand, and Don Joaquín would bless him. The other children didn't appear.

3

At the Marist school, Claude Théwissen noticed the intelligence of the de Tena boys and communicated it to his superior. In minutes they were able to solve problems that it took others hours to do. They also brought up new and surprising ideas.

"Imagine, *mon père*," Théwissen told Father Laville, "I had Juan de Tena divide the globe, and he did it exactly and then asked me why two straight lines never meet. In the middle of class he raised his hand and inquired, 'Does the sun have a final destination?' When I told him that it was to cool down and stop emitting light and heat, which would cause us to die, he had this surprising response: 'Professor, I think you are only giving us a partial view of the universe. Besides Earth there are other suns, other planets, and some of them could possibly have life.' The truth is, the boy amazes me. It's fascinating to work with children like that. I'm going to tell them about Abbot Lemaître, who was so knowledgeable on the subject. Lorenzo, the eldest, is more aloof, but he has become passionate about the study of light-years. He does research on his own, and the other day he told me radiantly, 'I read that Earth has been orbiting the sun for more than five million years at the speed of thirty kilometers per second or a hundred and ten thousand kilometers an hour.'" The Belgian seminarian couldn't contain his enthusiasm. "What good fortune to have those two minds with us!"

"What did you say their names were?" asked Father Laville. "I'm going to give Tomasito Braniff's parents their names. They have asked me to find intelligent friends for their son."

The Braniffs' house intrigued Lorenzo and Juan because the boy had a little electric car that he could drive along the garden paths. When they were seated at the Braniff family table with another school friend, Diego Beristain, and his father, Dr. Carlos Beristain, a waiter stood behind the seat of each diner.

The food didn't taste good to Juan because he was being watched so closely, and he turned his head to the big man behind him: "Are you going to leave?"

"I'm here to attend to whatever you may need."

The boy sunk down in his chair. "Are they going to take me to jail?"

"You seem to have a guilty conscience," said young Diego Beristain, who was perfectly comfortable.

Juan's comment made the Braniff boy laugh, and after dessert— a chocolate cake that melted in your mouth—he addressed his new friend like a benevolent prince. "Do you want to ride in my electric car?"

"No. It's not even dangerous."

"Dangerous?"

"What's the thrill of riding around at twenty miles an hour in a garden, when I've hung from the back of cargo trucks that go seventy?" Juan said.

Tomasito Braniff looked at him admiringly. The waiters looked at one another, and Lorenzo asked for a second helping of Black Forest cake. When they left the table, Juan de Tena conceded to get into the little ruby-red Ford, the only one in Mexico, and take a pompous ride around the family park.

Juan's rebelliousness—a new phenomenon in his life—appealed to Tomasito, and Diego Beristain liked Lorenzo. The older brother, who was so serious in the classroom, so pensive, so tied up in his thoughts, would wildly throw his dice at recess and become suicidally daring. "You won't tolerate having anyone beat you," Diego told him. "That's why you take risks." The day of Lorenzo's First Communion, Aunt Tana, Tila, and the other servants had cautioned him to swallow the Host very gently, caressing it with his tongue, because if he chewed it, frogs and snakes would come out of his mouth. "Not only did I sink my teeth into it, but I spit it out and stepped on it," Lorenzo said to his friend.

Diego was shocked. "Oh my gosh."

"They liiiied to me. They lie to us, Diego. You try it yourself— not a thing came out of me."

"No, Lorenzo, your doing it is enough for me." Diego was dis-

concerted by his friend's rage. Why so much hatred? They discussed
the dogmas of faith, the mystery of the Holy Trinity, of the Immaculate Conception, the last rites, the heavenly promise. For Lorenzo,
the great mysteries were the universe and what were called natural
phenomena. He felt that the mysteries of faith, even God, could be
products of human invention.

Diego knighted Lorenzo, and with that endorsement he became
part of Diego's gang. It was a traditional gang, with the fat kid, the
skinny kid, the rich kid, the poor kid, the one that always wears a
cap, the kid that's always late, and the dandy. Besides Víctor Ortiz,
the beggar, the other four—Pedro "La Pipa" Garciadiego; Gabriel
Iturralde, the giant; Salvador Zúñiga, called Chava, the short one;
and Javier Dehesa, the fat little capped one who always raved about
his mother's Spanish tortillas—all followed the powerful Diego
Beristain and his inseparable philosopher Lorenzo de Tena.

Their lack of money was tolerable because they were all penni-
less in those days. Not even Diego had enough for a cheap cup of
coffee at the Chinese coffee shop.

Lorenzo made a suggestion. "Let's take Víctor's glasses off him so
he looks more messed up than he really is, and he can stick his
hand out and beg."

"A little charity for this poor cripple, for the love of God."

With some four centavos they would go into the little coffee
shops. If Víctor—the one with the black circles under his eyes—was
lucky, they'd get enough to go to the movies. If not, they'd walk
down avenida Juárez, joking around, and go into Sanborn's, the tile
house, but just to use the bathroom. One lucky afternoon at the
four-o'clock show, Lorenzo and Diego both spotted an Eversharp
pen lying in the aisle. Diego kicked it so that Lorenzo couldn't reach
it; then Diego threw his entire body across the aisle. Lorenzo dove
also, but too late, because Diego had it under his belly.

"It's mine. I found it," argued Diego.

"No it's not. You kicked it, but I saw it first."

Diego put the pen into his shirt pocket, showing it off, and
when he least expected it, Lorenzo grabbed it.

"It's mine, you thief!" Diego said.

"Come on, man. Let me watch the movie!"

When Lorenzo was distracted, Diego took it back again. Another grab, and Lorenzo got it back. At the climax, Mary Pickford and Douglas Fairbanks resolved everything with a final kiss. After the movie the gang went back to Diego's house, and when he wasn't paying attention, Lorenzo recovered the pen.

"Listen, brother, this is getting serious, eh? You can't leave now. That pen is mine," threatened Diego, who was taller and more muscular than Lorenzo.

"Well, you can go right to hell, because I'm not giving you a thing."

"In that case, you're going to spend the night on the roof. I'm going to sleep."

The gang watched as Diego threw Lorenzo over his shoulder and carried him up the stairs to the roof garden and locked the door leading to the roof.

Just as he was about to fall asleep, Diego heard flowerpots falling like meteors, bursting against the roof. Furious, he went up. "Hey, stupid! What are you doing?"

"Well, see for yourself. I may have lost, but you're the one who's going to be in trouble."

"No, you're the one who's going to get hurt." He gagged him and tied him to one of the pergola columns. "There we go. Now you'll stay put."

Diego went down to his bedroom to sleep, but he had nightmares, because he realized that when he was carrying Lorenzo up the service staircase, he could have dropped him and hurt him.

The next day, Diego got up and ran to untie him. "Come to breakfast." He had asked the cook to make a monstrous brunch with huevos rancheros, cured beef, beans, quesadillas, sweet bread, and coffee. It was served by José, the manservant, who had set a beautiful table.

"Oh my gosh, this is some breakfast," Lorenzo said, and after the orange juice, he reached his hand toward Diego. "Here's the pen, take it."

"That pen? What would I want it for?"

"Well, if you don't want it, I don't either."

"Then let's give it to José."

"Hey, Lorenzo, did you sleep at all?" asked Diego, ashamed.

"Of course. You can sleep great standing up. You had me tied up really well."

When they were out on the street, Lorenzo confessed, beaming. "The truth is, I had a fantastic time. The sky was really black. I could see the constellations, and I knew them all; I never fell asleep. I think it was the first time I've felt good since I've been in the city. You have no idea what you've done for me, Diego."

Diego was overwhelmed as Lorenzo told him that he had recovered an image buried in his memory, the train trip with his mother to see where the world ended. When he finished, Lorenzo said, "Do you realize what you've given me? I haven't been this happy in years."

"Are you going home now?"

"To the terrifying House of Usher? No way! Let's walk."

Diego was going to tell him that he was crazy as a loon, but something in Lorenzo's eyes stopped him, an intensity that scared him, perhaps the same thing Amado had seen in the garden the night Florencia died.

At school, Claude Théwissen asked Father Laville if Lorenzo could become his assistant. "He's perfectly capable of teaching my classes in my absence. The two brothers, Lorenzo and Juan, come to class knowing as much or more than I do. You can't believe, *mon père*, how they study."

And so it was a big surprise when, at the end of the year, *Mon père* Laville announced that Fernando Castillo Trejo had won the first-place prize. The second went to Lorenzo de Tena, and the third was awarded to that good-looking, wealthy boy, Diego Beristain. The same thing happened in Juan's class. They cheated him out of first place.

Lorenzo was furious. "What animals! They've rewarded someone who doesn't deserve it," he protested to Théwissen. It was easy to figure out that Castillo Trejo's father was one of the school's benefactors.

Théwissen was ashamed. "I would have given you the prize, but

I'm only a teacher. I promise to make up for this injustice, which I feel in my own flesh. From now on I'll focus on the two of you."

"Is that all you're going to do about this iniquity?" yelled Juan.

"Unfortunately, justice is not part of our world, but I assure you that within a few years, when you are both lawyers, the others will bow to your superiority."

"You're contradicting yourself. How will they bow before us if justice isn't part of this world?" Lorenzo said sarcastically.

"I want to assure you both that as long as I'm in Mexico, I will protect you."

Juan objected. "We've just witnessed your protection, thank you very much."

Lorenzo and Juan didn't believe him. Théwissen would return to Belgium, abandoning them, just as Florencia had done.

4

Without Lorenzo's realizing it, Juan had distanced himself from school little by little. And from the house as well. They still talked on the bus about light and about the heat emitted by the stars and of going to the observatory in Tacubaya to see the universe through the telescope, but the three-year age difference separated them. Even though, thanks to Lorenzo, Juan joined in with "the older ones," on certain occasions they would tell him, "We cannot take your little brother to this."

"I can't waste any time, brother. I can't go with you today," Juan would say before he was left out.

"What are you going to do?"

"Work."

It was true. He fixed radios here and there, and the shopkeepers and bakers in the neighborhood paid him. What did he do with his money? Who knows? He also stopped sleeping at the house on Lucerna, and it didn't bother Cayetana in the least.

"Leave him alone. He's a man," Tila said to Lorenzo, patting him on the shoulder. "He wanders around. Don't worry, everyone in the neighborhood loves him."

"What about high school?" yelled Lorenzo.

"There's no better school than life," Tila philosophized. "Your father isn't upset, and Juan is his responsibility."

Even though Lorenzo started each day with a declaration of hate for Doña Cayetana and came home at night mulling over the anger accumulated during the day, he was drawn to his father's sister. He once heard Dr. Beristain say, "Cayetana Escandón de Tena is quite a character." And she was. It was impossible not to acknowledge it. And Tana had said the same thing about her nephew. She turned to him for advice, and for the last three years she had asked him to escort her to different government agencies, in hopes of reclaiming her hacienda in Morelos, seized in 1910, during the Revolution.

The de Tena family was not rich, although they lived as if they were. They would not have changed the course of their lives for anything in the world, but no one was to know that Tila turned Joaquín's and Manuel's collars and cuffs inside out and that they owed her three months' salary. That's why there were charity raffles, carnivals, charity sales, and childhood friends. "Do you have any clothes that no longer fit your children that you can give me for the orphans?"

Cayetana and Lorenzo rode the streetcar on their different errands, and Doña Tana never lost a whit of dignity, holding on to the handrail with her gloved hand. She carried a cane or an umbrella, depending on the season, and she handled that instrument like a scepter, which distinguished her from the common folk. She impressed Lorenzo the day she banged her umbrella on the imposing desk of the manager of the Bank of Mexico because he did not stand up to receive her with sufficient haste.

"A gentleman stands for a lady," she said in voice that exalted her.

The banker dissolved into excuses.

Tana maintained her irate tone, and of course she secured the loan. On the front steps of the building leading down to calle Venustiano Carranza she said haughtily, "That's how you have to treat the lackeys."

For her, the Mexicans were divided into gentlefolk and lackeys, but a good supplier could be a gentleman if she decided he was. "Christian values belong to the aristocracy," she would say, holding on to her nephew's arm. She smelled of rice powder and violets, and Lorenzo would always associate that smell with old age.

"Try on my shoes, Lorenzo. See how well they fit you?"

"They're women's shoes, Aunt. They have a heel."

"It's almost nonexistent. I'll have the cobbler remove them. Listen, to save some money, ask Tila for the hammer and take them off yourself. With a little work, they'll be as good as new. I barely wear out my shoes at all."

"But Aunt—they're women's shoes."

"You'll get used to them. You'll never own a finer pair of shoes, I'll tell you that, Lorenzo."

Annoyed by his lack of appreciation, she insisted that wearing them was a privilege conceded only to him. On the verge of tears, Lorenzo wore those torturous ankle boots, turning his feet inward. He did everything imaginable to hide them under the table or an armchair; so much so that his buddies noticed his torment, and they never, ever commented.

Diego spoke with his father: "Let's give Lorenzo a pair of shoes."

"Don't be insensitive," Dr. Beristain replied. "That would mean we are aware of the situation. Someday he'll buy himself a pair, and we'll act like we never noticed."

Three years later, Aunt Tana wouldn't notice her nephew's grave disappointment when she told him with a triumphant air that thanks to the support of the renowned Guilebaldo Murillo, attorney to the Archbishop Mitra, Lorenzo would enroll in the Escuela Libre de Derecho to study law.

Heading to the Libre de Derecho, on calle Basilio Badillo, while the rest of the gang went through the doors of the university's National School of Jurisprudence, plunged Lorenzo into desperation.

"Don't worry, brother," Diego told him. "It'll be the same as always. There's a way to get around Cayetana de Tena, and I'm going to show you how. You can still spend time with us. Listen, you're only there Mondays, Wednesdays, and Fridays from eight to eleven in the morning, and on Tuesdays and Thursdays from six to eight in the evening. Don't complain. You have two mornings and three afternoons free. Besides, we'll all be in court at the same time."

Lorenzo used a great many trolley transfers. Five trips for twenty centavos. The Roma–Merida tram ran down avenida Chapultepec toward the last stop, the Zócalo, or central plaza, which was under construction. The government wanted to make both it and the National Palace grandiose and to increase its stature from that of "A Child and a Thimble," as the poet Lopez Velarde had written. The promenades and walkways, the profusion of bushes and palm trees, the pornographic card vendors—all made the downtown entertaining and enticing. Lorenzo walked the rest of the way along calle República de Argentina between the bazaars, the Porrúa bookstore, the Robredo, and the Pax, shoe stores, small coffeeshops and inns, the wax museum, and the newspaper stands on every corner, to reach the National School of Jurisprudence. The small printshops at San Idelfonso would make copies of theses and course notes that the students purchased for classes. A Chinaman offered cakes at his coffee stand, and students who were dressed in coats and ties lined up in front of a public phone booth. It was unusual for anyone to wear a jacket. "The ones without ties are low class," commented Chava. The first-year "initiates," who were humiliated the day they registered, wore berets or hats to hide their shaved heads.

By eleven o'clock in the morning, not even a skinny man would fit into the First Appearance and Misdemeanors Courts at 100 Donceles, next door to La Enseñanza, called "Christ's church between two thieves."

In order to get the judges to sign their agreements, the students had to look for them in the canteens and the pool halls in the area, and that's how Lorenzo learned to play billiards. "Man, it's low-class entertainment," Chava would say.

Diego and Chava developed a liking for Café Fichot and ate empanadas as they came out of the oven and were served by a girl wearing an apron and a hairnet. That was until three women in hats and gloves caught them: "Dieguito and Chavita playing hooky!"

"Can those miserable witch friends of your mother's get back on their brooms and leave us in peace?" protested Chava.

Sometimes Lorenzo got annoyed with his friend because Diego had such an easy time of it. He loved life in all its manifestations—horses, cars, women, in that order—and he shared it with an ease that was foreign to Lorenzo. For Diego, living was a personal accomplishment. The only thing missing was the ability to maintain balance between his ego and his sudden impulses. Unlike Lorenzo, Diego chose to remember only what was pleasant. Or maybe he just didn't mention the bad, not even to his best friend. His financial situation made the Beristain family home the center of energy.

Each of the children had his or her own room and the opportunity to bring in their friends, who practically took over the dining room, the library, and the gym. The French-style house on Bucareli was complemented with a ranch in Xochimilco, surrounded by canals, chinampas—or floating gardens—boats and rowboats, pastures, stables, flowers, a fruit garden, and an Olympic-size swimming pool. It wasn't the house itself that impressed them, but rather its smell of happiness. Finding a place among the Beristains was easy. All you had to do was take refuge in their warmth and affection, in the magnitude of their embrace, to delight in a glass of wine in Dr. Beristain's shadow as he encompassed them like a benevolent god.

Carlos Beristain, a Basque with light eyes and abounding health, simmered like milk about to spill over, and he became a father to all of them. On one occasion, when Lorenzo arrived late and the family had already finished eating, the doctor insisted on keeping him company while he ate, and the boy felt such a strong sense of communication that a knot formed in his throat. "Would you like more?" asked the doctor. "You took very little." The fact that Dr. Beristain waited on him made him feel special, and Lorenzo would never forget the casual way Diego commented when he saw them together, "Ah, Lorenzo, here you are with my father, Herr Professor."

Could life really be that easy? Dr. Beristain spent his fortune on books and on trips that re-created and confirmed what he had read. Greece, Italy, Egypt. He had even traveled to Ferrières to pay homage to Rousseau. "All right, think now," he would say, "come to a conclusion. Think. Put your brains to work." He would raise his arms. "Be gods. Don't be children of a lesser god. Read Tennyson. You're young, unseasoned. Make this house a palace of ideas."

Lorenzo had great regard for the doctor, mostly because one afternoon in the library they spoke about time, and together they took down books on Aeschylus and Saint Augustine from the shelves. For Lorenzo, returning to a subject from his childhood was to come to terms with his life. He had survived Florencia's death, and, guided by Dr. Beristain, he returned to the mystery of life and death. Saint Augustine asked, "What is time? Who is capable of explaining it simply and briefly? When no one asks, I know what time is. When someone asks what time is, I don't know. What I do know is that some things will happen and other things will not happen any longer, and therefore they are the past, and the present is nihilism." That definition caused an almost uncontrollable euphoria in Lorenzo.

"Only the present can be measured," Dr. Beristain assured him, criticizing the Church—cruel stepmother, persecutor of Galileo, and of Giordano Bruno, who was also an astronomer. Saint Augustine, one of the four fathers of the Church, asked for forgiveness every step of the way: "I am searching, Father. I do not affirm. Lord protect me." He begged the All-Powerful Father to allow him to investigate. He implored that he not be condemned for trying to understand.

"Fucking religious shits, fucking church," mumbled Lorenzo.

"I contemplate the dawn. I predict that the sun will rise. What I contemplate is the present. What I announce is the future—not the future of the sun that is shining, but rather its rising at dawn. If I couldn't imagine this in my spirit, as I am now while I'm saying it, I wouldn't be able to predict it. But the dawn that I see in the sky is not the rising of the sun, although it precedes it. Nor is it created by my imagination. Both are perceived as the present, so the future rising of the sun can be predicted."

Saint Augustine asked God to give him the explanation, and he came to the conclusion that time measured the length of a movement rather than the other way around. Others believed the opposite, as they affirmed that "time is composed of the movements of the sun, the moon, and the stars."

"Lorenzo, come play Ping-Pong."

The shouts of his friends broke through to their ears, and Dr. Beristain said, "Go ahead if you want. You're free to leave."

"No, Doctor, I would much rather stay here in the library with you." He had anxiously asked himself how many hidden places there were in the sky. Could the heavens be measured like the Earth? The Earth is divided into cultivated fields—rectangles, triangles, pentagons, hexagons. Could the same be done with the celestial canopy? If you divided it into quadrangles, how many would fit? Could the stratosphere be measured in cubic meters? Lorenzo looked for answers.

Beristain didn't have them, and he returned to the subject of time, to ask himself, as had Saint Augustine, if the present came from a hidden place when the future became the present and then retired to a different hidden place when the present became the past. "The truth is, son, that it has never occurred to me to measure the heavens."

Lorenzo became indignant when Diego told him that the young poet Porfirio Barba Jacob had written:

> "Life is ending
> And it is not a time to learn."

"Do you agree with that, Diego?" Lorenzo asked. "Learning is the only thing that excites me."

"More than women?"

"There's no comparison."

"That's because you haven't gotten laid yet."

At the ranch in Xochimilco Diego could swim the length of the pool underwater in the blink of an eye. He'd get out and towel off his strong torso, his athletic legs. The others wore bathing suits but didn't get into the water. Lorenzo did. To test himself, he'd dive from the highest diving board. No belly flops, even though his "crawl" left a lot to be desired, and after two strokes he preferred to dunk anyone who came close and to prove his power by holding them under the water. "Die, cowards!" Chava, Víctor, and Javier were afraid of him. They nicknamed him Moby Dick. Lorenzo was competitive to a fault. Diego won every tennis match, with one hand tied behind his back. It was the same with horseback riding. His haute école style made him stand out.

Lorenzo, on the other hand, took his life in his hands. "I'll kill myself if I have to," he'd say furiously as two blue veins swelled at his temples.

Colonel Humberto Mariles, Diego's instructor, offered equestrian classes to all the members of the gang. He'd take them crosscountry, and every weekend he raised the jumping hurdle a little higher for Diego and Lorenzo.

"Stop, stop, Lorenzo. You're crazy. Stop," Diego begged. No challenge could go unanswered. Their friends contented themselves with following at their own mounts' pace.

"Let's go steal ourselves a nun!" Lorenzo would yell as they crossed Tlalpán at a gallop. Mariles had no choice but to watch as that crazy boy took every possible risk in spite of being so off-balance in the saddle. "I'll die before I give in," he told them. "No one is going to beat me." A frantic opponent, he kept up with Diego, and everyone paled at his fury.

"That boy is going to kill himself," Humberto Mariles concluded.

"I can do anything you can," Lorenzo challenged Diego.

Although Diego's new Ford was black, it reminded him of Tomasito Braniff's electric car. The first week, the buddies practically slept in it. Diego would raise his head to look out the window and prick up his ears, his hair glistening, maintaining his flock. As driver and owner, he ruled. His character attributes made him the indisputable leader. "Young wolves, I am the first one to choose the prey and the moment of attack." Only Lorenzo never lowered his head like the rest of the pack. Diego wasn't about to concede his rank in the hierarchy of the gang. "Natural selection," he'd say between guffaws. Inside the Ford, the tribe argued, filling the streets with their impertinence. On Uruguay, as they passed the police station, Diego yelled, "Go fuck your mother!"

Chava, already little, made himself smaller yet: "Hey, you just called the police bastards."

"No way," was all Diego was able to say before the police caught up with them and took them to the station.

"We all swore. It wasn't just him," Lorenzo stated.

"Then you'll go to jail too. Where are all of you from?"

"Mr. Army Commander," Lorenzo addressed the commander, "I don't think jail is the right place for us. I think rather La Castañeda, the insane asylum."

The man smiled. "What happened, sir? Were you all not swearing?"

"Yes, we were, but it was because we were discussing Reform Article 27 of the Constitution. Does it seem right to you, Commander, that the Constitution is for the use of the president and is a dead law before the will of the people?"

"You weren't swearing at the police?" asked the commander in a reserved manner as he was subjected to Lorenzo's know-it-all onslaught.

"No sir. That's why I said you should send us to the madhouse. Do you think we're crazy?"

"No."

"Then if we're not crazy, you should let us go."

Not even Danton would have been as persuasive as Lorenzo.

"Go on, then," the policeman said, "but let me make a suggestion: fight for your beliefs without swearing at anyone."

5

Years earlier, after high school, Lorenzo had started smoking. The smoke lifted the veil of shyness he felt with others and allowed him to be bolder with women. In truth, he was tortured by the very presence of the opposite sex, because even exchanging looks with women made him blush. On one phenomenal drinking spree, Lorenzo, Diego, Chava, Gabriel, Víctor, and Javier ended up in a whorehouse, and Lorenzo was the first to follow the fat woman who approached him.

"Come over here, little one," she said when they were in her cubicle. "Climb on top of me, come on . . . Sonny, take your pants off."

All of a sudden he was completely sober.

"Move it, kid. I don't have all night."

His socks had fallen down on top of his shoes, and she slipped off both shoes and socks. Then she opened her legs in the harshest gesture imaginable. "Climb on. Come on, what are you waiting for?"

Terrified, Lorenzo froze.

"Put it in and move, little one."

Lorenzo came, and she ordered, "Now clean yourself off and hand me some of that paper too." It was toilet paper. "Hurry up and get yourself out of here."

Diego would never forget the pain he saw as Lorenzo told him what had happened.

"Listen, Lencho, it's not so bad. We've all gotten stuck with those fucking old broads."

For years Lorenzo would remember the fat woman, her yellowed eyes ribbed with red veins, her swollen belly, and her spongy legs opening to reveal the horrible treasure. "And the room, Diego. That room, the curtain . . ."

"Lorenzo, be understanding."

"It's disgusting, Diego, just disgusting."

"But you came, didn't you? Everything worked, and you came."

"It's a phenomenon that I still don't understand."

The gang was tortured by the danger of getting syphilis. "The broads," as they called them, were an obsession. The boys took off after them like wild horses escaping from a barn. Unlike other oversexed boys, who had to take care of matters themselves to control their adrenaline, the gang could turn to Dr. Beristain.

"We'd like to see my father," Diego greeted the secretary in the doctor's office, just around the corner from the house on Bucareli.

Sheathed in his white coat, his stethoscope hanging around his neck, Beristain was even more admirable. "Sit down and relax. I'm not going to judge you, as you all say. You, Diego, pull down that screen. I'm going to show you some transparencies. Look here, gentlemen. Here you have a case of gonorrhea. Now this is a form of chancre. Look closely. It's devouring the penis, precisely in the glans penis."

No one moved.

"Look at this liver, Diego. You didn't put the sheet into the projector very well; make it sharper. I want you all to notice, this is a healthy liver, gentlemen, and this one, to the right, is that of an alcoholic. Look carefully. He has cirrhosis." As he turned on the light, Dr. Beristain kept haranguing. "Your health is your business, whatever your highnesses decide. If you want to die, go ahead right now. I'm not going to restrain you. I'm just pointing things out. Do you wish to have families someday? Take care of yourselves. Do you want to smoke? Finish off your lungs? I have brought you here not to prohibit you from doing these things, as the Marist priests did, but rather to inform you. The choice is yours."

The silence made accomplices of all of them.

"If something happens to you, don't keep it to yourself. Come see me immediately."

Lorenzo lit a Delicados cigarette with the butt of the one he had just finished.

"My dear Lorenzo, what would you say if I took dirt and put it into this watch?" He took out his pocket watch.

"Doctor, I'd say you were a savage . . . Well, no, no, no, I—it's just crazy."

"Well, this watch is nothing compared to what you're doing to your lungs. Destroying them, sending them straight on the path to pulmonary emphysema. Do you know what it's like to die from asphyxia?"

Diego turned to his father. "You don't know who we're involved with. We could have caught something . . ."

"I'll cure you, but don't you know about prophylactics?"

"It's just that you lose sensation, Father."

The gang frequented a brothel called Montparnasse, which they nicknamed Monpiernás, or Mountlegs. To build up their nerve, the future lawyers, who would soon become Secretaries of State, senators, or even president, would meet first at a bar on the corner of Insurgentes and avenida Chapultepec to see who could drink the most. They were all well dressed except for Lorenzo, who could not emulate Mero Bandala, the *arbiter elegantiarum*, as Diego called him. But Diego could—as the owner of a navy-blue blazer, a Prince of Wales shirt, a London Fog raincoat, and a substantial number of striped shirts, sweaters, and cashmere jackets from Burberry's.

Of the group, only Pedro Garciadiego, a true dandy, could compete with Diego Beristain. The crease in Garciadiego's pants fell perfectly; his shoes were gleaming; his hair was smeared with Vaseline, Carlos Gardel style; and his cuff links were gorgeous. Everything, including his umbrella, was name brand. He took great care with his profile, front, three quarters. He practiced posing in front of the mirror. One night an admirer said, "You should be in the display window at El Palacio de Hierro. You're a mannequin." The nickname La Pipa—the pipe—suited Pedro because it was what he smoked, and he'd lay his Dunhill tobacco on the table for everyone to see.

Garciadiego drank as much as the rest, but he didn't hold it as well. On one particularly infamous night, he went to the bathroom, saying, "I'll be right back." In the men's room, he took off his jacket, but he couldn't hang it up, and it landed at his feet. He wasn't able to get his pants down, and he wet himself all over and threw up on his jacket. Completely inebriated, he put it back on, left the bathroom, and attempted to sit down at the café table among his friends.

"What is this?" said Chava, alarmed.

Víctor, the most compassionate, stopped him. "Don't sit down, Pipa. Let's take you home."

"I'm not taking him in my car," protested Diego.

"But you brought him," insisted the easygoing Víctor.

Accustomed to excess and drunkenness, the waiters laughed. But they'd never seen anyone vomit that badly before.

"We need to get one of those Ford taxis that cost fifty cents per stop," said Diego as they stepped outside.

"No, there isn't time. Let's take him right now," insisted Víctor, who was holding Garciadiego up as he was about to fall.

"Hey you," said Diego in a commanding voice to the first taxi that came along. "Can you take this gentleman?"

"No."

"We'll give you a peso."

"No."

"Okay, two pesos."

"Five, but you have to lay newspapers down on the seat."

Diego and Lorenzo covered the backseat with paper, and once Víctor had Pedro all settled in, he said, "Lie down. Don't move. We're going to follow you. You're not alone." They pulled out behind the taxi, driving toward the house on the corner of Álvaro Obregón and Orizaba.

They all chipped in to pay the five pesos that had been meant for the Monpiernás whores, and they woke the doorman up. "Listen, we have your young master here, and he's pretty sick. It isn't serious. Just don't tell his parents, and please bring us the hose."

Víctor Ortiz, the only one who dared to touch Garciadiego, leaned him against the huge ash tree in the garden. Diego aimed the hose at his friend's body. Even the drowsy doorman couldn't help but smile when the stream of cold water hit Pedro's face and appeared to wake him up, although not very successfully, because he toppled to the ground like a piece of rotten fruit.

"Take him up to his bedroom." Diego told the doorman. "You're in charge. Make sure his parents don't find out."

Diego handed him a two-peso tip, at which point the doorman asked, "How did this happen to the young master?"

————

The euphoric sensation that Lorenzo felt with the first drink was something he wouldn't exchange for anything. Being with his buddies in a festive environment made him feel lyrical. My buddies, my chums, how clever! What great people. They shared everything; they were a commune—everything for everyone. He hugged them; their words guaranteed that Mexico would be a great country. They would redeem it. How he loved them. What swell guys—so smart. Chava Zúñiga was a prodigy; Diego couldn't be a better man; Gabriel Iturralde would defend them if necessary. Lorenzo congratulated himself for it all, even the head of foam on the mug of beer. No time was as worthwhile as the hours spent at Montpiernás, the school of life. They danced, and in a little while each disappeared with one of the whores: home, sweet home. Iturralde, the Basque, would ask himself, Is there anything more inviting than a cunt?

The four of them decided to rent a room the size of a closet in the Atenas y Abraham González building, which was close to the place where Julio Antonio Mella was assassinated. The gang's den was better attended than they had expected: "Let me borrow the keys, let me borrow the keys." "Well, I'll be there tomorrow morning at eight." "That's a terrible time." "It's the only time she can make it. She starts work at ten." "Let me have the keys. I want ten at night." "If you get there early, don't knock. You wait until I come out." All of a sudden, a sly one would knock: "No way, man, not a chance, Chava. You've destroyed the mood." Their great passions were subject to circumstances—a ringing bell or a yell that floated up from calle Abraham González.

Thanks to his ease with words, Chava Zúñiga was able to convince the Secretary of State, Oscar Molina Cerecedo, that he was indispensable to the newspaper *Milenio,* and he immediately persuaded the director that his buddies, budding geniuses, would make a fabulous contribution. Chava had the gift of making people laugh, the grace of irresponsibility. Playful and seductive, he could entertain them for hours.

"What a great street hawker! His words can even rip the calluses off your feet. I'm taking you to the Zócalo to perform." Lorenzo laughed.

"Little brother, I'm going much further than you, so treat me right," Chava said. For the present, he had moved ahead of all of them and was distributing the earth's bounty. In front of Secretary Molina Cerecedo he exaggerated the deplorable financial situation of poets, the horrifying loft where the best Latin American novelist produced his masterpiece, the small, dismal room where the immeasurable genius painted. "Redeem yourself," Zúñiga warned the Secretary, and, amused, the Secretary conceded favors. Chava embellished his private life. The most beautiful women on Earth resided in his empire, and the description of his amorous conquests, which oscillated between challenges and pleas, delighted his listeners. He was a courtier to the very tips of his toes, but he had developed his own style. He distributed his salary among the haberdasher, the tailor, the cobbler, and the jeweler. "But not to women. They pay for my services. I'm an amazing lover. I'm sure that one of them told me that Gabriel Iturralde doesn't last long. Premature ejaculation, my dear." From the time he was a child, Zúñiga had inspected the size of the penises he observed in the school bathrooms. He would point them out: big, little, tolerable, nonexistent. He never criticized Lorenzo, but he was moved to tears by his friend's wardrobe.

"Little brother, how can you wear that abominable suit? What woman is going to give you a second look if you're wearing khaki? Aren't you aware that fashion is a manifestation of culture? My supreme elegance is revealed in these vertical lines, the blazer, open to the imagination. No, Lencho, you're very wrong. It's not just narcissistic merchandise. The camel-hair coat identifies me. It gives me power."

Gabriel Iturralde, on the other hand, counted only on his pleasant personality, and Víctor Ortiz on his kindness and the habit of eating leftovers from his buddies' plates, although obesity was lying in wait for him.

Zúñiga gave them all the opportunity to publish in the newspaper, but the happiness of knowing they were friends continued to be greater than seeing their names in print. With a total lack of envy, Zúñiga praised the gang, inflating their attributes. The group's spirit of camaraderie made him happy, and he shared that same happiness. The editorial room of *Milenio*, with his great buddies, would be the brain of the country. "Have you seen the modern machinery at the Cable Office, Lorenzo? Since you like science so much, it'll bowl you over."

Through their editorials, the gang thought they would direct the government, nourish the nation, and if things didn't work out, it would be because the leadership hadn't followed their advice. To be young was to be omnipotent, to belong to Mount Olympus, to run with the torch in your hand. And win.

"How am I going to become a journalist if I've never written an article in my life?" Lorenzo asked.

"It's the easiest thing in the world, Lenchito. The editorial room is swarming with people who have abandoned their studies in all the careers—doctors, lawyers, architects. They all find satisfaction here. Since they haven't been successful, they're journalists. Your sense of culture is superior to any of those fiddling with their notebooks here. I'm going to give you an assignment. You interview Bart Jan Bok, the astronomer. Tell him that you're a reporter from *Milenio*."

"But I'm not."

"Tomorrow you'll have your credentials, and in a week you'll stop by to see the cashier."

Lorenzo had never expected to be so fascinated by Bart Jan Bok; nor had he imagined that the scientist would end the interview by saying, "Young philosopher, thank you for your excellent questions."

Lorenzo was more gratified by the conduct of this man than by the publication of the interview. On that day he decided, I'm going to learn to write. His drive helped him prolong each day, drawing as many hours as he could from it. There was even enough time to go all the way to Monte de Piedad to pawn Princess Radziwill's emeralds. The princess was an intimate friend of Aunt Cayetana's. Every six months Lorenzo took the Russian leather jewelry box, with whatever the princess put in it, to be pawned. Six months later, the princess, a friend of Aunt Tana's husband, Manuel Romero de Terreros, would give him a bundle of bills to get it back. To show her appreciation, she offered Lorenzo a cup of English tea and unloaded her problems onto him, speaking all the while in French. Her troubles were so different from his own. Incredulous, Lorenzo came to the conclusion that each person had their own hell to deal with.

What am I going to be a lawyer for—to pawn jewels at Monte de Piedad? he asked himself angrily. He hadn't lost his inexhaustible critical ability to expose the truth, to find the motive for this or that apparently disinterested action. He was observing the spectacle that Chava Zúñiga was staging in the newspaper room as if it were a circus performance. As the others were applauding, Lorenzo was watching the ashes scatter and fall.

"Brother!" Zúñiga was yelling. "Free yourself of that nihilism. Take off that expression of death. Don't have such contempt for your fellow man! Be magnanimous, like me."

Zúñiga was as enthralling to Lorenzo as he was to everyone else.

"You, Lorenzo, are committing the greatest crime against humanity!"

"What?" he asked, dauntless.

"You're not happy. Watch me, brother!" He was hanging from the curtains, practicing dance steps. His favorite was to take an invisible woman by the waist and, bending her backward, pretend to kiss her passionately, then break into a tango to the tune of "Don't devalue humanity; don't underrate human beings." Even Lorenzo couldn't help but laugh.

No one in the house on Lucerna knew about Lorenzo's activities. None of them knew what the others were doing. They preferred to float above events, like Don Joaquín, who lived attached to his routine—the drink at the Ritz at one o'clock, the Rosary at seven, bridge on Thursdays, Sunday mass at La Profesa followed by the family meal at Carito Escandón's.

Aunt Tana asked Lorenzo to accompany Lucía Aramburu y González Palafox home every Thursday night after they played bridge. Of all his aunt's friends, she was the one with the reddest lips. Her youthful movements made her jump from her seat like a spring. Lorenzo liked to escort her to her house on avenida Insurgentes, and he liked that she called him darling. One night she asked him to come in, and she invited him up to her bedroom. Lorenzo had learned from Cocorito, a waitress he knew quite well, that women were more daring than men. He came to the conclusion that they had an element of craziness in them. They jumped headfirst, ignoring where they were going to land, the poor things. When Lucía said in a singsong voice, "Undress, darling," and then, at the end, "This is a secret just between you and me, love," he agreed immediately. How could she think he would be anything but a gentleman? He wouldn't tell her, either, that the waitress's breasts were more playful, because hers had fascinated him—two mature, fully ripened pears.

As he returned to his attic on Lucerna, he felt as if he owned the streets. The houses were his partners in crime, and they winked at him. The sidewalks under his nimble feet repeated with every step, "You are the master and lord, master and lord, master and lord." The apparatus between his legs, aggressive and well formed, had taken that woman, probably quite experienced, to an orgasm. Thanks to that perfect weapon that made him a man, he had a woman under his power who was at least thirty years his senior. Lucía would kneel at his feet. Every bridge game would end in an orgy. What a task he had. He was curious to know what Diego would say when he told him.

Expressing himself through desire was something totally new for Lorenzo. Thursday became the high point of his week. However, the following Thursday, after crossing the five streets that separated the two houses, Lucía said good night without even a glance at his erection.

"Good night, little boy. Sweet dreams."

The rejection deeply humiliated him, but she continued to intrigue him. Why sometimes yes, and not others? His aunt's yell, "Lorencito, please come down and walk Lucía home," became a siren's song.

Lucía took his arm familiarly, and he would try to guess what would happen. Sometimes she was terribly distant; other times she was wildly passionate.

She possessed him; she mounted him; she became a male goat. He was her object, her lover, and her son at the same time. She rocked him like a child in that flowered canopy bed. The only thing Lucia did not do was walk around the bedroom naked—unlike Cocorito. Her order was final—"Don't turn the lights on"—and the darkness made her more of a promised land, playing hide-and-seek, eluding reality.

He surprised himself one night, screaming, "Lucía, Lucía, don't ever leave me!" And he asked himself how it was possible that he had never felt anything like this before. Losing himself in Lucía, losing himself over Lucía. He never imagined he'd lose himself over a friend of Cayetana's, whom he considered practically an old woman. How disrespectful to himself and to them! After being with Lucía, he saw his aunt with different eyes. Who was she? What did she do in her bedroom? Did Don Manuel, so gruff, reach for her at night under the sheet? And what about the good Tila? What did she do when she went back to her village? Women! What an incomprehensible mystery. Dense like swamps. Nevertheless, all he could do was wait feverishly in the attic for his aunt Tana's yell, opening the doors to paradise with her sharp "Lorencito, do me a favor and accompany Lucía," to which he threw himself down the stairs and arrived in the living room, cheeks red, which made Doña Cayetana exclaim, "Look at him; he looks like a little apple!"

Lucía, the savage mare—would she sink her teeth into that little apple, or would she send him home without any reward? One night Lorenzo decided to win the game. Lucía had hardly opened the door, saying good night, when he stuck his leg in the way.

"Listen, young man . . ."

Lorenzo threw himself on her, right there in the hallway, before going up the stairs, and she laughed, delighted, her lips a little swollen, with that slow gesture of a body that prepares to give in. Lorenzo remembered Diego's advice: "Go for it. They may tell you no, but they're always grateful." Fucking old women, fucking Lucía. That night he had her as never before, and he was the one in

charge. He did it the way he wanted, and at one point he turned on
the light and saw her. Her full breasts had the beauty of fruit—
honey trickled harmoniously and sweetly, extending over her entire body. More beautiful than Cocorito, this woman was the Earth
itself, with her armpits a little loose and her thighs ready to give in.
She covered her face, and he looked at her, enraptured, loving her,
without hearing her desperate palpitations. How beautiful, my
God, how beautiful. The fact that she didn't believe him only
made her all the more desirable. Fool, little fool, beautiful little
fool, you're the most beautiful thing I've ever seen. Iztaccíhuatl,
Popocatépetl, Pico de Orizaba, Nevado de Toluca, crater of honey
and black grapes. No fifty-year-old woman should be ashamed of
her body. He would accept it like a long-awaited rain shower. Lucía
noticed the surrender in his eyes. This youth was giving her back
her self-confidence, although he probably had no one to compare
her with. How wonderful. He would become more ardent each day.
She would know how to keep the flame going, feed his devotion.
Lucía would set the rules. No, no—let him set them. Let herself
surrender to the width of his shoulders, to his gift of command, to
the hair that curled at the nape of his neck, to the wisdom in his
eyes, to his ardor, and, above all, to his audacity, which no one
would have suspected. For the first time since her youth, she was
not ashamed of her nakedness in front of a man. Lorenzo should
have been the first, she thought tenderly. He was the one who deserved to have made the blood run through her thighs. Was she
still tight enough? Her lover's convulsions, his legs that trembled
right down to his heels, proved it. He had taken her out of her own
body. What a tender and violent man, both at the same time. She
had known bold men, but none like this little boy, none. Her esteem for Doña Cayetana de Tena increased.

6

Lucía's activities, written down in a tiny Hermès agenda, filled Lorenzo with surprise. Her *affaires d'argent*, as she called them, seemed strange to him. She had several *maisons de rapport* downtown, on calle Donceles, and on Isabel la Católica, and her *homme d'affaires* collected the rents, which allowed her to travel to Spain three or four times a year to cultivate her friendship with Alfonso XIII. The great ones of Spain reigned in her house, although Lorenzo was on the verge of replacing them. She no longer lived only for "the king and queen," although the inertia of habit would immobilize the silver-framed photograph of Alfonso XIII on the piano with its inscription "To Lucía, my love." To be worthy of the king, she frequently visited Casa Armand to renew the trousseau destined for the Eastern Palace in Madrid, where you couldn't wear the same thing twice. The king, the queen, the princes, the entire court would remember the previous designs. Renew yourself or disappear. The fashion show started aboard the *Queen Elizabeth*, where, from the first night, the captain requested that she sit at his table. She was also in the habit of inviting European diplomats to her house, as they traveled constantly and might in turn be invited to the court, where they would mention her name, as well as the fact that she entertained like a queen and that her salon was the most exclusive in Mexico.

Although she never went overboard, Lucía held her salons several times a month. So as not to spend money on help, she turned to Tana: "Could Leticia help on Friday for the cocktail party I'm throwing for the ambassador from England? It's a great opportunity for her to mingle with the upper class." She did the same thing with her other friends. And Lorenzo was always invited.

Leticia went in her party dress, covering a beautiful body, and later she told Lorenzo that Lucía was in a league of her own when it came to being cheap. She mimicked Lucía: "The watercress sandwiches are just for the diplomats." The help wasn't to pass the silver platter among the nationals. The Old Parr whisky was re-served for the diplomats as well. Lucía served the Mexicans a vile beverage disguised in cut crystal decanters. Leticia, Elsie, Inés, Concha, and Mercedes burst out laughing in the kitchen while they stuffed themselves with the finger sandwiches that the chef at the University Club had delivered two hours earlier and the petits fours from El Globo, "just for the diplomats."

Lucía dazzled everyone with her theatrics—gold sparkles on her skin and in her hair. "How do you make yourself look younger every day?" her guests exclaimed as she walked by. Sometimes she caught Lorenzo's avid gaze on her thighs, or she herself looked to meet his eyes. He was obviously bored. The only purpose those evenings held for him was to get to the final mutual destination—to make love. When will they finish saying good-bye? he wondered. They talked about the jeweled Fabergé Easter eggs, the tercenten-nial of the Romanov dynasty. In Mexico, there were collectors of eggs that held semiprecious stones—lapis lazuli, iridescent topaz, serpentine, turquoise, and onyx. Never opal. It brought bad luck. Why so much attention to the eggs? Anastasia's fate was another inexhaustible topic. The word *czar* filled their mouths. The age of the Virgin of Guadalupe painting in La Villa, its authenticity sci-entifically proven, was the Mexican topic of the moment. To hurry them up, Lorenzo handed out fur stoles, black coats, hats, canes with silver and ivory handles, and umbrellas from Harrods. Leticia would give him a pinch as she passed by. When they commented to Lucía, "What a good-looking assistant!" she responded excitedly, "He's a de Tena, Cayetana's nephew. You have no idea, he's a peach of a thing." Listening to her, Lorenzo could have strangled her right then and there, and when Leticia repeated it, imitating the entire scene—"peach of a thing, I tell you, such a peach, you just can't imagine"—he chased her vengefully.

Like Colette with Gigi, Lucía instructed him on the function of clothing, on the purity of an emerald with or without flaws, on per-fume. Lorenzo's dream was to someday buy her Shalimar by Guerlain. In the meantime, he attended to her bath: her tub surrounded by sponges, powders, and moisturizing creams. "I'm my best investment," she repeated flirtatiously. "If I don't take care of myself, who will?" She was not at all cheap on herself. Lorenzo scrubbed her back. "Ay, not so hard!" Devotedly, he dried each part of her body, mostly her sex; he passed her a peignoir and watched her put perfume behind each ear, between her breasts, at her right wrist, and on the crease of her arms. What devotion as he caressed Lucía's long thighs, covering them with cream. "I do it for you, my love, and this is for you, sweetheart," she would respond with a little yelp.

Although Diego would have been amazed at his friend's sexual prowess, Lorenzo never confided in him about this. It didn't fit his gentleman's code. Besides, not rushing things relaxed him. He could go back to what was most important to him without any hindrance—his studies.

"I haven't seen you very much these last few months," commented Dr. Beristain, and in spite of his seventeen years, Lorenzo blushed.

"It's because they give me so much work to do at the law office." It was true. What he didn't tell Dr. Beristain was how much he hated going to the trials on calle Donceles, and that the depositions were repugnant to him. There was nothing worse than repossessing furniture on the sidewalk—stripped armchairs with the legs up in the air. What a misfortune it was for humanity to display its wretchedness.

The evictions made him express even more hatred against the landlords. Pack of rats. "Don't send me on another eviction. I refuse. I'll resign first," he warned the dispatcher. Because they knew his character, and in order to avoid his long sermon against the bourgeois, Lorenzo was exempted from seizing property for the repayment of debts. Did the lawyer he worked for have any idea what it was like to go into a dark room in one of the most unsanitary neighborhoods of the underworld of Mexico to order a woman who has already been rejected, and is already a loser—condemned from the minute she entered the store—to return the Singer to the vendor, who knew for certain in the first place that she would never be able to pay for it? The client's mere appearance was enough for anyone to evaluate her financial situation. On the day of the repossession, he, Lorenzo de Tena, had to confront this creature, who also lost her center of gravity when she lost her machine. That's what the Mexican Christian society was like. He wanted to resign right then and there from the disgusting law firm.

Curiously enough, any agent who happened to visit the debtor after that would have found her sewing on the very same machine. Lorenzo had settled the debt, and if he could have gotten the seamstress out of her hovel, he would have done it. He would suggest it to Lucía, but he doubted that his lover would ever give up her collection of little boxes, teaspoons, elephants, frogs, Redouté roses, and other talismans, to which she attributed sentimental value.

"It's the perfect claim," he said to Lucía. "The truth is, the rich justify the accumulation of possessions with sacrifice, saying, 'I do this for my children.' "

"You have a father, Lorenzo."

"My case is different. I don't know where I came from, and I don't know where I'm going. I'm fine alone, and I follow my own rules—although I'm probably lying, Lucía of my soul, because I now follow you."

There's nothing you can do about it; that's just the way she is, he would repeat to himself as he recounted her faults, which disappeared as soon as he saw her. That woman whom he gushed over was his thirst and his relief; through her, through her warm body, he reached the exclusive estate of his manliness. After that would come the perplexity, the justification, the search for explanations to himself, but in the meantime, he didn't want any obstacles. One day he would have to reflect on his relationship with Lucía, because what was important to him was not the life of the emotions, but the life of ideas. Yet this relationship had thrown him headfirst into the world of sensation, a whirlwind from which he could not escape. In a trance, he had given himself senselessly to Lucía.

At one point he thought of confiding in Dr. Beristain, saying, What should I do? I'm drowning, Doctor. I love this woman. I love her like a barbarian! Or better yet, in a reasonable tone and reflectively, more appropriate to the doctor's age and experience, he might say that he, Lorenzo, understood very well that he was pussy-whipped—excuse the vulgarity, Doctor—and if the doctor thought there was a cure, a bromide or whatever it might be called, that they give the soldiers, could he provide it, please, a normal dose, and if he, Beristain, could inform him how long this type of phenomenon lasts . . . I mean the passion. I mean, falling in love (he knew very well that the thing with Lucía was not going to last a lifetime, of course not). In the meantime, if he, Carlos Beristain, had a cure, Lorenzo was begging for it, just to lower the fever of his concupiscence so he could go back to being the way he was before.

One night Lorenzo asked Lucía what happened to Felipa, the maid. She worked to support a string of brothers and sisters, although she was far too young to do so.

"I fired her because she stole my brooch, the one with two sapphires and two diamonds," Lucía answered.

"That's impossible. Have you looked for it?"

"Everywhere, sweetheart. Under the bed, in the living room, in the kitchen, and in the maids' room. Besides, I have proof that she's guilty."

"What?"

"She never stopped trembling and bawling. She left a disgusting mess. An innocent person doesn't shake like that. Black as she is, she turned white when I told her I was going to call the police."

"Lucía, let's look for it together. What you've done is very serious."

"All righty, darling, but I tell you that I'm sure, little one, sure. I'm positive, okay? Positive. What hurts the most is that the jewel was given to me by the Duke of Albuquerque in Madrid."

Lorenzo shook the rugs, went through the closets and the dressers. He took the brooch out of the corner of the third drawer. "Look, your stolen brooch."

"Ay, that's wonderful, darling. You would be the one to find it."

"You should go after Felipa."

"What's wrong with you, child? Are you crazy?"

"Lucía, if you don't rectify this injustice, I'll never see you again, in spite of the fact that I love you."

They didn't make love that night. Or the next day or the day af-

ter that, although Lorenzo was at the point of breaking his promise
and running to avenida Insurgentes. On the third day, Lucía came
to leave him a little note in a perfumed envelope, written in her ta-
pered Sacred Heart schoolgirl script: "I have done all I could to
find Felipa. She has turned into a Wells character, invisible. Love
Lucía."

Lorenzo didn't respond. On Thursday his lover showed up to
play bridge, and even though Lorenzo swore he wouldn't be at
Lucerna when his aunt Tana yelled "Lorencito," he went downstairs, trembling, to accompany her home. She told him that she
had put on her oldest dress and gone through seventy-seven
dung heaps without finding the girl. Lorenzo declared that she
had to keep looking. She had known how to find her to hire
her. At the door, Lucía invited him in. "Come on, darling. Don't
be a silly."

Biting his lip, he said no, and he left, crying from anger.

The same thing happened the following Thursday. Lucía gave
him a detailed recounting of her difficult ordeal in the Guerrero
neighborhood. "I've done the ridiculous for you,. sweetheart, just
for you. Forget the annoying child. She was swallowed by filth. Let
it go now, Love. As you can see, I did everything that was humanly
possible. Really, this is ridiculous."

But Lorenzo didn't go in, and he never would again. To do so
would have betrayed his mother. He went back to seeing his buddies, and when the memory of Lucía became pressing, he would
look for Cocorito.

One afternoon after dinner Aunt Tana informed them that
Lucía had left for Spain without telling anyone. "That's what she
does when she has some kind of a setback. She just leaves."

A telephone call shook the de Tena house: "Miss Lucía Aramburu
y González Palafox has been murdered."

Shaken, Cayetana ordered her nephew, "Please, run over to
avenida Insurgentes. I thought she was in Spain. It must surely be a
mistake. Why are you still standing there like a fool? Come back as
soon as you find anything out."

A world of people blocked his way to number 18 avenida Insurgentes, proving that the news was true. Lorenzo was able to reconstruct the crime from the different phrases he heard. A light in the house being on day and night had intrigued Arcadio Diazmuñoz, the street sweeper, who had climbed onto the balcony and looked through the dirty glass to see an elongated black shape, which appeared to undulate, thrown to one side of the piano. A grease stain on the floor. The stench of the cadaver—which now, according to Arcadio, encompassed the whole block—reached him. "Unmistakable," he said. "I know about that." It had been several weeks since anyone had answered the bell at the two-story house. As Arcadio got closer, he could see greenish potbellied flies emerging from the doorjambs. He ran for the police. "Something strange is going on in there, and I tell you because I know about garbage." An hour later, Efrén Benítez, an agent from the Public Ministry, and Alfredo Santos, the director of Criminology and Identification, showed up. It was necessary to break one of the windowpanes to get in. "How horrible. What a terrible thing. A person of the best society." "They say she was single." "They've been inside a long time. The family members already went in."

A woman approached Lorenzo: "Are you a family member? You look a lot like the ones who went in."

Lorenzo made an effort to control himself, and with his press credential from *Milenio* he went up to the bedroom with the others. He remembered the household furniture—"horizon gray" as Lucía used to say, French style—and he looked around the room for the first time, because in truth, the only thing that had been important to him about Lucía was her body. Her house always seemed just like the house of Aunt Tana or Kiki Orvañanos or Tolita Rincón Gallardo or Mimí Creel—the same inlaid wood furniture, the chairs made out of apple and pear wood, the colonial mirrors, the porcelain from the Compagnie des Indes, the Catherwood engravings—mass-produced houses, cut with the scissors of good taste. Now Lorenzo noted the disorder, the great confusion of objects thrown on the rug, the dresses in the open closets, the shawls and the handbags all rummaged through, the drawers open for everything to be seen, and the jewelry in plain sight: a ring with an enormous diamond, no less than twelve carats in weight, but fake; an emerald wrapped in tissue paper, fake like the diamond; boxes with fake pearls in tissue paper; bracelets adorned with twinkling stones. He remembered Lucía saying, "*C'est du toc, mon cher.* What I wear looks fine, but it's junk. My good appearance legitimizes any illegitimacy. I dignify an imitation, darling. What I wear only in Madrid, I keep in the bank. They're such peasants here in Mexico that they don't know the difference. There is no one easier to deceive than Mexican high society."

According to her, God had endowed her with a superior intelligence that she was to use to restore His Majesty Alfonso XIII to the throne, and to that end she wrote numerous letters. Another letter, addressed to her lawyer, was an interminable complaint against Monte de Piedad, where many wealthy clients sold their jewels and expensive items on consignment: "I am perfectly capable of creating a scandal. I have influential friends in the press . . ." She wanted at all costs to have a painting that she had pawned a year ago returned to her. The papers had expired, and it had not been sold. There was also a message written in green ink, from Miguel Maawad Tovalin, agent of a photography enlarging studio, which stood out: "I'm sorry I did not find you at home. I will return tomorrow between ten and twelve." According to the criminologist, it was dated the eve of the crime.

A reporter said, "This is going to be the scandal of the year." Unable to speak, Lorenzo followed his colleagues like a phantom. The cadaver was visible through the glass doors to the living room, dorsal decubitus, lying next to the stool at the foot of the piano, as the expert noted. Everyone stopped when the door was opened, horrified by the frightful number of fat green flies on top of the cadaver, with their clumsy wings and their noisy buzzing. They were also buzzing inside her innards under the black silk slip. The burned corners of two folded quilts hid her face. The cadaver, arms spread open, had one hand wearing an old glove with all the fingertips ripped; the other hand, naked, displayed a *chevalière* engraved with a family coat of arms. "Darling, I read *El Universal* with gloves. It's such a dirty newspaper."

When the expert uncovered the face, a horrified "oh!" ran

through the crowd. The worms formed a whitish, moving mass; the black-and-red larva fell, making an unforgettable noise. Something even more horrible was awaiting them. A ray of sun struck the gold molar in the mandible. The hair spread out over the Persian rug was all that was recognizable.

"She's been dead for at least a month," the expert was heard to say.

Lorenzo felt the impulse to throw a sheet over her. Wasn't that how they covered people who were run down on the street? Lucía lay in complete view of everyone.

"Let's hope she didn't suffer when she was killed," Lorenzo said, surprising the forensic expert, who looked at him strangely.

"You knew her, right?" The expert asked when he saw the decomposed face. "Young man, you'd better go out and get hold of yourself. You don't have the stomach to be a criminal reporter."

Lorenzo walked through the city all day, constantly repeating to himself, "I killed her. I killed her." If he hadn't abandoned her, Lucía would still be alive. He walked until late into the night, the cadaver in front of his eyes. He had slept with that body, those black stockings that now lay thrown in a pile of filth. He had watched them slowly climb Lucía's thighs. Step by step, the refrain resounded in his head until he lost his mind: "I killed her, I killed her." She was a marvelous, crazy little thing. I killed her. I felt like killing her so many times. I hated her so much that I wished her dead. I shouldn't have judged her so harshly. If I had stayed with her, surely I would have killed her; so, based on that logic, I killed her. She never went to Spain. She never went anywhere. She shut herself up with her pain and wanted to take a picture of herself to send to me. Fucking Lucía. I shouldn't have condemned her, the poor, unconscious, abused, miserly, parasitic woman.

When his feet and legs began to hurt, Lorenzo wondered how many kilometers he had walked. Crazed, he reached the door of the house on Lucerna that looked so much like Lucía's, and he went up to his attic. A deep sleep overcame him, and he awoke at dawn. He went out very early. He didn't want to see the family. On the third day, he returned to the house, which was crackling with the brutal

news, and he heard Aunt Tana call, "Lorenzo, is that you? We're
here in the living room reading the newspaper. Come in and join
us. *El Universal* has the best news."

"They know who killed her," said Uncle Manuel. "They're following the trail of a Miguel Maawad Tovalín."

"She had a secret life that none of us suspected. Who would
have thought it. Such a respectable woman," murmured Joaquín.

"Look who's talking. It happens in the best of families," Tana retorted sarcastically. "During Porfirio Díaz's government, she was
considered one of the most beautiful women in Mexico, and her
beauty was recognized at all the Centennial dances."

"At the Centennial dances?" asked Lorenzo, bewildered.

"Yes, she was my age. I also was popular at the Centennial
dances. Don Porfirio wrote his name on my dance card."

"In spite of her appearance and her talent, her rages and eccentricities and her improper remarks kept her from marrying. No beau
chose to be her husband," said Don Joaquín.

"Lucía would have been a good match for you, and if you had
wanted, the orphans could have had a mother today. After waiting
for you for so long, Lucía saw that her youth had passed by when
she turned fifty—the age she had to die."

Lorenzo felt the urge to cover his ears, but he couldn't prevent
the fragments of conversation from continuing to reach him like
arrows.

"Everyone was dying to be invited to her Louis XVI salon."

"There was a rumor that Lucía would be secretary to the King of
Spain. She was able to get several audiences with Alfonso XIII,
who was impressed with her intensity. That's why she made so
many trips to Madrid."

"Lucía hated the Republicans. She said they were her personal
enemies and fought to have them thrown out of all the social centers."

"She was totally unbalanced," Don Joaquín commented again.
"A hysterical woman. When Julio Alvarez de Vayo, the ambassador
from the Spanish Republic, visited Puebla for the first time, she
stepped in front of him and yelled, 'Long live King Alfonso!' 'Yes,
ma'am, for as long as he likes, and as long as it's at Fountainbleau,'

he responded. There were comments about that episode at the Jockey Club for months."

Lorenzo had never heard his father speak so volubly. Other incidents gave credence to Lucía's eccentricities, and the boy was painfully adding them up. It had to do with intolerable remarks, with nervous prostration. She had no maids. She'd throw them out. Yes, that was Lucía. "Her income got as high as twelve hundred pesos a month." She, who always complained about not having enough money!

What kind of life had this woman led? Lorenzo wondered. He asked for *El Universal* and went up to his room. The paper was certain that the author of the crime was a man, and that the man, from his long and narrow footprint near the body, wore elegant footwear.

In the days that followed, Lorenzo's nightmare kept getting worse. Perhaps Lucía had seduced him because she couldn't have his father. But no, Lucía was part of his being, his intimate self, the real him. She could be totally useless, a snob, as cheap as they described her, but they had shared a secret life, and he knew her to be sweet, sometimes laughing, sincere—a clean Lucía, a child–older woman, an older woman–child. "Good-bye, Lorenzo. Thank you, and take care of yourself," she had sleepily called out one night as she heard him going down the stairs. "Good-bye, boy. You make me happy," came the unexpected gift of acknowledgment. Only Lorenzo had seen something pathetic and disconsolate in her that was now crushing him. Many times when they were alone, Lucía looked at him as if she wanted to permanently set his features in her mind, and he could read the love in her eyes.

Once again Lorenzo felt the sensation of leading a double life, initiated the day he entered the house on Lucerna. Everything that was indispensable to him was a secret. Everything else, the everyday routine, he had to tolerate. He hid what he was really passionate about. No one was aware of the extent of his interior life. Even Diego didn't know his quintessence. Lying across his bed, Lorenzo heard someone knock on the door.

It was Leticia. Seeing him crying, she sat on the edge of the bed to sob as well, and when she caught her breath, she humbly told

him, "Brother, brother, you're all I have. Little brother, I'm pregnant, and it's going to show soon."

At that instant Lorenzo resolved that as soon as he could, he
would leave the attic room that Aunt Tana had assigned to him,
get an apartment, and take charge of Leticia.

7

Lorenzo had been oblivious to Leticia's roundness, but not to her creativity. His younger sister had become a woman very quickly, like street children who age from living always on the defensive. She filled the house with her exuberance, her unbroken health, and the ease with which she shared her affection. She kissed everyone, and when she said good-bye, you could still hear her crystalline voice softly singing to the sound of the five fingers of her hand, from which she threw kisses: "Kisses! Kisses!" She was an arrow of kisses, her reddish hair following behind her like the train of a bishop's robe.

"Hey, your sister has gotten really good-looking," Diego had said to him one day. At that moment Lorenzo saw her in a different light.

As proof of her favoritism, Aunt Tana had decided to look for a private tutor for Leticia from the Marist order, a saintly male to instruct her, to communicate his piety and his temperance, and to lead Juan down the right path as well, for who knew where that boy wandered. The "good" families generally have faith in the heavens; all solutions fall from there, and Tana accepted the novice like he was the Savior. Raimundo was included in family life. He was charged with saying the blessing at the table, delivering the thanksgiving, and assembling the community of patrons and servants for the Rosary ceremony.

Besides, impressed in the evenings by Juan's notable talent for math and for abstract thought, Raimundo was, himself, edified. It was almost like a communication with God. He would wait excitedly on the street for Juan to arrive. That quiet and sneaky boy knew all the answers. "He could be an inventor," the tutor told Aunt Tana. "He has extraordinary ability."

"An inventor of what, evil? Because I've had several things disappear, and Juan is the only one who always has money in his
pocket."

"Doña Tana, I assure you, he has a privileged mind."

It surprised Leticia when Tana answered, "But not more so than
Lorenzo, of that I'm sure."

Raimundo's presence at Lucerna was beneficent because the
whole family lived at the mercy of events, and since Don Joaquín
was incapable of making a decision, Raimundo became a substitute
paternal figure. They lived "by what God dictated, what God said,"
and they prayed, devoid of all free will. Anyone with gall who
came to 177 Lucerna could become captain of the ship without
even intending to. "Whatever Raimundo says . . . Raimundo knows
. . . Raimundo's in charge."

Raimundo decided to take all the children—even Santiago, the
youngest, whom he carried with ease—on an excursion. "So you'll
know about the countryside, see the sunset, hear the tolling of the
bells, and study the baroque artwork created by Indian hands in the
village churches. We're going to leave the city to breathe the good
mountain air of the great volcanoes, Iztá and Popo." Everyone
liked the proposition, even Lorenzo, who would have gone with
them if his presence hadn't been required at the Beristains' on Saturdays and Sundays.

Preparing the knapsack . . . what fun! Above all because Ray
(as they now called him) warned Aunt Tana, "If we're not back
by Saturday night, it's because we're spending the night at a
farm."

They came back, their arms loaded with fruit and wildflowers,
talking about truncated, inverted, pyramid-shaped supports; about
the Mudejar style; about open chapels and baptisteries; about vir-
gins brought from Spain and dressed in silk by the devout church
mice of the village. They could distinguish Saint Francis's rope belt
in the heights of the churches, and they learned which order had
constructed each section. Santi collected butterflies, river rocks,
little idols found at archaeological sites. On the bus, they sang
Spanish songs, led by Raimundo, who had asked them not to call
him Father or Brother, but just Ray. He even taught them a few

poems that were a little unorthodox, like the one about the Virgin of Begonia:

> *Virgin of Begonia,*
> *grant me another husband,*
> *because the one I have,*
> *because the one I have,*
> *doesn't sleep with me.*

No one noticed the influence the tutor began to exercise over Leticia, except for maybe her brother Juan, who was as abstract as physics, and for whom Raimundo felt a special partiality. Maybe Juan thought there was nothing you could do about those things. Women are pretty at fifteen merely because they are young, but Leticia was pretty because she wanted to be, and she wanted everyone to notice. The only one who could have controlled her natural impulses was her eldest brother, but Lorenzo spent all his time at calle Bucareli, at the courts, at the *Milenio* newsroom, at Dr. Beristain's library, or who knows where the hell else. He wanted to think, to reflect, to live in the world of ideas, and thanks to the presence of the future priest, he could focus on himself with a clear conscience because the future of his brothers and sister was in the hands of a guider of souls, a man of the Church.

When they went on excursions, Leticia started to take Ray's hand on the steep paths, and to hold on to it longer than necessary. Then, with the insolence and impetuosity of youth, she threw herself into his arms one day until he hugged her back in a distinct embrace—that of a man and a woman who desire each other. Aunt Tana noticed that something was happening. Leticia always placed herself near the instructor, her eyes too bright or tearful. Aunt Tana had read Stendhal's *The Charterhouse of Parma* in French, and this seemed like the most brazen debauchery. She returned the seminarian to his order. At a family meeting she warned Lorenzo, stunned, that his sister was shameless and that from now on, he would be responsible for her future. "I wash my hands of this. I did everything for you orphans, but nothing has turned out the way I planned. You run away from the house, Juan steals from me, and now Leticia loses her head. I can't take any more."

Lorenzo looked at Leticia with true horror. He wanted to rationalize his hatred for "that fucking little priest"—which is what he called the banished cleric—but if he had come across him, he might have beaten him to death. Leticia's weakness was also repugnant. Of course, men were opportunists, and none of the family had known how to take care of his younger sister, including him. But Leticia was contemptible. He protested to Juan, who showed up every now and then.

Juan replied dryly, "You who study all the time. Haven't you read anything about human nature?"

It turned out that Juan knew a lot more about life than Lorenzo did. He went to the damned brothels, to Plaza Garibaldi and to calle de Órgano; the prostitutes held no secrets for him. He was their soul mate, he did them favors, he had power over them, and they looked to him to keep their money, because somehow Juan would double it. The world suddenly confronted Lorenzo. Not only was Leticia a loose woman; Juan, his brother, with such an aptitude for abstract thought, had dedicated himself to something very concrete—the dens of iniquity. Practically a pimp, Juan's low-life friends had dragged him to the depths, while he, Lorenzo, read *The Brothers Karamazov* and *Crime and Punishment* in Dr. Beristain's shadow.

"Mr. de Tena, you're not giving a speech. This is demagoguery."

"Me, a demagogue?" Lorenzo choked out.

"Yes, Mr. de Tena, yes, absolutely. Knowledge inherited from centuries ago is absolute. Questioning everything is a provocation. Please, come down from the podium and return to your seat. At this institution we demand that beliefs that are thousands of years old be respected—"

"You are the demagogues and opportunists," Lorenzo interrupted, at the height of indignation. "This is just a breeding ground for public office. No one discusses anything, because they all aspire to power and they fear they will not be considered if they rebel. A government post is a fountain of riches, and in order to drink from it, subservience and corruption are indispensable. Power in Mexico denigrates the individual. Lack of discussion or research is an obstruction of scientific progress. We have to go back and question everything. You're just social climbers, opportunists, third-rate politicians."

"Mr. de Tena, I ordered you to get down."

"If we don't think with our own heads," he shouted, "we're never going to progress. If we let ourselves be used, we'll not know how to apply our conclusions to the reality of the country. I just want to use my head—"

The professor raised his hand in the air. "Mr. de Tena, I'm going to have to call the director."

Lorenzo definitely had not adjusted to the Libre de Derecho. Something like that would never have happened at the university, where there was freedom in the courses. Each teacher could teach the material he wanted. Lorenzo had already provoked another controversy when he affirmed that knowledge and faith were two different things.

"If your classmates have faith, I don't see why you subject them to interrogations that don't concern them. Planting doubt in people's minds seems to be one of your goals, Mr. de Tena, and we're here to learn, not to take the wrong path. There is also an inflection of arrogance in what you say, which many of us teachers particularly dislike. In any case, I'm sure that life will take care of bringing you down a peg."

Lorenzo delivered blows left and right. He felt Lucía's death in his own being. His lover's decomposed flesh covered him in filth. Leticia's pregnancy was also indecent, and the comments people made about the crime at the house on Insurgentes plagued him. This high-class woman's intimacy fascinated the aristocracy. *Boccato di cardinale*, what a juicy tidbit, said Uncle Manuel, placing a petit four into his big mouth at the bridge game, and that pedestrian gesture in a reserved man submerged Lorenzo in confusion. How disgusting. If Manuel reacted that way, what must the rest have thought? Now that Lucía was not alive to defend herself, her most innocuous gestures were torn to pieces, and what Lorenzo had to hear on the street, at the courts, at the *Milenio* newsroom, plunged him into a stupor. He felt as if his body were stained— and everyone else's as well. If someone put his ugly face close to Lorenzo's to gossip, he would back up, as if he had suddenly discovered that men sweat, defecate, become shapeless and bloody masses. The pavement on the street also smelled of urine. The horror of Lucía's death accompanied him, and he asked himself, shooing away nonexistent flies, if he was going crazy.

Several blocks from the house on Lucerna, Lorenzo settled in with his sister in a building on calle Marsella that seemed to disintegrate each time someone pulled a toilet chain. Lorenzo sank into a depression as he regarded the three measly rooms, their dimensions and the fact that the windows looked out onto a wall. He did not attend the Libre de Derecho any longer, and although it exasperated him to have to show up at the law office of Rosendo Pérez Vargas, who exploited him, the salary was even more indispensable now that he had to pay rent and support his sister.

At 35 Mesones, he bought a Smith-Corona with a double tabulator so the margins would stay vertically aligned, and with the help of another legal assistant, José Sotomayor, who was an excellent typist, he wrote up the complaint briefs.

"De Tena, go collect what's due from El Rápido Fleet Company today. The insurance company already came to see me about it."

"Those bills can't be collected. They're so small and old," protested Lorenzo.

"Go today. Do you have the written complaints?"

"No. There's nothing worse than writing up these complaints," Lorenzo said anxiously.

José Sotomayor got him out of the mire. "Give them to civil court. They work fast there and don't ask for much in the way of a tip."

Lorenzo became furious. "Since I came into this office, the only two words that I hear are *tip* and *bribe*." The law office always put him in the worst mood. He would start boiling as soon as he arrived in the vestibule and would grumble his rancor during the long hours of waiting for the judge's signature.

Accompanied by the clerk, agreement in hand, he went to notify El Rápido, the freight company on 64 Moneda, of the complaint. They didn't find the building, but there was a surprise waiting for them. On the sidewalk in front, piano and violin music could be heard through the windows of the academy run by maestro José Montes de Oca at the House of the Seven Princes. Why didn't I ever study music? Lorenzo thought. If I had learned to play the violin, I'd be inside there and not here collecting on beggarly invoices. Several trucks were parked in front. "Son, there is no such number," said one of the drivers, "but maybe Saúl with the freight company on the corner would know." Saúl's fleet was the Mercury, and farther ahead was the Arrow. They had never heard of El Rápido. The owners of the trucks had invoices printed with fictitious names—Pegasus Freight, Rapid Transport, Reliable Moving, Condor Fleet, Greyhound, Thunder—all of which disappeared at the speed of light. The clerk looked at Lorenzo. Embarrassed about wasting the clerk's time, Lorenzo offered to treat him to the white and airy tortilla-like *garnachas* from the woman who made quesadillas on the corner of Moneda Street. This was where the drivers and loaders fed their faces. Lorenzo dipped his *garnacha* in green sauce; the clerk preferred red.

Crestfallen, Lorenzo accompanied the clerk to Donceles and said good-bye at the door to the courthouse. "As soon as I find something out, I'll let you know," Lorenzo said. "Please forgive the waste of time." How inexperienced he was, and how corrupt the fleet owners were, and how infuriating this life of a legal assistant— pencil pushers! How did Diego and the rest of the gang tolerate it?

Nevertheless, on the way home, Lorenzo was compensated for his trouble. A little fat man wearing a felt hat had set up a telescope, and he was stopping pedestrians in front of the Guardiola building on the corner of 5 de Mayo: "Come talk to the stars . . ."

Lorenzo stopped. He adjusted the telescope, carefully focusing it, and the moon appeared through the lens. The street hawker kept yelling out, "Come see the moon. Come on up. There's enough for everyone."

At times there were as many as three or four people and even a dog in line. Then the asphalt astronomer would let loose with his spiel. "See the moon for fifty cents. Visit the moon, get to know her better; make her your own. You never know, there's a chance you could see God!"

The idea that a biological God existed, who intervened in everyday life and directed organic evolution, permeated the corner of 5 de Mayo. Lorenzo was about to contradict the man and assert that biology, astrophysics, and other sciences proved the opposite, but the street hawker would have resisted the explanation, just like Lorenzo's buddies and fellow students at Libre de Derecho, as well as Aunt Tana. When the real world of space, time, and substance was discovered, what would happen to the men genetically predisposed to accept only one truth? He, Lorenzo, gave almost everything cosmic importance, including the most common daily events. Maybe he was the crazy one. Many times he had thought he would like to melt into something bigger than himself, maybe into the cosmos that was observed by this deficient telescope. Perhaps that's what happiness was.

On his fourth visit, the sidewalk astronomer recognized Lorenzo. "You, young man, really do like walking on the moon."

Leticia's presence and the magnitude of her belly did nothing to help his frame of mind. She weighed him down. As she got heavier and heavier, she made him fatter as well. They ran into each other in the hallway, in the bathroom. I'm sorry. Excuse me. I didn't know. There's no lock on this. I'm sorry. Leticia didn't sing anymore. Her corpulence confronted them at every instant. They were no longer the winged and transparent brother and sister in front of the mirror, but two sweaty and embarrassed bundles that restricted air circulation as they expanded. They listened to each other's footsteps with apprehension. Here he comes . . . he's leaving . . . he closed the door. They anticipated the sentences they would interweave with resentment. Lorenzo stayed out of the house as much as possible. Sometimes, in order not to see his sister, he sat on a bench on avenida Alvaro Obregón.

Leticia served him lunch on a small wooden table in the kitchen, and unlike the blessed Tila, she didn't do it particularly well. Besides, it nauseated him. One morning Lorenzo interrupted her endless string of comments about the workings of the building. "Leticia, just shut up. I can't even think!" When he heard her crying behind the closed door to her room, rage pierced him. Determined to be through with her, he yelled ruthlessly, "You had your fun, right? So don't cry now."

His younger sister never acted offended. One of the rules of women of her class was to overlook incidents, without establishing a connection between good and bad and without drawing any conclusions. The same mistakes could be repeated until death, without a lesson ever being learned. Leticia's restless and senseless conversation revolved around the subject that affected Lorenzo the most—Lucía's murder. With the meticulousness of a certified public accountant, she made it her business to know everything. It turned out that Lucía was not who everyone thought she was, but just the opposite. "Lucía—and you should know this better than anyone—had a dreadful secret life."

"Why should I know that?"

"Because you walked her home every time she came to play bridge with Aunt Cayetana," Leticia answered maliciously.

The milk that was forming inside Leticia, the streams that were born under her breasts and furrowed through them like a poisonous system, formed an atrocious net that trapped Lorenzo the same way it had trapped Leticia. Taking responsibility for Leticia was like taking responsibility for Lucía's murder. Concentrated in this fatherless child were the deception and the abandonment to which he and his siblings had been subjected. In this child lay Santiaguito, with his devoted "Papá, can I bwing you your slippews?"; Juan's stealing; Lorenzo's rage. The only survivor was Emilia, in the United States.

In order to avoid his sister's verbosity, Lorenzo would say, "I'm leaving now," or "I'm here." Every now and then, when he'd return home, he would stifle the impulse to tell her, "I was offered this job . . ." Maybe if he hadn't stifled it, they would have fallen into a familiar conversation, the kind that nurtures intimacy, but when he saw her, the desire would vanish. At first, when she served his coffee, Leticia would sit at the wooden table with him. Now she went back to her room, her gait heavy with pregnancy, her legs separated. Wearing a robe, always the same one, Leticia awaited childbirth. Once she was free, her luck would change.

Lorenzo began to lie. He hid his sister's whereabouts, and he lied about everything. He didn't even tell Diego that Leticia was going to have a child. Something like this would never happen to the Beristain sisters. They had too much self-respect; they hadn't been degraded by their mother's death. Lorenzo repeated to himself that hiding the truth was not lying; many truths were hidden in the universe. If men debated in a swamp of moral and aesthetic judgment, what in hell could a measly lie matter? Besides, to whom did he owe the truth?

Surely, if he went to Dr. Beristain, the doctor would help him, but his pride wouldn't allow it. Ask someone for something? The very suggestion made him sick. But he was strapped for money. Leticia did the impossible in keeping his shirts and trousers in fairly good condition. Should he write to Emilia in the United States and ask for her help? Now a newlywed, she would have to ask her husband, and they were already responsible for Santiago, whom she had sent for, as promised.

In his rage, Lorenzo committed himself to destroying everything he had once loved. He magnified his buddies' faults, exaggerating their traits to the point where they became worthless. How easy! I'm like the illustrator José Guadalupe Posada, he thought. I capture men at their most unfortunate moments. He pictured the gang members in front of his eyes—grotesque, dislocated puppets—and he stopped them right at the edge, the better to push them into the abyss. He repeated the motto that they had touted with such jubilation: "May the weak and those who have failed perish. And let us help them to disappear. May this be our first principle of love toward our fellow man." He fulfilled it literally. No one was spared.

His friend Diego threw himself into law with a vigor that Lorenzo didn't share. Although they had been very young at the time, they had both heard Alejandro Gómez Arias request autonomy for the university. "I hate this career more and more," Lorenzo told Diego, "and I want out of it more than anything."

"You're crazy. That's where our future lies. We're going to be rich and happy. We'll do great things for Mexico. Lawyers are the ones who matter the most."

"I'm not interested in being like the ones who matter."

"Don't be an idiot. They run the country."

"That's why we're going straight to ruin."

"Lorenzo, please . . ."

It was really better for the friends to avoid Lorenzo. "Brother, you're going through a bad time, but you'll make it. Maybe, without realizing it, you miss your aunt Cayetana," Chava said.

Lorenzo was about to kick him, but his friend cracked up laughing, and for a moment they were back to the way they had been before—two boys, arm in arm.

Lorenzo had divorced himself from Diego ever since the night they were walking along avenida Álvaro Obregón in front of the Catroviejos' French-like house, through whose tall windows they could see gigantic mirrors, chandeliers with hundreds of lights, soft parquet floors, and golden chairs worthy of Versailles.

"You have to marry a rich woman!" exclaimed Diego.

The house was just that—a marble woman covered in lace and fluff. The daughters of the family, accompanied by a good dowry of beams and fine wood, were of marriageable age. The young men had to catch them. Lorenzo turned into a panther, and for the first time in his life, he remembered his French.

"*Macros*, that's what you all are. Pimps!"

"What's wrong with you?"

"You're kept whores."

"Listen to me, Lorenzo."

"You make me sick."

He was so angry that the others stopped, except for Diego's colleague Alberto, who, full of fury, threw himself on Lorenzo. Before he could raise his hand to strike, Diego took his friend by the arm. "Let's go, Lorenzo. Come on." He took him straight to his car. "Calm down, buddy of mine! With remarks like that, you're going to end up all by yourself. Alberto was just joking."

"It was no joke. Everyone knows he's after the richest girl. That boring Sandra Orvañanos!" Lorenzo yelled.

"Lorenzo, you need to calm down, or your reputation is going to be the end of you. I'm telling you this because I've known you for years. The guys have been saying that you've become unbearable. There's going to come a time when no one will want to have anything to do with you."

"I don't want to be around those freaks anyway."

8

"Father, you have to speak with Lorenzo," Diego told Dr. Beristain with concern. "I'm telling you that there are moments when he seems to lose his mind."

"It's because he's extremely intelligent and very sensitive."

"He may be as intelligent as you say, but someday he's going to do something crazy."

"That I know. Of all of you boys, he's the only one who could commit suicide."

"What?"

"It's true, Diego. Your friend de Tena is capable of the most extreme actions."

"If you know that, why don't you help him?"

"Of course I'll help him, to the extent that he will allow me. In the meantime, nothing would be more beneficial to him than to be our friend and to be in our house. He's a noble boy, but there is great arrogance in him. I don't know what will happen in the long run."

What perception his father had. No one had Lorenzo's ability to concentrate. Once he became lost in a book, no human power could convince him to do something he didn't want to do. How many parties they'd had without him. But it was never the same when he wasn't there. His originality, his daring made the parties unpredictable and more fun.

Once, Lorenzo had told him that sex could be a heavy burden for a man.

"A burden?" Diego laughed. "A burden? It's a pleasure, man. The best there is."

"I'm not referring just to coming, you fool. I'm talking about something much deeper."

"What, Lorenzo? Tell me, what? Come on, because I'm not in the mood for philosophizing."

"We have a responsibility to the woman herself—to the woman. We should protect her."

Diego remembered his friend's disgust when he had gone to the whorehouse for the first time, and how he had cried, "I detest what just happened." Diego was confused, and Lorenzo looked away.

One time, when Lorenzo had severely criticized his classmates at the Libre de Derecho, Dr. Beristain said to him, "There is no bigger tragedy in life, Lorenzo, than to become a champion of good and believe in it."

The boy's orphanhood moved Dr. Beristain as much as his atheism—which he declared over and over. The more Lorenzo claimed that he didn't need any god and that he was a free man because he didn't believe, the more he quoted Nietzsche. It made Dr. Beristain want to embrace the boy, and tell him that he needed everything, and that he was willing to give it to him. However, it wasn't that easy.

"I still haven't developed a scholarly routine, Doctor. I can't hold on to anything. You, on the other hand, are a thinker. You have work habits and training that I haven't attained. Your conclusions always surprise me."

"I have reached a compromise, and that is something that you, de Tena, my friend, ignore, and not accidentally. Someday you'll appreciate that, and you will remember me, I have no doubt."

"I broke with the Church, and that torments me," said Lorenzo.

"You know very well I'm a Juarista. The path you have chosen must worry your family."

"Doctor, I don't have a family. I have younger siblings, an older sister in the United States, that's all. If I have to answer to anyone, it is to you, who have treated me like a son."

"In any case, Lorenzo, it must have been difficult to leave them."

"Why shouldn't there be a price for freedom, for those who want it?"

"Are you sure you have freed yourself?"

"Yes, Doctor." He smiled a juvenile and beautiful smile. "That I am sure of."

Lorenzo had crushed Leticia's lover like a cockroach. He spent several days demonstrating scientifically that Raimundo was not worth a second thought. "Listen, love exerts tremendous control over life. It imprisons you. It shoves you into a tunnel that is impossible to get out of." He hugged her. "We all have at least one chance in life. The trick is not to let it pass you by. You can forge a future from where you stumbled, and I'm going to help you. I swear we'll get through this together. Once your child is born, you'll get back to normal."

He told himself the same thing he told her, but he couldn't forget that the night Lucía had humiliated him, he had fervently wished her dead. The newspaper wrote of a spiteful lover. Maybe Lucía had insulted the man. She was an expert at demeaning people.

That was how Lorenzo entered the world of suspicion. His motto became "Distrust and you will succeed." Life and the actions of others infuriated him, but what tormented him most was that they invaded his ideas, they never left him alone, and they obstructed his train of thought, through which he proceeded as if toward some goal. Space . . . time . . . could it be measured with a ruler the way you measured distance? At night he planned his work for the following day. "Tomorrow I'm going to the university; then I'll stop at the library to check—" He slept, content with the possibility of discovery. Life, cruel as it was, decided otherwise. Leticia was another mountain in the middle of the road, impossible to tunnel through. Lorenzo could have murdered her lover. "The only thing I ask is that you let me work," he demanded.

To which Leticia responded, "Work on what? All you do is read, and when you aren't reading, you sit there staring, deep in thought."

"I think, Leticia. I think."

"I can't stand your great silences, Lencho. It's as if I didn't exist."

"You're right. You exist only in your capacity to create problems for me."

"And when you marry? And when you have children, then what? The only thing that matters to you is that a woman lets you work?"

"Yes. That's what I would most appreciate from anyone."

"What about your children?"

"I'll never have children."

Leticia wasn't aware of the effort it took to bring money into that tiny apartment, Lorenzo accumulated jobs, ran from one place to another with his briefcase hanging from his arm. The tempo of the judges, the secretaries, the bureaucracy all made him furious, and he had to keep repeating to himself, Calm down. Calm down. Don't raise your voice. But he would turn red, and acerbic criticism would fall from his lips onto the desks like asteroids. "Where is our poor country going to end up, with people like you?" "Bad tempered," a teacher had correctly written on his report card once. The rudeness, the idiocy of everyday life interrupted the flow of his thoughts and kept him in a state of perpetual annoyance.

When Leticia had her daughter, Lorenzo became more violent. "Don't breast-feed her here. Have a little modesty." Leticia's enormous breasts disturbed him. When the child was twenty days old, he asked if she was going to start eating with a spoon. The birth of the calf that Florencia had lifted onto its four legs was much better than this slow process in which he was forced to participate. The smell in the apartment changed for the worse. Leticia, her daughter in her arms, left a trail of dirty diapers.

Six months later, Leticia met him at the door. "Lorenzo, I'm leaving."

"What do you mean, you're leaving? Where are you going?"

"With my son's father."

"What?"

"Yes, I'm leaving, with my son's father."

"With that derelict?" Lorenzo wavered between disbelief and hatred. "Besides, why do you call her your son? It was my understanding that you had a girl. You named her Leticia like yourself."

"I'm sure now that this one is a boy." She pointed to her belly.

Leticia was leaving, but with someone else. Lorenzo couldn't believe it. "Who is he? Where did you meet him? When? How, when, and where? Bitch! Of course you're leaving me. Apocalyptic beast. I can't tolerate your being here one minute longer. You're an imbecile as well as a bitch. You aren't worthy of my mother's memory. You're nothing—just a female in heat, like all women. Whores, whores!"

Leticia was no longer listening to him. She had everything ready. The scum was waiting for her on the corner.

"On the corner? The asshole!"

"That's life, Lorenzo. Women take off with the one on the corner."

How despicable female nature was.

Leticia's absence didn't bring him the calm he had expected. It took a lot of effort to concentrate on reading.

At one in the morning Lorenzo was reading Goethe's *Faust* when the doorbell rang. After Leticia left, Lorenzo had given Diego the address to his apartment. The bell rang again, and Lorenzo ran downstairs. Nobody rang like that at this time of night.

It was Diego. "Lorenzo, come on. Let's get to Lucerna. There's bad news."

In the Ford on the way, Diego broke the news. "Your father is dying. I'm not sure if you'll make it in time. Your aunt Tana called the house and asked us to find you."

"What happened to my father?"

"They're going to say it was cardiac arrest."

"But what did my father die from?"

"He was hit by a rock."

Lorenzo's face burned. "What?"

"What I just said. He was hit by a rock."

"Where? How? We're not out in the woods. Who dies from being hit by a rock?" Lorenzo put his hand on Diego's arm.

"He was walking along the street, and as he turned the corner, someone threw a rock. It was just a stroke of bad luck that it hit him on the back of the head. Of course, there was a lot of blood. I'll spare you the rest."

"This is crazy. Did they catch the person who threw it?"

"Of course not, and they never will. Some neighborhood kids who knew him picked him up and took him home."

What kind of death was this? Was it the Stone Age? Like the death of the adulterous woman from the Gospel who was attacked by a condemning mob? That kind of death, in the twentieth century, in the middle of the city? A blow to the head? Lorenzo was indignant. Such humiliation inflicted on his father. Stoned like a dog. That such a delicate man should die this way injured Lorenzo in his most intimate being; his heart pounded, and his temples were bathed with sweat. "I don't understand. I don't understand anything. A rock?" he repeated.

Diego sped through the empty city, and they got there in a heartbeat. Doña Tana, Tila, and two women dressed in black were around Don Joaquín's bed. The flickering of the light from the candlesticks against the walls made the bedroom seem like a chapel.

"You didn't make it. He had a heart attack," said Tana, upset.

His father's face, his head on the pillow, his eyelids already closed by Tila's merciful hands, had a nobility that struck Lorenzo. How was it possible that he had never noticed it? Don Joaquín's flawless profile was accentuated, his ample forehead, his thin lips drawn up in a slight smile on his white face, giving him an unsuspected spirituality.

He never did anything in his life, thought Lorenzo. How is it possible that he has that nobility? But he did. Tila's thick hands arranged the sheets and smoothed Don Joaquín's hair back with a confidence that made Lorenzo stare at her. So Tila loved this man who had never worked and was given to idleness and irresponsibility? Never had he noticed that an affectionate tie existed between his father and Tila. It had always seemed as if the maid didn't even exist to Don Joaquín.

Tila murmured in a quiet voice, "We should send for the boy. Santiago loved his daddy so much."

Juan, undaunted, stayed in the shadows.

There was a sob from the corner of the room. It was Aunt Tana.

Lorenzo, surprised by her crying, was crushed by two revelations—
the nobility in his father's face and Tana's capacity for emotion.

Guessing his thoughts, Tila, who continued to fix the bed, said,
"She loved her brother like a son. She always protected him. She
can't accept that he has gone before her. It's hard for her, Lorenzo.
It's the worst."

Seeing her beaten like that made him afraid. He approached
and put his hand on her shoulder. "You've always been strong,
Aunt. Don't fail us now."

Aunt Tana, neck bowed, hair white, face soaked with tears, only
made an affirmative gesture with her shoulders. Or had she raised
her shoulder to say, What does it all matter now?

Tila approached Lorenzo again. "Isn't Leticia coming? The people from the funeral home are about to come in, and after that,
everything will happen very quickly. You're going to have to leave.
I'm going to dress him."

Lorenzo was startled once more. Tila, with the round, strangely
smooth and young face, was his father's caretaker. ("Dark skin can
tolerate more than white skin," Leticia told him once, when he
made a comment about it.) She also made the decisions. Tila, who
had never married, would now embalm his father. She would wash
him and dress him in his best suit; she would knot his tie. Lorenzo
remembered how Don Joaquín, standing behind him in front of the
mirror, had tied his tie when he wore his first dinner jacket, years
ago. When four black magpies came up the stairs, Tila shut herself
in with them.

Lorenzo was surprised at his aunt Tana's composure during the funeral. Not a single sign of depression. Stiff, she smiled haughtily
under her lace mantilla, which was held tall by a comb that gave
her the bearing of a defeated queen.

"She looks like a Velázquez painting," said Diego.

"More like a Goya," corrected Lorenzo.

The usual people filed in. Leticia appeared suddenly at the
cemetery, wearing a skirt that was too short, her hair tousled, looking outrageous. She breathed health, and her aura enveloped them

all. Her curly, disheveled reddish hair made a halo around her face, as if she had just awakened from sleep. Nobody paid any attention to poor Joaquín, and Lorenzo heard the Marquesa of Ciruelillo say out loud, "She looks like an Italian film star."

The Count of Olmos focused his binoculars on her, as if he were at the opera, and he said to Mimí Roura Reyes, "She has the face of an angel."

Leticia's legs, without stockings, were like two magnets, tanned by the sun, standing on the black earth next to the four cemetery employees who were shoveling dirt into the grave. Nobody could look away from those cedar towers, or from her bare arms that emerged from an ordinary blouse. As the gravediggers scooped up the dirt, they also raised their eyes to the woman gleaming in the sunlight, her recently bathed skin luxuriant. She was pure radiant energy. No wonder the atoms crowded around her. There were no ghosts at this burial. Lorenzo watched in anger how they all went to hug Leticia and give her their condolences, even before speaking with Aunt Cayetana. *Gloria in Excelsis Dei*, Leticia. Men, women, and children wanted to press against that creature of delight. The elderly men all called themselves her uncles. They covered her face with kisses, saying, "Don't cry, my pretty child. Don't cry. I'm here for you." They wiped her tears with their lips (Leticia, sentimental and noisy, shed tears copiously). In the end, the younger sister of the de Tena family, Don Joaquín's daughter, stole his funeral honors.

The young people, who never thought about praying, inquired hastily, "Where are they going to say the Rosary? When is mass?" And they asked Leticia, who didn't have a clue about any upcoming services.

When she said good-bye, Doña Tana said to her niece, "I hope you attend the Rosaries in another skirt and a long-sleeved blouse."

"Yes, Aunt." She hugged Tana. "I just grabbed the first thing I could find. I didn't even have time to put hose on."

"Yes, we all saw that. Stop by the house first so I can look you over."

"Of course, Aunt."

"I'll lend you an appropriate mantilla."

"Thank you, Aunt."

As it turned out, the most conspicuous member of the proud de Tenas was the outcast, the fallen one, the one who did whatever she pleased. Lorenzo, incredulous, watched Aunt Tana put her arms around Leticia's waist, despite her long absence. Did Cayetana de Tena suspect something? Surely she did, because she didn't ask her, when are you getting married? She could never admit that a de Tena had fallen into disgrace. In the meantime, the smartest thing to do was to ignore it. In spite of everything, her niece's presence made her face light up. Aunt Tana raised her powdered cheeks so that the girl's swollen and fruity lips would rest on them, and she returned the kiss at the speed of sound.

Lorenzo had no alternative but to conclude that nature overcomes all prejudice. "Are you all right, Leticia?" he asked seriously.

"Yes, brother, I am."

"Do you eat well? Do your children eat well?"

"Yes, we eat well. If you come to the house, I'll serve you five poopy meatballs with pee sauce, puree of wax, and snot gelatin."

The same Leticia as always. She couldn't change even under these circumstances. Lorenzo turned his back on her.

Diego confirmed the general reaction: "My God, what sex appeal your sister has. Believe me, I had a great time. So great that I'm going to La Bandida right now. What are your plans, Lorenzo?"

To Diego's amazement, the young de Tena responded, "I'm going with you. Fight death with life is a good rule of mental health. I have an enormous urge to fuck too."

"You've never used that word. Let's go. Man, what a sweet thing your sister is. I hope you'll excuse me, but she's hot—what a lay. Not very often have I seen such an angel, and believe me, I do know about women."

"And I don't?"

"Not you. You live in another world, Lorenzo."

9

A year or so after the death of Don Joaquín, Aunt Cayetana's husband, Manuel, also passed away, as quietly as he had lived. Every two or three months Lorenzo visited Cayetana. Leticia also kept her company some afternoons, without the children, of course. Juan had vanished. Santiago, the youngest, was now an economist, living in the United States. "His future is on Wall Street," the brokers told Emilia, who sent them pictures of a tall, thin boy on whose shoulders the banking trade sat quite well.

Welcome, welcome, Mr. Buckley . . . Lorenzo would greet him that way when he returned to Mexico.

Lorenzo forced himself to go to the house on Lucerna. When he crossed the threshold, the walls molded to his body like an old coat. Enter the kitchen; hug Tila. "Lenchito, can I get you something before you leave?" Up to the bedroom to see Cayetana sitting in the sun. It was a conditioned reflex.

"Aunt, you're so quiet."

"Since you all left, there's no activity. I have few guests, so I don't get invited out much."

"And your big dinner parties?"

"Not anymore, Lorenzo, not anymore. Without your father and without Manuel, I don't have the energy. I died along with them."

"Aunt, don't say that. What about bridge?"

"I do that. You see, it distracts me, but that's only once a week, with friends who are just as alone as I am."

As he left, Lorenzo promised himself that he would visit her more often, but his daily hustle and bustle didn't allow for it, and besides, he held a grudge against her because she had enrolled him in the Libre de Derecho. Only once did she look Lorenzo in the eyes, when he announced to her, "Aunt, I don't want to be a lawyer. I can't tolerate the corruption, the fraud. The jobs they assign us are degrading. And I don't have the stomach for evicting people."

When he gave up law, Lorenzo didn't have anyone to share his fears with. Asphyxiated as he was under the gray cloak of his depression, the streets no longer distracted him. He walked deep in thought. How easy it was to feel lost in the city that had been like home the day before.

One morning he noticed Chava on calle Bucareli, and he took refuge in the first shop he could find. He didn't want anyone to see him. The last time he had seen Diego Beristain, his buddy had said, "Oh, my God, man, you look awful! You're all skin and bones. What's wrong with you?"

Lorenzo anticipated Chava's exclamations and his fondness for hyperbole: You've left the law office? Brother, where is your savoir faire? If you don't assimilate, you're never going to get anywhere.

The gang's direction was ascendant. Chava Zúñiga spent more and more time with the politicians. Víctor Ortiz found work with the United Nations. La Pipa had also entered into the diplomatic service: "My salary is paid in dollars, brother." Of course, Diego had the most brilliant career, as he was the most gifted.

"How is Lorenzo?" Leticia said when they asked her about him. "The worst ever. Terrible. You can't believe how bad. He's never been in this severe a crisis. Everyone runs from him." She did Lorenzo the favor of repeating the gang's comments to him, laughing. She later clarified: "You can divulge the sins, but not the name of the sinner."

"So now you're an accomplice to my friends? You can keep them, Leticia."

"They prefer me anyway. Before, they needed you at *Milenio*; now you seem dangerous. The last time they saw you, the only thing you talked about was the seven million dogs that had to be killed because seven hundred Mexicans had died of rabies. You even gave numbers—two hundred thousand dogs produce two hundred and fifty grams of crap apiece. Since you never dropped the subject of feces, about which you had such precise details, they thought you had rabies." Leticia laughed.

Lorenzo growled to run her off. Leticia could take her life and pass it on to someone else as if it were a stone. In his case, no one would take responsibility for him. He didn't have his sister's charms. Women can cling to the male body, belong to it, live the other's life. He had to find his own life. While the others took off spiritedly, he withdrew, incredulous, desperate.

Leticia, on the other hand, was as happy as an abundant river, a smile on her lips. You could even hear her hair growing. Everything about that woman moved, everything. Each pregnancy made her sparkle. With one child in her arms and the other by the hand, she walked along on her high heels with the grace of a debutante. No wonder they take a fancy to her, thought Lorenzo. She left pieces of herself everywhere, like gifts. She attended to her children between laughs and jokes. She never mentioned the lover of the hour, "so you won't be annoyed, you're such a big grump." When Lorenzo would say good-bye, she kept throwing him kisses from the doorway.

"You're so irresponsible."

"That's why you're here, to be the conscience of Mexico," she'd respond, making a face.

"Where are you going to end up, Leticia?"

"What about you? With your deep thoughts you're closer to hell than I am."

Maybe she's right, thought Lorenzo, astonished. She was irresponsible, and yet, how sure she was of herself. The memory of Florencia stuck him like a lightning bolt. "Where do you live, Leticia?" he asked. "No, don't tell me. I don't want to know."

"I live in a house with a garden and the children, and we throw ourselves on the grass to look for four-leaf clovers. I also have a magnolia tree, the kind you like so well, and it flowers every year."

"Well then, you honor your name with that smile."

"Really? The only time I was truly unhappy was when I was with you."

"Why, Leticia?"

"Because I had to stop being myself to share your life. I feel sorry for whoever marries you."

"I'll never marry. I'm not made to have a family."

"You'll see, Lorenzo, that life can decide differently. Your poor wife will never able to dance naked."

"What woman wants to dance naked?"

"I do, Lorenzo, and many more like me." She was different, a natural phenomenon that was impossible to classify.

He would have liked to see Juan, although he didn't really know anything about him. He supposed he was doing well, and besides, in his particular state of mind, he sensed that Juan was the only one who would understand him.

"Our brother set up a foundry in the Tablas de San Agustín neighborhood. It's on the way to Pachuca. He'll be here soon to ask us for a loan," Leticia told him sarcastically.

"I'd like to talk to him."

"That surprises me. You always say he's a good-for-nothing."

"See, Leticia, I can surprise you too."

"I doubt it. You have everything but an imagination."

While leafing through a magazine in a barbershop, Lorenzo saw Diego Beristain's smiling face next to a sophisticated young woman at the "Black and White" dance at the Jockey Club. Lorenzo felt betrayed. He detested the three-hundred-and-one most-photographed people in the society section of *El Universal* and *Excélsior* more and more.

The root of it was his discussion with Diego, when Diego speared him with, "Brother, you're facing an anticommunist. Vasconcelos was right when he said that Russia is dishonored by the dictatorship of espionage and brutality without precedent."

Lorenzo left the table profoundly disappointed.

Diego went on. "You're becoming as radical as Narciso Bassols, who refused to be Secretary of the Supreme Court of Justice and told Ávila Camacho that not only was he not in agreement with his government, but he was going to fight against it."

That was what Lorenzo wanted to fight against. And he wanted to do it alongside men like Bassols, who was incapable of chasing a political position.

"So you're a supporter of the resignation champion?" Diego laughed.

"Is that what they call Bassols?"

"Yes. He even refused the job of Secretary of Education in 1934, which had been held by both Ortiz Rubio and Abelardo Rodríguez. He also said no to Secretary of State, because he was against gambling. Listen, I admire his civil courage, but Bassols doesn't live in the real world."

"Because he doesn't play the game with that pack of rats in the government? Because he wants to modernize education in Mexico? Because he has demonstrated against layoffs? Because he's opposed to the ostentation of the privileged class? Because he doesn't want Mexico to imitate Paris and be mired in trying to be French, which really makes us look like idiots? Don't tell me you've become a right-wing lawyer."

"Don't go on anymore, brother. Don't go on. Your poison will reach all the way to calle Bucareli."

Without knowing it, when he spoke to Lorenzo about Bassols, Diego had opened a door. Lorenzo had almost missed the announcement about the establishment of the Political Action League, which was headed up by Bassols. He showed up for the first meeting. Víctor Manuel Villaseñor and Manuel Mesa Andraca, Ricardo J. Zevada and Emigdio Martínez Adame rejected any approximation to power a priori, which, by being just that, was corrupt.

"Are you familiar with the Workers' University, Diego?" Lorenzo asked when he saw him next.

"To tell you the truth," Diego said, "I find Lombardo Toledano repulsive, no matter how eloquent he may be. He pretends to be with the masses, live like the masses, when in fact what he wants is to impose himself on them. But enough of that! Let's go to your Workers' University."

The lecture was bad, the indecisive teacher spoke in front of a worker who was sleeping under his railroad hat, and in the back of the room, knitting needles clicked. "The project is good, but the issue is, how to put it into practice," said Diego, sincerely sorry. "I would gladly come teach classes, but I think I'm more useful at the University of Mexico."

The worker's cry—"How can I be free if I don't 'know'?"—at the Political Action League assembly moved Lorenzo right down to his bones.

At his side, a young man who was more or less his age, José Revueltas, stood up immediately. "The comrade is right. The illiteracy that afflicts the country is horrendous. We don't even have books!"

The next day, anxiously, Lorenzo gave them his own books. They had been read so many times that some of them were sacred to him. Dostoevsky, Tolstoy, Romain Rolland.

Pepe, which was what they called José, the skinny one, leafed through them lovingly. "So you're one of us, comrade? I aspire to write a novel like these. I started one titled *The Ruin*, but it was trashed. They probably blew it up. Now I'm working on another one, *Walls of Water*. I think Chekhov and Gorky are bigger than Tolstoy. I dislike his style because it's filled with pity—that stupid passion, that condescending feeling—without thunder, without lightning, without the exaltations of a storm."

Neither José nor Lorenzo had participated in the Vasconcelos movement. They had been too young, although Lorenzo had witnessed the overwhelming movement in the city in support of Vasconcelos. He had been incensed with the electoral fraud. Vasconcelos called for an armed uprising but then became as invisible as the eye of an ant, going into exile and leaving his followers hanging.

"I wasn't a Vasconcelista, but as a philosopher, Vasconcelos is a good novelist." Pepe Revueltas smiled.

"He could still surprise us," protested Lorenzo.

"Not anymore. No, not anymore. He's an old man of forty-nine."

Pepe smoked nonstop, just like Lorenzo. Between cigarettes they talked about the proletariat, which irritated them like a burning spike between their eyes, which were reddened by the smoke. "I'm a nonconformist, a spoilsport, staunch enemy of the government, Comrade de Tena."

The phrase he quoted from Goethe stirred Lorenzo, and he would later repeat it himself: "Gray is every theory; green is the golden tree of life."

"Do you know Goethe's *Faust*?" Pepe asked him. Thomas Mann's *The Magic Mountain*? That's an exceptional novel. Read it: Settembrini's philosophical disquisitions will inspire you." Revueltas had read it in the original language. "I studied in a German school until fourth year."

More and more intrigued, Lorenzo waited impatiently for Pepe at the League headquarters. "Revueltas!" he greeted him as he saw him enter. "Revueltas!"

And the young man smiled at him. "Comrade, I really like that you call me by my sonorous last name instead of Pepe, like everyone else does."

I feel much closer to Revueltas than I do to the gang, Lorenzo concluded. His admiration for Revueltas had no limits once he discovered that in 1932, at seventeen, after a long imprisonment in the Islas Marías jail, he was released because he was a minor. Three years later he went back to the Marías in a raid; there he caught malaria. Revueltas still had scars and knots on his head from being kicked when he was detained, two of his ribs broken by the toes of his captor's shoes. He knew what a hunger strike was all about. He had slept on the concrete slab of a jail cell. He could incite a crowd and fire a weapon. His brother Fermín carried a gun. Politics was a man's business. For the Revueltas, protesting, riots, and persecution were daily events. Where was he, Lorenzo de Tena, when Revueltas, imprisoned in the juvenile courts, was studying Marxism? De Tena didn't even know what the Seventh Congress of the Communist International was, and Revueltas, a designated member of the Mexican delegation with Hernán Laborde and "El Ratón"—Miguel Ángel Velasco—had traveled to Moscow and shaken hands with Stalin himself. "The Russians are quite a people, brother! What great people! The only tragedy was that I learned of my brother Fermín's death during that time."

Because of his relationship with "El Pajarito"—Little Bird Revueltas—Lorenzo began to realize what it meant to live clandestinely. He had never before felt danger. "If you're against the government, they'll pursue you," said Pepe. "You must decide if you want to continue or stop here."

Lorenzo's clothes no longer distinguished him from the rest. His hunger either. El Pajarito and he came and went, sweaty, understanding the fatigue of the stooped-over porters. Revueltas called them comrades. "Let the comrade by, Tena," and the woman with the thick torso, her basket piled full of sheets, would pass by. So many people. The multitude agitated and repelled him. "You have to get lost in it, comrade." The city—what an eagerness for survival, even though on the corners, leaning against the posts, the vagrants hung around for hours, scratching their crotches. Lorenzo called them assholes. José Revueltas called them unemployed.

"Alcoholism, filth, lack of responsibility, how do you fight that?" Lorenzo asked.

"I'm not so sure that alcohol is damaging, Comrade Tena. It's given me my greatest enlightenment; it's launched me into sidereal space."

"And what do you know about space?"

They became less formal with each other through their conversations about space, and the immeasurable space made them two peas in a pod. They lived feverishly. Unable to say no to anything, exhaustion was gaining ground. "We'd feel terribly guilty if we didn't attend this meeting," Revueltas contended. They walked like crazy men to the Guerrero neighborhood to help a family get their things together—things that had been thrown all over the sidewalk—and to attempt to find them new lodging. In the meantime, the police were compiling a file on them.

"Could militancy be an introduction to insanity?" Lorenzo asked. They lived at the mercy of their lack of foresight. They spent time and energy looking for the reason why Mexico was lagging behind.

"Mexico has to situate itself on the revolutionary vanguard of the continent, comrade. We have an advantage. We've already lived what Europe is going through right now. We sent our masses to death in the Revolution of 1910. The Soviet Union survived it also, and that's why the proletariat union will win. To increase our production, we first have to create a social consciousness, a mystique. In Moscow, many young people of the Komsomol participated in the construction of the metro without pay. These are people truly filled with purity!"

According to Revueltas, what was important to the work of the

Party in the provinces was to have contacts. He had wasted a lot of time looking for transportation. Usually there wasn't even a ditch for a road. Not even for a horse. He'd have to wait until a rancher agreed to let him sit in the saddle behind him. "Can you believe, comrade, that most of the effort is spent just trying to get there? And when you get there, you have to find comrades willing to listen to you, something to eat, a place to sleep, because the guy from the Communist Party is never anywhere around, or he didn't leave the key. You waste your energy trying to figure out the logistics. There isn't any sound equipment, and everyone walks around inattentively. One night you finally ask yourself, What am I doing here? and you can't even stand yourself anymore. 'Ah, so you've come to teach us all something,' one of the local leaders of the shrimp workers' labor strike said to me, and then he proceeded to slap me across the face, as a bonus. Don't expect them to thank you, Lorenzo. That's a petit bourgeoisie reaction." Nevertheless, Pepe still exclaimed with an enormous smile, "All of this makes me happy to have been born!"

The image that Tena and Revueltas had was unrealistic. They didn't accept themselves or forgive themselves. "Distrust, and you will succeed," Lorenzo would say, and José would finish his thought: "The first person you must mistrust is yourself. Who knows what atrocities we're capable of? Now, give me a ticket for the ride."

"I don't have one, brother. Let's walk."

They walked the entire city. Of the two, Revueltas had more experience living day to day, and he could sleep peacefully on any park bench. He could even go four days without eating. With a laconic "I've gotten used to it," he would erase the bad times. "Fill up on liquids; water tricks the hunger. Besides, you're younger than I am and therefore stronger."

Just as with Bassols, his theme was the workers' struggle. He insisted on rural secular schools and focusing on the fields. "All Mexicans with the ability should be rural teachers."

Lorenzo offered to teach mathematics at the Octavio Silva Bacenas High School, located on the road to Puebla. Getting there was an odyssey that excited him. But there was no sign of acknowledgment in the classroom. "It's insulting," he commented to

Revueltas. "They're stone-faced, and I feel really bad." Was that so-
cialism, making someone do what they don't want to do by moral
obligation?

"I don't like to teach either, comrade. I like to think out loud,
with a beer in front of me." They never had money for beer or for
coffee, or even for rides. "We're dead broke, comrade." Revueltas
smiled. "We're poor, poor, poor. Why are we so poor?"

"There are people who are poorer than we are."

"There are also those who get out of poverty. Ours is an interminable poverty."

Poverty brought them together.

"Do you have anyone to borrow from?" Pepe asked.

Lorenzo blushed. "No."

Whom would he turn to? To Diego? He'd die first. The last
thing he wanted was for Diego to find out about his situation.
Lorenzo, allied with the vanquished, would be a loser, a dissident,
"an outsider," as Diego would say in his stupendous English.
Lorenzo swore he would not join the game or the system. Besides,
Diego had thought that the newspaper *Combate* was supine foolishness. "It looks like a recipe from a popular inn or for economic cuisine. It's a disgrace. Lorenzo, did you even analyze it? Bassols is
asking for soap, a bed without lice, food and the necessary clothing
so as not to be hungry or cold, a good sex life in place of the misery
that inhibits drive or debases the emotions, a minimum degree of
culture, which guarantees balance and the happiness that only science can give. He wants us to look to the different corners of nature and the different nuclei of human life in order to have a total
sense of the universe. It's so simplistic, it borders on pathetic. I
don't understand what you're doing there, or what those 'corners'
are, brother!" Diego kept repeating, "What riches are you going to
distribute? First you have to create them. We have to 'do.' You're
one of the doers. Foreign investment is flowing in; we're the future
of the world. Inter-American Development Bank believes in us:
'Mexico is the most viable country of the continent.' Are you going
to waste this magnificent moment?"

The moment? The PRI—the Institutional Revolutionary Party,
which was the ruling party—treated the country as if it were its

own settlement. The presidents had secret accounts, with funds in excess of a hundred million dollars a year, with which they lined their pockets. Created by constitutional right in 1917 by Venustiano Carranza, that money was part of their tremendous power.

"We have to end presidentialism, Diego. It's drowning us with its corruption."

"If they do something good, it doesn't matter if they're getting rich."

Having become wildly impulsive, Lorenzo went from joking to derision, from laughter to anger. Unable to control himself, he threw his darts. Many commented on his cruel wit. "Don't get near him. If he doesn't like you or you say something he disagrees with, he'll rip you to shreds in front of everyone." "If anyone knows how to humiliate, it's de Tena."

At one of the last parties, Chava grabbed Diego by the sleeve, saying "Take him with you, anywhere. You're the only one who can get him out of here. Just look at Beba's face. Everyone is shocked by his behavior."

Irascible, Lorenzo wanted everyone to think about training centers, community development, technical training, potable water plants, school construction, and workshops where the poor could discover their potential. "We need to support national development with science." But after a few people said, "How interesting!" the friends went back to the latest political rumor, to their own stories, to gossip. "Where is your sense of social responsibility?" screamed Lorenzo, until Chava said, "Brother, we're with you, but you always pick the wrong time to bring it up."

When was the right time? When would the moment come? Didn't they live in chaos and caciquism?

Diego did not share Lorenzo's inclination toward the Communist youth. "What's wrong with you, Lencho? You exude animosity. Who would have thought it? Those who knew you before would never have suspected that you would turn into a fanatic. With your lucidity, your strict sense of perfection, the way you control your ideas—you were going to make your life a work of art. Are you doing that? You were doing well, Lencho, but for some obscure reason you've chosen to betray your social class."

"These are my kind."

"No, Lencho. No. You'll find out. At the first opportunity, they'll kick you out."

"Your classist arguments don't belong in the twentieth century," Lorenzo answered.

"Be realistic, Lencho. You have to be suspicious about the Glorious Russian Revolution. Be suspicious of any political system, right or left. Why have you become so committed to the left? Capitalism creates sources of work. Look how the Mexicans cross the Rio Grande because our revolutionary country isn't capable of feeding them. We have to give them jobs, but the main thing we need to do is to stop being a protectionist state. The working class? Don't make me laugh. In the depths of their little hearts, the workers want what everyone wants—a good life. Have you spoken with Josephus Daniels, the ambassador from the United States? The other day I heard him speaking with Ezequiel Padilla, in the Department of Foreign Relations, and I agreed with some of his points."

How was it possible that Diego went to foreign relations meetings, when the gringos wouldn't give in and wanted to take possession of the land along the Rio Grande.

Diego Beristain, Chava Zúñiga, Gabriel Iturralde, Víctor Ortiz, La Pipa Garciadiego—all inserted themselves in the business world.

"This is a war to the death, between the rich and the poor, Diego."

"Don't be simplistic, Lorenzo. Remember that in revolutions, the poor aren't winners either. The smart ones win, brother. The ones who were down at the bottom yesterday are on top today, and they attack exactly what they were defending yesterday."

Brother? Was he still one?

Money was essential, but Lorenzo and Pepe were exactly where it wasn't. It became an obsession because of its absence. "Can you do anything in life without money?" Lorenzo asked.

"Look at Gandhi, Lorenzo. Look at the Franciscans."

"Our needs are concrete—paper and ink for flyers; cold, hard cash for the printer." How was it possible that no one joined forces

with the Political Action League? Weren't they aware of its importance? Didn't Bassols have money? Why not ask him for it?

"Are you crazy? Work, comrade, work. He'd send us to be
porters in La Merced. Haven't you noticed that he never delegates
any jobs? He's the one who empties the garbage in the office."

"He must have something. No one holds a government position
for free."

"He lives day to day. I'm telling you, it's the truth."

Bassols kept a low profile, as Chava would later say. Looking at
him, no one would have believed he'd been a minister or an ambassador. One afternoon Lencho saw him hanging from the running board of a bus, traveling outside with the rabble. Lorenzo
would never have suspected that, years later, he too would adopt a
proletariat bicycle.

Lorenzo was fortified by listening to Bassols expound in such a
matter-of-fact way about a problem as heartrending as the exodus
of the Republicans from Spain in 1939. Bassols was capable of
making decisions. Hearing him, Lorenzo concluded that it must
have been very comforting for the refugees, after three years of war,
to meet up with this dry, precise man who took tangible measures,
talked to them about the future as a certainty, consulted with the
Mexican government by telegraph, and within ten days had an answer that was crucial to their lives. Hearing his penetrating words,
it was pointless to complain. He helped these people rebuild themselves. He told them that Mexico was waiting for them. They
would find work in a country where there was much to be done.
Nothing about him was charitable or sentimental. He would look
at his watch, and he seemed to be saying, Time for crying is over.
It's time to set sail and start a new life. He kept watch to ensure
that the food would last and that they took sanitary precautions on
the transatlantic liners *Ipanema, Sinaia, Méxique.* Intellectuals, laborers, farmers, they were all needed, even though Mexico was es-
sentially an agricultural country.

Bassols didn't do anything without consulting the Popular
Front, for which he felt immense respect, and they took turns with
the petitioners in the concentration camps. Everything had to be
resolved as quickly as possible, with maximum efficiency. Time was

key to the destiny of the losers, whom Bassols called heroes without realizing that he was also a hero. He had gotten more than ten thousand Spaniards out of concentration camps in France. Making a big fuss, without romanticizing, he had sent them to Mexico and was starting all over again now. Starting from zero, when it would have been so easy to be the Secretary of the Supreme Court.

Austere, agile, decisive, prematurely balding, Don Chicho Bassols made quite an impression on Lorenzo. Chiseled like a diamond, his brilliance cut through the boy. I have someone to look up to here, he said to himself. Bassols wants to serve Mexico without making any concessions—in other words, without giving in to power.

"How about going out and distributing *Combate*, Comrade de
Tena?" Bassols asked him. "You'll be out in the provinces, getting
to know your country."

Lorenzo thought it was a unique opportunity.

"The travel allowance is almost nonexistent, but from what I've
been told, you are a frugal man."

Lorenzo smiled. "Like a Franciscan monk, Mr. Bassols, a Franciscan."

Bassols looked at his watch. "You can plan on leaving within
twenty-four hours of accepting the offer, Comrade de Tena."

Lorenzo had gotten used to Bassols announcing, "We're going to
talk for an hour now," and in an hour he would look at his watch.
"It's two o'clock. Let's go eat. We have to be back in the office at
three." At ten to three, no matter how feverish the discussion was,
he'd asked for the check, look the waiter in the eye, leave a generous tip, and start back to calle Donceles.

The comrades made fun of him. "He's an overseer." Nevertheless, they followed him.

When Lorenzo met Chava on calle Edison and told him that he
was going to be out of Mexico City at Bassols's request, Chava
raised his arms to the sky: "He's abominable; his telegraphic prose
is vile. He's a just man. You have to keep your distance from just
men; they'll make your life bitter. To believe a newspaper can
change a country where illiteracy prevails is unforgivable."

"His language is like a scalpel. He cuts right to the bone."

"Don't outline his virtues for me, Lencho. Such human and political righteousness bores me."

———

Two large packages of the weekly edition of *Combate* were tied to the grille of the bus, wrapped in oilcloth. It was a tabloid—about forty-five centimeters long and barely eight pages, printed with little letters—that the government considered subversive.

Leaving the city forced Lorenzo to think about practical things, which scared away any dark thoughts.

"Remember, after Mexico City it's all jungle," Chava warned him. "You're going to find yourself in a void."

"That's what I want, a void." Traveling into the plains by bus was also a journey in search of nothingness. The driver put his own life in danger along with everyone else's. When could he have learned to drive, if he ever had? He forced the engine, each shift of gears torture, the noise of the metal fittings and the shaking of the sheet metal setting nerves on edge. The troglodyte took the curves as if they were squared, hitting the brakes at the last second, and the vehicle would lean toward the precipice. The passengers didn't react. Maybe the smell of gasoline had made them sleepy, or maybe it seemed normal to them that life was hanging from a fucking thread. Trapped in a sheet metal cell, they shut out any sense of comprehension. They were forms without human features, except for one who slept with his mouth open.

At the first stop, Lorenzo got off, relieved, and went toward a sign, lit by a single oil lamp, that read MEN. The stench forced his eyes and his throat to close. The waiting room, with benches against the walls, was also filthy. Everything seemed to be heading toward death, without protest from anyone. Lorenzo, who had been thinking of buying a soft drink, knew that he'd never be able to swallow a drop. Disgust made him clench his teeth, but the resignation of his fellow travelers, who lived as if they were already dead, was even worse.

The plains extended for as far as the eye could see, and the straight lines were endless during the day. Unlike in the city, they were not cradled by the mountains. They went on and on and on, like the bus engine, roaring louder and louder all the time. Free, the plains unrolled themselves, naked, sterile. Lorenzo eroticized the landscape; the hills became breasts, the valleys the back, the curve of the belly, the gracefulness of the neck. Lorenzo had gotten out of the bus to find refuge in the leafy woods, in the concavity, the cave, the unexpected disorder of nature. He was surprised at what the landscape could do to men. "This is the face of Mexico," he repeated to himself, incredulous.

In the seat next to him, an engineer wearing a felt hat was on his way to supervise the construction of a road. Seeing the laborers on the side of the road, Lorenzo asked him, "How do these people live?"

"When they need money, they work digging ditches."

"But how do they live?"

"Haven't you realized, my friend, that seventy-five percent of our country suffers from inanition? This is India, my friend. India, with a disadvantage. There are no cows; otherwise we would have eaten them." The engineer was annoyed.

Lorenzo's spirit began to absorb the sight of the starving dogs, the hungry oxen behind wire fences, the barren lands and dried-up rivers.

At the first village, after finding a room in the only house with brick walls, he asked the owner of the shop, "Where do people get together around here?"

"At the cantina. They're there now."

Lorenzo shouted out the newspaper's name on the main street, as he had seen the paperboys do on calle Bucareli: "*Combate!* Buy *Combate!*" His heart contracted in fear. "Turn your heads toward me. You don't have anything to eat, and I come along offering you sheets of paper. I can't turn around and escape. *Combate!* Buy *Combate!*" His voice bounced off the mountains and against the misery that was even greater than the mountains. The comrades were also a little like mountains, but unmovable. What is it that allows the development of intelligent beings?

Lorenzo traveled from town to town, from cantina to cantina. The sound of the jukeboxes gave him goose bumps. The smell of urine and beer permeated every crack. When he entered a cantina, you could cut the smoke with a knife. Sometimes there was a billiard table.

"I don't know how to read."

How was he going to sell the newspaper?

"I never went to school, and I never needed it."

The men clinked glasses with glassy stares. Lorenzo sensed that they would drink until they fell over. Alcohol was the only thing that could give meaning to their abandonment and keep them around the table, even if they didn't know what to talk about. When Lorenzo got up, one of them, the drunkest, hugged him. "No, man, don't go. Don't leave us."

His legs became stoic, his stomach as well. As he went on, the desolate immenseness of Mexico's hunger was only equaled by the horror it produced.

The great starry nights were his compensation. He looked to find in the sky what he had seen on Earth. The empty places of the Earth would have their equivalents in space, which now served as his roof. There were vast regions, apparently empty, but nevertheless full of gas, interstellar material, green oases, well-cultivated fields, sources of light and energy. The stars were grouped in crowds like the men around a table in the cantina. These stars would spin in a spiral until extinction, like the farmers who clinked glasses— a collision of galaxies. Could the stars be as exhausted as the farmers? Lorenzo followed the parallels. He converted the sky into another Earth. If every day interplanetary matter fell to Earth, then men should reciprocate, rising and expanding into the atmosphere. Swallowed up by the emptiness, would they have life? If we were all the result of a great explosion, an unimaginable ball of fire that came from nothingness and belonged to an always greater universe, what cataclysm would return us to the starting point—if there had, in fact, been a starting point. The next morning, Lorenzo felt more love for these weak pieces of matter who lived ten seconds—compared with the age of the universe—and he wanted to embrace them, but he had to wait until the meeting at the cantina to break down walls and form a stellar cumulus.

The potholes that pitted the roads of the Mexican Republic shook his very neurons. One afternoon in the Altar Desert, after days of traveling through a landscape where there was nothing to be seen, an image struck his eyes and almost shattered him. A ramshackle tomato truck had crashed into another truck. Heaps of smashed red tomatoes lay on the road outside of their wooden crates. The red-stained boards of the crates were upright. Next to them lay two bodies muddied with another red—that of their own blood. Suddenly, from who knows where, from the center of the Earth, came ragged men and women running to pick up the tomatoes. The dead thrown on the road didn't matter—only the tomatoes.

What a Dantesque image! Lorenzo saw his country for the first time, and everything about it hurt him. The great Mexican emptiness, the useless stations, the destitute towns, the cube of a house lost in the immensity. The groups of houses looked like bellies exposing their intestines, and above them, the vultures. The vultures were always there.

Thinking about the celestial dome saved him. He did mental calculations, compared the brightness of the stars. He recalled that Copernicus had refuted Aristotle's theories. He'd have to bring that up with Revueltas.

It seemed as if life were escaping from him, dripping away, leaving crevices and cracked, dry pavement, where the potholes were craters at earth level. A strong man with a challenging stare advanced along the street with a limp that is common to children born with their feet turned inward and no orthopedic device to correct the condition. They end up walking on their ankles to overcome it. Were it not for those ankles, which were turned into stumps that were even with the ground, the man would be a giant. Not being able to count on his legs, he had developed a powerful upper body, but the strongest thing about him was his gaze. Lorenzo concluded that the poor triumph over misfortune with greater will than everyone else. Any one of his gang, pampered as they were, would have given up. This man understood his own fragility and the coldness of the universe, yet he didn't feel inferior. His contact with the earth had taught him that the sparrow was faster than he was, the dog could hear better, the insect detected honey way before he would detect the kindness of others. But he wasn't going to let a stinking illness defeat him.

Sometimes a face opened into a comforting smile that wasn't aware of its own seductiveness, and, for that very reason, was even more charming. That smile, the red gums like the tomatoes over-turned on the road, was much like a wound.

Even Lorenzo opted for silence. It was his armor, but it was also a weapon that would later become dangerous. In the years to come, he would maintain a reproachful silence when all yearned to listen to him. In the future, the faces would raise up toward the presidium, and he would withhold judgment.

Upon his return to 25 calle República del Salvador, he would make his doubts known to the Party members. He would have liked to speak directly to the big shots—Martínez Adame, Mesa Andraca, Villaseñor, Zevada—but they rushed in to see Don Chicho Bassols and barely said hello. The caricaturist, José Chávez Morado, came slipping in with his cartoon in hand. Villaseñor, hair combed down with cream, seemed to ignore Lorenzo. How were they going to write if they were never in contact with the reality of the slums? What did they base their directives on, if they never went out into the countryside to see what he, Lorenzo, had endured? *Combate* challenged President Manuel Ávila Camacho—a Catholic, a believer, and a declared anticommunist—and the commercialism of the great press. But how could *Combate* talk about the miners of San Luis Potosí without ever having gone down into a shaft? It's true, they did support the miners' strike of Nueva Rosita, in Coahuila, against American Smelting, but missing were straightforward and reliable articles. *Combate* bitterly criticized the United States and the Yankee demands to Mexico to pay for the use of the Rio Grande.

"Not only should we look for another way to distribute *Combate*, but we have to change its entire concept," Lorenzo told Revueltas. "Whom are we addressing? This country isn't Russia. We have to write in terms that are intelligible to the peasants."

"Talk to Don Chicho. I'll go with you."

Of the comrades, Revueltas was the only one who understood him. You had to read José María Luis Mora's *Mexico and Its Revolutions*, Bertrand Russell, Henri Barbusse, Romain Rolland. "What an era ours is," Lorenzo said. "The legendary heroes live among us and are our contemporaries!"

"Do you know what Mora requested in 1824? That the word *In-*

dian be removed from the official language so that we would speak only of poor Mexicans and rich Mexicans. When they received complaints from Tlaxcaltecan communities about being plundered, Mora reminded the deputies that they had agreed that the Indians did not exist; therefore they could not demand agrarian rights."

One afternoon Revueltas entered Bassols's private office accompanied by de Tena, who was ready to challenge the boss's severe look.

"I've come to ask for permission to be absent this afternoon," said Revueltas. "My wife, Olivia, is about to give birth."

"How inconvenient, my friend, since we need you in a matter that can't be postponed. Can't she deliver the child later?"

Lorenzo didn't know whether to laugh or cry.

"Comrade de Tena, remember, you're on the road tomorrow."

"What's the point? What is the value in what we're doing?" There was anguish in his voice.

"Comrade, what are you saying?"

"This country is damned, Mr. Bassols. Nothing can be done."

"Remember, comrade, that feelings of defeat are reactionary. You're playing into the enemy's hands."

"I'm a realist. There is another way. You have to bring the people out of the ignorance and the poverty. The first thing to do is to feed them, then teach them to read, educate them. No one can think on an empty stomach."

"Well, keep your certainty to yourself. It's your reactionary origin that makes you speak this way, comrade."

"It is my conviction after the experience of distributing *Combate*."

"If we all had that certainty, where would our country go, young comrade? In *Combate* we criticize the government's actions. I've had a lot of patience with you, de Tena, and I order you to leave tomorrow morning to fulfill your commitment."

"Don't worry, sir, I'll go, but what we're doing isn't worth a crap. After all, I console myself thinking that a billion years ago, bacteria created life on Earth, and within another billion years it's likely that the Earth will disappear altogether, along with the human race—"

"Don't be a smart-ass, de Tena."

"Excuse me, sir, but isn't it *Combate*'s moral obligation to warn about the risk of not taking action in time to avoid irreversible damage?"

"I know that you're interested in science, but right now I don't have time to listen to you, de Tena. Tomorrow you're going to Puebla, and don't tell me that it's a lost town where *Combate* cannot make a difference."

In Puebla, Lorenzo looked for the Socialist Student Block, which defended the Spanish Republic and received the children who were sent to Morelia from Spain. According to Bassols, they would help him distribute *Combate*. Two men, Gastón García Cantú and Antonio Moreno, were subscribers. Getting two subscriptions was an astounding feat. Not only that, they invited him for coffee. A little less discouraged, Lorenzo set out toward Punta Xicalango, near Ciudad del Carmen. In Villahermosa, Tabasco, he would make contact with Garrido Canabal's followers.

When the air coming through the window of the bus emitted vapors hotter than the engine's, Lorenzo reconciled himself to the trip. The thick bushes of the coffee plantations, with their little red fruit, crowded up against the road, and the vegetation was overabundant and luxurious. The ceibas appeared to reach for the heavens. A storm made it dark, and Lorenzo thought that the issues of *Combate* would get soaked in spite of the oilcloth cover. He definitely liked going south better than going north, and Bassols had sent him to Veracruz, the most resplendent state in Mexico.

Lorenzo's spirit was calmed when he reached a fishing town on the ocean, very poor, on a protected bay surrounded by palm trees. As soon as he felt the sea approaching from the horizon, he accepted the infernal heat and the smell of gasoline. "There, next to the beach, is the place where you stay," the driver told him. Several metal tables with chairs, courtesy of the Corona bar, and four or five little rooms made up the hotel, which wasn't much of anything. But the presence of a woman dressed in black, wearing black stockings, caught his attention. The black clothing made her look tall and slender, and the well-shaped legs in high heels intrigued him. He observed her as he did the ocean and the scorpions (against which he had no antidote), and he watched her fan herself languidly, then jump into the only hammock, spike heels and all. You're going to break it, he thought. Could she be the owner? Only the owner would dare do such a thing.

That night Lorenzo went out for a walk and raised his eyes to the sky. What luck—the Milky Way! What could it be made of? When he returned, the woman in black was still in the hammock. Lorenzo decided to approach her. "Can I buy you a drink?"

She agreed with the same listlessness with which she had rocked herself in the hammock. "Fine, but right here. I don't frequent the cantinas."

"Are there many?"

"That's what there is the most of." She smiled a half smile.

Lorenzo smiled at her openly, and she had no choice but to respond to his charm.

"Boy, you have an irresistible smile."

"Boy?" He was annoyed. "Not hardly." That *boy* was a challenge. Perhaps if it had not been for that, Lorenzo would not have decided to show the proprietress what a man he was.

"What's your name?"

"Who cares!"

"I need to know."

"I'm Lucrecia."

"Really? Come on. Let's go in the ocean."

"At this time of night?"

"The best time is between three and four in the morning."

When she took off her stockings, legs whiter than milk emerged. "I'm never in the sun. I never go out during the day. I don't like it. Sunburns damage my skin. I only walk at night in the moonlight and starlight."

The word *star* made him accept her long, thick black hair—like that of María Félix, the famous movie star—as well as her lack of imagination.

Sure that she would follow him, he started off. Behind him, Lucrecia walked on the cold, hard sand: "There are shells." When the sand became damp, Lucrecia took off her dress and went into the water, which was darker than ink. He left his only pants on the beach and followed her, naked. In the water, Lucrecia embraced him. She clung to his body, belly against belly, legs intertwined, her chest against his. They were the same height. He heard her breathing, which sounded like the black water. Standing there, he took her. Then she rolled over on her back and moved her arms toward his waist: Now, like this, impale me, lift me out of the water, like that, with just your strength. Covered by the water and the night, the woman became the essence of mystery to him. The waves splashed sweetly against her sides. It was a long navigation through the salty walls of this portentous woman. An immense silence fell from the vault of the heavens. The woman enveloped him in darkness, as if she were blanketing him. He didn't know if they were going to die. The woman disappeared, then appeared more rotund with every resurgence. She was a colossus; she moved so powerfully that he feared they would both drown. A continuous shuddering seemed to come from the water and her weight. I wouldn't care if I died now, thought Lorenzo. He immediately recalled, I have too many *Combates* to distribute. There were always too many. Wrapped in her large, liquid thighs, Lorenzo almost didn't hear the ocean any longer, or this woman into whom he had rained. Water was now raining on him. The sound of the water swelled and was like a heel tapping. Lorenzo felt that he was excavating a furrow in the sea-body of the woman. Suddenly he no longer felt her, and he began to search with the gestures of a blind man, until he heard her voice.

"Come," she said to him. She got out of the water and walked into the night.

He imagined her whiteness on the sand. She picked up her cast-off dress and pointed. "Here are your pants."

"Witch, how can you tell? Everything here is invisible."

They walked without hesitation toward the straw tiki hut. The woman stood motionless at the door. "Go to your room now."

"I don't want to leave you."

"Then come to mine."

When Lorenzo awoke, the sunlight blinded him. It was two in the afternoon. There was no one in the hotel. He heard a noise that sounded like pots and pans, and he went toward what he assumed was the kitchen. It was filthy. "Could you give me a cup of coffee?" he asked. "And the lady?" he added.

"She left."

"For where?"

"Oaxaca."

"When did she leave?"

"Early this morning."

"Ah." Lorenzo decided to leave the next morning, and he asked for the check.

"Mrs. Lucrecia left word not to charge you, and you can come back whenever you like. You're always welcome."

At the Political Action League, Lorenzo was drawn to a man with an intelligent expression who listened intensely to Bassols speaking. Besides wearing a conspicuous hearing aid in his left ear, he made a screen with his hand to cover his right, so as not to miss a word of what Don Chicho was saying.

When it was this man's turn to speak, Lorenzo was amazed. He was an extraordinary orator, even more persuasive than Bassols.

"Who is he?" he asked Revueltas.

"His name is Luis Enrique Erro. You can't imagine the knockdown he just gave the Finance Minister at the financial planning convention for rural schools in Querétaro. The audience protested angrily with shouts, whistles, and stamping. Erro began to speak without anyone listening, but at a certain point the audience quieted down. His argument was so brilliant that they gave him a standing ovation. His style was of English irony. There is no one like him. He wants to change education and make it widespread, for everyone. He was chief of technical training with Bassols at the Department of Education, and he created the National Council of Higher Education and Scientific Research."

"Scientific?"

"Yes, it's radical. The founders of the Polytechnic Institute are all of the extreme left. He's one of those who believe in socialist education. That's where his interest in technical schools comes from."

What Lorenzo never knew was that Erro also noticed his enthusiasm.

When Luis Enrique Erro invited Lorenzo to his apartment on calle de Pilares in the Del Valle neighborhood, Lorenzo accepted, flattered. "I'm going to the old man's house," he told Revueltas. "What an honor!"

Like de Tena, Revueltas lived in conflict with himself. "Do you think it's all right not to attend the League meeting tonight?"

"Of course. Don't be a fool; you're not on duty, or are you? I, on the other hand, have to stay until late, because if I don't, Rafael Carrillo will hold it against me."

To his surprise, at Erro's house Lorenzo was not overcome with the anguish of politics. For the moment, the exaltation of the street missions he and Revueltas had been involved in since dawn ended. No one predicted catastrophes. The conversation was lively, and at around nine o'clock that night, Erro said—with the particular inquisitive look of the deaf, like someone sharing a secret—"I have a telescope set up on the roof. Would you like to see it?"

Of course Lorenzo wanted to.

Erro maneuvered the Zeiss telescope and aimed it at Sirius, the brightest star in the sky. He pointed, then located Ursa Major and said, "Look. You can see it better than ever tonight."

"I don't see any bear."

"The Greeks saw her, friend, and that's good enough for us."

"I thought Andromeda was a girl."

"And she is, young de Tena. She is. Use your imagination. Very few constellations look like their name."

Lorenzo realized that Erro had another life aside from politics. "I belong to the Astronomical Society," he said. "If you want, I'll take you to a meeting."

The young man had spent months between depression and exaltation, and now, like an unexpected gift, the heavens were opening up for him. He breathed more easily.

"If you like, you could be my assistant, work here at night," Erro said. "I would give you a key to the main door, and you'd have direct access to the telescope on the roof. The work consists of taking plates during the night and developing them the next day. I have a darkroom right here. You would give me the plates, and I could teach you to how to study them."

Luis Enrique Erro was not aware that he was changing the boy's life.

"Ours is a country of servants, de Tena. The Indians are at the service of the whites; the poor, of the rich. If we don't change each one's situation, this country is going to shit."

With men like this, you can build a different country, thought Lorenzo.

Erro's battle cry was socialist education. "Owing to its very nature, public school has no substitute. It is fundamental because of its equalizing action." Erro started to talk badly of the liberal professions, the opportunistic lawyers, the businessmen, dizzy from their prosperity, and even the revolutionaries who opposed social change. "Zapata is my hero. The land belongs to whoever works it. Land and liberty." The country would be buried in the hands of the dandies who swarm in the State Departments. "We're a poor country, de Tena. Apparently the system gives opportunities to all, but it gives its favors to those already privileged. Our society looks down on mechanics, electrical work, chemistry, accounting—any diploma of a qualified worker. We need to eliminate the idea that the only thing that counts is a university career. See for yourself where the liberals are taking us. They're selling the country—"

"Luisín"—a woman named Margarita interrupted—"let's go eat. Is your young friend going to stay?"

Margarita Salazar Mallén lived only for her husband, and she added another chapter to his biography, "Did you know, young man, that Luisín studied accounting by correspondence in order to survive in Havana, and he increased the merchants' sales?"

"Woman, enough of that," said Erro, annoyed, but Margarita insisted. Deafness had removed Erro from Congress, where he had been the presiding member. When he became unable to rebut, his deafness made him turn his head and look at the stars, and they fascinated him even more than politics. Before, when Luisín returned from Congress, he had commented on events, just as in *El Universal*, but now he talked only to the stars.

"President Cárdenas, who held him in high esteem, sent him to Paris in 1937 so that a specialist could operate on his right ear." Doña Margarita kept talking. "The operation helped somewhat, although they thought they would probably have to do a second one. Cárdenas insisted on it and paid for it in advance. To my husband—you see how he is—it seemed useless to spend it on a probability, and he invested the money in a twenty-five-centimeter Zeiss reflecting telescope! That is the very one he has set up on the roof, waiting for his great dream to come true—to move it to a new observatory where it will assist modern science."

The first night Lorenzo stayed alone with the telescope, he felt he had found his spiritual home.

"You already know how to handle it, my friend," Erro said to him. "Don't forget to cover it, and lock the door when you leave."

Yes, that vast space before his eyes was his; it paralleled the space inside him. Millions of creatures moved and spun around, as they did inside his body. They wove a network of circuits that preserved his life on Earth. He was his own universe, and much more. Mexico City was deserted. Nothing moved on Earth. The silence came from the stars. Where am I? Lorenzo wondered, and he breathed deeply. On a cosmic scale, in the celestial vault, the luminous objects that he photographed and would examine tomorrow under the microscope were another body that palpitated like his. The particles had radiation, energy, magnetism. Lorenzo aimed the telescope toward Orion and stopped observing only when he saw the white light of dawn. As he lovingly covered the Zeiss, an immense gratitude toward Erro and toward the night overcame him.

He urgently felt the need to raise his doubts with Erro about the luminosity of certain stars. Erro generously pointed out that light passes through a prism to display its spectrum. When a light source withdraws, its spectral lines shift toward the red side—in other words, toward the longitude of the longest wave. And inversely, if the source comes closer, its spectral lines move toward violet. The displacement is proportional to the speed of the luminous source. When an ambulance approaches, the sound of its siren is sharper, and when it gets farther away, the sound is deeper.

One problem led to another, and Erro welcomed his student's proposals with true curiosity. He now had a first-class collaborator, someone as possessed as himself.

"Ah, brother," Revueltas said as he listened to Lorenzo. "You have found something that you will not be able to live without! Your life will become the best and the greatest in the world. Everyday life will become tolerable. You will now fulfill your destiny."

"Edwin Powell Hubble," Lorenzo repeated with reverence, and at night he raised his head to see the expanding universe, where everything moves away from everything, and no one, nor anything, is the center. How amazing was the dome of the sky, deep and limitless. He was thrown into its immensity. If the Earth on which he was standing was barely a dot, what was he, with his tossing and turning and his absurd anguish? He felt great sympathy for Humason, Hubble's assistant. He had only gotten through elementary school, and he worked herding two little mules to bring water to the builders of the Mount Wilson Observatory in California. Hubble, who was impressed with his natural intelligence, hired him as a janitor. Humason dared to ask everything; his curiosity was stronger than he was. He learned to handle the instruments; he developed and set the plates; and finally he was made Hubble's assistant. What proficiency. Science wasn't so inaccessible then; poverty or backwardness didn't matter. It was possible to do research. Everyone could study the universe. Intelligence was enough, and that he surely had.

At five in the morning Lorenzo descended from the roof to the street like an automaton. He raised his gaze to see what had appeared so amazing—the unfathomable darkness overhead. Nevertheless, there on the sidewalk, it seemed more familiar, maybe because he lit a cigarette, something he had had no desire to do up there.

The long nights of watching began to swallow up his life.

Contrary to what Revueltas had said, everyday life became intolerable in the light of day, and reading *Combate* made Lorenzo more furious with each edition. "We're way behind what is happening. We need to raise the issue of the land along the Rio Grande differently. That land is ours according to the flow of the river waters." No one seemed to listen to his energetic protests. Militancy became monotonous, and he didn't like his comrades, who adhered to their routines.

"No, Comrade Lorenzo, bylaw 17 says . . ."

"Damn the bylaw; we don't need it. We can do this without consulting the bylaws!"

"Discipline above all else, Comrade."

The atmosphere that surrounded them was disturbing. Persecuted like rats, they lived clandestinely. The press put them on the red page, among rapists and murderers, and their misfortunes didn't bring them any closer to one another. Lorenzo felt like kicking them.

"Your predicament is normal," Revueltas assured him. "I too felt incompatible with this environment."

"They're hairy beasts, Revueltas. When you aren't here, I have no one to talk to."

"De Tena, when you have a mission to complete, no one can stop you."

"But it's hard!" Lorenzo became alarmed. Was the same thing going to happen with this group of friends that happened with Diego and the gang? Where could his brother Juan be? He sensed that Juan had lived everything that Lorenzo was just beginning to experience, without ever mentioning it, and had also asked himself, What's the point?

Revueltas smiled. "Devote yourself to the cause. The problem is that you've never read Marx."

How strange were the men who came and went with infinite complacency, focused on their small affairs, without questioning what was happening in the heavens.

Lorenzo found Erro more fascinating every day. Maybe he associated him with the location of Earth in the physical universe that he was now discovering. Lorenzo remained rooted to the telescope night after night. He depended on it like a drug. At three in the morning the cold struck his face and hands like a knife, but it didn't stifle his determination. He had entered an unknown world, parallel to the celestial dome—the world of astronomy.

Luis Enrique Erro had come into contact with Leon Campbell from Harvard as a result of Erro's observations of the magnitude of variable stars that formed his roof. Campbell used data from "amateur" observers in the American Association of Variable Star Observers. The association trained innumerable lovers of astronomy to measure the magnitude of variable stars and then employed their data in the construction of the light curves of the stars. The amateurs— some as scrupulous or more so than the professionals—mailed their results to Harvard and supplemented the academic insufficiency. Their devotion to the Harvard College Observatory, which allowed them to contribute to discovering the sky, was boundless. They were so afraid of being wrong that they excelled in their meticulousness and delivered stunning results owing to their accuracy.

Erro had also developed a friendship with Cecilia Payne and her husband, Sergei Gaposchkin, who became two great stimulants in his life. In their correspondence they had encouraged him to attend Harvard. And that was exactly what he did, thanks to the fact that Lázaro Cárdenas named him Mexican consul in Boston.

At Harvard, he met Harlow Shapley, who was called the modern Copernicus. Shapley had taken the privilege of being the center of the universe away from the sun when he discovered that the sun was on one edge of the Milky Way. Shapley agreed with Kant: if the Milky Way was made up of millions of stars in the shape of a disk, maybe other Milky Ways existed similar to ours, as far away as the stars are from the planets. In that case, neither the Earth nor the sun nor our galaxy could be the center of the universe.

"We're only a little piece of garbage in the immensity of a universe that is still expanding," Erro told Lorenzo.

Shapley was the first to measure extragalactic distance using variable Cepheid stars in the globular cumulus for that purpose, and he deduced that these stars were situated in an imaginary sphere around the galactic center. According to him, the Cepheids varied due to diametrical changes of the sun.

How could one not be drawn in by Erro's eloquence and his interest in setting up a new observatory in Mexico? Before the war, the Tacubaya Astronomical Observatory provided good results with an antique refractor telescope. It had a five-meter focal distance and a thirty-eight-centimeter lens. But the war suspended all possible production. Before the Revolution in 1874, the Mexicans went on expeditions and set up camps and played a significant role in astronomy. The Revolution put everything on hold for more than fifty years, and today everyone concentrated on the Carte du Ciel and the ephemerides.

Although Shapley knew the Aztec calendar, Luis Enrique Erro taught him even more. If any people on the continent had an ancient knowledge of the sky, it was the Mexicans, and that tradition should continue. Long before the discovery of America, the Maya, short and large-headed, climbed El Caracol in Chichén-Itzá to observe the heavens. They documented their novel hypotheses in their codices. They studied Mars, Saturn, Venus. If they had known how to decipher and predict natural phenomena, they would surely have made new contributions to the world of astronomy.

Shapley took Erro seriously and invited him to one of the meetings of the Hollow Square to analyze the project. If young Mexican scientists were all of his caliber, then what was happening over the border could not be ignored. Turning their eyes toward their neighbor—the unknown—was indispensable now that Europe struggled in uncertainty.

It would be magnificent to develop a new Mexican observatory. If North American politics had failed in Latin America, maybe scientific cooperation would prove fruitful.

Harlow Shapley looked carefully at the annual reports from the Tacubaya Observatory, which Erro had given him. Shapley laughed wholeheartedly when he heard about their problem consolidating time after the Mexican Revolution. National telegraphs had one time; railroads ran on United States time; the 105th meridian and

California time completed the dance of the hours. "What an imaginative country. Everyone has his own time!" It confirmed the proverbial Mexican lack of punctuality. The hours floated in the air; no one was able to capture them. One of the tasks of the Tacubaya Observatory was to unify them all. José Alva de la Canal, the mechanic there, adapted at full speed. He set up an antique clock in Tacubaya to make electrical contacts every sixty minutes with the United States. Tacubaya then gave the time telephonically, and there was such a great demand for it that the two telephone operators received eighty calls per minute, almost going crazy. XEQR alleviated the task at the observatory by broadcasting the time.

"Can you believe, Dr. Shapley, that announcing the time would be the mission of a scientist?" Erro imitated the voice of the radio announcer. "It is 2:33 in the afternoon, official National Observatory time." He made Shapley laugh. Thanks to the Tacubaya radio, music from San Antonio, Texas, was heard in Mexico for the first time. "The observatory almost disappeared because the public preferred to listen to gringo music. 'Daisy, Daisy,' and 'Oh my darling, oh my darling, oh my darling Clementine' were in demand."

Shapley, an antifascist like Erro, wanted to bring European scientists who were in danger to study in the United States. Hadn't Einstein been in Princeton since October 1933? Jews and non-Jews, expelled from their countries by the war, would keep coming. On the other hand, the North Americans treated Mexico as if it were their own backyard, and he was curious about this vast territory where time was measured differently. The Mexicans made up for their lack of academia and of facilities with inventiveness. Maybe their very virginity would allow them to draw unexpected conclusions. Erro had charmed him. Shapley believed in the community of nations, and as Europe was entangled, he now looked to Pan-Americanism. Joining Latin America and winning them as allies was better politics than that of the Big Stick.

Another visiting Mexican astronomer, Carlos Graef Fernández, contributed to Shapley's fondness for Erro. Had Shapley noticed the hearing aid Erro wore? Graef reenacted the scene at Congress.

Erro, representative of the XXXVI Legislative Congress, was in the middle of one of his celebrated polemical dissertations when shots were fired. The legislators threw themselves under the red velvet curules while Erro continued speaking. When he finished his magnificent address, his fellow representatives congratulated him: "How brave you are!"

"Why?"

"When the shooting began, you didn't even duck."

"What? There was shooting?"

On another occasion, when his hearing aid fell off, he bent down to look for it, and a bullet meant for him hit the backrest of the seat in front of him.

Graef repeated the dialogue between Erro and the future president of the Republic: "What post do you want in my government?" asked Ávila Camacho.

"I want an astrophysical observatory."

"You can have it under one condition; it has to be in my state."

It was unthinkable that such a thing would happen in the United States. Shapley had never put his own money into his research. Things didn't work like that. The state provided. What guys, these Mexicans. Graef was brilliant, rigorous, and objective. Manuel Sandoval Vallarta had worked with Nobel prize winner Arthur Compton, and Norbert Wiener admired him as much as he admired Arturo Rosenblueth, a luminary in cybernetics. Not just anyone graduated from MIT. At twenty-six, Sandoval Vallarta was a reputed top-notch researcher. He and Georges-Henri Lemaître were the authors of a theory of cosmic rays. Damn, these Mexicans had something inside them . . . and they had to be helped.

12

Lorenzo felt that the opportunity to listen to Erro speak was an un-deserved gift. Without suspecting it, Erro offered him a way out of his anguish. "Don't you go thinking we're good-for-nothings," Erro told him. "Manuel Sandoval Vallarta took Albert Einstein's relativ-ity course, Max Planck's course on electromagnetic theory, and un-dulatory mechanics with Erwin Schrödinger. For three years he stayed in Berlin, which was the center of the world of physics. Car-los Graef worked with the most eminent physics theorists in the world, and he brought the young Félix Recillas, who had great promise in mathematics, to Harvard. Chandrasekhar took an inter-est in Recillas as well. In spite of our lack of equipment, de Tena, there are first-rate people at the university. The Mexicans have been exceptional at Harvard, but Sotero Prieto molded Graef and Alberto Barajas and Nápoles Gándara and López Monges here in Mexico. Scientific research and higher education have united, but we have to get the government interested so they'll help us. If the gringos do it all, we'll lose our autonomy."

Lorenzo's nationalism coincided with Erro's. "Welcome, wel-come, Mr. Buckley," was one of the worst embarrassments of his youth.

"If we don't convince the government to promote science, there won't be an observatory," Erro said.

"But how? They're apocalyptic beasts."

"If you call them beasts, you'll never get anywhere. You have to show them that we'll never get ahead without science. We can't be fainthearted. Sandoval Vallarta wasn't when he was at MIT, and look at the results. He transformed that institute from a simple en-gineering school into a center for the advanced study of physics and mathematics. Of course, he had the collaboration of other great minds. Imagine if we had here in Mexico, my friend de Tena, what MIT represents in the world of science. There's no reason for us to lag behind. We have to convince the government."

"That's a good job for you. You know them and how they work."

"They realize that it is a primary duty to humanity and themselves. Otherwise they are in big trouble. In the meantime, I have proposed to recruit astronomers for the new observatory. Tacubaya is no good anymore. I need brains. Come with me to Tonantzintla; you won't regret it. You have what it takes to be an astrophysicist."

How surprising life can be and how wonderful. Revueltas was right. Lorenzo was dying to tell him about it. He felt as if he was finally living, while Revueltas debated down there in the cultural and hormonal stew of his recent paternity, in which women trapped men with their tiny brains and their uteruses that swell up each month. *Combate* was also moving at the cellular level. It needed new blood, and it needed to get in touch with reality, which it would certainly find horrifying. It was better to extract himself from the situation, and Luis Enrique Erro offered him that option.

Now the days became only a transition period in which he unwillingly fulfilled the tasks entrusted to him by Bassols, tasks that would never lead anywhere. Of that Lorenzo was painfully certain. The night became day, and the day a drowsy rhythm of waiting.

On Erro's roof, Lorenzo opened his eyes at the chirping of the first bird and repeated to himself, "This is life." He ran feverishly to develop the plates. At eleven in the morning, after examining them under the microscope, he ceremoniously closed the door to the temple that offered him so many riches, and went to the first inn he came across to have lunch. He then headed to the Political Action League. The images from the microscope pursued him every moment. They were music and painting: he saw Miró, Klee, Kandinsky. He heard the melodies of space, flute sounds that had soared for seventy thousand years and had come down to mix with the oxygen, the rain, the rays of sunlight. As he walked along the streets, every detail acquired a new dimension. He found a connection with the leaves on the trees and the cracks in the surface of the walls. The effects of the light brought out the true structure of the objects he had seen in the sky. He saw spirals and the arms of galaxies in the smallest and most ordinary cells. The celestial phenomena had erupted in his daily life, and even a pair of crossed logs looked like a star or the axes of a supernova explosion.

His life was now guided by the Southern Cross. Rich in stellar clouds, it orbited to the vertiginous rhythm of the Andromeda nebula. Orion's belt held him prisoner, his sword a symbol of Lorenzo's knighthood.

From that moment on, the stars governed his habits. At four in the afternoon he returned home to sleep. The street noise, the slamming doors, and the light disturbed him, but fatigue overcame him. He no longer thought about anything but that extraordinary organization of thousands of millions of suns, of which he was a part. Everything returned to its rightful proportion. There was a reason for Florencia's death, as well as for that of Joaquín de Tena. Certainly his mother's aura was out there in the oxygen, and in the carbon dioxide exhaled by La Blanquita the cow. The delicate molecular combinations were what had pushed Emila to San Antonio, and the cosmic rays were the authors of Santiago's life. Leticia's existence no longer seemed as objectionable. She obeyed rules—as did the composition of methane, water, ammonia, hydrogen, uranium. And if it seemed primitive, it was because Emilia, the eldest, with her rebellion, had succeeded in saving herself from the evils of the feminine condition and its vegetative decomposition. Lorenzo now thought more about radioactive isotopes and chemical properties than about bus tickets. The spectroscopes that Luis Enrique Erro showed him replaced the structures that he had believed to be immutable—the cruel, hierarchical Mexican society that had rejected his mother.

Aunt Tana! I completely forgot about Aunt Tana. He woke up with a start one afternoon and decided to go to see her. It had been six months since his last visit. How strange that he no longer held the least bit of a grudge against her.

His aunt's health, considerably worse, alarmed him. "It's the years," said Tila, who couldn't have been any more robust. "The dog got old too." Fifí's white forelock was no longer as tall, and her coat was yellowing on her belly, on her paws, and around her eyes, which had become black circles, hollowed out like caves. It was the same with Cayetana's ivory countenance; her eyes had disappeared. "We all have to die," said Tila. "You see, Don Joaquín, who was younger, died first. It wasn't his turn," she protested angrily. And Lorenzo wondered again what kind of relationship there had been between her and his father.

Unlike Tila, Lorenzo had the feeling that he would miss Cayetana. Juan was going his own way, Leticia too. Emilia and Santiago were in the United States; only his aunt tied him to the past. Tana was his blood. He needed her memory and her time. He tried to explain it to himself. His aunt was going to take something with her that only she could give him, and only he was capable of understanding. Suddenly he wanted to know more. Who was his father? How had he met Florencia? Where? When? He was full of questions without answers. In a thread of a voice that went from her mouth to Lorenzo's ear, Tana attempted to breathe air from the space near her lips; the bloodless face paled. Arranged among the cushions on her chaise longue, her hair pulled up messily, Fifi lying on her legs, Tana appeared to wait. No one needed her except Leticia, who entered violently and danced through the house like a sunflower, filling it with oranges and yellows. Stoically, Tana never enumerated her pains or disappointments. Never a complaint. Not even a single reproach. Quite the contrary. "Life has been generous with me."

One afternoon she took Lorenzo's hand and murmured in her broken voice, "I'm proud of you."

Lorenzo raised her transparent palm to his lips. "And I of you also, Aunt." He kissed her, smiling.

He would have liked to have taken some lessons from that cadaverous woman's innermost resources, but it was too late. In the last days, she began to get chills and to shake.

"It's the illness," Lorenzo said, to calm himself.

"It's fear," observed Tila cruelly. "Your aunt is afraid to die."

Lorenzo was annoyed. Tila did not wipe his aunt's soaked forehead with sufficient urgency. She didn't change her bedclothes quickly enough.

"She's not aware of anything anymore."

"Yes she is, because she shivers."

"It's the fear," Tila repeated.

Fifi, the little dog, also shook to the bone. They both shared the same fallen white locks of hair, smoothed down with the fluid of their ruined bodies. One afternoon Leticia came in, slamming the door, and leaned over to kiss her aunt.

Tana grabbed onto her neck with unexpected strength and said in an almost inaudible voice, "Don't leave me."

"Of course not, Aunt. Lorenzo and I are here."

Death was executing Cayetana de Tena, nailing her to the cross of the Sacred Heart, La Profesa Church, the University Club, the Jockey Club, the Polo Club, whose trophies were getting dusty in the living room. As the Virgin of Lourdes looked to the sky, the fervent prayers were only babblings, the counting of the rosary beads became thorns on her head. Is that how the human experience ends? Lorenzo asked himself. Torn, he could do nothing for that open mouth, the exposed palate, all modesty lost, the death rattle invading every chink. "Can't you close her mouth?" he asked Tila.

"No, boy, no. Have pity—that's what death is like. Just don't look."

Lorenzo tried to imagine her palate as the skeleton of a tiny ship under construction, but that didn't help, so he opted to look out the window. The rasping breath was never going to stop. How could the lungs of a dying woman produce such a powerful sound? "I hope it ends," he murmured to himself.

"Fear gives you a lot of strength," Tila concluded.

Leticia, absent, was missed. Lorenzo lit a cigarette without thinking twice. Tila didn't protest. At this point, what did it matter? Then he turned to Tila, his eyes full of tears, and said, "I can't stand for this to happen to her. I don't think I've ever felt as much respect for anyone as I do for her."

Tila didn't respond. That night Tana did expire, in the presence of Leticia, who overflowed with life and optimism. A few days later, at the seventh Rosary to be exact, Fifi died too, and Lorenzo ordered Tila to bury her in the garden. "She will fertilize the land."

Tila said to them, "I want to go to my land also. It's time. I'd like to take the furniture your aunt gave me, but I don't know how to do that."

Like a flash of lightning, Lorenzo remembered the night when he had donned a dinner jacket and was fighting with his bow tie in the big mirror in the living room. His father had stood behind him, put his hands around his neck, and tied it perfectly, saying, "These things I do know about." He had tried to hug his son. Without saying thank you, Lorenzo had gone out to the street to wait for Diego. For a split second his conscience stung. Poor Father. Deep down he was harmless.

Lorenzo rented a moving truck, and when he shut the door to the house on calle Lucerna for the last time behind Tila, he knew that if Aunt Tana had taken her poor secrets with her, he would discover others. Those, by definition, would be crucial.

The events surrounding Cayetana's death were characterized by the exclusivity and modesty dictated by elegance. The house was soon dismantled. To Lorenzo's surprise, he learned that it had been rented. Out of pride, Tana had never revealed this. No wonder she watched her money so carefully. Aunt Almudena took the most beautiful furniture to Houston. Some of it she would give to Emilia, if the girl asked for it. Or to Santiago. Did Lorenzo want to unload it, the way he'd gotten rid of the particle "de" of his last name, or did he want to keep the colonial screen or a carved credenza? Lorenzo wanted nothing. He was never even home. "Aunt Almudena, it's all yours. You'll take better care of it than anyone else."

Three months later, as he passed by the house on Lucerna, he saw a sign hanging out in front: FOR RENT. Without inhabitants, it was just another house, like all the others in the Juárez neighborhood, gray and somewhat small. It didn't even seem as if the sun reached it.

13

"I'll pay you back later; here is the title to the car as a guarantee." Debts, cheating, street fights, run-ins with the police. "Look, I'm just an idiot. Let the cops catch me." Violence and jails. "Damn it! Six months in the black Palacio de Lucumberi again!" That was Juan's life. It took four men to arrest him; they couldn't handle him. Who knows where such strength came from? He defended himself like a lion. But he never protected himself from his abusive and cheating partners, who made him the scapegoat to save their own skins. Juan had to answer to the charge, and he, the youngest, was going to end up in the slammer. "I've had it with partners," he said once when he got out of jail and set up a small refrigeration shop on avenida Observatorio. Within a year he had to shut down owing to a number of problems with the taxes, the workers, the night watchmen.

Erro had immediately detected Juan's potential, as well as his restlessness. It was obvious that he was Lorenzo's brother.

"Brother, do you want to come work in Tonantzintla, Puebla?" Lorenzo said. "Luis Enrique Erro is setting up an observatory."

Luis Enrique Erro had inscribed a Greek phrase from Aeschylus' *Prometheus* above the door of the main building: "God liberated men from the fear of death, giving them illusory hope." The view of the Cholula valley was unsurpassed. You could contemplate the volcanoes from there most of the year. And *contemplate* was the word. Nothing could be more propitious for meditating than that landscape, which connected the valley and the mountains, giving weight and reason to the lives of the inhabitants. A number of people rode their bikes to the Talavera pottery factory in Puebla and worked eight hours a day. Life passed to the sound of the church bells. Their tolling brought the poet López Velarde to mind, his slow conversation with the bell ringer. There were three hundred sixty-six bells—one for each day of the year and an additional one for leap year—housed in the belfries of three hundred sixty-six churches. How would they sound when rung in unison? The cornfields had begun to grow; the cows mooed, and a donkey brayed. The brothers looked at each other nostalgically. "Emilia's donkey." Maybe they thought about Florencia, but they never said it aloud.

"De Tena, you may find what you're looking for here," said the director to Juan. "These are difficult times, and I know you've seen your share. I offer you a discipline that is based on the rigor and the exercise of reason."

"Reason, in a country where everything is escapism?" Juan said sarcastically, just as his brother would have.

"Yes. Here you will observe and study a fraction of what exists beyond what we understand. I need good mathematicians. Your brother Lorenzo is an observer, and according to your elders, you have a gift for abstraction."

Juan was surprised.

"I've discovered variable stars, Juan, and I keep looking. I believe in the human race."

"I don't."

"At twenty-five? You'll believe again, my friend. You'll believe again. As you study what was previously believed to be divine, and as you get closer to the planetary system, you'll realize the importance of our brains. What you'll see up there will make you believe in men. You'll realize that there is communication between the physical and chemical processes of your brain and those in the sky. Your brain can unravel enigmas. The sky below belongs to us. Down here, we live what happens up above. Through this telescope you will see a distance of ten million light-years or more, and out there, galaxies that will influence your biological evolution are waiting to be discovered."

So this bald hill was the observatory? When he arrived in Tonantzintla, Juan looked at the village, which appeared uninhabited, as did all villages in Mexico. The slope on which Erro was having the observatory built was a solitary mushroom. Not even a hint of a cornfield next to it. "Up there you'll only find pebbles that roll down the hill with the rain," Don Crispín would tell him days later at the general store. His small suitcase weighed him down. Where would he live if no one opened their doors, if no one came out to meet him? You could hear the chickens cackling in the pens. Someone must feed them. Suddenly, around the curve, he saw a pine tree. He would tell Erro: "You can plant trees up there, since there is already a pine tree." The astronomer would probably respond that he had come to do astronomy, not reforestation.

The winter of transparent air was beginning—long nights and icy mornings. "It's the best season of the year to observe, brother," Lorenzo said, happy to see him.

That afternoon Erro had tea with the two brothers. "Doesn't it seem like an ideal site, Juan? Look, over to the east, Popocatépetl and Iztaccíhuatl; to the west La Malinche; the Pico de Orizaba way over there; and Cortés Pass here. What more could you ask for? Have you noticed the quality of the air? An indispensable condition for observing the sky, Juan. You can make out the Cholula pyramid to the north. Do you see it there—the colonial church built on top of it? Farther down in Chipilo, there is a group of Italians who make the best butter and cheese. So, Juan, my friend, you have the privilege of working in one of the most remarkable places in Mexico."

The only thing that stood out on the hillside was the observatory's main building, with the grand staircase—"of Greek proportions," Erro boasted, smiling. "We would like this to be the Parthenon of Mexican astronomy. We'll set the equipment up behind it, a Zeiss telescope, a darkroom, an archive room for the plates."

Standing next to Erro, Lorenzo looked toward Puebla de los Ángeles, which seemed to be ever expanding. "Sir, don't you fear that the same thing will happen in Puebla that did in Mexico City, and we'll be invaded by more intense lighting in time?" asked Lorenzo, still squinting to see even farther.

"No wonder you have the reputation of being a pessimist, Tena, my friend. Graef says it will be a long time before we have to deal with such misfortune."

Erro depended on Carlos Graef Fernández's insight. Graef had great leadership qualities and was good at bringing people together. As soon as they heard laughter in the hallway, everyone knew. "Here comes Graef!" "Graef is one great big chuckle!" He was the only one in Tonantzintla with a doctoral degree in mathematics from MIT, where he had been Sandoval Vallarta's student. Erro had gone to Massachusetts to get him to help with the Tonantzintla project. They made an odd pair—Erro, thin and elegant, with a hearing aid that bit off part of his ear; Graef, small, round, and prone to a cordiality that made him lovable.

Trained by the North Americans, Graef was used to group discussions, and some nights he stayed up with Erro until very late. The door to the office was open, and their heated voices could be heard in what sounded like an argument. When Lorenzo stopped at the door, Erro called to him, "Come in, Tena, come in. Pull up a chair. We're talking about gravity. We could use you." After that first night, they included Lorenzo in the group. Fernando Alba, calm and reflexive, inspired confidence. Recently married, he lived in Puebla and spent the night at Tonantzintla only on rare occasions. When Alberto Barajas came from Mexico City to see his friend Graef, the discussions became even more passionate. Graef pulled the writing table up in front of him and took notes on loose-leaf paper. His writing was so large he filled a sheet with one or two calculations formulated out loud. Barajas stretched out full length, his feet on Graef's desk; leaning back, he looked at the ceiling. Graef dictated his calculations until someone suddenly said "No!"

"Why not?" Graef would roar, getting to his feet.

Barajas condescended to sit up and explain before going back to his original position, and Graef went back to his loose-leaf paper.

It drove Lorenzo crazy that there would always be two possibilities in science, and that both were good. Graef was the first to shoot his ideas into arenas Lorenzo had never even contemplated. Graef taught him about physics. Alba shared his knowledge as well. Sometimes Erro had flashes of genius, but he was respectful in front of the scholars—those who were trained doctors, who presented their hypotheses, not waiting for the rest to discuss them. Tena raised his thrilled eyes toward Erro, and that single look gratified the man more than a thousand words. It would have been good to have a son like that, Erro said to himself, but he wouldn't have said it for anything in the world to the proud apprentice, who showed a greater aptitude to confront him than to give in to him. Graef, with his usual good humor, inquired curiously, "Let's see what our friend Tena thinks," and Lorenzo became involved in a violent discussion once the floodgates were opened.

"That can't be, my friend, because an electron advances through time and through space."

When Erro indicated that he had missed something owing to his deafness, they spoke more slowly, but seconds later their ideas were running all over one another at a gallop. Lorenzo was now one of them. His cup of black coffee got cold. When no more butts fit into the ashtray, Erro would get up and empty it, and no one noticed.

Lorenzo asked permission for his brother Juan to attend the improvised discussions, and Graef and Alba, who had him in their classes, agreed immediately. "He has made spectacular progress. In three months he knows more than a second-year student in the College of Science. Bring him. What are you waiting for?" Alba was very enthusiastic. That night Lorenzo was the one who was surprised. Juan jumped into the debate like someone jumping into a bullring. How did he know so much? Where had he learned it? Unlike Lorenzo, who had waited five days to intervene even when he was encouraged by Graef—"Come on, come on, friend; speak up; your eyes are shining"—Juan disregarded respect for his elders.

The fervor of the two brothers was good for Graef, and for Alba, Erro, and Barajas. Juan spoke from intuition, and he almost always came to the same conclusions as Barajas did. "How do you arrive at that, de Tena? Tell me. Write your calculations down right here." And Barajas would take a sheet from Graef to give to Juan, who couldn't put anything down on paper. Nevertheless, his conclusions were good. Alba would lean back, satisfied. There was a future for science in Mexico, if you could count on minds of this caliber.

"Sports are very good for scientists," Shapley had said when they were at Harvard, and Erro followed his advice to the letter. In the afternoon, they played basketball. Erro jumped around like a grasshopper. A consummate athlete, Graef also played. Since the director took off his hearing aid, it was impossible for him to hear the swearing that went back and forth with the ball.

Happy about the chance reunion with his brother, Juan never ceased to amaze Lorenzo. His presence unleashed endless images, the buried movie of their childhood—Juan behind him in school, Juan dancing frenetically in front of Aunt Tana, calling her a damned witch, Tila covering each glass of milk with a little white sweet roll.

Puebla also amazed them, especially the Tonantzintla hillside, scarcely thirteen kilometers away.

Graef and Alba sized Juan up. "Your brother could become a noted mathematician. He's lacking theory, but no one can beat him when it comes to practice. His ability has provoked some envy here," Erro told Lorenzo.

Of his four siblings, Juan was the one Lorenzo knew the least about, and now they were competing in the field of mathematics. Juan's lean face held traces of suffering, but he joked around, never said anything about himself, avoided every subject except mathematics. He wasn't concerned about Emilia's or Leticia's life; he cared only to hear news about Santiago. He scoffed at the past, and he challenged Lorenzo. The older brother recognized traces of his own character. Juan initiated each conversation with a dare: "I bet you can't . . ." Little by little Lorenzo realized that no one had ever given Juan the credit he deserved, not even their old teacher, Father Théwissen. No one, not even he, had done the young man justice. Juan was an above-average student, but since Lorenzo also stood out, his brother's talent went unnoticed.

At the house on Lucerna, science or culture had less value than good manners. Cayetana signed the report cards without looking at them. She never congratulated her nephews; the only one she acknowledged was Leticia. When Joaquín de Tena gave out allowances on Sundays, he passed Juan over. "That boy is just bad," Doña Cayetana concluded. How alone little Juan must have felt. No wonder he lived on the street.

"I have a well-founded distrust of that boy," Cayetana de Tena used to say, irresponsibly cruel. "I never know what he's doing and even less what he's thinking."

Juan's teachers had rejected him because he questioned their declarations. He asked questions they didn't know how to answer, or he insisted that such and such a problem had another answer. Every time he raised his hand, the teachers ignored him because they were afraid that he would confirm their ignorance. The geography teacher had attacked him when Juan proved, in front of thirty-seven students, that she didn't know where the equator was: "You're crafty and tricky." She was determined to hurt him, to isolate the remarkable boy, and the community went along with her.

By sixth grade, the last year before high school, Juan had decided to look for another world, and without telling anyone, he headed for the street. He made friends with the storekeeper, the paint-shop owner, the pharmacist, the people he saw en route from his house to school. He asked one for wire, another for alcohol, and in a back patio he set up experiments that caused a sensation. "Light on the street, darkness at home." Juanito was a hero everywhere but at 177 Lucerna and at school.

Now, at the Tonantzintla Observatory, Lorenzo was filled with amazement. The two brothers shared a mute rage that exploded sometimes and made them tremble, distorting them and their vision of the world. "Where were you, brother?" Lorenzo asked one day when they were heading down to the village and decided to go eat in Puebla. The two were smoking. They each lit their cigarettes with the butt of the previous one. Lorenzo punched him. "Let's quit smoking one day."

"I'd rather quit eating." Juan laughed.

Once again Lorenzo saw himself in Juan.

Riding on the bus, expounding on the enigmas of squaring the circle, enthused by his elder brother's interest, Juan began to talk about his businesses. As he listed them, Lorenzo grew sullen. Juan, the owner of a foundry, would have another one someday. He had acquired land to construct high-temperature ovens, but since his permits were not in order, the inspectors closed the factory. There was no bribe large enough to keep it open. "I'm only going to be here at the observatory for a season, brother. I'm thinking of traveling to the border to sell sponge iron that I invented for special construction, like overhangs for gas stations, and roofs shaped like wings. I named my invention the Tenalosa. What do you think,

brother? If this business doesn't work out, there's another one waiting for me in Tampico, importing and exporting rods." In his free
time, Juan had designed skates.

"Skates, man?"

"Yes, with only one plate, like the ones for ice, and not four
wheels but six tiny ones. I know they have potential." At the first
opportunity he said he would visit Emilia in San Antonio and
make her a partner: manager of the North American branch.

Lorenzo would have liked to say to him, you're just like me,
brother. Where could this folly take him? Juan never said a word
about his personal life, but since Lorenzo also guarded his privacy,
they had a gentlemen's agreement. "We are not more than what we
are not," Sartre had said.

Juan lived in a house in Tonantzintla, just as Lorenzo did,
but he never said which one. Although it was easy to find out in
such a small village, Lorenzo refrained from asking. Like his aunt
Cayetana, he kept his distance from his brother. Without saying it
openly, he knew that he did not trust him. He preferred to walk
alone than to walk with Juan, whose plans concerned him.

Lorenzo couldn't conceal his anxiety when Juan didn't show up
one day. According to the residents of Tonantzintla, Juan had un-
dertaken an excursion to Popo, the volcano. Alone? Who knows?
Was he bundled up? Who knows? When he left the shop, where he
had been standing at the bar drinking beer, he yelled to whoever
cared to hear, "I'm going to climb Popo. I'll make it to the top. See
you later." He said it as though it were no big deal, as if he were going to the cantina in Cholula. Lorenzo got so angry with that
brother of his. Aggravated, he kept asking everyone, "Did he go
alone or with others?" How irresponsible to take off on an adventure having no ability or skill. Was he a mountain climber? Did he
know how to climb? Fucking Juan, I'd like to choke him. How
could he risk his life when they needed him at Tonantzintla? Could
he become a mountain climber? Did he know the three rules of
climbing: first save yourself; second, save whomever you can; and
third, if you have to choose, save the person with the best chance
of surviving? Would it occur to him to at least save himself?

On the fifth day, beside himself, Lorenzo decided to go after his

brother. Sheathed in a heavy sheepskin jacket, he and Don Candelario, who had offered to accompany him, started to climb. The
simple act of thinking that each step Juan took could hurl him to
his death sent Lorenzo into a state of extreme tension. At the end
of the day, the tension disappeared, and his thoughts were confused. Surely his brain must be deprived of oxygen, because when
he stopped to take a breath, he didn't understand what he kept repeating, no matter how hard he tried. He needed air. Don Cande,
on the other hand, seemed alert, although he was breathing rap-
idly. "You need to drink water," he said, and passed him a bottle.
"Dehydration is dangerous."

How wise! Lorenzo had a prolonged coughing attack.

"It's because your lungs get dry up here," Don Cande explained.
"Your throat gets so dry that your ribs can crack from coughing so
hard."

Lorenzo heard his voice in the distance, as if he were twenty
meters away. He couldn't feel his toes or his fingers.

"Professor, you're as white as a sheet of paper. That's a bad sign.
Let's go back."

As if he had been given permission, Lorenzo got up and vomited.
When Candelario turned around to descend, Lorenzo followed him
without a word. He was silent on the bus to Tonantzintla.

He didn't even hear Candelario say, "It's like your brain needs
more air or more blood, don't you think, Professor?"

Lorenzo couldn't think of anything but Juan, up there, wherever
he was.

At the entrance to the observatory, Guarneros, the handyman,
said triumphantly, "Professor, your brother arrived right after you
left to look for him . . ."

14

The Toxquis' house, where Lorenzo lived, was made of dirt, the floor as well—rocks piled on top of one another, the stone wall turned white in the sun, the toilet a paradise of buzzing flies. From the ceiling of his room, hanging next to the lightbulb as the only luxury, was a yellow strip blackened with flies. But Doña Martina had lined the exterior walls with Mobil oilcans in which geraniums flowered, and fragrant herbs grew in chipped washbasins. She spent her time washing. The first day, with a fresh smile, she gave him a bar of Palmolive soap, informing him that soon the bath with a shower would be ready. She kept her promise, the tiles arrived within a month. "In the meantime, Professor, the bath is a bucket under the fig tree. No one will peek at you."

Even though Martina scolded her children, "Shhhh, the professor is resting," Lorenzo never slept more than six hours. Two black hogs grunted in the patio, the chickens cackled, the dogs scratched themselves, and the little donkey waited for its daily load. Florencia again? Her presence was stronger in the countryside than in the city, and living in Tonantzintla was a return to the garden at San Lucas. Maybe that was why Lorenzo felt so good.

When the sun was on its way to the summit, Lorenzo, in a splendid mood, went into the observatory darkroom to develop his plates and then sit in front of the microscope and examine them. The seemingly inanimate world that he had watched sleeplessly the night before was concentrated on a plate, and Lorenzo marked a star with a tiny *x*.

He felt a cosmic repulsion for earthly things, sometimes even for Juan and his preposterous projects. Nevertheless, on Sundays when Don Lucas Toxqui invited him for turkey mole, he went with pleasure. Don Lucas was a *tiempero*, a caretaker of time. Don Lucas's strongest relationship, the decisive one, was with the volcanoes. Popo and Iztá ruled that man's destiny. During his walks, Lorenzo had discovered the power the mountains held over the town's inhabitants; these peaks were god and goddess to whom altars were raised with offerings: corn, fruit, flower buds, incense, and pulque. They were truly greater gods than the Christ brought by the Spanish, who died on the cross like a pitiful thing. Like any man, Popocatépetl had his own temperament. Toxqui called him Don Goyo. The villagers at the foothills of the volcanoes didn't fear the Sleeping Woman, her hair a white train of snow. Popo was the only one that could end it all. That was why the offerings were essential—so the rivers wouldn't run with lava, taking away houses and crops.

Some certainties weakened in Lorenzo. He was no longer sure that the volcanoes didn't have powers. The story about the *tiemperos* initiated him into a world of popular wisdom. Hadn't Toñita, the girl who cooked and cleaned for them at the observatory, predicted that they wouldn't be able to observe that night, when she had seen him and Erro sitting on the main step to the building?

"Why, Toñita?"

"Because the flies are flying very low."

She was right. They couldn't observe. These natural phenomena were intrinsic here like corn, beans, and their children's growth. The volcanoes were husband and wife, walking hand in hand. They sat together at dusk; they fought; they made up and slept in each other's arms. Their presence defined the life of the inhabitants of the village. The volcanoes, mother and father, could avert the wind and the sun.

The certainties in the minds of the caretakers of time compensated for Lorenzo's visceral anguish, which was provoked by the expanding universe discovered by Hubble, and by the thousands of miles of galaxies, of which his was just one. No one shared his efforts to understand it, and Lorenzo asked himself if the universe would continue expanding.

Talking with the farmers was like going back in time. He listened to Don Lucas Toxqui, to his friends Honorio Tecuatl and Filomeno Tepancuatl, and to his cousin David Quechol de Pancoatl. One of Don Lucas's ancestors had died as an infant and was buried in the atrium at Santa María Tonantzintla. The prayer on the blue-and-white ceramic plaque said, GOD WANTED ANOTHER ANGEL, MICHAEL, FOR HIS GLORY, OCTOBER 8, 1918. Another even older plaque read MONDAY THE 1ST OF FEBRUARY DON ANTONIO BERNABÉ TECUAPETLA ESCRIBANO FROM IBICA, TONANRIN, DIED IN THE YEAR 1756. Deeply rooted to their land, the villagers not only walked on the bones of their dead, they also had a tranquil wisdom. They understood that if the night stars looked tiny, it was because they were farther away than people were capable of understanding. They accepted the sun for what it did to the earth, to their bones, to their very skin. They studied the seasons of the sun to know when to put up adobe walls and when to put roofs on their houses. They carried the solar cycles in their veins, and the questions they asked Lorenzo were not in the least artificial. On the contrary, they came from ancient knowledge. These people did not speak of the sun as a god, but rather of the day in which man will reach it without burning himself. "But that day there will not be a sun. It will have cooled, and we will be dead," said Lucas Toxqui. They worried that the sun might disappear. "It could disappear, and then we'll die or have to go somewhere else."

"Where else?"

"To a place like this, if we can find it."

"The sun moves; the sun spins. It doesn't stop just like that."

"Without sun, the cornfield doesn't grow."

"Without sun there is no green."

"Without sun we'll die of cold."

"I think the sun gets bumps all over it. That hillside that you see from is also a bump, and surely up there on the sun there's another one like it. I've seen the holes on the sun."

"Look, Professor, with the naked eye you can see that the stars change place. I've proven it, because as a child, I picked my star, and now that I'm fifty, I've lost it. I don't know if it went out or where it moved to, but it moved." Everyone followed Don Lucas, with his slow speech, which offered him an unexpected peace as he sat having one beer after another right out of the bottle, while the women hastened around the stove.

From the moment Lorenzo began to observe, he realized that the cosmos was changing him. Of course he would live among the others; he would walk with them, eat with them, and smile. But he had his own world. He tolerated the everyday only because he knew he could return to the telescope at night. The life of the stars was more genuine to him than that of men, to whom he listened, estranged, without the least bit of curiosity. He couldn't observe them under the microscope as he could his plates, to predict their coarse conduct compared with that of those objects in the sky. Like the men, the stars were born, grew, and died; they had a fascinating life. To his surprise, the largest stars were the ones that shone for less time, and the tiny ones, like white dwarfs that were very, very dense, lasted a long time. Maybe someday, in a billion years, the sun would contract into a white dwarf. Or could the stars have been born before the universe itself?

Lorenzo was obsessed with the death of stars. Surely Florencia had exhausted her fuel before her time, and her extinction was the result. But she was out there combining helium and hydrogen, and every now and then she blinked so he would recognize her. Just as with men, the longevity and the lifestyle of a star was determined by its initial mass. From the time they were small, some people promised to be creatures of strength; others wore out. They burned their internal fire and died before their time. That's what would happen to him. He would explore the sky until he exhausted himself; he would continue taking measurements between one star and another; he would calculate their angles, reconcile his tables. He must surely need glasses by now. He would become the detector of stellar objects, and even if he had to write down millions of figures, he would not weaken. He would specify the positions and movements of more than one hundred thousand stars. Erro assured him that there were more stars in the sky than men on Earth.

Lorenzo developed the habit of thinking during the day about the problems from the previous night, mulling them over while he lived alongside everyone else. The young Braulio Iriarte, nephew of the observatory's benefactor, would greet him: "And how is the absentminded professor today?" Lorenzo continued on his way without even noticing.

The comments of Don Lucas Toxqui's belligerent cousin brought him back down to Earth. When Lorenzo had been at the observatory for a year, the man surprised him by saying, "You are all up there buying and buying devices, writing and writing little numbers, and our children have to go all the way to Atlixco to school because we don't have one here." The statement struck him. He'd build them a school. But with what? He had to find a solution to their poverty.

"Why don't you grow flowers, Don Honorio?" Lorenzo asked his neighbor. "They do so well here."

"The flower?" (They said "the flower," "the egg," "the pea," "the shoe"; they never used the plural.)

"Yes, devote yourselves to the flower. You yourself, Don Honorio, told me that visitors always want to buy your roses. Instead of getting into corn, try flowers."

"Are we supposed to eat flowers?"

"Honorio, don't play the fool! You'll earn money. Your loved ones will eat much better if you sell flowers rather than corn."

"Where can I get money to build a school?" Lorenzo asked his brother.

Juan was blunt: "Galileo had to court dukes and marquises from Venice like a bulldog to secure donations and buy the lenses for his telescope. He traveled from Venice to Florence, from Rome to Venice, to visit his potential patrons. In exchange, he placed models of his inventions in their hands. You only have to go as far as the Federal District. See your tycoon buddies, or the Secretaries of State. Swallow your pride; arm yourself with courage, brother. Turn to the politicians and the businessmen. There's no other way."

"I can't. I've never asked for anything."

"Don't give it another thought. If you want to help the village of Tonantzintla, you'll have to bend over backward and pay your dues just like everyone else."

Erro advised, "Use your eloquence, Tena, my friend. You can be persuasive when you want to. Employ your gift of convincing others."

But up until that point Lorenzo had never even knocked on a single door to ask for donations. He hated any administrative task.

He wanted to sink into the night, live for it, become part of the agreeable symmetry of the sky, and not argue at ground level, among human weakness.

It was barely daylight when the incipient white light impeded his ability to distinguish the planets. Lorenzo reluctantly prepared to close the cupola. Stiff, he stretched his arms, moved his legs. He smiled when he heard the roosters crowing and the sound multiplying throughout the village. Then came the chorus of crickets still rubbing their elytrons, chirping in the semidarkness. Crickets bring good luck, he thought as he slowly descended to the town, still dizzy from his high night of radiant energy. Now it was the stars from below that shone in the grass, in the branches. There were hundreds of minute particles of light that struck up a new dialogue with him.

Lorenzo associated everything with the sky. His true existence was up there, and it began at night. For him, the sun enclosed the Earth in a deceptive circle of light. When night arrived, the darkness gave the universe its true dimension: the abyss, the emptiness. It made him exclaim, "Son of a bitch! Where the hell am I?"

Once, when he spoke to his brother about his cosmic solitude, Juan answered sarcastically, "Don't be crass, brother. Don't kid yourself. You sound like Aunt Tana. Facts. Astronomy requires facts, not feelings. Your solitude is laughable. You're not living with the Aristotelian sky from four hundred years before Christ, which consists of a thousand twenty-seven cataloged stars. This is the twentieth century. It doesn't ask you to become ecstatic about the craters on the moon or allow for sentimental drivel. You must discover the origin of the universe. We still don't know how it emerged five billion years ago."

Luis Enrique Erro put Lorenzo in charge of obtaining permission from the Department of Communications to pave the road from Acatepec to Tonanzintla. It was a small stretch, but it was indispensable for the trucks to enter, especially for transporting the Schmidt camera. Shapley was sending them this telescope, which was capable of reaching greater areas of space, of photographing large regions of the sky, and of seeing celestial objects that were previously indistinguishable.

After he was kept waiting in the reception area, which irritated him, Lorenzo met with the department undersecretary, who arrogantly responded, "Tell your boss there isn't any money for special requests. Besides, we don't have any reason to spend a cent on research that will always be behind that of our neighbors to the north."

Lorenzo lost his temper. "If we let others think for us, we'll never get ahead. All I want is to use my own head, Mr. Secretary, and it appears that you would rather live borrowing the work of others." Any chance of paving the road went down the drain, and Lorenzo gained a powerful enemy.

Erro was furious. "I'll go the see the president myself to fix this vexing matter. You're a terrible ambassador."

"Let's see what horseshit that idiot gives you."

"Listen, Tena, don't you be a smart-ass."

Control of Tonantzintla was Erro's business, and without realizing it, he also intervened in "his" scientists' personal lives. Fernando Alba went to mass with his wife simply because he loved her. Erro was indignant and missed no opportunity to tell him so.

"I'm not a believer, Don Luis," Alba responded, "although I had the same religious upbringing as you did at the Sacred Heart. For me Jesus Christ was a man who fought for others in his own way and was killed, like so many. But I respect my wife, and if she wants me to go with her, I'll go."

Erro kept on, cruelly. "Come on. Come on. Let the church mouse speak," he said in a sarcastic tone.

Lorenzo intervened. "Leave him be, Don Luis."

"Listen to me, young man . . ."

"Don't get involved in what doesn't concern you, Don Luis."

"You are disrespecting me."

"You are abusing your authority," Lorenzo said.

The incident caused quite a commotion, and if it weren't for Graef's intervention, it would have escalated. Graef's humor, his continuous jokes, were indispensable in Tonantzintla.

Graef laughed. "Listen, we're all nervous about the arrival of the telescope, and I recommend that we go down to the Santa María church and flutter around among the angels and cherubs, even if Erro won't go into a church, even by accident."

The telescope traveled in pieces by truck from Cambridge, Massachusetts, to the border in Laredo. It was overseen by Harvard graduate students—one Mexican and the other North American. Who was going to be responsible for the transfer from the border to Tonantzintla?

Erro chose the de Tena brothers. "It is proof of the trust I have in you."

Lorenzo lived through the journey vacillating between states of terror and euphoria. The precious cargo that Juan was ferrying would change the lives of many Mexicans. In their truck, the brothers advanced like pachyderms under the sun behind other tractor-trailers, Lorenzo biting his nails. The telescope, built during wartime—like the ones at Harvard, the Technical Institute of Cleveland, and the observatory at the University of Michigan—was a greater treasure than all that Montezuma had accumulated. Would they conduct First World science in Tonantzintla that would be capable of competing with the United States and the Soviet Union? After today, Tonantzintla would possess one of the largest Schmidt cameras in the world.

Would the pieces fit together correctly? Would the mirror work? It wasn't the traditional type, but a spherical one. The Perkins-Elmer optic—the most advanced in the world—would it be effective? The Schmidt camera encompassed an area of five degrees by five degrees. Would it allow them to reach very weak objects?

When Lorenzo switched with Juan and rode in back, he had placed his hand on the lens and left it there during the entire trip. He protected it as if it were a child. Any incline or curve that was too pronounced made his heart accelerate. For him this was a warrior's vigil. Juan took it more in stride. "It looks like you're praying to the Schmidt, brother. Don't be so fanatical. There are other venerable objects in the world."

"Like the Tenalosa?" barked Lorenzo, and he immediately regretted it. He had wounded his brother. How stupid I am, he thought. But instead of admitting to his pitiless sarcasm, he closed up inside himself. It wasn't the first time. Surely Juan had gotten used to his darts. From the time he was a child, the harsh words of his elders had entered the depths of Juan's being.

In the months that followed, the mounting of the telescope distracted Lorenzo, and he didn't have time for Juan. He forgot about him. The atmosphere in Tonantzintla was electrified. All they talked about was the strength of the platform that would hold the cupola of the telescope, the circular rails on which the dome would revolve, what would be achieved with the telescope once it was functioning, and, most of all, the glass. Fernando Alba was the expert; he had already installed the measuring apparatus of the first cosmic-ray laboratory at the Engineering College of Mining.

Erro feverishly pressured him. "Do you know a good mechanic in Puebla?"

Lorenzo was dazzled by the ingenuity of the young Eduardo Miranda, who without any formal education always came up with the right answer. Each dawn Miranda arrived in the dark on his bicycle, which had no lights. "You're going to get hit by a car on the road, Eduardo," Lorenzo warned. Luis Enrique Erro exuded enthusiasm and, alongside Alba, followed the process until the late hours of the night. Lorenzo would lie down to sleep next to the telescope. One day they would polish the optic glass themselves, which required infinite precision. They would understand the properties of the materials—silicon, quartz, pirex—the manner in which they contract and dilate.

Erro repeated that the primary virtues of a telescope should be its power to absorb light and its resolution capacity.

During those days Lorenzo felt very close to Erro, in spite of Erro's mood swings and his unpredictable reactions. It was wonderful that there were older men like him in Mexico. What a privilege to work with him.

Erro sent him to Mexico City to look for a missing piece. "I trust only you, Tena. I know you won't make a mistake." The recently founded Physics Institute at UNAM, the National Autonomous University of Mexico, also boiled like a cauldron in the city.

Alba smiled. "The situation is radically improving. We're going to publish our results in the engineering journal, but soon we'll have our very own publication."

"So will we," said Erro, "for astrophysics."

"The main thing is to send students outside the country," maintained Graef, "so they can come back and train others, like Félix Recillas."

The arrival of Félix Recillas and his wife, Paris Pishmish, sent Erro into seventh heaven, because Paris had advanced theoretical training. Erro knew her from Harvard. She had been educated by a German mathematician taking refuge in Turkey, a disciple of Professor Erwin Freulich, Einstein's assistant. Sergei and Cecilia Gaposchkin were in the habit of having tea with her. Cecilia was typically English, and they didn't invite just anybody. Paris could easily communicate with the high-level academic researchers.

Félix Recillas had a gift for adapting to any surroundings. Aside from his talent in mathematics, which was confirmed by George Birkhoff and Oscar Zariski at Harvard, he had learned to handle the telescope at Oak Ridge. The astronomers watched him with curiosity because Graef had told them that he had taken Félix out of an Indian village and, through him, was planning to demonstrate the intelligence of the Mexican Indians. An orphan, Recillas was from San Mateo and spoke Náhuatl. Graef had put him on the mathematics track and recommended him to Harvard.

Recillas identified with Juan de Tena. He said to Juan, "Listen, you don't seem like you're from the same family as your brother. You're a hooligan, just like me. That's why I like you; you and I are of the proletariat class." Juan hadn't surrendered to authority.

Lorenzo, on the other hand, put great effort into completing everything Erro assigned to him, unlike the academics, who considered Erro simply a good promoter.

All that Lorenzo desired was that life not swallow up his eagerness for science, that life would allow him to think about the stellar cumulus. How did the other researchers tolerate the presence of a wife, of children? Lorenzo didn't want anything or anyone to interfere with the sky or with him.

15

The day of the inauguration of the telescope finally arrived, February 17, 1942. Soldiers stood on either side of the road from Tonantzintla to the observatory, holding the national flag to render honors to President Ávila Camacho and his guards. Next to Puebla governor Gonzalo Bautista and a tense and pale Luis Enrique Erro, the president walked over the last stretch of the now paved road that would take him to the telescope. The guests followed between the impassive soldiers. More than ten thousand people from Puebla and Mexico City waited. Domingo Taboada, the contractor and amateur astronomer, had given part of the land for the observatory. This was a personal triumph for him. Thirty scientists from the United States and Canada accompanied Harlow Shapley, godfather of the new observatory. Bart Jan Bok, his second-in-command, who was in charge of the Schmidt camera at Harvard, was among them. Journalists and photographers ran in front of the committee, competing for the best snapshots.

The North Americans had great hopes. They climbed Tonantzintla's steep hill under the beating sun and felt the warm embrace of Mexico, and they were grateful, in light of the war. Shapley read a message from Henry Wallace, the vice president of the United States, who one year earlier had attended Ávila's swearing in. Wallace confirmed that Roosevelt wished the conference to take place in spite of everything that was happening in the world.

Governor Bautista's speech had a profound impact on the listeners. He said that Mexico would defend education and scientific research alongside the United States, and that this meeting would seal the pact between two neighbors who were more than friends. Allied in science and technology, they would fight for progress, health, and social equality.

Luis Enrique Erro vowed that the whirlwind of the war, of a sick world, would not hinder advancement; on the contrary, scientific progress would be the future of humanity, free of all wars. Eloquent, Erro gave his best speech.

At that moment Lorenzo—standing in the back next to Eduardo Miranda—saw their friends Tecuatl, Toxqui, and Tepan-cuatl, dressed in their sandals and cotton pants, coming up the road, followed by more than seventy peasants. One woman from the city took off her bracelet and put it in her purse. The women advanced, united, alongside one another, their straw hats on their heads, and skinny dogs bringing up the rear. Once up the hill, they came closer. "It is also our telescope."

Lorenzo smiled. He understood their pride. It was the same as his. When the two large doors of the cupola slid smoothly open, the farmers, hats in hand, kept an expectant silence. George Z. Dimitroff, standing next to the team of mechanics, asked Ávila Camacho to press the buttons on the command console. Upon see-ing the telescope elevate, an *"Aaah!"* ran through the crowd. Luis Enrique Erro's features relaxed, his hands too. Dimitroff gave an ex-planation of the functions of the Schmidt camera, and many bare-foot children raised their curious little faces toward the apparatus.

Shapley smiled. "Maybe the astronomers of the future are among them," he said.

The town band followed with the joyous and deep sound of the bass drum while rockets exploded deafeningly in front of the church below. There would be fireworks that night. The cele-bration banquet took the visitors by surprise. On red and yellow tablecloths, under crepe paper streamers, were glass containers of fresh fruit water in strident colors: Jamaica flower, tamarind, orgeat, lime, alfalfa—fruit shakes crowned with pineapple and watermelon. Harlow Shapley sat in the place of honor next to the expert on nebulae, Dr. Donald Howard Menzel, who exclaimed with a smile, "I never dreamed I'd eat chicken with chocolate sauce."

Chandrasekhar bit into one chile after another. "In India they eat very spicy food," explained Blas Cabrera, who looked ill and ate very little. The presence of the refugee scientists from the Spanish

Civil War piqued the curiosity of the North Americans. They sat next to Pedro Carrasco and Vicente Carbonell, and Marcelo Santaló, who was preparing a guide for observing the Mexican sky and at that moment was describing his trip on the transatlantic steamer *Sinaia* that had brought him to Mexico. They talked a lot about Pan-Americanism and the union of Latin America with the United States. Alba Andrade initiated a long conversation with George Birkhoff. Head straight, eyes self-confident, Luis Enrique Erro attended to everyone. This was a very big day for him. He showed Otto Struve how to drink tequila with lime and salt. Erro's inventiveness caused Shapley to remark, "What a complete man. He knows science, politics, history, and even Mexican cuisine." At that moment he was expounding on the glorious epazote herb, which gives the beans their unique flavor. The two González sisters, Graciela and Guillermina, who would work as secretaries at the new observatory, touted the beauty of Puebla to Walter Sydney Adams, who came from Mount Wilson: "You can't miss the Casa del Alfenique. It's as special as a kiss."

"A kiss?"

"Yes, yes, a kiss."

Braulio Iriarte made them all, including Cecilia and Sergei Gaposchkin and the Canadian J. A. Pearce, laugh out loud.

Well into the afternoon, they descended to the Santa María Tonantzintla church, oohing and aahing with admiration. Was it the effect of the tequila or a hallucination? A waterfall of little angels and cherubs, with yellow pineapples and red pomegranates, stretched out their arms impetuously. Unsuspected paths and inviting curves opened inside the round and powerful columns; the supports were interwoven like palms; the stucco rose like half-baked bread. "This sanctuary makes me delirious!" exclaimed Iriarte. "It's baroque art, but created by Indian hands."

"From which century?" asked Shapley, his gaze fixed on the innocent saints and the rain of large golden flowers.

"The sixteenth."

"Why did the Spanish entrust the decoration of their churches to the Indians?"

"Because the Indians instantly reproduced any design. That

was when the Spaniards realized that these were extraordinary artisans."

"The polychrome of the angels is the same as the colors in the tablecloths and the bandolier on the tables up there," Bok commented. "What a wonderful sense of color." The scientists wanted to know about indigenous art. Were there other similar chapels? Of course. The Rosario was right there. Mexico was ultra-baroque because it was afraid of emptiness, and that was the reason for the excess. Nothing could be left blank.

"Why do the angels have yellow hair?" asked Cecilia Payne.

Iriarte answered that he himself was blond and Mexican, and he had the face of an angel.

Cecilia replied that she shared Paris Pishmish's preference for the dark-skinned ones.

Iriarte ventured the hypothesis that perhaps the profusion of children and sculpted flowers was an homage to girls and boys who in the month of May dressed in white and offered flowers to the Virgin Tonantzín, their little mother, the indigenous goddess.

"Hey Braulio"—Lorenzo passed by him—"you've spouted off enough. Erro is waiting outside. He's furious."

Lorenzo's admonition had the opposite effect and gave Braulio wings; he became lyrical. "Did you notice the orchestra of cherubs?" And he went on to describe each one of the instruments. "Isn't it marvelous? And you won't believe Cholula when you see it. It's a great ceremonial center from after the fall of the Teotihuacán Empire! On Thursday I'll have the honor of being your guide."

Braulio informed them that the observatory was constructed on top of what must surely have been a ceremonial center. The peasants went up one or two times a week to sell artifacts made before the conquest, crying, "Buy it from me, please!" The artifacts were authentic, and during their walks Lorenzo and he had found obsidian arrows, ceramic fragments, vessels, even a mask with the features of Tláloc, the rain god.

As they left the church, an explosion of fireworks made them raise their heads. Bok stopped in front of a woman who was taking ears of corn out of a steaming vat. He asked for one and bit into it.

Delicious! Many followed his lead. "This is the best party I've been to in my life!"

It was time to begin the Inter-American Science Conference at the University of Puebla, and the translators had not arrived. The grandiose project was falling apart. Ay, Mexico, what a traitor you are!

Erro approached Graef. "You're the only one who can save me."

With his customary good nature, Graef accepted. "I believe that the most appropriate course, in order not to interrupt the presenter's train of thought, is to translate when he is finished." Graef waited for Dr. Otto Struve to complete his presentation and then gave a clear synthesis of his ideas. Next came Fred Whipple. Graef listened attentively and made a precise outline of his paper and even interjected clever comments. The same with Joel Stebbins, the pioneer in photoelectric photometry, and Robert Reynolds McMath, the solar astronomer who proved the existence of light curves for different solar eruptions.

Increasingly impressed by Graef, George Birkhoff invited him to teach relativity and gravitation at Harvard. At the same time, Birkhoff accepted an invitation from the University of Puebla. He would come to work in Mexico. In exchange for his teaching, Graef had promised him a group of good students: Javier Barros Sierra, Roberto Vázquez, and Francisco Zubieta, who was attempting to explore a new path in differential geometry. With Alberto Barajas, an unsurpassed teacher, they could work on the gravitation theory, since both Barajas and Graef had solved the difficult problem of two bodies in the theory of gravitation.

Erro meanwhile congratulated himself for having integrated Paris Pishmish into the Tonantzintla team. The students felt comfortable with her. She generously introduced them to the important guests who came to visit.

"Is he approachable? Can we introduce ourselves to him?"

Paris guided them, smiling. Fred Whipple, the North American, proposed a process he had discovered for the formation of stars through the condensation of clouds of interstellar dust. Joel Stebbins spoke about photoelectric measurement, through its color index, of the interstellar material that formed clouds. Walter Sydney Adams (Juan de Tena asked if he was a relative of the discoverer of Neptune) expounded on the topic of interstellar material, which he believed took the form of a cloud because of the multiplicity of interstellar lines in its spectrum.

The degree of complexity of the papers by the Mexicans and the Spanish refugees surprised the North Americans. The presentation on magnetism by the physicist Blas Cabrera especially impressed the younger ones. And when he left Spain, Pedro Carrasco, a professor of mathematics and physics, had decided, "I can find a country in Mexico; I will only find work in the United States." Many of his students said that it was a delight to hear him speak. They had requested "theory classes" in order to keep listening to him lecture.

The conference continued during meals and during the visits to the Palafoxiana library and the Puebla cathedral. While Braulio pointed out the painting of the great cypress with the four doctors of the church—Saint Augustine, Saint Jerome, Saint Gregory, and Saint Ambrose—the scientists returned to their favorite subject: astrophysics. Nothing satisfied Lorenzo more than these discussions, which were a continuation of those in his youth with Dr. Beristain; the ones with José Revueltas about *Combate*; and the ones with the guys as they set up the telescope. From the words came the experiments. The beautiful camaraderie of research and the interchange of ideas struck him like the electrons of an atom.

At the end of the sessions, Juan offered to take them for a ride, and Cecilia was fascinated by the landscape along the way to Atlixco. "I feel like I've entered a painting from the fourteen hundreds. All that's missing is for them to speak Italian."

Braulio laughed. "If we go to Chipilo, you'll hear Italian. There's an Italian neighborhood there where people make butter, cheese, and salami."

"This country seems so much like mine that I feel at home here," said Chandrasekhar, whom his colleagues had nicknamed Chandra.

In the colonial building that housed the hospital for the poor of San Juan de Dios in Atlixco, a little boy showed them an oil painting that was in a terrible state. They could barely distinguish the characters he described in the archaic language of Lope de Vega. "Look at these indecent and lascivious beauties. See San Juan de Dios here, on the verge of recovering some prostitutes from the voracious inferno."

"Boy, you're really taking us back to the fifteenth century," commented Erro, amused. "All that's missing is for the Celestina to appear."

"You're amazing. What's your name?" Cecilia Payne asked the child.

"Héctor Azar. Atlixco is my land, and I'm going to remove the dust from all these paintings."

Braulio Iriarte recalled how, years earlier, Aldous Huxley had exclaimed about Tonantzintla, "This is the most sensual temple of Catholicism!" Cecilia agreed.

Mexico, what a contradictory country! The visitors went from one surprise to another. Puebla de los Ángeles was comparable to any city in Spain. Throughout Mexico they discovered the culture of a country that was treated with disdain. They felt ashamed.

"What have we been thinking?"

"Where were we two hundred years before Christ?"

Iriarte explained that the Great Pyramid in Teotihuacán was much taller and covered a larger area than the Pyramid of the Sun, which was four hundred meters on each side and sixty-five meters tall. "Archaeologists have dug tunnels and discovered tombs, murals, friezes, and carved stones."

Birkhoff climbed the sixty-five meters of the pyramid. From the top he looked out over the plaza and its impressive construction, proof of a superior culture that the conquistadores had slashed to shreds. Who were the barbarians—the Spanish or the Aztecs?

Mexico, with its fields where the water evaporated because no one knew how to retain it, its cornfields that were consumed by the sun, its dried-up fruit, was getting into the veins of these visitors. They walked in the dark humidity through the longest tunnel inside the pyramid, thinking that they might be asphyxiated. Emerging into the sun, they were confronted by children with bellies big from malnutrition, and by vendors with idols, willing to hand over their treasure for a few cents.

Sergei Gaposchkin squeezed his wife's hand as he suddenly bent his head. They were no longer comfortable about being westerners. The weight of Catholicism on an entire race was devastating. Of course, the regal art was a marvel, but it had been built on the damp ruins of another wonder: the indigenous culture. In Cecilia's head, the Aztec gods and the angels danced macabre dances, and the cascade of gold on the baroque altars overwhelmed her, making her dizzy. "We've all been affected," said Henry Norris Russell. "We never expected anything like this."

Lorenzo was honored that Shapley would call *him*—a student— to walk by his side. Lorenzo was also used to meditating as he walked along the road. Erro had the same habit. They walked around the perimeter of the observatory three or four times, deep in thought. Lorenzo's steps on the earth helped him undertake a systematic analysis of a problem, one foot after the other, in step with his train of thought.

Graef had been a three-hundred-meter-dash champion, the strongest rower at the German Club, and a first-rate diver, but lately he refused to walk. However, on this occasion he joined Shapley, strolling in the splendid landscape, and Lorenzo accompanied them happily.

Donald Menzel summed things up: "There is no doubt that this conference is one of the most important in the history of science. The relevance can be measured by merely looking at the great number of discoveries reported for the first time here in Mexico."

The conference was to continue at UNAM and to end at Universidad Nicolaita de Morelia, where Harlow Shapley, Manuel Sandoval Vallarta, Henry Norris Russell, and Walter Sydney Adams were to receive honorary doctoral degrees.

The Mexican effort had borne fruit. "We must treat Mexico differently," the scientists said. They wanted to publish the Mexicans' work and invite them to be part of the international scientific community. Russell, director of the observatory at Princeton University, extended an invitation to Erro. Adams offered the Mexicans observation time at Mount Wilson. Otto Struve at the Yerkes Ob-

servatory in Chicago did the same. Dr. J. A. Pearce, from the Do-
minion Astrophysical Observatory in Canada, called the Mexicans
colleagues. "With fewer resources and more ingenuity, they have
achieved what many in their great laboratories have not."

With the elation from the unveiling of the Schmidt camera behind
them, Erro now realized that he needed people. Little by little the
euphoria diminished. The Tonantzintla institution, which had
come out of nothing, awoke with empty arms. Its researchers faced
a new and unfamiliar challenge. The only ones with any academic
background were Graef, Paris Pishmish, Alba, and Félix Recillas,
who was about to graduate. Graef, as brilliant as he was in theoretical physics, did not have any training in astronomy; he wanted to
work on gravitational phenomena, which, he frequently pointed
out, he couldn't do in Tonantzintla. Besides, they were clamoring
for him at UNAM.

Erro, who was previously absorbed by the immediate problems of mounting the telescope, now recognized the weaknesses of
the brand-new observatory. Then Shapley approached Erro to invite Lorenzo Tena to come to Harvard. They needed young astronomers, and it would do Tena a world of good to become
familiar with other telescopes and to see the North American way
of conducting scientific research. Besides, Shapley realized during
his days in Mexico that the idea of change was not unappealing to
the boy.

"What do you mean you're going to the United States?" Erro's
voice trembled as he checked his hearing aid with one hand. "Who
is going to study the magnitude of stellar colors and the spectra of
the austral Milky Way? You belong to the southern sky, the galactic
pole, to Carina, to the constellations of the Southern Cross, to the
Magellanic Clouds. You're indispensable to me. On top of everything else, the Schmidt camera has defects, and although these
don't hinder its operation, they cannot be corrected until after the
war."

Lorenzo remembered his first night in front of the telescope and
the emotion he felt at seeing the sky. When he went by to say

good-bye to Erro, he decided to say good-bye to the Schmidt as well. His fate was sealed. He would devote himself to the science of the stars. From his planet Earth, he would study the objects in the sky: the sun, the small planets, the comets, meteors and meteorites, and interstellar matter. From the moment he had opened the cupola of the telescope and aimed it at the sky, he had begun advancing toward that still elusive place that made him feel he was beginning to be happy.

16

From the very first moment, Lorenzo knew that he would love Harvard, where the students grew just like the orchards. Among the well-pruned trees, the apples peeked into the classroom windows. Even a glass of milk was a cultural experience. Lorenzo sat at a drugstore counter and asked in his beginner's English, "An apple pie and a glass of milk."

"A glass of what?"

"A glass of meelk."

"What?"

"Meelk."

"I don't understand you."

"Meelk, meeeelk, milk."

The waitress stood looking at him fearlessly. Lorenzo then began to milk the udders of a cow in the air. "A glass of cow juice."

The sadist brought him the glass of milk to accompany his apple pie, and Lorenzo swore he'd never return.

During the first weeks, he felt very alone. Everything at Harvard was calculated so that the young people would do nothing but study. Cambridge, what a pretty redbrick city. He went into the courthouse, attracted by the memory of the Escuela Libre de Derecho and of the movies, where very pale witnesses swore on a Bible and an impassive judge banged his gavel. The mahogany dais was imposing; the twelve good men who would hand down their verdict—honest. They followed the process, interrupted by the cry of the defense attorney: "I object, Your Honor." A murmur of approval arose from the spectators. Just like in the movies, thought Lorenzo. He admired the beauty of the surroundings, the polished banisters. The lighting re-created cinematographic illumination, but he couldn't stop thinking about a painting he had seen—*The*

Literate Ass, a judge with the head of a donkey. When the spectators raised their voices, the square-faced judge with gray hair like Goya's donkey threatened to clear the room, and Lorenzo took the opportunity to leave. Once outside, he took a deep breath. What a relief to have traded legal codes for the telescope.

Reports about the war in Europe were constantly in the news and in the streets of Cambridge. People spoke in mysterious tones about nuclear energy. Mostly they talked about the losses suffered by the English Royal Air Force and ways to prevent them, of the bombardment of the German war industries, and of planes whose pilots and rear gunners were attacking Berlin. Some pilots had flown more than thirty missions. How heroic England was as it faced the bombings. Lorenzo heard the old physicist Tom Brandes say that this war was a continuation of the one in Spain against fascism, the one made up of brigades of free men who came from all over the world. Brandes had lost many friends, stupendous guys, in the Lincoln Brigade.

Because of Brandes, Lorenzo began to buy the newspaper *The Masses*. A pacifist, Tom maintained that no war is just, and its consequences are atrocious. Hitler personified evil; they had to put an end to his dementia. Tom alleged that in war, more people die as a result of the stupidity, ignorance, and cowardice of the high command than in combat. Distrust of those in power and creation of a society critical of its governors was the first step toward civilization. How insane to send so many young men to the slaughterhouse. Enlisting in any army was foolishness, not love of country. His words did not sit well in the atmosphere of patriotism that existed among the young men who were waiting to be recruited. "Old codger. Decrepit old man, your brain has gotten soft," they said.

Tom Brandes perceived that Lorenzo shared his anguish.

Aside from listening to Brandes and watching Movietone newsreels, Lorenzo spent his time at Harvard's Oak Ridge Observatory. Revueltas had talked to him about the Spanish Civil War. Revueltas's brother Silvestre, who was a congressional delegate in Valencia in 1937, had returned with passions inflamed for the Republican fight. The Spanish refugees had begun to arrive while Lorenzo lived in Tonantzintla, and he was proud that Mexico was one of the countries that offered them asylum. Luis Enrique Erro, indignant because the clergy and most of the Catholics supported Franco, became impassioned about the fate of the antifascists, and if it had not been for his excessive preoccupation with the telescope, he would probably have placed a bomb at the Mexican Military Fascist Union.

Spain's civil war had been fratricide, unlike this one, in which the English, the French, all of Europe, and now the North Americans united in their implacable opposition to the German Nazis. Lorenzo left the movie theater in disgust in search of Tom Brandes: "This is butchery and a crime!" But the probable victory of the Allies somehow still encouraged Lorenzo.

With the Oak Ridge telescope, Lorenzo experienced "the other way to do science" Shapley had mentioned to him in Tonantzintla. This was the most powerful telescope he had ever encountered. No wonder Shapley was able to do what he did. Facing the splendid command console and all its buttons, Lorenzo felt a healthy envy. When will we Mexicans get to this point? he wondered. How great it would be if telescopes were mass-produced and sold like bicycles or refrigerators, and all you had to do was choose the best brand. This telescope reached the weakest and farthest objects Lorenzo had ever seen. He knew he must learn to handle it at any cost. A mirror collected the light from the celestial bodies; the rings of Saturn were spectacular; and seeing Jupiter's moons, like seeing the moons of Mars, was an unexpected gift. He had become impassioned about planetary nebulae, gaseous wrappings of stars in the last stages of evolution, just before they became white dwarfs. Bart Jan Bok had indicated that planetary nebulae were essential to the study of the chemical evolution of the galaxy. Lorenzo set out to look for objects with emission lines directed toward the center of the galaxy, and he found sixty-seven new planetary nebulae.

He spent much more time in front of the telescope than was required. The war gave him that time. Not even for a moment did he consider giving in to fatigue. He'd die before he'd admit defeat.

Besides the telescope, seeing the modern buildings, the laboratories with unsurpassed equipment, the workshops—all operating to perfection—was a joy. The personnel seemed numerous and competent, in spite of the fact that they told him there weren't half as many as there should be, since so many had gone to war. At Harvard they explored the cosmos with all possible instruments. The researchers had everything at their fingertips—visible light, radio, X-rays, ultraviolet, infrared, and cosmic light. The physicists, the astronomers, and the biologists exchanged information. Norman Lewis, rejected from the army because of his poor health, was an expert in radio astronomy. "It's the only way to find a new civilization," he told Lorenzo, who bit his tongue so he wouldn't reply that as far as he was concerned, there was no life on other planets and that extraterrestrials were purely science fiction. He had been amazed in 1938 by the credulity of the people in New York, who ran from their homes, crazed, when they heard Orson Welles announce a Martian invasion on a CBS radio program. So far, no being from other worlds had presented itself on Earth. There wasn't a single indication or the least bit of proof of extraterrestrial contact. "Let's share our thinking on this. Come to my house," Lewis said.

"There are many, many dead planets," insisted Lorenzo.

"Yes, but there are even more that we have yet to discover. You stick with your extremely weak objects, and maybe among them you'll discover an artificial one. And if you do, it will be the work of intelligent beings, and then you'll have to admit that I'm right."

That night, Norman Lewis reinitiated the discussion. His raised left eyebrow made it seem as if he were always listening for a message from another world: "We radio astronomers are like that." He laughed. He was very pale, with delicate features and skin as translucent as a porcelain cup. But what Lorenzo noticed the most were his hands; they looked like they belonged to another man—the hands of all of humanity, a worker's hands, large and callused. When Norman lowered them, Lorenzo missed them.

These days, scientists talked about destruction. Although Norman rejected the military axiom that "the best defense is a good offense," he declared, "We have to be realistic. Are we going to allow ourselves to be murdered?" An admirer of Oppenheimer, he was dazzled by the supremacy of the United States. There was good science and bad science. He didn't think it was right that the Russians hid their discoveries.

At one point Lorenzo declared his admiration for the U.S.S.R., as El Pajarito Revueltas would have done, and he thought, This will be the end of the discussion.

But Norman, who was the authority, put an arm around his shoulders and leaned toward him: "You and I have a lot to discuss, but let's go have dinner first. My friend Lisa is going to make us spaghetti." Then Lorenzo noticed that there was an insipid blond girl in the laboratory, and she was staring at him.

The next day, when he came out of the darkroom, ready to examine his plates, he saw her again in the hallway. She gestured with her hand. "You'll see, the gringas are really easy," Chava Zúñiga had told him. Crass gringa! thought Lorenzo. She was nothing like the brown-skinned women he knew. Young girls with that white linen hair that was so blond and straight—it seemed like wet rags. However, Lisa had set her eye on him from the moment she saw him in the astrophysics department with Norman Lewis. She was attending a philosophy of science seminar for her master's degree. Her tenacity turned out to be so effective that by Friday night, Lorenzo led her to his monastic room, its window looking out onto the orchards. There she seemed more appealing. Her hair smelled of lemon, her white skin as well, and the rosy tips of her nipples were like the noses of those little cats that enchant everyone.

With complete naturalness Lisa found her place in Lorenzo's minuscule apartment, and a week later the Mexican wouldn't have known what to do without her. It was true, he observed less, but the Harvard sky became more accessible because of her.

In Tonantzintla, he had begun his true relationship with the sky. In Mexico the sky was his hat, his buddy up above. It belonged to him; it was an animal that included him; it blanketed him, a bear sky, a cow sky, a dog sky. At Harvard it seemed sumptuous and haughty, a sky that did not invite him to enter. It was truly magnificent, but it didn't breathe with him or give him a big, familiar hug. They were not intoxicated with each other. Here, the Harvard sky observed *him*: Let's see what you do with me, little astronomer. It wasn't fat or affable or round; it didn't rain or even sprinkle; and sometimes it even tasted like beer.

"Lisa, Mexican beer is the best in the world." Lisa listened without blinking while she cleared the dishes, and her charitable presence anointed Lorenzo with a sense of security he had never before experienced. He shared his most intimate thoughts with her: "The starry sky lives, it beats, it isn't unchanging; the same thing happens to it that happens to Earth. Everything moves down here, up there too."

"The sky isn't water or earth or air or fire. It isn't any of those elements, so what is it?" she asked. "Could the sky be a fifth element?" And Lisa would answer herself because she was a good philosophy student. "Aristotle believed that the stars were immovable and that the celestial dome was fixed for eternity." When she spoke of God, she declared, "God must be adored and not ever mixed in with geometry, astronomy, and philology. The heavens are for the theologians; the stars and the planets are for the astronomers."

Thanks to her, Lorenzo's English made rapid progress. He read Tennyson in English. They went to the Harvard University library, where Lisa took out William Blake's slim volume and made him memorize "Tyger! Tyger! burning bright / In the forests of the night." She introduced him to the pages in Joyce's *Ulysses* that dealt with science. Lisa was growing inside him, encompassing a bigger space all the time. One night she yelled as she came in the apartment door, "I cut my hair!" The mischievous locks, purposely messy, made her look like a little boy. She didn't wear high heels. If she had, she would have been taller than he. Her long legs looked good sheathed in jeans; she strode, hips forward, hollowing out her waist and chest, which gave the impression of fragility, as if she had to protect her insides.

Lisa taught him the pleasure of making love slowly, settling into Sunday leisure. She pointed to the bed. "We're going to spend all day here today. We're going to eat here. I'm going to beautify myself with your semen, your bull's blood." At first she shocked him. "I want to enjoy the pleasure. I won't take your quickies. I'm not going to have sex your way. I refuse. I hate your cleanliness, your rushing, all your reasons to do it fast. I want to enjoy; it's my right. Leave your rushing in Mexico. That doesn't fly here."

Lorenzo realized that until then, he had made love on the run. Cocorito, the waitress, had accepted that he hurried to the bathroom and stayed under the shower longer than he stayed inside her.

When the gang headed by Diego had proposed renting an apartment on calle Abraham González "as a group," Lorenzo hadn't thought about Cocorito. "You're driving her crazy. Aren't you going to take her there? If you don't, you're an asshole," Diego had chided.

When he first saw the waitress, Lorenzo had decided that she was a queen, with her tight belly, her high rump. She moved between the tables as if she were navigating. He watched the graceful movement of her proud head, her pale cedar skin, her radiant mahogany hair. She was a goddess. He could have kissed the floor of La Habana Café, where she spun flirtatiously, the ties of her tiny apron around her waist. Whenever Lorenzo talked, Cocorito was there, coffeepot in hand, ready to listen to him. She left the table only when the manager scolded her. "She's really got a thing for you, brother. Your gift of gab has her under your spell." It made Lorenzo's heart skip a beat that Cocorito would choose him over the rest. She made him into a god, Jupiter, the seducer, the Casanova. When he walked into the café, he would blush, and his heart would race. He, who had never been inhibited in a classroom, barely raised his eyes, confused, and his friends had a field day making fun of his shyness.

The first day, when he took her to the apartment, he was ashamed as he held her hand and they climbed the worn-out stairs. But when he realized that she wasn't a virgin, all his pleasure vanished. A horrible feeling of loss filled his eyes. He penetrated her a second time, hating her, when seconds earlier he had put her on a pedestal. Even Diego had teased him when he heard Lorenzo say, "Listen, I'd kill for this woman." He kept taking her while he complained about the deceit.

"What deceit? You didn't even know her." Diego laughed at him. "I can't believe you thought that Cocorito was just waiting for you. You could tell she was experienced from a mile away. You can't be that naïve. Were you planning to ask for her hand in marriage?"

The last time Lorenzo undressed next to her and told her that he would not see her again because he was leaving for the United States, Cocorito snuggled against his chest. "You'll never know how grateful I am that you've loved me," she said. Then she told him about her life, a violated life. Lorenzo felt his nerves in torment and wept in her arms because he was going to leave her.

And what would become of Leticia?

And of Emilia, the eldest?

And of all the women on the face of the Earth?

Now, with Lisa, he had the same sensation of loss. But what he shared with Lisa was the closest he had felt to happiness. Everything went right for her. She chose good movies, books, friends; she carried herself with confidence. Their conversations were good, and the meals were good. She was more mature than most girls her age. Having her at his side, with her concave chest and her tousled linen hair, was a certainty comparable to knowing that the Earth revolves around the sun. And she offered him a different Harvard. Some of the greatest people had been at Harvard—Igor Stravinsky, Bertrand Russell. "Look, this was his house; they lived here; they walked along these pathways. How lucky you are to be here. Lorenzaccio. What luck to belong to the elite—proof that you possess a better mind than the rest."

On weekends Lisa took him to concerts. Conferences came one right after another without a breath in between, and Lisa didn't allow him to breathe. "Let's go, come on, it would be a crime to miss it; we can't give ourselves that luxury."

Norman Lewis knocked on their door with those hands that didn't belong to him: "Where are you going? I'll go with you."

The conversation would then exclude her, and Lisa set certain conditions. "Come on, Norman, but I won't allow you to talk about astronomy." That was impossible to stick to. Under Norman's influence, even Lisa imagined how she would greet an extraterrestrial and what she would pull out of the refrigerator to feed him.

She never tired. "Your electromagnetic waves are killing me, Lisa," Lorenzo told her. "There's no doubt, you are a solar woman." She went from one activity to another, and if Lorenzo hadn't gone to the observatory, she would have dragged him along with her at night as well. "Let's stay peacefully home today," begged the Mexican.

"No, no, Lorenzaccio. The only way I'd miss the Corelli *Concerto Grosso de Navidad* is if I were dead. You have to hear it. It's essential to your mental health."

"What is hurting my mental health is all your bustling around, Mrs. Dynamo, widow of acceleration."

"We'll be sitting, Lorenzaccio. I have just confirmed that you emit lethal radiation, like X-rays." Lisa was a human shooting star. Maybe she had a greater number of mobile cells, and her supernumerary structure led her to exercise with the same ease with which her practical spirit and her diligence resolved everyday problems. Without her, Lorenzo would have slept—and how he missed that. But she brought him out into Harvard life. With her he got to know Boston and the other Ivy League universities. The Peabody Museum of Archaeology and Ethnology. It was wonderful, in spite of the fact that Lorenzo saw it all at a gallop, worried about his work, about meeting Bok!

"The closer I am to you, the more energy I receive by the minute, Lisa." Years later he would ask himself how it was possible that he never got sick. He came to the conclusion that Lisa, purveyor of light and heat, prevented it, and that he had been very fortunate.

Thoughts of Mexico didn't cause him pain, nor did thoughts of Leticia, because he couldn't see them. He had entered into the feverish rhythm of competition. He had to show the gringos his worth. Anything you can do, I can do better, he told them with his eyes. Once, on the street, a gringo called him a little Mexican jumping bean.

And they said Cambridge wasn't a racist town. He would make them see what little Mexican beans were capable of. He was the last to come down from the telescope platform; it was he who closed up the cupola and turned off the console. He spent the entire night standing, in spite of the intense cold. He wouldn't even use the heater. The frigid weather cleared the sky; it was never better for observing. He never complained. Pushing himself beyond his limit made him wonder if the cosmos forced its own nature on him. What more could he ask for, since he didn't belong to the kingdom of feelings? Feelings, what a great hindrance!

One night Lisa pointed upward: "Look at that sweet little star!"

Lorenzo became angry. Stars weren't sweet or cute or brave or intelligent. They just were. That was why science was so conclusive compared with the humanities.

One night a snowstorm pounded against the cupola. He was so absorbed in his calculations that he didn't notice. During the night the wind rabidly struck the closed cupola, under which he was making his measurements. It burst against the windows of the building. Only when a six-pointed star fell on his sleeve outside did Lorenzo notice. "It's snow! It's snow! I've finally seen snow." He took shelter under a canopy to study it. When the furious flakes stopped spinning in the air, Lorenzo moved into the middle of a vast white desolation that came up to his knees. There wasn't a soul around; it was too early in the morning. Only the vapor of his breathing kept him company—and the snow. He finally knew what it was. What he had seen on Popo when he went searching for Juan was barely frost. At Harvard, more than just snow-covered, the Earth appeared to have returned to the Ice Age. Two hundred million years ago the Earth was blue ice. The polar caps expanded and froze the oceans; immense winters brought by glacial winds settled on the surface of the Earth. Then came the Pleistocene, and with it, a pale sun, under which humans attempted to survive. How nature had raged against them. As he put one shoe in front of the other in a foot of snow, Lorenzo thought about the concentration of natural forces that governed the world. Could man handle them? This snow was a bomb. What fun the decrease in temperature brought. Where were the animals? How did they protect themselves? A shiver made him lose his footing. If I don't hurry, it'll be good-bye astronomy. The shape of an animal was outlined in the distance. What if it were a mammoth? The violence of the storm seemed to come from the beginning of time. In Mexico during the rainy season, the sky had fallen in, but it was a tropical deluge. This cold that came in from the Arctic made him think that maybe he was the only survivor. All this snowy whiteness defined purity for him for the first time. Feeling like a polar bear, Lorenzo found refuge in Lisa's arms.

The next day the storm grew worse.

It wasn't long before the other observers told Shapley, "The Mexican guy is really tough. He hasn't missed even one night."

He'd die before he'd miss a single night observing. The Oak Ridge station had a variety of telescopes, and having access to them thrilled him. From the beginning, Lorenzo's passion was the discovery of very red or very blue weak stars. He spent many hours tirelessly cataloging objects of very pale light, even though he preferred to spend all his time in front of the telescope studying, with great detail and fascination, the most tenuous objects that originated from diffused sources. That was when he detected a new kind of galaxy, of a very blue color, in the halo of the Milky Way. How many of these galaxies were there? Surely a great number. Lorenzo was thrilled because scientists thought that the majority of the galaxies were yellow in color—the nuclei in particular—which indicated that they were dealing with old stars. The existence of blue galaxies signaled their recent formation on a grand scale. This could also mean that he, Lorenzo, was discovering new astrophysical processes. Maybe he could find galaxies with intense ultraviolet radiation. He applied the Tikov method of discovery to the eight-inch Ross refractor. The lens had a color curve with the appropriate slope to discover extremely weak luminous objects. Later he moved on to multiple-image plates that were developed through three successive emulsion filters. If he continued this way, he might discover planetary systems in regions of space close to Earth that were very different from our solar system.

17

Lorenzo was pleased when Bart Jan Bok and his wife, Priscilla, invited him to have dinner with them and their children. He wanted to discuss his recent discoveries with them in depth. Being included in the bosom of a family was comforting, and Bok's support was indispensable. Besides, Bok inspired confidence in him. "Very good, Tena, my friend. Very good. Everyone is impressed with your work. I believe you should think of publishing your first article with these results." The Dutchman was moved as he said, "Harvard needs men like you. I wish you could stay forever."

His face red with emotion, Lorenzo replied, "The truth is, I'd like to do my studies here. The thing that bothers me is that we're so beaten down in Mexico, and Erro is waiting for me. He probably feels that I've betrayed him with my absence, and he has every right to feel that way. I'm here because of him, but if it were up to me, I'd do my Ph.D. in Cambridge."

"That's what we all wish. In the meantime, Shapley has written to Erro to extend your stay."

Nothing could have pleased Lorenzo more. He felt that Bok's desire for his presence and the fact that he expected an article from him was unwarranted encouragement. He had conquered scientific English; writing it would not be too much of an effort.

What he never dreamed was that Shapley would ask him to be director of the Oak Ridge station. Lorenzo didn't realize that he reminded Shapley of his own youth. Shapley saw himself in the Mexican's temerity. He had begun as a reporter for the crime section of a Kansas newspaper, writing articles about drunken oil workers, until he decided to attend the University of Missouri. Since the journalism school had not yet opened, he chose the field of astronomy, simply because he couldn't pronounce the word *archaeology*. "I opened the catalog of courses," Shapley had told him. "The very first course offered was *a-r-c-h-a-e-o-l-o-g-y*, and I couldn't pronounce it. I turned the page and saw *a-s-t-r-o-n-o-m-y*. I could pronounce that, and here I am." With the advantage of large telescopes, Shapley had been able to design a radically new model of the galaxy. It was so drastically different from traditional theories that only his strong character saved it from its critics. In 1921 the *Boston Sunday Advertiser* had published an eight-column article on the Harvard astronomer Harlow Shapley, who could prove that the universe was a thousand times larger than it was currently believed to be. Like Shapley, Lorenzo didn't fear anything, and he was furiously competitive. The war of 1914 had concerned Shapley; the Mexican too had started his work in an era of war. Like Shapley, he defended himself like a cornered bobcat.

The telescope at the Oak Ridge Observatory gave Lorenzo a sense of power that disappeared at dawn when he returned home. Galileo Galilei, the messenger of the stars, must have felt the same way in 1609, when he invited the Senate members to look from the tower of San Marcos through the two-lens telescope at the Venetian ships several kilometers away. To see them with the naked eye, the viewer would have to take a three-hour trip. What a wonder. The ecclesiastical authorities in Rome must have been amazed when they saw how Galileo dismantled the telescope after having them observe Jupiter and its satellites. To the genius! To the genius! In the years that followed, they only shouted to demonize him, denying all support and finally condemning him. Nearly three hundred and fifty years had passed since then.

Harvard needed a young man with a persevering character. Harlow Shapley offered Lorenzo the job of director as if Lorenzo were doing them a favor. Shapley had expected him to refuse. It was a great honor. Lorenzo doubled his workload. The *Astrophysical Journal* would publish his article. He had never been so happy. In spite of the fact that the cold lacerated his chest, there was nothing better than working all night.

As the months went by, the results in the lab were the jubilant proof that confirmed his hypothesis about weak stars. "Things are going so well for me," he said, "that I'm afraid something bad is going to happen." The news about the war saddened him, but his life really had only to do with the nocturnal sky. "Lisa, Lisa, you are living with a happy man."

"You still have your shirt on."

"I'll take it off right now."

In memory of the garden from his childhood, Lorenzo wanted to see a garden with a tree. Lisa showed him the apple orchards. "An apple a day keeps the doctor away." They ate more than one a day, and the entire house was filled with the fruity fragrance. As in the New England fields, there were apples in people's gardens, and Lisa would just jump a fence to pick them.

"So you're the thieves," one homeowner said as he came out one day.

"I'm sorry, sir. We won't do it again," Lisa said.

"I suppose you aren't students. If you were, you'd know that there is a code of ethics."

"Sir, I'm an astrophysics student," Lorenzo said hastily. "I'm from Mexico."

"From Mexico? You're Mexican?" The man's face opened into an enormous smile. "What great fortune! Are you Mayan, by any chance?" He looked at Lisa. "You, on the other hand, look American. My name is Eric Thompson, and I'm wild about the great Maya. I've published several articles about Chichén Itzá and Kobá, where I spent my honeymoon."

"We've stolen Eric Thompson's apples!" exclaimed Lisa, covering her mouth with her hand.

The man with the graying hair smiled. "Let me invite you to steal a cup of tea from me. I don't have any tequila."

In 1926 Eric Thompson had disembarked from the ship *Progreso* and from then on had dedicated his life to the Maya. "Young man, do you speak Maya?"

Lorenzo made excuses for himself. "No, but very few people in Mexico know it."

"Of course they do! Almost two million between Guatemala, Honduras, Belize, and Mexico speak it. Come into my library. I've built an altar to Mexico that you need to see."

Photographs of Uxmal, Chichén Itzá, and Teotihuacán peppered the bookshelves, which were crammed full. "I'm working on my book *The Rise and Fall of Maya Civilization*, but I still have a lot to do."

"What is a lot?"

"Six or eight years of consistent work, and that's if things go well. If I finish in the next ten years, I'll be pleased."

Lorenzo and Lisa looked at each other.

"I've been in Campeche, in Chiapas, in Tabasco, in Oaxaca, in Veracruz. What a country, my friend, what a great country. I still have many trips to take to Mexico and Central America."

When Lorenzo repeated that he was studying astronomy, Thompson sprang up like a grasshopper. "Of course. How did I not guess that you were an astronomer? You had to be. The Maya predicted eclipses, recorded the passing of time and the movement of the celestial bodies, and developed the calendar. Surely you both know who John Lloyd Stephens and Frederic Catherwood are."

They both shook their heads no.

That didn't seem to dishearten Thompson. "That's what's bad about specialization; you lose the big picture. Friend, you come from a fabulous civilization that you must learn about in depth. Stephens and Catherwood opened the path for Sylvanus Morley and myself. Surely you'll be interested to know, young astronomer, that the passing of time—the interminable flow of days slipping from the eternity of the future to that of the past—fascinated the Maya. Their calculations on a stela in Quiriguá take us back thousands of years; others probe the future.

Lorenzo was amazed. Time had been the theme of his adolescent imaginings, and the magnitude of the Mayan astronomical codes piqued his curiosity. He asked Thompson if he had written any articles on the subject, and when Thompson handed him a reprint, Lorenzo showed his appreciation with a Mexican hug. What had happened to the grandeur of the Maya?

Thompson's face saddened. Palenque emptied out, and the ancient cities just dried up. A great epidemic? A collapse?

Enthralled, Lorenzo made no motion to leave until Lisa tugged on his sleeve.

They left with a basket of apples and an invitation to return:

"Come back whenever you like. It nourishes me to talk about Mexico."

"You see," Lisa said, "if you hadn't come walking with me, you'd never have met him."

Lorenzo hugged her. The sky at Harvard and the perfection of this university—with libraries where you could find the works of Stephens, review Catherwood's engravings, read Leibniz and Kant—made him happy. Stretching out your hand, you could take these books right off the shelves, just as Lisa had. "North American universities," bragged Lisa, "have incomparable libraries. I'm going to show you all there is here about your country. And the University of Texas at Austin has more. You may even feel like reading a Mexican author."

Harlow Shapley called Lorenzo to his office. "Luis Enrique Erro is asking me anxiously when you will return. It's been almost two years—"

"I wanted to speak to you about that. I would really like to do a doctoral degree, if you will allow me."

"Listen, Tena, your determination takes me back to my youth. There is nothing I would like better, but unfortunately, I have to play the devil's advocate. A doctorate will take at least two or three more years. My friend Erro will feel like I've stabbed him in the back if you stay. It's your decision. If you stay, you will have my complete support, but my moral obligation is to tell you that Erro is not prepared to lose his best scientist. You have remarkable intuition, and you are a splendid practical observer."

"And if I don't graduate?"

"Academia isn't everything, my friend. There are astronomers who have doctoral degrees who have not achieved a fourth of what you have done. You must continue with your blue galaxies, your blue stellar objects, and the planetary nebulae. Your investigation will take you to other stars, other discoveries. We're proud of you. No one has ever observed for the number of hours that you have accumulated in twenty-seven months. You can learn theory from practice. Galileo wasn't born an astronomer."

Lorenzo didn't sleep all night. He knew he would return to Mexico.

When he decided that the moment to leave had arrived, one thought bothered him. If he took Lisa to Mexico (like a package), she would be his responsibility. His lover would face language problems. She'd have to adapt. Still, independent as she was, she would overcome the obstacles. But Lorenzo knew he wouldn't study as much, having to come home earlier. What a hassle. Fucking women! More out of a sense of honor than from conviction, he proposed marriage to Lisa while they were listening to a Bach fugue.

"No," she responded laconically.

"No?" repeated Lorenzo, stunned by the rejection.

"No."

"But why not? What will happen to you? What will you do without me?"

"The same as you'll do without me. I'll survive. Don't worry. I've gotten used to your presence, and I'll do the same with your absence."

Lorenzo was totally thrown. He had never imagined such an answer. This was an extragalactic phenomenon without explanation. If he had been able to discover the lines of emission of stellar objects, how had he missed them from this creature who was part of his everyday life? The woman must be crazy, poor thing. She was irresponsible. What would become of her? From the very depths of his being came a lament he had not anticipated. "Lisa, I don't want to leave you."

"But you are leaving, and I could not live in any country besides my own."

"It's impossible for me to stay, impossible to betray my country. I wouldn't be able to face myself in the mirror. I'm taking you with me," Lorenzo said angrily.

"I don't want to go."

"Lisa, I don't understand. I never imagined you would do this to me."

"And I never imagined you'd be so naïve."

"Your tone hurts, Lisa."

"You're the one who's leaving. I'm the one who's hurting."

"I've asked you to marry me. I'm suggesting we go together."

"You're a macho Mexican, Lorenzo, and I'm Anglo-Saxon. It would be too hard for me to adapt—"

"I'm macho?" he interrupted, indignant.

"You are, even in the way you fuck. Thanks to me, you've gotten a little better, but even after a hundred thousand light-months, you still run to the bathroom to conscientiously wash yourself after making love. Shit, I'm the one who could get pregnant, not you. What is so repellent?"

"What? Why didn't you tell me?"

"I'm not a prostitute. I don't have an infection. Instead of taking me into your arms, you run to disinfect yourself."

"You should have told me."

"I did tell you, but it's a Pavlovian reflex. You do it automatically. You and I are different. I like to walk around the house naked; the freedom is liberating. You're trapped by obligations. You always have a debt to repay to yourself. I don't owe myself anything."

Shocked, Lorenzo hid his face in his hands. "I don't understand. I don't understand any of it."

"Of course not. All you understand is to go running out every night to your telescope. There isn't anything else for you. It's your true phallus, the one you know how to handle, because the one hanging between your legs doesn't work. I'm not going to miss you. Anyway, our sex life isn't what it could be."

Such brutality and such indecency. Was this another Leticia? Lorenzo reeled. "You're really crude for a woman."

"Don't start with that, Lorenzo. We live in my country—not yours, where the women are slaves. Here the sexes are equal. Sperm and eggs are the result of a primitively identical evolution, remember that."

Lorenzo hated her. He wanted a woman who did not create problems for him. That's why he had hated her every time she contradicted him. "Don't be argumentative. Let me work." He hated her feminism. He hated her criticism. While she was his accomplice, he accepted it, but the moment she confronted him, he felt she was a threat. On the other hand, it was impossible to live at Harvard without Lisa.

Lorenzo moved to the couch in the living room. He couldn't sleep. At one point he got up and opened the door to the bedroom a crack and saw that she was sleeping placidly. I think she's even smiling, he told himself as he stood there freezing. Maybe she's a Martian. Maybe she's only reached the bottom rung of the evolutionary chain. In the morning he saw her leave for her tennis game in shorts. He watched her through the window. Had he really wanted her immobile, waiting—he, the agile, the impatient, the creator, the transcendent? She wanted to dominate him. That was it. She took away the peace he needed for research. She was spoiled, just like Leticia; her whims drove him crazy. Nevertheless, when Lisa came back in time to make dinner and skillfully set the table, he didn't have any desire to run to Oak Ridge, as was his habit. He delayed taking the last bite. She spoke very little, but there was nothing in her attitude that gave any indication of the discussion the night before. And if I stay? Lorenzo wondered.

Wearing his jacket, he went out into the dark night. When he returned, desolate, at five in the morning, the door to the bedroom was locked.

The last days were sad. Lorenzo left for the station with two suitcases. Only a disconcerted Norman Lewis accompanied him. They embraced. "Although I'm not Lisa, I'm going to visit you in your marvelous country. I want to see if you're right."

As the train pulled away, Norman's figure kept getting smaller on the platform until he raised his hand for the last time.

18

It was impossible to sleep. The desert that devoured everything seemed to come to the window and cover the sleeping people. The sand was going to swallow the train and the few passengers. Few, because not many could handle the long trip from the United States to Mexico in third class. Who were these people? Day and night they abandoned themselves to sleep, legs spread out or curled up. The children, little bundles of misery, awaited the end. Which end? Whichever. Other children would have run between the seats. These didn't dare. The slap across the face that one father gave a little boy who ventured toward the caboose still resonated in the air. There was an atmosphere of disapproval, of monotony, of slowness. Immersed in his thoughts, pencil in hand, Lorenzo studied the hypotheses that obsessed him more than Lisa and his very life—the flare stars in the Orion nebula. What was stellar evolution if stars didn't die or if they turned cold like the planets? Lorenzo was a man possessed.

If he hadn't been so absorbed in his papers, perhaps some traveler might have spoken to him, but it never occurred to Lorenzo that he was isolating himself.

He felt the rhythm of the rocking locomotive, the windows suddenly covered with a profusion of branches and sap, but the greenery did not bring respite. The jungle, its hot humidity, made the smell of urine rise from the bottom of the train car. The tropics harassed them as much as the desert had. When they reached the high plains, Lorenzo rested, but the memory of Lisa—Lisa's belly, Lisa's eyes—was inescapable. How different it would be if she were traveling by his side. She would have struck up a friendship with this one and that one. She'd know the conductor's name, not to mention the porter's. Lisa, he now realized, was his communication with the world. He, on the other hand, lived incarcerated. How long is the sun going to live? he wondered. Answering this was a much greater challenge than anything that could happen on the train.

The sun is like a nuclear electric plant that produces energy and transforms its hydrogen into helium. What will happen in five billion years when it has consumed that energy? Will we die from the cold? Lorenzo thought about other stars, younger than the sun, or of an even more advanced age, and he plunged into conjecture again. When would it be possible to postulate if the universe was finite or infinite? When would it be proved one way or the other? How did the universe begin? Humbled, Lorenzo could only respond as Galileo had: I don't know.

Disheartened by the events in the sky, he returned to Earth. He would have liked to have seen Emilia in Texas, but a stop for even a few days made the trip impossibly expensive. Besides, he felt an urgency to continue observing the blue galaxies with the Schmidt camera in Tonantzintla. He did not ask himself how he would make a living in his country, but rather how the telescope would respond.

Seeing the spectacle of the cornfields and the great blue mountains of the high plains, Lorenzo made peace with himself. Even his sister Leticia's lovely face danced in his imagination. I feel an unexplained force inside me, he thought. I could knock over a bull. Rich with what he had learned, his gaze across Mexico was like that of a pioneer. He felt as if he had the power to get water out of the desert. He loved Tonantzintla, how he loved it! A great task was awaiting him. He would propose one reform after another to Erro at the observatory. His brother Juan should also go to Cambridge, put his knowledge to the test outside the country, have access to the devices at Oak Ridge, listen to the modern mathematicians. Norman Lewis would protect Juan. He was a dependable friend.

The first thing Lorenzo did upon his arrival in Mexico City was to take a bus to Puebla and another slower and broken-down one to Tonantzintla, his true home. Don Lucas Toxqui opened his arms: "Your room has been waiting and lonely. No one has occupied it."

The town seemed to be asleep under the tolling of the bells. Its rhythm never accelerated to Lorenzo's tempo. The passage of time ate away at him; it seemed to thicken in the blood of the people. "Hey, what's the big hurry!" said a peasant whom he inadvertantly pushed out of the way as he ran up the slope.

"Where's my brother?" he asked Guarneros, the handyman, when he arrived at the entrance, smiling.

"He's not here."

"Where did he go?"

"He's not here."

The observatory was strangely empty. No one was in the cubicles. Finally, in the main office, after embracing him effusively, Luis Enrique Erro said, "I had to ask your brother to leave, and believe me, I'm sorry."

In the commotion of a basketball game with the villagers, Juan had pushed someone to the ground. It turned into a fight, and they were about to come to blows. Since Erro didn't tolerate any insult to the locals, he fired Juan.

"Why didn't you write to me about it?" Lorenzo said.

"There was nothing you could have done, Tena. My decision was final."

"I want to know where my brother is."

"No one knows. This happened more than a year ago. We've lost touch with him."

"I'm leaving right away to look for him!" exclaimed Lorenzo, red with anger. "And Fernando Alba?"

"He's at the observatory at Tacubaya with Joaquín Gallo."

"And Graef?"

"At UNAM, in the College of Science."

Somberly, Lorenzo decided to return to the city. He went first to Tacubaya to see Alba.

"Listen, I'm sorry to tell you," Alba informed him, "but Erro has lost his mind. He not only threw your brother out of the game, but out of Tonantzintla."

"I don't understand any of this, Fernando. Shoving someone in a game isn't anything out of the ordinary. It happens all the time."

"The truth is, it was a pretext. Erro couldn't handle your brother's intelligence because it surpassed his own in a short time. He jumped on that incident to get rid of him. It was intolerable to him that a boy who didn't even go to high school would be better at everything than he was."

"Where is Juan?"

"Graef and Barajas have asked me the same thing. He hasn't been in touch with Recillas either, who was such a good friend. That incident was quite a blow to all of us. I lost my best student. Who was there left to teach? Julito Treviño and the other two who weren't worth the time. Graef was coming to Tonantzintla less and less because he was so upset. The only ones left were Don Luis and myself, and I kept at it for a time until he said to me, "Alba, if you're not happy, leave. See what else you can find." After that I taught classes in Mexico City at the Polytechnical Institute, at the Military School, and at UNAM. I've gotten away from astronomy; now I focus on Birkhoff's theory of relativity."

"What about Félix Recillas and Paris Pishmish?"

They're going to the Paris Observatory. The only one worth anything in Tonantzintla now is Guido Münch. You know, the one who's half Chiapaneco Indian and half German. But he's been awarded a Guggenheim Fellowship to study with Chandrasekhar at Yerkes in Chicago. Tonantzintla is dead, Lorenzo. None of the scientists are left, and the young people are not going to be properly trained by conversing with Erro. You know, you can't create a research environment by decree. I'm convinced that astronomy is not like physics. It's impossible to teach it to students who don't have some background in it. Erro is an amateur, and to make matters worse, the Schmidt camera's optical lens is failing. If we don't send the mirror to Perkins-Elmer, we'll never get any results. That's how things have been since you left. After the 1943 conference, everything has gone downhill."

Lorenzo became obsessed with finding Juan, but how? Surely Leticia would know. Where was Leticia? He had never even sent her a postcard.

It took two phone calls to find her living in the front part of a boardinghouse on Orizaba Street.

"Bye, Leti, see you tonight!"

"Leti, sweetie, don't forget my cereal for breakfast tomorrow."

"Leti, you know I adore you, but it's been two weeks since my sheets and towels have been changed."

A hoarse voice responded from the depths of hell: "Good-bye, my precious . . . Yes, darling . . . Don't worry, doll."

Lorenzo followed the voice to find a woman lying on a bed in a room converted into an office where she ate and drank, she did her hair, she did her ironing, and she entertained. Lorenzo stopped. The voice encouraged him to enter. "Come on in, honey. What can I do for you?"

Lorenzo slowly backed up. Leticia immediately buttoned her blouse and ran her fingers through her disheveled hair. Panda-bear circles blackened her eyes; it was amazing how much she had aged in a little more than two years.

"Brother, when did you get back? How did it go? Can I give you a shot of tequila? I'll have one with you and see if it helps me get rid of this nasty flu I've had for more than a month. That's why I look like this."

"I'd rather talk in the living room."

"Go on then, darling. I'm going to put a robe on right now."

Without waiting for him to leave, she jumped off the bed, put on slippers, and picked up a rag off the back of a chair. Lorenzo was repulsed.

Sitting across from him in the living room, Leticia lit a cigarette. "Want one? I do. I feel nervous around you—now, isn't that unusual."

"Letiiiiiii," rang out a voice from the doorway, "if I don't come back tonight, don't worry. Okay, love? I'm going after that one I told you about."

"Yes, sweetheart. I hope everything goes well, and I'll wait for you in the morning, all right, doll?"

"You're really very friendly with your tenants."

"You want me to hate them?" Leticia responded. "Tell me how it went for you in the States. They pay in dollars there, right?"

Leticia seemed so vulgar. What she had gained in experience, she had lost in freshness. Her children? All in school. "That's good, right? Because they annoy me like you can't imagine. How are they doing? Ay, who knows. I think they're doing well. At least they haven't been expelled. Emilia came from Texas, gorgeous like you wouldn't believe. The years don't show on her, and what a figure. And me with all these rolls. She was wearing divine gringa clothes. She left me a really fine dress, but it doesn't fit. Thanks to her, I was able to start this boardinghouse. Santiago is at the bank, and he's doing great. And the suits! You can't believe the suits he wears. He looks like a model. Much taller than you. Of course, he's driving the girls crazy. You're going to see him, right? He comes by here every now and then for lunch and always leaves me some dough. You know what I mean by dough? Don't worry about it, brother; you'll figure it out. You wanted to see Juan? Well, you're going to have to visit him in jail at the black Palacio de Lecumberri. He set up his principality there six months ago, and I hope he doesn't die, because he owes me money. No, of course I don't go! I don't want him to hit me up for more. The only one who has the balls to see him is Santiago—when his girlfriends don't keep him out too late. Stay for dinner. Come on, it's on me. Ay, don't be so stuffy. I thought you'd be easier to get along with when you came back from Gringoland. You're leaving already? All right, sonny, drop by anytime. I'm always here, playing mother to the tenants."

Lorenzo went to sit on a bench in Plaza Rio de Janiero in a state of shock. He lit a cigarette. It took a minute for his heart to settle down. Why am I shocked? he thought. Leticia has always been like that. At least she found a modus vivendi. He noticed that the red-brick buildings that Don Porfirio Díaz had imported from France during his presidency, with their attic rooms and eaves for snow, seemed incongruous. What snow? And what ridiculous railings. How absurd it all was. He took a deep breath. Mexico is a victim of Europe, he told himself. He walked slowly toward the white Sagrada Familia. On the steps of the church a flock of beggars raised their hands, and he thought he saw Juan's among them. Two women in black, their heads covered with mantillas, wearing ostentatious Virgin of Guadalupe medallions between their breasts, passed in front of him. Lorenzo crossed avenida Chapultepec. Then he took calle Florencia and continued along Paseo de la Reforma for a good while to Cuauhtémoc at Insurgentes, where he saw Lucía's house. Freshly painted, it was home to new tenants. He kept walking until he stopped under the Chinese clock on Bucareli. Oh, Mexico, how you hurt me. He felt a pressing need to walk the city, although by then, aside from having tears in his eyes, his legs were numb. Am I going crazy? He inhaled the smoke of his last cigarette deeply and asked himself, How many packs have I smoked since I've returned—three, four?

Before leaving for Harvard, he had distanced himself from his friends. Now he yearned to get back with them, most of all Diego.

When the two men saw each other, neither mentioned Dr. Beristain's death, and when they embraced, both closed their eyes. "Later, brother," Diego murmured. "Later, not now." They began an intentionally frivolous conversation about Diego's tennis matches, a game that he won because his serves were phenomenal and about his work at the Finance Ministry. He had added bridge to his social activities. "It's very intelligent, almost like chess. With your memory, you'd be a marvelous player." As Lorenzo remained quiet, Diego said, "It seems you haven't changed. You're still the same red-hot intellectual."

Lorenzo had the unpleasant feeling that his friend was flattering him. During his absence, Diego had become more worldly. He was infinitely social, and diplomacy was second nature to him. Saturdays and Sundays he went out with the two luminaries, Hugo Margáin and Juan Sánchez Navarro, who were good-looking and easygoing, groomed for success. Life in Mexico had a varnish of urbanity that concealed people's feelings. How pleasant they all were. How refined. How diplomatic. Lorenzo missed the scientific discussions with Norman, and Lisa's frankness.

Life in the capital had gone on without him, and everyone was involved in their own things. The interests of the old gang seemed childish next to his great ambitions. They didn't care to do anything now but champion themselves. Dr. Beristain, the only one with whom he could share his ideals, was dead. El Pajarito Revueltas was being held in jail. Lorenzo noticed an atmosphere he had never detected. His friends were what the gringos called too good to be true. Something was going on behind the scenes. Did they lead double lives? What masks did they wear?

Within a few days he realized that his experience at Harvard was incommunicable. The memory of Lisa pierced him like a knife in the belly. What am I supposed to do here? he wondered. Why did I come back? Why did I accept La Pipa's and Chava's invitation to go out with them? What do I have in common with them anymore?

He was surprised by the slow, unpunctual, and copious meals that annihilated the afternoons for anything other than a boa constrictor's siesta. "You've already become a gringo? Mexican food is the best in the world."

At Harvard, lunch was barely a pause between two tasks, an impulse between two ideas. There was no time to lose. Here, time was a little pig's foot in vinaigrette that you were to suck right down to the bone. Then some roasted pig's feet and pork tacos. "This pork is out of this world!" Pork rinds in green sauce; pork and pork and more pork. Pass me another tortilla to cover my porcine head. "Lencho, how did you survive without *tlacoyos* or *pambazos*?" Mexico seemed like an immense tortilla frying itself in the sun.

How could they stand to listen to one another saying things that demeaned them? They have to be smarter than this, thought Lorenzo uneasily. I remember them as being brilliant. But no. They continued with their inanities, which at times Diego, ironically, refuted. Finally, thanks to the alcohol, nobody listened to anyone anyway. Why were they content with so little? At the same time, Lorenzo reproached himself: Why am I so critical? Some of the women were extraordinary knitters of commonplace yarns. Pleased with themselves, they described their day in minute detail, right up to their arrival at the party. Lorenzo soon realized that his friends applauded them, but there were ulterior motives. "Put up with her stupidity and then take her home with you. She's really dim-witted but great in bed," confirmed Chava.

The uneasiness Lorenzo felt at age eleven in his aunt's house on Lucerna returned. That was when he believed that adults had explanations for what happened in the world. Wouldn't Lisa and

Norman be stunned? Maybe it was because of Lisa that the women seemed like incomprehensible globular cumuli, distant conglomerations he had no way to measure.

Mexico struck him in the face like a rock. At Harvard he had never noticed men hanging around on the corner with nothing to do. Poverty made the Mexicans settle for watching life pass them by. Like my father, he thought. What had the Revolution done for them? If I had never left, would I be aware of so many flaws? he asked himself. At Harvard all the stars were novas; here he only saw the nebulae.

Diego put his arm around him. "Brother, you're like a fish out of water. Either join in or you'll sink. You can't blame others for what happens to you. That will only serve to isolate you even further."

"Join what, Diego? You want a country where a few share the pie, decide for the rest, and complain because they have to pull the miserable multitude behind them like an anchor. I want to appeal to the peasant, the laborer, the mother, the housewife—to encourage them to participate in science, regardless of whether they belong to any party or whether they know how to formulate their desires. I want to make them willing participants. I want them to say, Here I am. This is my country! I want to make a difference."

Everything his buddies enjoyed was repulsive to him. The Archbishop Luis María Martínez appeared in *Rotofoto*, sprinkling holy water and blessing warehouses, cabarets, dance halls, restaurants. "Look at him in his robe at Sears & Roebuck, the salesclerks kneeling as he passes."

"Lorenzo, you're wrong," interjected Chava. "He's a good man. Two days ago they offered him a first-class seat, and do you know what he said? 'You can hang me on any nail.' "

Lorenzo kept insisting that the only difference between Tongolele the prostitute and the archbishop was the neckline. "She just shows more than he does." Matching Chava's wit, he answered, "This is the country of Agustín Lara, José Alfredo Jiménez, Jorge Negrete—'El Charro Cantor'—and the little Indian wrapped in his serape sleeping under the shade of the maguey. When are we going to step out of this postcard?"

Lorenzo resented Chava. Apparently his buddies' ideals had gone by the wayside. They lived the high life, but Lorenzo accused them of being low.

Chava retorted, "If you keep that up, we'll never meet your requirements; the entire country will never reach your high standards. Tolerance, brother, tolerance."

"You say concede, Chava, concede, but I don't do that. I demand."

"Well, don't be so demanding, and you'll have a better life."

The first drink didn't affect him, so Lorenzo drank another. After the third, a slow euphoria came over him and increased with each sip. Why hadn't he ever thought of alcohol to calm his anxiety? He and Lisa never drank. Norman either. Occasionally he had a beer.

Norman Lewis would probably have liked to debate with Juan. Like Norman, Juan believed in the possibility of intelligent life on other planets. "There"—Juan would become excited, pointing at the celestial dome—"there are many resources to explore. Just as we extract gas, petroleum, and minerals out of the earth; up there unexplored veins await us, fields that go beyond the quasars and the black holes."

Juan took great pleasure in the perfection of instruments. He repeated to whoever wanted to listen that the microphone is truer than the ear, the movie camera more exact than the eye. If technology could go beyond human limitations, if machines were much more sensitive than nerve endings, then surely our brains could be replaced by mechanical techniques. Didn't Pavlov demonstrate that the sacred will of man could be nothing more than a conditioned reflex? Juan's speculations irritated Lorenzo, but to Norman, who compared the brevity of human life with the years of a planet, it seemed feasible that a society of extraterrestrials, for whom a year could equal a thousand or a hundred thousand years, could colonize our galaxy. Juan and Norman would get along, and Lorenzo yearned to see his brother's intelligent face debating with his friend.

He decided to return to Leticia's boardinghouse and ask her to invite Santiago to dinner.

"Of course, brother; you don't have to ask twice. Would Friday be okay?"

How Santiago had grown, and how right Leticia was. He was handsome and self-assured, and Lorenzo fell under his spell. The youngest brother's gratefulness to Emilia was infinite, and that made him even more likable. "I can never pay her back for all she's done for me." He had the same worldly aura around him as Beristain, Chava, La Pipa—of the triumphant Mexico. At the end of the meal—delicious, of course—Lorenzo expressed his desire to see Juan, and they agreed to meet at the entrance to Lecumberri on Sunday. "Take identification, or they won't let you in," Santiago said.

Lecumberri was the most abandoned place in Mexico. Like simians in cages, the prisoners grabbed the bars, roared insults, or begged for money, reaching out their hands or a sardine can. One of them latched on to Lorenzo, who imprudently had gotten too close. They reached F ward, where the thieves were housed, and Lorenzo shivered when he heard his last name resonate in the shit-filled air. He didn't recognize his brother. Juan had shrunk. He almost had no face, only eyes under a shaved skull. "Brother." Juan allowed himself to be embraced; his arms hung at his sides. Then Lorenzo pulled himself together so as not to shout out in protest, What have they done to you?

Juan looked at him impassively. His uniform was worn and dirty, his arms a disaster of scars, not to mention his bruised cheeks. Juan waited, a cigarette butt between his fingers.

"How long before you get out?"

"I don't know. The public defender, who represents everyone here, says by the end of the year." At no point did he try to get closer, not even when the three started to eat the contents of the basket Leticia had prepared.

"That sister of ours sure knows how to cook," Santiago said as he lifted the spoon to his mouth.

Juan didn't smile. He ate in silence.

"I brought you cigarettes, brother." Lorenzo handed him a pack.

Juan didn't even extend his hand to take the gift. Only at the end did he turn his face to Lorenzo and ask, "Did you work on blue objects at Harvard? Did you go back to the emission lines of those stars that impressed you so much at Tonantzintla? Maybe you'll find the fundamental elements of stellar evolution there." When Lorenzo was about to answer him, content, as if he had revived a dead man, Juan headed to his cell, saying, "Save it for next time. That is, if you come back," and with that, the green metal door slammed shut.

"Will he recover?" Lorenzo asked Santiago in the park in front of the jail.

"Yes. Don't worry, he always comes up smelling like a rose."

"He looks like he's drugged."

"It's better. That way he can tolerate life in there."

"Why doesn't he have his own defense attorney?"

"There's no point. They're all rats, and besides, Juan is about to get out."

"What can I do for him?" shouted Lorenzo desperately.

The younger one had an answer that seemed out of place for his age and his lifestyle: "Nothing, brother. Nothing. Be yourself and continue your life. If we don't do that, how will we get Juan out of this hell?"

19

Lorenzo took the bus back to Tonantzintla that same afternoon, rage in his heart. He thought about Juan for a while, but halfway through the trip, the T Tauri stars recovered their empire. Surely, in spite of Alba's pessimism, there had to be someone at the observatory to talk to about stars. "If you concentrate on the study of the planetary nebula, Tena, my friend," Bok had told him at Harvard, "you'll determine the abundance of heavy elements like argon and sulfur, as well as the pre-galactic quotient of helium to hydrogen. This is so very important!"

My God, it seemed like time had stopped in Tonantzintla. The stillness of the observatory grieved him. In the sleeping town, the Toxqui family had not moved ahead either. Even the children had stayed the same. After Cambridge, they all seemed tiny to him. The potholes on the street were still there, and the same metal rods were still exposed on houses that waited for a second floor. There were demolished or half-constructed fences—everything half finished. "What happened to the idea of growing flowers?" Lorenzo asked Don Honorio Tecuatl.

"Well, we'll see," was the halfhearted response.

That was it! Inertia had conquered them all. Lorenzo's irritation grew and beat furiously against his temples. My science is useless, since I'm the only one who is discouraged by all this.

He got into one of his endless discussions with Erro and noticed that Erro's left ear, his good one, was hearing less. The effort to hear made his face contract as if in pain. The convincing polemist no longer had the same drive.

Enveloped in smoke from his chain of cigarettes, Lorenzo confided his anxiety about Mexico's falling behind. It was visible in the valley before them. How was it possible that the celestial dome had more movement than this tiny fragment of Earth? When would the sky influence the lives of men?

"The heavens and the Earth are one. What is up there is part of what is down here," Erro had told him with a smile. It brought back the memory of the time when Erro had asked him to be his assistant—the teacher who had spoken to him on the roof at calle Pilares.

"Tena, would you like to occupy one of the bungalows here rather than live in town?"

"A bungalow for just one person? That doesn't make sense."

"That's right, Comrade Tena. It's time for you to look for a wife. Haven't you thought of marrying?"

"I want to work," grumbled Lorenzo.

"It won't interfere with your work."

"I'm perfectly fine living with the Toxqui family."

Possessed by his galaxies and his blue stars, Lorenzo had no one to discuss them with. Erro had aged. At Harvard, Bok was his best sounding board, but here . . . Who? Diego would listen to him like a good friend, but he wouldn't be able to respond. He missed the ferocious discussions of Harvard. Oh, Norman, where are you?

But on Lorenzo's first night in front of the Schmidt camera, Mexico immediately recovered its magical spell. The sky was his skin, his bones, his blood, his breath—the only thing he would give his life for.

"I don't think there is anything that makes me happier than the Tonantzintla sky," he told Erro.

"Then dive into it. It is your salvation."

"Things really do happen there."

They both knew that Juan stood between them, victim and ghost. Lorenzo blamed Erro for ruining his brother's life, for the loss of the team of people, and for the inertia of the observatory, the same inertia that was mirrored in the country.

"I could leave for ten years and come back to find the same fruit rotting under the trees."

"Why are you admonishing me? I'm not responsible for man's inconsistency," said Erro.

The best mathematicians and physicists, trained by Sotero

Prieto, were absorbed by UNAM, whose colleges were dispersed throughout Mexico City: the biology building in Chapultepec, geology in Santa María la Ribera, the Physics and Mathematics Institute in the Palacio de Minería, philosophy in Mascarones.

Those who had been at Harvard and MIT during the Second World War returned to teach subjects that were previously unknown in Mexico. Raúl Marzal took charge of promoting the College of Engineering; Alberto Barajas, mathematics. Leopoldo Nieto taught mechanical vibrations, although Alberto J. Flores, the future director of the College of Engineering, was the chair. The young Marcos Mazari took physics and engineering classes. Lorenzo visited Marzal's class and then stopped in at Raphael Carrillo's. "Professor, why don't you teach the theory of consolidation?" asked a student. What enthusiasm there was. That was how the professors who would later teach at the College of Science began to strengthen their course work.

In Mexico City, the colleges planned to join together on the immense expanse of the volcanic land of the south. "It's beautiful, brother, just beautiful," Graef said ecstatically. It would be called University City, and the campus would surpass that of any Ivy League university. "Join us. We don't have an astronomy program yet. You could start it. Your place is here, not in that village."

"I'm going to make it work. You wait and see," Lorenzo responded angrily.

"Don't be blind. You don't have any people. Who's going to want to get all dusty out there?"

With Graef, the College of Science would lead the country's progress. The artists Diego Rivera, David Alfaro Siqueiros, and Juan O'Gorman walked around the campus. O'Gorman had been entrusted with painting the library. Alfaro Siqueiros was doing a super-dynamic mural for the tower of the dean's office with materials that had never been used before. Rivera was painting the stadium. Three works of art, as well as the university museum, the botanical gardens, the Olympic pool, and the athletic fields.

The beautiful edifices built on the sea of lava, the immense windows, the space, and the nobility of the landscape enthralled Graef. "What a campus! Even unfinished, this University City is magnificent. Especially with the pyramid of Cuicuilco over to one side!" The incomplete murals shimmered. Recently bleached roofs shone. Some of the colleges were just being designed. The masons with their buckets of mortar looked like pigeons fluttering around crumbs of bread. "It's all ours"—Carrillo motioned good-heartedly—"but we are more than willing to share." Graef listed the subjects that were now to be taught at the College of Science. He said that they would soon have a nuclear reactor and a Van der Graaf accelerator to study atoms. Standing next to Graef, Marcos Moshinsky, a tall, younger man with black hair, made several brilliant comments.

"Graef, have you noticed that our university is as frail as a house of cards?" Lorenzo said. "Do you realize that this country's education is Third World? Not even twenty percent—what am I saying?—not even ten percent attend elementary school. In the United States it's eighty percent. Our dropout rate is extremely high."

"Lencho, don't be so negative. What's important is that we get scientific and higher education started. We've received several requests from North American universities to collaborate with us."

"Of course, because our scientific activity is so limited that it isn't a threat to them. The number of scientists in the United States is almost one hundred times higher than here, so it's convenient for them if we do scientific studies, because we're far from competing politically or economically."

"You're the competitive one, Lencho, and your pessimism is going to kill you."

"We don't have an elite. To achieve that, we have to increase education at all levels."

"I assure you, Lencho, that we're going to develop top-class people."

While the development of science was flourishing in the city, Tonantzintla was being extinguished, along with Lorenzo's spirit. How many times he wished he had stayed at Harvard for three more years. "How can you discuss that if you don't have a doctoral degree?" Juan Manuel Lozano had retorted once. Lorenzo could only discuss the subject of his degree with Norman Lewis. He kept a hostile silence with his colleagues, thinking, My country has betrayed me. A large majority of the young people cared nothing about the invention of models or of hypotheses that explained what happened to the Earth and to the sky. Not everyone could make an equation, and all preferred to do what was safe. Besides, where were the laboratories, the equipment, the instruments, the scholarships? Certainly not in Tonantzintla. Not a single politician would ever even glance in this direction, no matter how well intentioned he was.

Before, pedestrians on the street could raise their eyes to the night sky and locate Sirius, the brightest star in the celestial dome. Now, not only streetlamps but automobile headlights obscured the stars. In their zeal for modernization, men had erased the sky from their lives. Who was even aware of planets, stars, meteorites, or comets except for a number of scientists?

Tonantzintla, a village lost on the map, was also assailed by the light from the city of Puebla de los Ángeles. A halo of light rose from the buildings and the advertisements, a sort of fine orange dust covered the sky, impeding observation, when before it had been black and clear. There was not a single protest. Braulio Iriarte, Luis Rivera Terrazas, and Lorenzo Tena confronted the apathy alone.

When Lorenzo had wanted to build an elementary school in Tonantzintla, Don Lucas Toxqui said indifferently, "There isn't any interest or any means. The government officials never show their faces around here."

Lorenzo had become indignant. "Couldn't the children study outside, under a tree? If it's so urgent, the physical location is the least important part."

"We want a formal school."

Thanks to Lorenzo's efforts, they now had a school. But what a toll it had taken on him. I'm going to die young, he'd say to himself. But I don't care. Let come what may.

Tonantzintla and Tacubaya's backwardness was becoming more evident to Lorenzo while his former teacher and friends, Alba, Graef, and Barajas, worked enthusiastically at University City. They had drawn students who previously preferred to follow safer paths in law, accounting, or medicine. The sciences no longer seemed unappealing, incomprehensible, or uncertain.

In the months that followed, Lorenzo absorbed himself in the nocturnal sky, as Erro had suggested, but he then found that the Schmidt camera did not respond. Oak Ridge, where are you? The telescope had an alarming defect. Could it be the tube, or the structure that held the powerful lens?

"Lorenzo, Félix Recillas is coming to the University of Puebla next week. Why don't you speak with him?" Rivera Terrazas suggested.

The meeting with Recillas in Puebla confirmed Lorenzo's suspicions. "Listen, Tena, gringo or not, the telescope at Tonantzintla is a piece of garbage. No one has been able to do anything with it. It's either the design of the tube, or else the mechanism is inadequate. You remember, craftsmen made it manually, and it was set up by inexperienced people whom Erro picked up here and there. The Schmidt camera was not working correctly when you left for Harvard. They've never been able to work with it. That's why everyone left. The only solution would be to send it back to Harvard."

On the bus from Puebla to Tonantzintla, Lorenzo repeated Recillas's last sentence to himself: No one has ever been able to do anything with the Schmidt. The mechanism doesn't respond because the people who set it up were amateurs. The optic lens wasn't defective; it was the structure, which was made with hammer and nails, that was defective. They needed an ultramodern design, the product of the minds of first-class engineers and mechanics, which Mexico had not yet produced.

Lorenzo remembered the fervor of Erro and his friends and the ingenuity and enthusiasm they had put into assembling and soldering the parts under George Dimitroff's strict supervision. Lorenzo hysterically repeated to himself that a machine would not beat him: What do I need to do here? I have to beat it. No matter how long it takes, I'm going to find a way. This determination set his nerves on edge. It was impossible to think of anything else. It was a duel to the death. "I'll die before I let this camera beat me." He said it aloud, with fury, scolding himself. He was incapable of leaving the ferrous empire of the Schmidt. You son of a bitch!

He climbed the hill in double time, seeing nothing but the Schmidt. Day after day, one aspirin after another, one moment of impotence defeating another, Lorenzo kept watching for the Schmidt to respond. How was it possible that he had so many projects, so many ideas, but he couldn't rely on a good instrument? Call Shapley? Leave Mexico? I don't have anything else, he repeated to himself. I don't have another country either!

One night, after he opened the doors to the cupola and aimed the telescope at the sky, he realized that the tube was wearing out. The construction may be deficient, he thought, but the optic glass is spectacular. That night he didn't take a single plate. His analytical mind calculated and calculated again, and finally, at five in the morning, Lorenzo went down to the village to sleep. He had barely opened his eyes when he was overcome with anguish. How could he work with this device to obtain the profundity of observation he desired? "This must be how mathematicians work on theorems, clearing the underbrush from the path until they reach the essence, the last step, the definitive, the solutions," he said aloud to give himself courage.

Without the least regard for his personal needs, Lorenzo made calculations, set up tables. Three packs of Delicados a day were not enough. At the general store, Don Crispín said to him, "I have your four packs here, my doc, so you can work better." Each night his determination took him further. He wrote down in a black linoleum booklet the inclination at which the telescope had responded, and he continued to make assumptions. If the tube wears out at twenty degrees and I readjust it, taking into account its flexibility, I'll get this result. By the end of two weeks he didn't need to take notes. He had it all in his head—the different variants, the steps to follow, and above all, Recillas's words.

He had already spent ninety days working fourteen hours each moonless night, obtaining new results, millimeter by millimeter, when he realized he could control the Schmidt. "Here we go, piece-of-shit telescope; let's prove that you do work." When he developed his plates, he was certain that he had reached as far as he had at Oak Ridge, and maybe even farther.

The distance from the Earth to the sky was unimaginable to the human mind. Some planets and stars were fixed, static, but many had changed during his time in Cambridge, almost in front of his eyes. At least that's what Lorenzo believed. They had moved in the southern sky. Proving it helped him tolerate the consequences. He confronted the telescope. He spoke to it out loud. He knew exactly how to maneuver it. And once he found the location, he took his plates without a single hesitation. Each night, he deciphered a new enigma, but then others emerged, and others and others. The flashing stars in the Orion nebula had entrapped him and led him to the T Tauri stars, whose strong emission intensity presented the red line of the Balmer series, red from the hydrogen.

When he showed Erro his first results, the astronomer hugged him. "Tena, you are everything I would have wanted to be."

And Félix Recillas admiringly addressed him informally, like a colleague: "I don't know if you made charts or if you have it all in your head, but the fact is, you have obtained a perfection of observation that no one else has achieved. Tena, you've gotten ten times more out of the Schmidt than the people in Cleveland and Wisconsin have. The gringos gave up too soon; they have used it less than half the time you have used here."

Recillas's words were good for him. It was a shame about the notes. He felt badly that he hadn't kept them, because that damned Schmidt had caused the disorderly flight of students and theoreticians who had waited for results in vain. "With such a fine lens, you have to find a real telescope," Recillas had declared.

Erro, nationalist as he was, believed that the telescope was a miracle of Mexican technology. "Neither in Holland nor in the United States would they have done any better!"

But something had failed. The same thing had happened in Cleveland, because their Schmidt wouldn't respond either. As a result of patience and mettle, Lorenzo had made it function.

"Devil of a boy," said Erro. "His prodigious intelligence would make him a genius in any First World country. They don't recognize his value here."

One afternoon Lorenzo decided to visit the chapel of Santa María Tonantzintla again, to see if the artisans had created their own cosmic order there.

At the general store, he picked up the keys from Don Crispín, who served as sexton, and when he opened the chapel door, sunny and warm juice oozed from the golden slices of orange, the honey of the pineapples, the red of the watermelons sculpted on the walls. Gluttony swelled the fruit bowl that spilled over from above— pineapples and melons, grapes so oversized that they looked like figs, bananas standing erect in their brazenness, carnivorous flowers with voracious petals. But there were also fixed points and an order decreed by mathematical law.

The chapel was enchanting. The people from the town were angels, and their mother was the Virgin, the consoler, the one who loved them and covered them with flowers and fruit in abundance. Glorifying her childlikeness, the Virgin had shrouded the inhabitants. Children of all eternity, like a great balancing force, they fluttered around inside this chapel that did them justice. The chapel had something of Leticia. "I couldn't care less," Leticia would have said. The cherubs would have greeted her with a round of applause. Leticia was part of the irresponsible, disorderly sky of the chapel, and for that reason, because of its lack of restraint and its abundance, it exercised the omnipotence that the faithful and the curious revered.

When Lorenzo noticed that it had gotten dark, he locked up the lascivious angels with relief and returned the key. The Schmidt camera was waiting for him, and as he climbed the hill toward the telescope, he thought about Lisa. Had she been in front of that altar, she would surely have said "Too much!"

20

The *Excélsior* headline grabbed Lorenzo's attention: STRANGE OB-
JECTS IN MEXICO'S SKY. In the article, Erro expounded triumphantly
about one of those unidentified flying saucers, a UFO, and supported his discovery with a huge spread of photographs taken with
the Schmidt at Tonantzintla. In the pictures, a white line passed
over the surface of the moon.

Surprised, Lorenzo intercepted Erro on his morning walk: "Are
you sure, Don Luis?"

"Of course I am. I'm not irresponsible." The director became irritated.

"You know very well that the Schmidt has oscillations and that
Braulio or Enrique Chávira could have moved it suddenly. Did you
consider that?"

"Of course. You are insulting me, Tena."

"You should have waited before going to the newspapers, sir."

"Why? I know what I'm doing, Tena, and I'm sure of my discovery."

Haughtily, Lorenzo warned him that he would take a plate of
the moon that very night.

Erro shook with rage. "You are defying me, Tena!"

The next day, Lorenzo put the photograph in front of Erro's
eyes. "It's a line. I took it over and over to prove that the light
came from a slight movement of the camera. That's what those objects are."

Completely disturbed, Erro threatened him: "Tena, I don't want
to see you again."

That evening, Lorenzo found him walking bent over alongside
Don Juan Prenso, the librarian, who would murmur into his ear,
"Nostradamus!"

"Didn't I order you to get out of here?" Luis Enrique Erro was trembling.

"Don't worry, I'm leaving."

On the bus to the Federal District, Lorenzo's conscience was eating at him. He felt sorry for the old man. Erro's contorted face appeared before him, and he repeated to himself, I was merciless. I should control myself, but I just couldn't let that happen. It's too irresponsible.

After that day, he didn't return to Tonantzintla. He couldn't sleep at night in his hotel in Mexico City. He looked for Diego, who said, "That was suicidal. The old man loved you like a son. What are you going to do now? I can give you work here, of course, but—"

Harlow Shapley had once offered him the directorship of the Bloemfontein observatory, run by Harvard in South Africa.

"Why the hell didn't I go to Africa? Bloemfontein is a thousand times better than this!"

They had proposed it to him again in the late forties, when he knew that Erro was getting on to such a degree that the only vigorous thing about him was his perennial bad temper. Now, after contacting Shapley, Lorenzo was on his way to pick up his ticket to fly from Mexico to Havana, Havana to Bermuda, Bermuda to the Azores, and from there to Madrid. Thirty hours in the air in a four-engine Iberia plane, making a stop in Madrid. After that he would leave for Casablanca in Morocco, then Dakar, Angola, and finally Cape Town. From there, he would reach Bloemfontein somehow—by camel if necessary. I wish I had learned to play the violin so I could be like Dr. Schweitzer, he said to himself, smiling. His footsteps resonated on the sidewalk, tap, tap, tap. He no longer wore Aunt Tana's shoes. Today I walk through the downtown streets, but next week I'll walk through an unfamiliar African city. He was curious about what that new life would be like.

"Lorenzo, I've been calling to you, and you haven't noticed. Where are you going so deep in thought?" It was Alejandra Moreno.

"To Bloemfontein."

"What is that?"

"South Africa. I'm going to run the observatory."

Alejandra stopped, incredulous.

Lorenzo laughed. "You look like a piñata that's just been hit."

"Just listen to what you're saying. You can't possibly have made that decision." Alejandra's face was stunned under her blue beret.

The traffic and the uproar of the street vendors around them increased. "Don't make such a face; it's not like I've died."

Alejandra pulled him toward her. "We need you in Mexico; you cannot leave." They reached calle Tacuba, and Lorenzo was about to enter the travel agency when Alejandra stopped him brusquely. "Before you buy your ticket, come say good-bye to Salvador Zubirán."

They walked to the dean's office at the university, on Justo Sierra 16. Alejandra, who came and went to and from the dean's imposing office at will, let loose her indignation. "How can we let him leave? There aren't enough like him around as it is." She waved her arms. "Our poor country! Really! When someone has the ability to contribute to moving it ahead, we don't even notice. Others recognize his value and know who he is while we continue to dictate letters and bury ourselves in bureaucracy." Her troubled eyes stared at Lorenzo, dumbfounded with disappointment.

Behind his ebony desk, Dr. Salvador Zubirán listened to Alejandra with the same benevolence he used with his patients. Although he was dressed in a dark suit, he seemed to be wearing his neat medical coat, which inspired calm in his dealings with others. He looked at the young scientist before him and at Alejandra, his defender, whom he had known for years. He wished all young people had that passion, although he wasn't sure if Alejandra's was for science or for that round-faced boy with red cheeks. He knew that, aside from the faulty telescope, what worked even less at Tacubaya was the human material. At this point a few amateurs still eagerly insisted on locating stars, although positional astronomy had been surpassed in all the observatories of the world: Mount Palomar, Mount Wilson, Kitt Peak, Lick. And Graef, Alba, Barajas, and other exiled Spanish scientists agreed that the Tacubaya Observatory so close to Mexico City should be renovated. Erro himself had indicated that after twenty-six years in administration, Joaquín Gallo was becoming the Porfirio Díaz of Mexican astronomy: "My last name is Gallo (rooster), and I'll defend my turf like a fighting cock." It was time to correct the situation.

Standing in front of these young people, Zubirán had no doubts. "I have an opportunity right here in front of me. Astronomy must be modernized, and Gallo has to go."

When Lorenzo and Alejandra descended the stairs of the venerable building hand in hand, Lorenzo Tena was the new director of the Tacubaya Observatory.

"Come to Donceles with me," Alejandra said. "Come on, let's go. Don't be a stubborn mule."

The only discussion in the corridors of the government buildings and among the Confederation of Mexican Workers was about industrializing the country. Talk about the new country took over like a fever. Mexico would initiate its endeavor with foreign capital and would be able to compete with the United States. From an agrarian society it would become an industrial giant. In the large pulque haciendas on the plains of Apam, where they grew maguey plants and fermented the juice into liquor, the peasants were transformed into workers who specialized in railroad-car construction.

In the United States, there were no longer men in the fields, only machines. The same would happen in Mexico. In the meantime, Mexico provided laborers to their neighbor to the north, laborers who crossed the Rio Grande out of hunger. Lorenzo was extremely irritated by the government's sense of triumph. If he didn't want to lose his mind, it was best to stay far away from these illusions, which were much more naïve than the song "Pretty Bubbles" that Florencia had taught them.

After his new appointment, Lorenzo Tena set himself up in the very provincial and unpopulated Tacubaya, some eight kilometers from the center of the city.

Diego visited him. "It's a shame not to see you presiding over the Castillo de Chapultepec Observatory, but this building is also worthy of you."

With its wide and tree-filled interior garden, tall ceilings, and large leaded windows, the Tacubaya Observatory not only had ex-terior gardens for the visitors to enjoy, but a tower with a cupola that opened to the sky as well. Through the telescope, with its five-meter distance refractor lens that was thirty-eight centimeters in diameter, they were able to see Saturn and its moons, asteroids, and stars. A jacaranda stretched the luxury of its lilac branches into the air during the entire month of March. The finest things in the entire building were the fifteen stained-glass windows brought from France. They glorified Copernicus, Kepler, Herschel, with their names written on ribbons held by cherubs. A telescope on a wooden structure and a tree of good and evil with five apples com-pleted the series of images. Save for the luxury of the leaded glass, everything else was empty boxes, dusty bookshelves, yellowed bul-letins, and row after row of the annual edition of the National As-tronomical Observatory bulletin that had been published since 1881. Nothing there could capture a young person's imagination. Nevertheless, the building inspired respect in the visitors: "You can see the sky from here, my son. The star watchers go up that tower there to observe."

In spite of all the dust, Lorenzo took his predecessors' reports off the shelves and read the texts with interest. In 1876 Díaz Covarru-bias and Francisco Bulnes, proud of their expedition to Yokohama, Japan, to observe the transit of Venus, wrote: "We presented our re-sults to the French astronomers." After that triumph they were in-vited by other countries, where there were telescopes much more powerful than the one at Tacubaya. During those years, astronomy became so popular that a cantina was even named Transit of Venus Through the Disk of the Sun.

One Monday, after seven in the evening, Lorenzo noticed the doorman allowing spectators in.

"Where are they going?" he asked.

"To see the stars."

"There are only two visitors' days, Saturdays and Sundays."

"Don Joaquín ordered us to open on workdays. He said it was the way to fight ignorance and superstition."

"Gallo is no longer the director, and visiting is no longer allowed."

When he saw the doorman's astonished expression, Lorenzo deigned to explain: "The telescope has to be for the use of the researchers, not for the curious."

"Researchers?" asked the doorman.

"Have you never heard that word?"

The Tacubaya Observatory was still being run the way it had been in 1914. Elementary and high school students burst in at will to see the stars or for an illustrated lecture on comets, eclipses of the sun, and the transit of Venus. Sometimes there were five, and sometimes there were twenty-five spectators. Logarithm tables were sold at the door, having been printed by the observatory "to help itself out a little." Lorenzo was indignant. "We might as well sell multiplication tables flyers too." People could come in to see the astronomical photographs under glass and the old instruments that were no longer being used.

As a result, Lorenzo ran into men, women, teenagers, and children in the hallways. They would ask, "Hey, can I use your bathroom?" And without fail, someone would always plant himself on a bench in the garden to eat lunch.

"This is not a picnic ground, this is a center of higher education, of *research*. What is going on is inadmissible, and I will not tolerate it."

Every morning, Lorenzo had to deal with some unexpected situation. One of the elder secretaries, Señorita Herlinda Tovar, warned him, "I am responsible for press announcements, and I also give talks on the radio. I teach in the province free of charge. My travel expenses and a small stipend for the talks are paid by order of Dr. Joaquín Gallo."

Lorenzo then discovered the true predilection that several of Señorita Tovar's friends had for the stars. They visited her to have their horoscope read.

"This has nothing to do with astronomy," roared Lorenzo.

"It doesn't hurt anyone, sir. However, your bad temper is poisoning the previously calm spirit of the observatory," said Tovar.

The Tacubaya personnel resented Lorenzo's impatience, and in a few weeks he earned the dislike of the librarian, who invariably arrived late. When it was brought to his attention, the man retorted that Joaquín Gallo had never reproached him. The secretaries were to be feared the most, as they formed a united front with Señorita Tovar. They wanted to institute a Secretaries' Day.

"What this country needs is twelve-hour work shifts, not more holidays," Lorenzo retorted. "Why don't we institute Asshole's Day? Everyone would be able to—"

To his surprise, Miss Tovar interrupted him: "Bastards' Day, Doctor. Bastards' Day." Thunderstruck, Herlinda saw Lorenzo smile at her.

The members of the Astronomical Society, founded in 1901, also felt rejected. The new director didn't offer them coffee as Gallo did; that great mathematician always had time to chat with them. Several businessmen had the luxury of having a telescope at home and were willing to help Tacubaya—if they received the attention they thought they deserved. Who did Tena think he was!

Only the young janitor was sympathetic to the new director, following him around. In the nocturnal solitude of Tacubaya, Lorenzo would observe, and in spite of the illumination from the city, those hours behind the telescope continued to be his best. But when there was a full moon, Lorenzo shut himself up in his office and looked at his watch hour after hour, desperately pondering the country's backwardness and, even more, the state of science in Mexico.

Lorenzo paced like a caged lion. Calm down, wild beast, he told himself. Calm down. Every now and then he'd reproach himself for his separation from Erro. He was still ashamed of the incident, but Erro continued to publish in *Excélsior* as if nothing had happened.

As a remedy to his despair, Lorenzo turned to the telescope. One night, when he saw the janitor, whom Gallo had employed as a messenger, he asked him, "Would you like to come up with me?"

He very patiently showed the boy how to focus the lens toward the stellar cumulus. Sharper than a tack, he appeared the next night at the same time. "What's your name?" asked Lorenzo.

"Aristarco Samuel."

"What?"

"Aristarco is my first name. Samuel is my last name."

"Who named you Aristarco?"

"I don't know. Probably my father."

"Did anyone ever tell you that Aristarco de Samos was the first astronomer in the world?"

"Yes, Dr. Pishmish did. But it didn't seem to be a big deal to her that I was named that."

If there aren't any astronomers, I'm going to train whoever wants to learn, Lorenzo said to himself. Maybe that's what science was all about in an underdeveloped country—grab onto the first one who shows an interest, especially if his name is Aristarco. After all, he himself had followed Erro to the roof on calle Linares equipped only with his enthusiasm.

"Listen, Aristarco, the night must be cloudless, without mist, without fog, to be propitious for observation. You have to open the cupola first so the optical system can stabilize with the environment. Look, the thermometer is here. To move the telescope, you use this rope and you point it in the direction indicated. Here are the position circles. Each morning we'll set up a schedule of what we're going to observe that night." He pointed out the exact square of the sky to observe: "Don't move from here. We're going to take plates. It's just like photography."

The next day, after developing the plates, he showed the boy how to compare them. No one was as passionate or as efficient as Aristarco Samuel.

The next night, in the waning quarter moon, they went up to the tower. They located the star they wanted in the immensity of the sky and remained taking plates at one minute, three minutes, six minutes, nine minutes, twenty-seven minutes. "You have to triple the observation time to reach the weakest magnitudes." With an expression of indescribable amazement, Aristarco Samuel focused the telescope in the indicated region. In spite of his mere fifteen years, he stayed awake all night. He had plenty of energy. Lorenzo explained to him, "We're going to work on high-luminosity stars, and you're going to help me classify them."

"I'd like to see farther," Aristarco said impatiently.

"Buddy, you have to wait for the light to reach you. If you had pupils that were four meters in diameter, you'd see forty times farther that this telescope, but since you don't, you're going to use a spectrum."

"In other words, if you say distant, you mean young?" asked Aristarco.

Lorenzo showed him how to determine if the stars were young or old, depending on their color indexes. "From now on, you're in charge of recording the position of the star, the type of plate, and the zone of the sky to be observed tomorrow night."

Aristarco's devotion was impressive. He asked how stars were made, what the dark material was, what the gaseous material was, and he became impassioned by the red stars. "I hate the moon."

"Why?"

"Because when it's barely a quarter crescent, we can't observe. Now I pray to the Virgin to give us a moonless night."

Lorenzo adapted a Rolleiflex to the telescope with a screw and adjusted it with the shutter open in order to take advantage of the movement of the telescope.

One night, sick with the flu, Lorenzo asked Aristarco if he felt capable of observing alone. Around midnight, coughing, Lorenzo climbed the stairs to check on him, and when he saw the boy work so attentively and so responsibly, he said, "Tomorrow I'll go over your material."

To his surprise, Aristarco responded, "I wish we had a bigger camera."

The next day Lorenzo found him sweeping in the garden. "What is your greatest ambition in life?"

"To be an astronomer."

"If you keep it up, you will be."

"How do you make a discovery, Doctor?"

"A great discovery is just the culmination of the work of a lot of people. At any given moment, the work of several men is concentrated in one brain that is more organized than and different from the rest. Newton, and later Einstein, reorganized what was already known and then articulated it in a different manner. That is discovery, Aristarco. All the necessary knowledge to take that step was already there."

Lorenzo made Aristarco write down the names: Herschel, Kant, Laplace, the English astronomer Thomas Wright, and finally Hubble, who photographed the first spectra of galaxies and demonstrated that they were very far from us—so far that they didn't even belong to our galaxy.

"Distance, Aristarco, is measured through other smaller stars or specific luminosity. With his marvelous telescope, Hubble had access to other galaxies, and he made his measurements based on variable stars. The light takes a certain amount of time to reach us, and the distances are counted in light-years. Andromeda, which is a galaxy close to ours, is two million light-years away. We receive light from galaxies sent ten, twenty, thirty, forty million years ago. The farther the astronomer sees, the more objects he is able to see as they were at the moment they were created. The ultimate goal is to understand the first galaxies, the ones that were formed in the very beginning."

21

Lorenzo was making a miserly salary after he left Harvard, but he was a frugal man. When one pair of shoes wore out, he always had enough to buy another. "It doesn't take a lot to live."

"When are you going to own your own car?" Chava asked him. "Don't tell me you've developed a liking for public transportation."

"I have, Chava. I'm in touch with the people."

"You like the smell of the people?"

Lorenzo shook his fist at Chava's jeering face.

"Don't you ever plan to marry, Lencho?"

"Yes, when I find a woman who will let me work. That's all I would ask of her: that she let me work."

"If you planned it right, you could have it good."

"I want to do science, Chava, be useful to my poor country."

"Things will be much better for your brother Santiago than they are for you. He's more realistic. It looks like you and Juan are both unable to adapt to the world. What planet do you two orbit?"

The mention of Juan shook him. Now free, Juan had knocked at the door of his apartment on calle Tonalá. "Lorenzo, you're the only one I can turn to. Lend me 579 pesos, or they're going to turn off my phone."

"What did you do to owe that much?"

"I made long-distance calls through Ericsson on a rush order for some conductors that you can't get in Mexico."

The mention of Ericsson reminded him of his father, who would ask his guests, "Do you have Mexicana or Ericsson phone service?" If they had Mexicana, he thought less of them.

Juan was excited; he was on the verge of success with his Mexican refrigerator.

"Why are you doing this if we already import General Electrics?"

"Mine will be much cheaper and will be the best. It's the invention of the century. All I need is your support while I finish it."

Lorenzo couldn't believe it. Juan was going from bad to worse.

He pleaded like a beggar. "Lencho, can't you sell a piece of Aunt Tana's furniture?"

"What? I didn't keep any."

"Leticia told me that you might have the armoire."

"Leticia is a liar, and you know that as well as I do."

"You could ask for a loan from one of your buddies."

"Which one, brother? Which one? Unlike you, I do have some pride."

"Ask Diego Beristain—579 pesos is like a fifty-cent piece to him."

Because he had accused the officials of nepotism and clamored for a law that prohibited employing a relative, Lorenzo had to shut the door on his brother, and he began to resent Juan's presence. Each time he saw him approach, he'd say to himself, Here comes the sponger. He was even more horrified when he saw how Juan lived. He had gone to see his brother's invention. On a vacant lot, inside a cave made of sheet metal walls and roof, Juan not only reigned over the refrigerator, but also over fragments of all kinds of tools. Balcony railings he had designed and soldered were beautiful.

Lorenzo held the railing up in the air. "Brother, this is really something." He walked between the stove, the refrigerator, the disassembled motor, and the turbine on the floor, not knowing what to say. But he was certain that most of Juan's inventions didn't have a chance, because no one would finance a Mexican automobile when it was cheaper to import one. In the middle of the patio, a little car, as red as a hemorrhage, caught his eye. "It's electric, brother; it doesn't use gasoline," Juan said. The stoves were electric too. Three boys worked with Juan—his "assistants," who listened to him attentively. "One day I'm going to discover the origin of the universe before you do," he told Lorenzo, slapping him on the back. "I'm going to beat you, brother."

Lorenzo held back. He didn't want to tell Juan that it was too late for him to discover anything. He felt like crying. They had once been able to discuss abstract astrophysical problems for hours.

Juan had much more to say than Luis Enrique Erro. But what was there to say about this trash heap of old iron? Cardboard boxes were filled with worn-out books—one about Edison, a calculus book called *The Semat*, Jonathan Swift's "A Modest Proposal," a pile of papers with mangled corners covered with his nervous scribbling, three celestial maps probably taken from Tonantzintla.

Lorenzo had also obsessively reread Swift. It was because of Swift, and not James Joyce, that he had wanted to go to Ireland. Of course, Joyce had wonderful pages about astronomy in *Ulysses*, but Joyce's work—he was sure—would not have existed without "A Modest Proposal." Nor without *A Tale of a Tub*. Lorenzo was still impressed with *Gulliver's Travels*, and he often compared the Mexicans to the Lilliputians. The fact that Swift was among his brother's old books saddened him. We read the same thing at the same time, he thought. Who could Juan discuss Swift with besides him? How big was the hell of his solitude? He, Lorenzo, had Diego. But Juan, who did he have?

Juan's young assistants didn't leave him even for a minute. None of them understood the equations he scribbled on sheets and sheets of paper, but their devotion made him feel respected. He shared breakfast, lunch, and dinner with them. Chufa's mother washed his clothes. What clothes? Lorenzo wondered. He looked so lost. And his entertainment, if you could call it that, was drinking beer on the sidewalk on Sunday afternoons. Lorenzo left with a disconcerting sensation that Juan had become a mad scientist. Once he totally lost his bearings, would he throw himself headlong into vice, in spite of his sparks of genius? Lorenzo would have offered for them to live together, but his brother had adapted to that marginalization; he was in his element. Living day by day, realizing at night that he had not eaten, was tolerable when he was young, but what would happen as the years passed? Juan dressed like an indigent; he had a poor man's face—scars of a poor man, hands of a poor man, eyes of a poor man. Prematurely worn out, he looked much older than his elder brother. It wasn't as if Lorenzo had money. Barely a year ago he was still living with the Toxquis in the town of Tonantzintla. But Juan's permanent poverty terrified him. If I'm out of touch with reality, as my friends say, my brother revolves in an unknown orbit, Lorenzo thought. Maybe the de Tenas had a touch of madness. Leticia and her inconsistency, Juan and his irresponsibility, he and his obsessions. What a mistake my mother made by dying on us, he repeated to himself, because when she left, she took our stability. There were the three of them to prove it. The ones saved from dementia were Emilia and Santiago.

He finally decided to turn to his eldest sister. "Write to her, Juan. She can save us," Lorenzo said.

Maybe Juan was impressed that his brother spoke in the plural. They didn't have to wait long for Emilia's response. With the generous intervention of her husband, she would send a money order. Within two months Juan needed another loan, and Lorenzo began to feel as if Juan were a constant threat. He was uneasy whenever Juan showed up, because Juan only appeared when the noose was already tight around his neck. "Brother, even Leticia is more responsible than you are," Lorenzo said to him.

"Leticia is a woman; she's taken care of."

When Lorenzo got together with his buddies, Diego's enthusiasm about the country's future exasperated him. "We're rich; we have oil, minerals, forests, water, kilometers of coastline, and a past more ancient than that of most of the countries of the Southern Cone, not to mention the United States. It all indicates that we are the leader of Latin America. Our popular heroes are more original and creative than those of any other country on these continents."

"Diego, please! Zapata has been appropriated by the PRI, the politicians, the parasites, not those to whom he truly belonged. And they have soiled and degraded him, using him for their dirty business. This Zapatista demagoguery in the PRI speeches makes me sick. They've done the same with Juárez. They've used him as a great historical reference, although while he was president, he and his cabinet lived a double life, which was evident in the newspaper society pages. They died and were buried with a papal benediction and the patronage of the Holy Church, their daughters were married in cathedrals, they visited the Vatican, and their hypocrisy permeated all their actions. It's such a great shame!"

"The displaced Europeans will come to Mexico as a result of the war," Diego said. "You wait and see the progress we're going to experience from this economic dispersion, the employment it will create. The age of iron will bring triumph. Fundidora de Monterrey and La Consolidada feed their ovens with mineral coal rather than vegetal coal. Both Tamsa and American Smelting yield high returns."

"High returns for whom, Diego? Corruption is an inherent part of public management. The PRI is a monopoly. It never loses an election because it doesn't have any opponents. If it did, the opposition would give us extraordinary power. We need fresh air. And although you say that they will create millions of jobs, for the time being, the poorest Mexicans have no purchasing power. I just keep seeing the same poverty."

"I'm dealing with Harold Pape, and in the meetings with the Altos Hornos de México steel mill I've seen measures being taken to increase the acquisition power of the poor. We're going to reach the same level as the United States and will be able to rationalize a tax system—"

Lorenzo interrupted. "Oh, come on. The truth is that here the rich are exempt, and the PRI government hangs the poor. How will they acquire purchasing power if they are barely surviving?"

"We have to liberalize commercial practices, and that can only be achieved with the fomentation of foreign investment. You should have met Gómez Morín, an exceptional financier, the founder of the Mexican bank. We're going to be swimming in foreign currency."

"And social discontent."

Lorenzo insisted on declaring himself a Republican, a socialist, a materialist, and an atheist.

"He's possessed!" Chava laughed. The gang didn't share the fury with which Tena defended his ideas. When Chava alleged that the eight-hour work shift was sufficient, just as in the United States, Lorenzo's indignation bordered on hysteria. "How are we going to push this country forward? How can we compare ourselves with industrialized nations? We need double shifts to overcome our backwardness, to train ourselves, to become competitive. If everyone else walks, we have to run."

"Lorenzo, were you at Harvard or in Japan?"

"If only we had Japanese mysticism to drive us ahead. The ideas of Japan shake me to the core. When I think about the amount of land they have reclaimed from the sea, I ask myself, Why don't we Mexicans, who have so much land, ever get ahead?"

Chava then launched into a story about the geishas and how he took a taxi on Meiji Avenue in Tokyo that looked like a honeymoon suite. The seats were covered in white lace, the backrests immaculate; the driver's head emerged, virginal, like a fluffy white meringue. "From the moment you get into the taxi, there's an insinuation that you're going to get laid. Eroticism on wheels, and the bed sure isn't as hard as stone, as in Mexico. You should find yourself a geisha, Lenchito."

22

"We have to catch the good students—grab them away from the Law College, from humanities, from economics," Graef advised. "I'm going to ask for their grades. It's up to you to convince them, reassure them. You, Lencho, the relentless, let's see if you can be as smart as old Sotero Prieto."

Lorenzo became convinced that the young people should get their doctoral degrees outside the country: the United States, the Soviet Union, Japan if necessary. "It's critical if we want to be competitive," Graef had said.

Dr. Pishmish was irreplaceable when it came to preparing the best science students. She helped them determine their vocation, persuaded them. There was no postgraduate study in astronomy in Mexico. Thus there was no one who could direct a thesis except for Paris, who couldn't do it all alone. The kids weren't afraid of her, but they went out of their way to avoid Lorenzo in the hallways. He would have to convince them to leave Mexico, but first he would contact not only Norman Lewis at Harvard, but also Walter Baade at MIT and Martin Schwarzchild, who knew all about stellar structure and evolution. Lorenzo's letters of recommendation carried a lot of weight, and he gave them only to the best students.

He would later invite the great astronomers to UNAM and to Tonantzintla, which had so fascinated Shapley, Chandrasekhar, Viktor Ambartsumian, and Evry Schatzman.

Each kid was a special case in which Lorenzo had to invest a considerable number of hours, laying siege and convincing them to continue their studies abroad. "But I'm going to get married, Professor."

"Take your wife with you."

"Doctor, my parents won't survive if I'm gone for four years."

"If you tell them you have to go, they'll visit you."

"They can't afford it."

"You can work in your free time; all the men do it."

"Professor, my English is horrendous."

"So what? Mine was too. Take an intensive course and finish learning it there."

"I'm anti-Yankee. I hate their culture."

"Don't worry, I can arrange for a scholarship to England, France, Italy, or Japan. Do you want to go to the Byurakan Observatory in Armenia?" The hours it took trying to convince them wore him out. "Each mind is a world unto itself," turned out to be an irritating commonplace refrain. So many obstacles. My Lord, they had more demands than excuses, depending on the personality of the candidate of the hour. What type of investment would this one require, Lorenzo asked himself as he listened to the oddest questions. At the moment of truth, they were all infantile.

The ones who had excelled in physics, and therefore were natural candidates, had such insolent answers. "Astronomy is the folklore of all the sciences."

"What?" replied Lorenzo indignantly.

"It is. It's really popular. Everyone likes it, but . . ."

"Listen, Graef," he told Carlos. "What kind of candidates are these? Send me different ones." The long, desperate conversations with the students confused Lorenzo.

Graef laughed. "You'd never make it as a psychologist, Professor."

Lorenzo talked with each one, and it was more unsettling and unbelievable each time. The candidate would begin to speak, delivering a lecture, with no compassion for the listener. Are they getting even with me? Lorenzo asked himself.

Fabio Arguelles Newman, who had a bad haircut and ripped jeans, watched him timidly, dark circles under his eyes. If it hadn't been for the desperation in the boy's gaze, Lorenzo would have kicked him out of his office. How many demons was the young man dealing with that made it so hard for him make a decision, in spite of the fact that he had one of the highest averages in the College of Science? Lorenzo had to control himself in order not to lose his

temper. Hadn't he himself been depressed at Fabio's age? As he listened to the somewhat shrill voice, he remembered his long trips
throughout the country, delivering *Combate*. Dr. Beristain's kind attitude was what had made the most difference.

"Listen, Professor Tena, there are only a few things I'm sure
about: it's better to love than to hate; justice is better than injustice; truth is better than a lie, although literature is a big lie well
told. The universe is the same everywhere. I'll have the same diffi-
culties at Berkeley."

"But not the same instruments."

"My brain is my instrument."

"There you'll have information that you don't have access to in
Mexico. You'll measure yourself against the best."

"Professor, Plato already said it all—"

"In science? Have you read Werner Jaeger's *Paideia?*"

"Of course, Professor."

Arguelles Newman was passionate about Kant and his concept
of the sublime. When man is able to make something of the infinite, the incalculable, the ineffable, and when he discovers that he
is made of the same material as the universe, then he calls his experience sublime.

"But this is astronomy, Fabio."

The young man responded, "Astronomy tries to explain the origin of the physical universe, and my concern is ontological in nature . . . To be or not to be?"

Lorenzo smiled. "The universe is where we are sitting."

"Listen, Professor, astronomy attempts to resolve doubts about
the physical nature of the universe, while philosophy formulates
those doubts. And what if the universe is only a dream? You want
to send me to Berkeley, but wasn't it Berkeley who said that the
world exists only when someone perceives it? I have more doubt
than certainty."

Lorenzo was going to respond that at that moment he did know
one thing for certain, which was that he, Fabio Arguelles Newman,
would go to Berkeley. But he restrained himself and agreed with
the boy—who sat ruffling his hair—that the principal mystery had
not been resolved, no matter how many scientific answers were
found.

"What are we doing here? Do the things we believe in really exist?"

Finally Lorenzo interrupted him impatiently: "If you don't believe that the physical is real, what in the devil are you doing in the science department?"

"It's exactly what philosophy asks. I don't know if this table is more real than my perception of it. And this can be extended to the entire universe. We don't know if it is different from the images our advanced devices show us."

Lorenzo held himself in his seat with both hands so he wouldn't get up, while Fabio continued in an ever more shrill voice. The boy must have seen something in the director's eyes, because he rushed ahead: "Of course, I'm not taking any merit away from scientific research. I can see what they have achieved, but it doesn't resolve anything for me."

Lorenzo became furious. "Ah, no?"

"Few things must be as fascinating in life, Professor, as discovering what stars are made of or if there is water on Mars. But does knowing it really eliminate our doubts about the existence of that same universe? I don't believe so."

This one is an asshole, Lorenzo thought, but he was careful not to say it aloud. He managed to lose himself in thought and only half listen. He was touched when Fabio said that as much as we may believe that we know what will happen within an hour or a year, we will never be able to guess "what will happen in the following instant, and paradoxically, all the rest depends on that instant." The boy asked compellingly, "Who is in charge of the existence of that instant?"

Lorenzo remembered how he had asked Dr. Beristain in his library, "So philosophy never dares to formulate a truth?" And the answer was etched in his mind: "Not without reservations, Lorenzo. Not without first asking if we are capable of assuming it, because sometimes the truth seems to be nothing more than an unsustainable hypothesis."

Fabio was gesticulating. "Maybe what happens is that time doesn't pass, much less take us anywhere. We strive to progressively count the years as if this will lead us to a better place." Defeated, he dropped his arms and looked at Lorenzo with anguish.

"In spite of all the uncertainties of the universe, Fabio, our own lives respond to an unknown order, and we are the ones responsible for finding meaning in that." Worn out, he concluded the interview.

Later, Lorenzo, who so loved philosophy, exclaimed to Graef, "All I ask is that you give me a good physicist!"

Tena was unaware of what family ties meant to other people, and that's what he told Graef. The family circle was becoming a knot if not a hangman's noose. None of those boys had a spirit of adventure.

"Of course they do, Lorenzo. And you must help them find it."

Lorenzo contended that a North American education seemed superior—taking sixteen-year-olds out of their "home sweet home," not to return until Thanksgiving holidays. That was liberating. Here, it seemed that none was willing to break the umbilical cord. "Man, they even intend to take their grinding stones with them. It's intolerable. Listen, the other day I lost my temper—"

"Let me interrupt. You, lost your temper? I can't believe that!" Graef said.

Lorenzo ignored him. " 'Do you expect your grannie to go with you?' I said to a boy, and I immediately regretted it."

One culture was confronting another, and Lorenzo was sinking into the immense lap of Mexican society. "How are we ever going to achieve anything of our own initiative? It wouldn't have taken Luis Enrique Erro so much work to find men and women for Tonantzintla." But that was a different time. His recruits had considered themselves fortunate. For Lorenzo at least, Luis Enrique Erro was providential. "I never made anyone beg me like these little boys do with me," grumbled Lorenzo.

Graef became serious. "We're losing our idealism, Lencho. We're no longer innocent or deluded. There's no doubt about it; we were better off before."

"Don't say that. You sound like an old man."

"You and I are cut from a different cloth than they are, brother."

Luis Enrique Erro, bitter and disenchanted, continued publishing articles in the *Excélsior* newspaper, and his books could be found in most bookstores: *Basic Ideas of Modern Astronomy, The*

Language of Bees. His novel, *Bare Feet*, was the best, written during his forced bed rest in the hospital and dedicated to Emiliano Zapata, "a light in the darkness of our history."

Visiting him at his sickbed, Lorenzo told him brusquely, "Your novel is better than *Axioma* and your treatises on the logical basis of mathematics."

Growling, Erro thanked him for his visits to the cardiology ward, but his wife did not: "This boy has always made you nervous. He brings up problems that you can no longer solve. Besides, he's arrogant."

"Just so you know," Erro said to Lorenzo, "I don't want any service or corny ceremony. I don't want a monument but rather something like a kilometer marker on the road."

At that moment Lorenzo could have told him how much he loved him, the gratitude he felt for him—Erro, I consider myself your son. You've been a formidable mentor to me. But he didn't. Nor did he confide that if he, Lorenzo, died, he would want to be right nearby, with a similar marker. What would the old man have said? No sentimentalism, Tena, my friend. Lorenzo regretted that he hadn't expressed his feelings, because two days later Margarita Salazar Mallén called to let him know, between screams and sobs, that her husband had passed away.

Erro died at the age of fifty-eight, on January 18, 1955. Lorenzo promised to provide Doña Margarita with a small pension, and he deposited Erro's ashes at the Tonantzintla Observatory, as he had asked.

In the end, nothing could have gratified Lorenzo more than the eventual success of the scholarship students who were studying in foreign countries. At Caltech there was one Mexican; at Berkeley, three out of six graduate astronomy students were Mexicans. Proudly, Lorenzo wrote to them to encourage them, telling them that their journey was similar to that of the medieval aspirants to the Round Table. They left to keep an armed vigil, in order to become knights. "You will compare yourselves to others, you will face your fears, and you will know who you are."

Jorge Sanchez Gómez wrote that two of his professors had been awarded the Nobel Prize, and that of two thousand graduate stu-

dents, nine hundred and fifty were foreign. "Can you imagine, Doctor, measuring yourself against Hindus and Chinese? This really is
a democratic country, because it doesn't shut itself off to foreign-
ers. Here I'm meeting the most intelligent people from Chile,
Argentina, France, England, Japan." Lorenzo smiled. "The competition is terrible, and I analyze and put my own intelligence, imagination, and above all, self-criticism, to the test. Sometimes I have
lunch with a really short Bolivian astronomer. Can you imagine, a
Bolivian woman at Caltech? I'm sending you my grades to see what
you think."

23

Lorenzo's articles were published in the *Astronomical Journal* and in the *Proceedings of the National Academy of Sciences* and were received in Mexico with growing acclaim as his fame grew. In the hallways of the Department of Education, at the university, at the Colegio Nacional, they spoke of the "extraordinary internationally renowned astronomer."

In 1948 Rudolph Minkowski had indicated that the numbering of planetary nebulae was complete, and the Draper Catalog increased the number of stellar objects from 9,000 to 227,000, adding only one planetary nebula. However, at Tonantzintla between 1940 and 1951 Lorenzo and his team had discovered 437 objects in a six-hundred-degree-square area. That contribution placed Mexico at the top of the ranking system.

Lorenzo now lived in a whirlwind. Named vice president of the International Astronomical Society and member of the Royal Astronomical Society, he traveled frequently to international conferences. Have all men become astronomers? he wondered. I can't believe I'm going to speak with more than two thousand people. He began his expositions with "I'm going to speak Spanish with a slight English accent. I'm an astronomer with a very good star." At the conferences they compared results, they learned of one another's specializations, they competed with one another, but above all, they discussed. Ah, blessed discussion.

He flew from Case Institute of Technology in Cleveland to the McDonald Observatory in Texas to work with Otto Struve. Speaking with Fritz Zwicky and visiting him at his home in Switzerland was gratifying, even more so because Zwicky was now studying the stars in the constellation known as Bernice's Hair. Lorenzo returned to MIT to attend a symposium on the composition of

gaseous nebulae, and from there he crossed the Atlantic to Mount
Stromlo in Australia to continue working on the T Tauri stars. Seeing the specters of the Andromeda galaxy and the Hydrus triangle,
Lorenzo discovered that the objects once considered stellar cumuli
in those galaxies were no more than nebulae from emissions similar
to that of Orion. Until then it was believed that the T Tauri stars
could be found only on the dark edges of the emission regions. But
in the Australian sky, as in Tonantzintla, a great number of T Tauri
stars shone in different regions, variable in their luminosity as well
as in their spectral characteristics.

The same T Tauri stars that Lorenzo worked on with William
Wilson Morgan, of the *Atlas of Stellar Spectra*, would lead him to
the discovery of those that would be called flare stars.

Based on the systematic study of galactic cumuli of different
ages, Lorenzo showed that flare stars occurred in a population of
young stars. He established their evolutionary sequence and described them as smaller and colder than the sun: "These flare stars
suddenly increase their brilliance. They produce gigantic explo-
sions in a matter of seconds or minutes, increasing their luminosity
thousands of times, in some cases to return to their normal state
hours later."

Lorenzo was admired for his discovery of novas and supernovas.
The blue stars in the galactic south pole already had the acronym
of his last name, as did other stellar objects—a comet and blue-
colored and ultraviolet galaxies. With more than seventy-four published works and an honorary doctoral degree from Case Institute
of Technology, he could at last feel satisfied. Case confirmed that
his discoveries had given his university and his country distinction,
and in future years, students and astronomers from many nations
would benefit from them.

When Walter Baade read the article on RR Lira variable stars in
the *Astronomical Journal*, he invited Lorenzo to Caltech. Baade, a
German immigrant and observational astronomer, had established
the distance scale of the universe, but with the discovery of two
types of RR Lira stars, Lorenzo determined that the universe was
twice as big. Certainly the universe was much bigger than Shapley
thought.

At Caltech, Lorenzo thought a lot about Shapley, whose claims had now been surpassed. That was what science was—a chain in which a scientist came to be a link to the following one. Only the older astronomers still talked about the debate between Heber Curtis and Shapley regarding the nature of galaxies. Hubble and the expansion of the universe were cult objects.

Directing Tacubaya didn't distract him from conducting his own research, and when, following Erro's death, the dean offered him the additional directorship of the Tonantzintla Observatory and the Astronomy Institute of UNAM, he was thrilled. Carlos Graef congratulated him. "What do you know? You're *the* astronomer. You can handle all this and more. We need you at the university; you're part of the inventory at Tacubaya; and with regard to Tonantzintla, you're the only one who can push it forward."

One Sunday at noon, Diego dropped in on Lorenzo at Tonantzintla: "If the mountain won't come to us, brother, we will come to the mountain. But first take me to meet your telescope, the famous forty-inch one."

Lorenzo was excited by Diego's enthusiasm, and they became involved in a discussion that returned them to their adolescence. They went back to their perennial topic—endless time. "Time will continue after our death, Diego," Lorenzo said. It consoled him that science was a process, that the experiments were linked; where one stopped, another continued on. He repeated, "Eternity is man's invention."

Diego reflected on the big bang and all the marvelous exactness of the universe: "It doesn't vary even a millimeter, Lencho. We're going to go to the moon, to Mars. We're going to see all that milk in the Milky Way."

Lorenzo reminded him of the millions of galaxies of the expanding universe.

"You see that? Where is the limitation?" Diego smiled with his little boy's smile.

"The limitation is in us," concluded Lorenzo, much less optimistic than his friend.

"Do you remember the discussions we had about religion, Lencho? You said that it gagged you to talk about it because you always ended up saying something stupid. Professor Elorduy's image of an old bearded man seated on a cloud with his son to his right was intolerable. 'How can you understand the cosmos without a vital and organizing force?' you asked. No one could talk you out of your need to organize the power of the universe, and you kept repeating, 'I don't believe in God, I don't believe in God, I don't believe in God,' as if you were possessed."

"I'm a little like Tennyson's King Arthur. Returning defeated from the war that had absorbed his life, surrounded by deception. The queen had betrayed him. His kingdom, which had once been the envy of all, was a disaster. He said that he could see God in the miracle of the stars and in nature. 'But I don't see him in men, blind with hatred and passions, capable of murder and the scourge of war, as if all this were the work of a lesser god, incapable of taking his plan to a higher realm.' I understand Tennyson. The perfection and order of the cosmos are impressive, but evil predominates on Earth. Man is capable of inconceivable crimes. In our time we have witnessed the diabolical concentration camps, the Holocaust, and the atrocious exterminations at Hiroshima and Nagasaki."

The discussion became tense when they talked about hunger. "Listen, Diego, democracy does not exist in Mexico. An illiterate cannot vote or elect anyone. How can they understand what a political program is? People need to reach a basic economic level to be able to defend their choices. What can a poor person without a salary defend? That's the reality."

"What is your solution, Lencho, if the Mexicans don't have a vote or a voice in the government's decisions?"

Lorenzo insisted on education, and he dissolved into criticism of the Church, the greatest stumbling block to social development in Mexico: Son, you must endure, and yours will be the Kingdom of Heaven. The Catholic Church had castrated millions of Mexicans, thrown them out into the street, defenseless, and Lorenzo would never forgive that.

"They're not all like that, Lencho."

In reply, Lorenzo told his friend that he would take him to Tepetzintla, in the Sierra Madres north of Puebla, three hours from Zacatlán, where the apples grew. "It's a valley where everyone walks barefoot, with their *mecapals* around their foreheads, carrying firewood. I have a good friend there who works for a pittance on a plot of land that doesn't even belong to him. He's told me, 'Eating is like drinking. It's harmful if you have too much.' His children are tiny and will never grow; they suffer from extreme malnutrition. One is ten and looks like he's six. Little as they are, they're so used to hunger that many of them don't want to eat. Diego, when I'm around, they hide. If you saw their stained skin and the big circles under their eyes, you'd feel the same impotent rage that I do."

"Brother, when are you coming to Mexico City?"

"I go to UNAM and to Tacubaya four days a week, but I feel more detached from the city all the time."

"You shouldn't isolate yourself so much. I'm having a dinner party next Thursday, come."

"The truth is, I behave like the abominable snowman."

"That's even better, because I have a snow queen to introduce you to. My wife welcomes everyone with open arms, and there are several volumes waiting for you in the library that you haven't seen."

Even at Diego's, Lorenzo was a fish out of water. Clara, Diego's wife, talked about books, concerts, exhibitions, but no one ventured to talk about scientific theory. By chance, they reflected on the weight of Einstein's brain. With three or four drinks under his belt, Lorenzo started to tell them about his adolescent euphoria when he saw James Maxwell's equations on the blackboard: "How was it possible that this guy woke up one morning and wrote out the formulas for electrical energy?" He got excited, although no one else shared his feeling. Diego would have agreed with him, but as the perfect host, he was going from one group to the next. "Surely Maxwell must have a brain different from everyone else's, which allowed for such a great discovery." After a while his listeners deserted him. Aren't they interested in understanding the universe? he asked himself, puzzled.

Lorenzo would become indignant when he heard people speak of the purity of Vasconcelism. Pure? Vasconcelos? Where was *"el maestro*"? What had he really done for Mexico? What the hell had he given the Mexicans? Nothing. He just confused them. Did he teach them to oppose the government? Come on. Let's pull our heads out of our asses. He deserted his followers like a groom leaving his bride at the altar—all dressed up and aroused. The dilemma of Mexican youth was precisely that—they had no one to believe in. There were no great elders to look to. Only traitors.

"What purpose did it serve to distribute the top one hundred classic books in the fields?" he asked Diego. "Who was going to read them? It's money down the drain. The farmers are dying of hunger in the midst of plenty. It is more important for them to learn to restore the land and preserve fruit than to receive copies of *The Iliad* and *The Odyssey*. Why don't we teach them to pick up the *tejocote* fruit that drop all over the ground and to use them? Why are other agricultural countries rich from their manufactured products? Remember the saying, 'Give a man a fish, and he eats for a day; teach a man to fish, and he eats for a lifetime'?"

"I believe I'm happier than you are, brother."

"Of course, because you have no idea what I've seen."

Diego's star was on the rise. He could end up as the Minister of Finance and, if the country deserved it, president of the Republic.

"By the way, brother, the Secretary of State considers your optic laboratory project propitious, and I believe it's time for you to pay him a visit to finalize a deal."

"That's great. I can go whenever you think is right, and this time I'll try to be diplomatic."

Diego embraced him. "You'd better!"

Curious, Chava, who was seated next to his old friend, said, "The world of science is foreign, difficult, and, to top it off, godless. No one follows you. Even if education is declared secular in Mexico, you scare away your audience."

"You always said you were an atheist and a freethinker, and now you come out with that, Chava?"

"Women don't tolerate my atheism. They want me to talk to them about God."

"In bed?"

"You'd better believe it—in bed. Listen, Lencho, you are undoubtedly an atheist with the vocation of a parish priest. Your sermons attempt to be the echo of the Holy Spirit, and they're really only a pain in the ass and the consequence of a bad hangover."

How frivolous Chava could be, and how opportunistic. And Diego too. As he left, Lorenzo swore to himself that he would never go back. But his affection for Diego made him return, always with the same result.

"Lorenzo, don't you plan to marry?" Diego asked.

"Get thee behind me, Satan! You're the only one I would tolerate such a question from."

"It's a normal question."

"Personal questions are never normal."

"What about Alejandra Moreno? Why not her? She's bright. You can see from miles away that she likes you. She's in your same field—education. Unlike you, she's always in a good mood. You yourself have said that she lifts your spirits."

Sometimes Lorenzo thought about Alejandra. He knew that she would marry him if he asked her. But attractive as she was, Alejandra was an activist and, not only that, a feminist. She was pictured in the papers wearing her Basque cap, revindicating women's rights. She was fighting to legalize abortion; she participated in marches for the workers. Give me a break! he thought. His life with her would be a hotbed of slogans, a lair for activists of any cause. Oh, solitude, blessed solitude, beloved solitude.

Chava persisted with the topic of his youth. "You don't look happy, brother. Do you know why? Because your way of life, your idea of the world, your erroneous ethics, your lifestyle—they all destroy your natural desire and your appetite for the things that bring happiness. If you continue with this cruel determination, you're going to destroy yourself."

"Oh, really? And what do you advise, empty-headed man?"

"Take a break from yourself. Your constant worrying is a form of fear."

Over time, Lorenzo had found it impossible to retreat from his life in the country. He had at least ten good friends in Tonantzintla.

"I have a little one on the way, and we'd like, with all due respect, for you to be his godfather," said Lucas Toxqui. "If it's a boy, we want to name him after you: Tena."

"But Tena is my last name."

"That's what we want to name him, Tena Toxqui."

The women got pregnant, gave birth, and appeared in public again, their bellies pushing out in front of them. "I've put a bun in her oven," Toxqui said proudly.

All these children confirmed Lorenzo's conviction. I'm never going to have kids, he told himself, wondering in despair, What will become of them? The birth of a girl filled him with even more horror. This world is not for women. Maybe in fifty years. Maybe, but not now. Their path is set; we have to create another path that has more options than reproducing.

He watched the children go to the elementary school built by his initiative, and he wondered, What do they have ahead of them? What will their future be? But they prospered nevertheless.

Don Honorio Tecuatl had planted delphiniums, and they grew tall, and he took them to sell in Puebla. "Doctor, your being an astrologer must have increased the production, which is why I need a loan to transport all these flowers. A lot of them rot on me," he said to Lorenzo one morning.

Lorenzo sighed in relief. For five years he had been running up against Don Honorio's stubborn "That's the way it is." Now, finally, laughing at the evidence, the farmers were beginning to yield. Until then a terrifying fatalism had made them immovable. The volcanoes had them tied down. Lorenzo had wanted to strangle the priest who passed through every two weeks to say mass. He was someone who could influence, educate, at least inform them. But he never said anything, because he didn't know anything. "It's what the Lord orders; it's God's will; God chose for it to be that way."

One day when he heard the priest ask a poor woman, "What did you bring me?" Lorenzo lost his head and yelled, "What do you mean, what did you bring me? What are you going to give her, you disgraceful parasite? You've never even told your parishioners to buy red lights for their bicycles so they aren't killed like bugs on the highway."

The little priest didn't learn the lesson. He didn't protect his flock, and he abandoned the lost sheep. He didn't warn them about the rivers of mud that flowed down from Popocatépetl, taking everything in their path. On the contrary, Lorenzo heard him speak calmly. "Once the mud reaches a gully, it stops, and that's the end of it." No wonder they all repeated, "That's the way it is." Enduring was their only form of survival. The priest also persisted with an almost biblical phrase: "The day that something truly happens, you'll hear the bells."

Now, after five years, Don Honorio had traded his inertia in for an enterprising spirit. And the others followed him because Don Honorio Tecuatl, with his strong jaw and his narrow forehead, was the leader of the group.

When Diego called Lorenzo at Tonantzintla to let him know about the appointment with the Finance Minister, Lorenzo was thrilled. He left for Mexico City immediately. Finally the optical lab project he had worked on for months would see light. In such a good mood, he stopped by to see Leticia after months of absence. When he said good-bye, his sister said, "I'm going to light a candle so that nothing goes wrong."

At exactly five o'clock he appeared at the Ministry of Finance, and for the first time, it didn't disgust him to be kept waiting for seven minutes. "The Minister is in a meeting, but he'll be with you shortly." But when he went in, the Minister's wrinkled brow seemed like a bad omen.

"Listen, Dr. Tena, the president feels that there are other priorities at this moment, but we'll examine your petition for the optical laboratory in Tonantzintla at a later date."

"Petition? I never asked for anything."

"Don Diego Beristain, whom we all respect, indicated that you were looking for funding for a laboratory."

"Diego Beristain is very mistaken. He told me that you were interested in the laboratory. But we'll put an end to this misunderstanding right here and now. Good afternoon, Mr. Secretary." He headed for the door.

He immediately called Diego. "Why did you lead me to believe that the Ministry of Finance would go for it? I forbid you to stick your nose in my affairs ever again."

With that, Lorenzo hung up the telephone. If this could happen with his best friend, what could he expect of these politicians, who didn't have the vaguest idea what science meant to Mexico? One door after another had been slammed in Lorenzo's face. "No, Doctor, there is no budget; the president is leaving on a tour." "I'm very sorry, Doctor, but it doesn't fit in with our priorities for public education right now; we've allocated all the funds to creating classrooms." "Doctor, you're internationally famous. Why don't you appeal to the scientific institutions in Holland, Sweden, Norway, or Australia, which are much more solvent than we are?" "Doctor, let's leave that chapter to the rich countries. We're headed toward globalization. It won't be long before we're all one; we don't have to spend money on our own science."

That night, Lorenzo returned to Leticia's house. From the expression on her brother's face, she knew he had failed. "Come on, a tequila will do you good. The sons of bitches don't deserve you, but if you'll allow me, I'll teach you how to fuck the shit out of them."

"I'll think about it on my way to Tonantzintla."

The hours on the highway to Puebla didn't weigh on him. The journey allowed him to think about what fascinated him the most—objects in the sky. The moment he left the last houses of Iztapalapa, he could lose himself in reflection. He drove the Ford to the rhythm of his thoughts, very slowly, then pressing the accelerator to the floor in such a way that the car, spurred on, would jump. When would they learn the distance of the galaxies? If the universe was expanding—in other words, if the concentrated matter at a point millions of years ago was expanding—and lines in the universe were not straight but curved, how could you calculate the distance, crossing through that space?

The trip to the observatory would relieve him from the bustle of appointments, pressures, and failures of the Federal District. It would get him back into the swing of studying the density of the universe over and over. Who would discover it? When would they discover it?

When he reached Huejotzingo, with its fragrance of apples, he had recovered the lost serenity and breathed calmly.

He passed through Puebla de los Ángeles almost without noticing it and searched lovingly for the hill of Tonantzintla. He didn't notice people, and he smiled deep down as he remembered Pablo Martínez del Río, who, when questioned about his vocation for archaeology, explained that man had stopped being of interest to him ten thousand years before Christ.

The noise in Mexico City had been unbearable to him. In Tonantzintla all he heard were the bells, and from time to time the hair-raising squealing of a hog. The silence was complete. Not even planes flew overhead. Nothing scratched the air; the firmament was the property of the telescope. He almost hit a cyclist on the edge of the highway near Acatepec. Oh Lord! Why don't they require bicycles to have lights? The truckers didn't worry about their headlights either, and many parked on the side of the road to sleep, or maybe to fuck. Mexico, a country that didn't take precautions.

He turned left and went up the small slope, which had been baptized with the name Annie J. Cannon, and he honked the horn. He wouldn't find Luis Rivera Terrazas around at this time—another one whose company he really enjoyed. Surely the secretaries, Graciela and Guillermina González, would have retired to Puebla. Since Guarneros was taking his time opening the gate, Lorenzo honked again, impatiently, thinking, there are only crazy people at this observatory, including me. Damned Guarneros. Where is that handyman? When he was about to honk for the third time, he saw a girl in jeans run down the hill, hurriedly put the key in the padlock, take off the chain, and open the gates with a smile. Lorenzo drove through and yelled furiously, "You—who are you?"

"Fausta—Fausta Rosales."

"Is that right? And what are you doing here, if I may ask?"

"I'm helping Guarneros."

"Can you please tell me what you're helping him with?"

"The garden. It's a lot of work for him. I offered to help, and he accepted."

"What did you say your name was?"

"Fausta, Doctor."

"Fausta," he yelled, raving. "A woman can't be named Fausta!"

"That's what my father named me," the girl responded, now quite frightened.

"I'm going to fire Guarneros right now." He got out of the automobile, took the chain and the padlock from her, and ordered, "Leave! I don't want to see you here."

She descended the rest of the slope toward the town without looking back. Lorenzo, beside himself, started the car and parked it in front of his bungalow. It had been a while since such a rage had come all the way up to his throat. He covered the entire grounds, calling, "Guarneros!" He circled the forty inches five or six times, as if possessed. He yelled again, "Guarneroooos!" But the handyman didn't appear anywhere, and he finally returned to his bungalow to make himself a cup of tea, to see if there was anything in the refrigerator, and to take down the thick leather jacket he wore to observe at night.

For ten years Guarneros was the only employee who slept at the observatory. Aristarco Samuel lived in Cholula and didn't come on moonless nights. Some afternoons Lorenzo invited his nocturnal companion to drink tea, and he would listen to the gardener's monotone relate one family catastrophe after another: his paralytic mother, his sick wife and handicapped child, his miserable salary, his health that deteriorated each day. There were so many misfortunes that one night Lorenzo was surprised to find himself secretly following Guarneros: I'm going to do him a favor. If he goes by the water pool, I'll push him in, and all his problems will be solved. When he realized what he'd been thinking, Lorenzo became terrified. It's the solitude—I'm going crazy. Tomorrow I'll go back to Mexico City first thing. He told this to Terrazas, who had a good laugh. "Don't worry, Lencho, you'd never have killed him."

When they both saw Guarneros come in with his soggy hat and his pruning shears, they looked into each others eyes, smiling. Guarneros didn't return the smile. He didn't have any reason to. "Doctor, the pump broke," he said in an irritated voice.

"Okay. Don't worry about it. Come on over here, Guarneros. I'm going to give you a shot of tequila."

Lorenzo now confronted an enigma as inexplicable as the age of the universe. What the hell was that stupid girl doing with Guarneros? How had she approached him? At what time, on what day of what week had she spoken to him? What relationship could they have? It was unbelievable. First thing tomorrow, when the good Professor Terrazas arrived, he'd ask him what the devil was going on. While he, Lorenzo, was working his tail off in the city, they were frolicking around here, and now Guarneros was even hiring a woman. A brazen one, no less. And named Fausta!

The next day, Luis Terrazas tried to calm him down. "The girl is living in the village. Everyone here likes her. She's very diligent and smart. You wouldn't believe the intelligent questions she asks me. Her father was a medical doctor, but he died. I don't know how many years ago. I gave her permission to go to the library, and I've found her lost in the *Semat* textbook a number of times."

"But what is she doing here? What is she doing?"

"She's the handyman's assistant. She sweeps all over the place. She works much faster than Guarneros."

"Where is that fool Guarneros?"

"He's around. Don't be in such a hurry. You'll see him shortly."

"And the girl?"

"Who knows about her?"

"Is she going to come back?"

"Don't be contrary, Lencho! Didn't you say you fire her?"

"Fired," corrected Lorenzo angrily. "Fired, not fire. Yes, I fired her."

"Well then, don't ask about her."

"I'm not asking."

No one had seen Fausta that day, and Lorenzo had the unpleasant feeling that he had again gone too far. But then he saw her walking with Guarneros. At six that evening, from his window, he saw her struggling to put a sprinkler on the hose. He was about to go out and say, Not like that, but he stopped himself. When he looked up again, the sprinkler was spraying water, and there was no girl. Four days went by that way. Fausta stayed far away from the office, and Lorenzo had to go back to the odious Federal District without speaking to her. He didn't want to be the one to go looking for her, but he thought he might run into her at any time in one of the gardens or the library, to which, according to everyone, she was addicted. Fausta was careful not to come too close to the director's space. "She can smell you." Terrazas laughed. "She has your number."

24

Fausta examined the Rembrandt self-portraits closely. The young artist was seventeen years old, proud, flashy, his eyebrows bushy, his chin strong above the white lace collar, his cheeks peach-colored with a golden fuzz, a sign of youth. Sixteen hundred twenty-nine, 1630, 1632, 1634; 1652, the wrinkled brow; 1659, the head protected by a helmet of golden reflections, the different plumed hats, the turban, the eyes more sunken each time, damn it. Life was falling into an abyss; the sketch of a smile of 1662 turned out to be just a truce. Time was ravaging him. Time followed his path, his hair becoming ashen, the beard becoming sparse, until the last portrait in 1669, when he was barely sixty-three and already an old man. Age, what an insult! In the postcards that Fausta pored over, Rembrandt tumbled into the void, his stare always more disenchanted, his features ruined, until he rushed headlong to death.

How do you create a self-portrait? What mirror do you look into? Centered in what kind of solitude, through what silence do the years pass? Fausta's father, Dr. Francisco Rosales, had also become saddened during his life. Defeat was imprinted in every pore of his skin, his eyes diminished by dark circles. Nevertheless, the look under the fallen eyelids summoned her fixedly, demanding an answer. But what answer? She recalled his questions when she was a little girl: "Will you be up to the task? You will travel alone, and the journey is long. Will you be able to endure it?"

When she was a child, swollen tonsils or a fever cheated her of any opportunity for adventure. It isolated her. "Fausta can't; she has the flu." Her father denied her opportunities. Fausta withdrew into herself. She read whatever she could get her hands on—medical treatises, oral hygiene advice, articles on vaginal douches.

Someday I'll leave, she thought. Her brother Alfredo also read, but he never lent her a book. Her siblings all ran off to their different activities: soccer, rowing in the Cuemanco canal, piano lessons, English classes—all except Alfredo. She envied her brothers the most, because they played sports.

Before she was seven, Fausta discovered her father's bathroom. He had a bathroom all to himself. The children called it the operating room, and no one was allowed to use it. Intrigued by the smell of cologne, Fausta came to the white door sniffing like a bloodhound, and without hesitating, she pushed it open. Bewildered, she examined the two showers, one with special jets, the modern toilet, the fluffy rugs, the enormous mirror, and another mirror on the ceiling over the tub. Why so many mirrors? The scales, the sponges, the plush atmosphere invited something . . . but what? On a glass shelf, a row of stainless steel jars offered different possibilities. Towels, prettier than the ones in the rest of the house, were a waterfall of whiteness. An indefinable modesty invaded Fausta, and she tiptoed out, hoping no one would see her. She came to the conclusion that a stranger was living in the family home.

Of all the children, Alfredo was the most withdrawn. They all yelled at the dinner table except for him. His very red and moist mouth stood out on his white face. One night Fausta stayed alone with him. "Please, Alfe," she asked him, "get me a lemon water. My lips are so dry from the fever."

"If I do it for you, will you let me get in bed with you?"

"Sure, get in."

What else would a seven-year-old girl say? Her brother, who was twice her age, slipped in between the sheets and started to touch her. Then he climbed on top and tried to penetrate her. "Alfe, you're heavy. Get off. What're you doing? Get off. It hurts!" In her feverish state, the little girl struggled, trying to repel a little piece of hose that made its way between her trembling legs. The next morning she told her mother, Cristina, about it.

"Now you listen to me," her mother exclaimed angrily. "That's not true! You're making it up. How can you even say such a thing?"

Nor did her father back her up. From that moment on, Fausta realized that parents didn't deal with anything that was painful for them. If you couldn't convince them of the facts, then the disgrace didn't exist.

If her mother saw her crying, she would ask, "Do you have a cold?"

"Yes, Mother, that must be what it is."

She never asked, Fausta, what's wrong?

As a child, in pain to the very marrow of her bones, Fausta tried to tell her mother of her failure at school, but Cristina would interrupt her. "You don't look well at all; you're tired; go lie down. We'll talk about it tomorrow."

But they never did. How could you trust someone who attributed everything that went wrong to illness?

From the time she was a child, Fausta went against the norm. She was drawn to secret passages that would take her to where she felt better.

Of the four connected bedrooms in the house, just as Alfredo had chosen her, an alley cat chose Fausta's room in which to give birth to her brood. Seeing the bloody mattress, Fausta took the newborn kittens and threw them into a tub of water, and she hung the mother cat from the fig tree in the garden. Was it Alfredo she was trying to kill?

"I'm bad, terrible," she repeated to herself. As if to prove it, she formed a gang, and they threw rocks at other children. Submissive and quiet at home, Fausta made up for it on the streets, all her energy concentrated in her right arm. She had such good aim that their rivals feared her: "Don't get close to that one; watch out for that faker." Throwing rocks was a catharsis. The battlefield was the safest place on earth, because there she felt invincible.

"Hypocrite, fucking bitch," a classmate yelled at her.

At eight in the morning the sister in charge of opening the door rang the bell for school to begin. Timidly, Fausta got in line.

"You're wearing two different-colored socks," the nun told her. "You stay out here until someone from home comes to pick you up."

Because one sock was a little lighter in color than the other,

Fausta was left at the door until classes were over. The waiting wasn't what hurt; it was the humiliation.

For revenge, and to destroy what the nuns revered the most, Fausta took to stealing the sacred Hosts. At recess she snuck into the chapel, took the key from the tabernacle behind the statue of Saint Joseph, climbed like a monkey until she reached the sacred goblet, and emptied all the Hosts into the pocket of her apron. Trembling, she went out into the patio, gulped down a number of wafers, and kept sneaking them during class. They stuck to her palate like crepe paper, and she would unstick them with the tip of her tongue. The risk eliminated the sensation of guilt. What a sin this is, she thought. What a sin, divine treasure. No one ever found out about the sacrilege.

> *"We are daughters of the incarnate Verb,*
> *Can there be anything more noble?*
> *Let us sing a sacred hymn*
> *Let us lift up a hymn to our Lord."*

"If you take Communion every first Friday of the month, you are assured of a place in heaven." Starting at age seven, the girls would kneel in the dark confession booth. The priest was deaf, and they all knew it. Since he was ashamed to admit it, Fausta would say, "Father, you know, two nights ago I killed my brother Alfredo."

"It's all right, my child. Go in peace. Say three Hail Marys and go to the first Friday Communion." Fausta continued to lie without fear of God. For her, the tabernacle was not sacred but magical, like Aladdin's lamp, and in the end, religion became as insubstantial as fairy tales.

When she spied on the nuns to see what they were like and what they did, Fausta again took risks. Did they have hair under their caps? It was easy to tell what they ate, because there was always a piece of spinach or bean in the teeth of Sister Marta of the Immaculate Conception. The habits they wore didn't make them otherwordly; it only accentuated their sweat, their flatulence, and other corporeal defects.

The subject Fausta liked the most as she was growing up was anatomy—because of her father's being a doctor. "Do you want to see an operation?" he asked. Accompanying him when he performed surgery was wonderful. She learned about cutting the skin open, about the insides, the underside of the skin, its shine and color, the organs that moved as the person breathed in and out, the mother-of-pearl color of the lungs—which in the case of smokers were covered with black shadows—the thorax, the side where the surgeon reached his hands in.

"I'm happy here," her father told her as they left the operating room.

"It shows, Father."

"It's the most demanding profession, child. You can't even rest when you sleep, because the patient in bed 211 may not make it through the night; the one in 417 suffered postoperative shock you should have anticipated; the one in 302 can't tolerate the medication and you have to give him something else. But I wouldn't trade my occupation for anything in the world."

While the family was on vacation in Ixtapán de la Sal, Dr. Rosales returned to Mexico City, convinced that he had left gauze inside one of his patients. Cristina shrugged. Irritated, the children resented it as well. Only Fausta offered to return with him. "No, child, I will not allow you to give up your vacation." And he took off down the highway in his MG, the only luxury in his life.

"Your father will not make it back, you'll see," Cristina declared.

In fact, Francisco had an emergency operation the next morning. "Do you know what it means to open up five bodies in a day?"

Fausta defended him. Her mother looked at her indifferently. "Well, my father makes me very proud, and my heart overflows with love and admiration for him."

"Are you ever corny," commented Alcira, the elder sister.

Fausta consoled herself. None of them would ever measure up to him. She intended to study medicine, follow in his footsteps. Live like he did, be the Dr. Rosales of her generation. She planned her future around medicine and her father's image until, when she was seventeen, adolescence burst forth, plastering itself all over the sidewalk, changing everything.

The well-known Dr. Rosales often went to calle Lopez, near marine headquarters, looking for sailors who came to offer themselves when they saw his sports car drive up. Then they extorted money from him.

Francisco Rosales was repulsed by his own homosexuality. Keeping his wife pregnant was one way to avoid making love to her. Nevertheless, he loved her, loved his children, and watched over his patients' progress obsessively. He would have given his life to discover a cure for his pain. He neglected himself, pushing the limits of endurance, but he couldn't keep away from the shameful encounters with the boys from calle Lopez.

Little by little Cristina became certain that she was not the only one in his life. When she intercepted a call from a young man asking for money so that she, his wife, wouldn't find out, it was the final straw. "So that's the way it is? You just watch, I'll destroy you!" she sobbed, humiliated.

The children were terrified and turned against him. They associated love with responsibility, because their father had always responded to their needs. What? My father? What are you telling us? They didn't understand that such a scrupulous man would have a family and at the same time look for pleasures considered evil. "We're the children of a queer," Martín, the eldest boy, said, and he left home the next day. Alcira did the same. The only ones left were Alfredo, who never worried about anything, and Fausta.

Unlike her brothers and sister, Fausta still wanted to see her father. She missed him terribly and visited him frequently at his office, even though they were unable to talk because he was attending to his patients. She watched him move, agile and delicate at sixty-four years of age, watched him examine a child's back, a mother's abdomen. "Don't worry, she's my daughter," he'd tell them. Fausta would look at him with such intensity that it made him turn his head, stethoscope in hand, to meet his daughter's black eyes before going back to the infant's shoulder blade, to the foreskin of an adolescent, the infection, the rash, the greasy hair.

"Look, Doctor, I have little bumps here." Bad breath, withered and yellowed skin, thick saliva were everyday occurrences.

"Do you want me to write the prescription?" Fausta asked him.

"Of course. Your handwriting is better than mine."

Ripping off the sheet with her father's name—Dr. Francisco Rosales, Universidad Nacional Autónoma de México, professional identification number 87997—giving it to him to sign, and handing it to the sick person made her proud. "I'm like him," Fausta repeated to herself, "in my fantasies, my desire to work myself to death for others, my timidity, and that blackness that I have inside and can't identify."

Of all his children, Fausta was the closest to him and the one who worried him the most. What did the girl know about herself? She lied, obviously. Fausta was the only one who went with him when he had double hernia surgery. She appeared at the hospital, and he had no choice but to accept her company. But his daughter's presence humiliated him.

"Give me your dental prosthesis, if you have one," she told him. "Open your mouth if you want me to take it out for you."

"I can do it myself. Give me a glass of water. Fausta, please go out." He was embarrassed by his modesty and by his chronic "sickness," which made him feel inferior.

For Fausta, his convalescence meant sacrificing herself to watch over him while he slept, changing the soaked pillow, the sweaty sheets, the towel around his neck that had to be wrung out every half hour because, ay, that body released so much water! His noble hands trembled, his arms as well. Most of the time he couldn't control the chattering of his teeth, which were now all back in his mouth. He would open his trembling eyelids and order, "Fausta, go eat."

"Father, I ate what you left on your tray. I'm not hungry now. You're the one who should eat."

The nurses took their own sweet time, just as in the welfare hospitals. One afternoon Rosales became so exasperated that he mustered the strength to put on his pants and shoes, walk along the corridor, and go out into the street. No one saw him, not even at the main entrance, where the police demand a release order. He took a taxi and paid for it at the house. The incident filled Fausta with admiration for her father.

"You could sue the hospital over this," said Cristina, exasperated.

They never sued, never complained. Maybe because he was a doctor, maybe out of laziness or skepticism—was it worth it?—or because deep down they didn't want a scandal and his homosexuality demeaned them.

Fausta felt rejected by her mother. Ever since she was a child, she had climbed the stairs to her mother's bedroom, four steps at a time, to talk to her, and she was always met with blankness. Cristina, distracted, barely listened, and Fausta's words fell lifelessly to the floor.

Fausta was also physically different. Her thin black hair fell on her shoulders in two braids. "Cut it, Fausta," her mother said. "Only maids wear it that way." Sometimes, at night, she put it up in a bun on her neck, but the next day she braided it again and meticulously made the ends very tight with a black ribbon, which she wrapped around several times so it wouldn't unravel. The expression on her darkly painted mouth was serious, but no more so than her eyes, like flaming coals, which made her mother exclaim, "Stop looking at me with that Emiliano Zapata stare. You make me nervous."

Her high cheekbones, sharp nose, and tight brown skin gave her the appearance of a warrior.

"Do you not own any other shade of lipstick besides Dying Orchid?"

Fausta had worn the same dark color since she was sixteen. "I like it, Mother."

One night when she had drunk two Cuba libres at Sanborn's bar in San Ángel, she snuck into the house and slipped quickly into bed so her mother wouldn't hear her, but a hoarse voice called, "Is that you Fausta? Come here."

"I'm really tired."

"Come here. I have something to tell you. Your father was found dead; it was a heart attack."

"You're lying. You witch, it's not true!" screamed Fausta.

"It's true, child."

It was the first time Cristina ever called her daughter that. With so many children, she was just too tired.

Fausta realized that the only bond she would have in life had been broken. To make his absence tolerable, she began an impossible dialogue. She consulted with her father in the morning, as if he were the *I Ching*. "What crap this is, Father. I don't want to go to school." She imagined him saying, Go, Fausta, go. She was closer to him now than she had ever been before. He became an accomplice. "You won't believe what a fool I've made of myself, Dad. This girl asked me to dance, and I told her no. What a fool. I was afraid of what people would say. Imagine that, just like my mother."

Only once, in the kitchen, did Fausta protest to her mother, "My father was extraordinary. Why did you destroy his life?"

"Maybe later I'll only remember the good, Fausta, but now I can't."

"You can't or you don't want to?"

"Child, I didn't know he was a homosexual. I thought they were men that dressed like women, and that was all."

"Mother, you're fifty-five years old and you talk like a child."

Her mother knew that Fausta studied theater, but how and with whom, she didn't ask. Why theater? Who knows, maybe it would make her lose her inhibitions, make her less repressed. Cristina saw Fausta come and go, barely eating at home, until the girl announced that she wouldn't be coming anymore because she was going to get her own apartment.

Fausta carefully put away her father's navy-blue tie and the prosthesis: two teeth with hooks mounted on a plate. She wanted the tailor to make some of his suits smaller for her to wear. "It can't be done, Miss. There is too big of a difference in size."

She got a job in the theater and found an apartment. With what she made at the theater, she could afford it. She looked after the scenery and the wardrobe, the lighting and the ticket booth. She did it all well. She was the first to arrive, the last to leave. One day when the lead actress didn't make it, Fausta, who knew all the roles by heart, stood in for her and did it better. She could have sent the actress packing, but that wasn't her goal; she wanted to help, like her father. Fausta didn't intrude, she didn't impose on anyone, she was surrounded by a halo of mystery, and that gratified her more than public recognition.

With the passage of time, her confidences to her father ceased. Now she spent hours looking at Rembrandt's self-portraits.

25

When Fausta invited her mother to the opening night of the play, she didn't warn her what it was about, but she felt pity as she saw Cristina leaving, livid, at the end.

"This just can't be," her mother murmured.

"It is, Mother." Fausta took her by the arm.

She shook her head. "No, no."

"Don't start to cry. If you do, I'll die."

"Just like your father, like your father," she mumbled.

Suddenly Fausta noticed that Cristina was old and bent over. She put her arm around her shoulders, which were covered by a beautiful alpaca wrap, and moved her head close to her mother's. "You don't want to see things the way they are. It's been like this for months."

"Months?"

"Maybe years, Mother."

"Do you live with that girl?"

Cristina must have realized that Fausta didn't only sleep with the girl, but that they displayed themselves publicly, to the disgrace of the family. In one scene, her daughter kissed a woman and undressed with her—Fausta, her daughter with black braids, naked, her small breasts next to the other one's bigger breasts; her sex, black triangle on top of the lighter triangle of the other one, the other one, the other one, the other one. Fausta, so quiet, so sneaky. Fausta, her eyes downcast, asking for a peso to buy candy at the store.

"The world isn't like you think it is, Mother. It's different. If you want to keep seeing me, you have to accept my homosexuality."

"But don't you have any conscience?" she screamed.

"I've never lived like it was a sin. My body is wiser than I am. My body takes me where it wants. My neurons—"

"Fausta, what will people say?" interrupted her mother.

"I don't think anyone needs to have any opinion about what I feel. It's my territory. My body is my freedom, my independent university, and besides, it fascinates me." Suddenly she said what she never thought she could say to her mother: "You're not going to do to me what you did to my father."

Alfredo, who had accompanied them, feigned absolute indifference, or maybe he was already past the evil he had instigated years earlier.

"Go get the car," Cristina ordered. "I want to go home."

Fausta was first attracted to women in elementary school. Although she had a boyfriend, they were never intimate. The intimacy with Raquel, her first lover, on the other hand, took her to another dimension, as if she were giving birth to herself.

Thin as a rail, Fausta won the athletic contests at school through sheer energy. The first to take risks, she responded to any dare. Death was always in the back of her mind, because she feared adults. She was afraid to acknowledge that they didn't love her. She lived with memories of a childhood of fear and deception. Her family had loved her, but not the way she wanted. No one gave her what she wanted.

Exercise drained her so that she would lose herself in it. It was a great relief.

When Raquel left her, she suffered the greatest shock of her life. At that time it didn't hurt her to think of spinsterhood. On the contrary, she took refuge in it. Until another girl said to her, "Come on." And not only that, this girl, Marta, had left a man to be with Fausta. Recovered, Fausta immersed herself in her new love's poems. Tall and slender, Marta opened the windows to the sea for her: "Look." At first Fausta couldn't see anything. Tears of self-pity blinded her. Within a year Marta finally confessed that she preferred men. "We're adults. It's not a matter of analyzing if you're a dyke or gay or bisexual. You're a person who loves, and that's that. Love will devastate you, no matter who you're with."

When Fausta separated from this lover—who always said "and that's that," the way the old telegraph operators said "stop"— Fausta sank into an exhausting routine backstage, behind the scenes, in the dressing rooms. She swept and picked up. Whatever anyone didn't want to do, she made part of her daily routine. It was vital to be of service to everyone, to keep a low profile, as the gringos say, not to have high expectations. She still acted, but she shunned the gaze of the others. What a contradiction. Above all, she rejected any possibility of success. "No, I'll stick with what I do. I want to serve, not stand out. It's not about me; it's about everyone else, what will happen to them if they don't succeed. I don't want to hurt the unity of the chorus."

The theater impresario told her, "They're mediocre; you're not. Think of yourself. I'm choosing you."

Irate, Fausta responded, "I'm not doing anything without them."

"Ah, then there's no deal. Stay with them. If you want to be the cause of your own misfortune, no one will stop you."

In a fiercely competitive world, Fausta forced herself to think of others first.

"What you do is more like social work than theater," Martín, her brother who most looked like her father, had told her. "You should stop killing yourself in that useless place. Do some traveling. Get to know your country, other countries."

"How can I leave them, Martín?"

"Just don't go back. I assure you, it will be harder on you than it will be on them."

With a pack on her back, a sleeping bag, an Everlast flashlight, blue jeans, and her Chiconcuac cap, Fausta took to the road. She would return to the city in September without the circles under her eyes, and not as thin. On the Mexico City–Puebla bus, the floodgates to the landscape of air and earth opened up to her. The green got into her eyes, her nose, her ears. By the time she arrived at the San Martín Texmelucán bus station, she was breathing deeply, and the smell of apples reached her. After three hours in Puebla, which was beautiful and big, she decided to look for the town where Salustia—the girl who had worked in their house for years—lived. She had told Fausta that she would always be welcome in Tomatlán.

———

As if in a fairy tale, Salustia opened the door herself. When Fausta asked if she could stay awhile, the girl said, "You can't sleep on the floor, Miss. I'll find a cot somewhere."

The family's entire life revolved around corn—planting it, harvesting it, eating it. Getting up at four in the morning was disorienting. In the dark, suspended in time, Fausta would ask herself, Where am I? Who am I? I am the creator of the world. I'm up even before the rooster has crowed. At night, after shutting in the animals, the family went to sleep, as there was no television. Adjusting to their lifestyle was easy. The daily repetition gave Fausta a sense of peace she had never had in the city. At five in the morning Don Vicente led his flock from the corral; Pedro, the twelve-year-old son, went to the field with the sheep, accompanied by the barking of Duke, the dog. Their relationship with the animals was like human to human; they seemed to read one another's minds. The birds were the greatest discovery for Fausta. At dawn their trilling welcomed the new day. Some were serious, others sharp, others shrill—hundreds of thousands of birds gathered under a piece of sky, singing their own particular happiness. The chirping was continuous, and it stopped magically when the sun came up. They aren't singing anymore? Where did they go? Why did they stop? Do they remember? What goes on in their little brains, in their bird heads? Some repeated the exact same brief melody; the songs of others were linear, a whistle broken only to take a breath. Did they take breaths? Fausta asked herself. If you taught them another tune, would they learn it? It made her want to learn more about their small and gallant humanity.

"It's the heat that makes them sing," Salustia informed her. At night, from the branches of the trees, the bevy of grateful songs arose. According to Salustia, it was instinct.

According to Fausta, they traveled in time, remembering what they had sung, and that's why they did it again with the setting of the sun. They're human, Fausta thought to herself, and they store their songs in a little dot the size of a mountain climber seen in the distance.

"Their brain is a little dot?" asked Salustia.

"It must be the size of their eyes," Fausta concluded.

The men went out to the fields to plant, plow, or dig up the cornfields, depending on the season, while Salustia and the other women went to the river with their tubs on their heads to wash clothes. Fausta went with them and watched how they put fleshy maguey leaves under their knees and then folded them up over their skirts to keep from getting wet. After beating the clothes on a rock, they bleached them, all soapy, in the sun. "That's the only way to get the stains out," Salustia explained to her. Once the clothes were rinsed, the women wrung them out and hung them from the branches of the tree, on the thatched stone wall, or on the tips of maguey plants.

Salustia would say to the sheets, "Dry! Hurry up and dry!" She would call to the sun, "Where are you? Don't be lazy; come dry the sheets."

How had Salustia tolerated the difference between life in the country and the city? To Fausta, the contrast was like a slap across the face. What relationship was there between the metal washer and dryer and the maguey leaves under the women's knees? What had the Rosales family offered Salustia in exchange for the tall pine trees she had given up?

Fausta adapted to their way of thinking. Why haven't I always lived this way? she wondered.

At one in the afternoon the women took lunch to the men in the fields. They protected themselves from the sun with their rebozos, the same ones they used to flirt with coming out of mass, the same ones they used to carry their children. It was a lovely hour when the men, women, and children sat in a circle to eat. Some went farther away to lean on a tree trunk and get some shut-eye— the worker's siesta. Seeing them, thinking about them, gave Fausta an intangible feeling of well-being, like an abstraction, a theorem, a theory.

Salustia, her mother, and her sisters treated Fausta with deference. "Wouldn't you like some tea, Miss? What would you like in your taco?"

"No, Salustia, I'm fine, better than ever." If she had accepted, she would have been the only one. Not even the children ate between meals. They worked hard, the same as their elders, and were thrilled when they could accompany their father, who left with his *acocote*—the long gourd used to extract the juice of the maguey. He would put the sweet water in his bucket with a little rag ball for it to ferment. The children participated in the different stages of making pulque. Later, Don Vicente would cure the pulque with prickly pear, with celery, with guava.

Fausta began to go with the children to deliver the pulque to La Marimba. On the road, the puddles were enormously attractive to the children. They loved throwing stones and seeing the tiny circles that formed in the coffee-colored water or just jumping right in and then suffering through the scolding. "Look what you've done to your shoes! You're not getting anything to eat for that!" They ran to the field to play *tixcalahuis* while the donkey, loaded down with small barrels of water, walked slowly along. The game consisted of sitting on a maguey leaf with the thorns removed and sliding down the hills, which were covered with pine needles and oak leaves. They hid their leaves when they were done so other children wouldn't take them. At night, after watering the animals, they did their homework by the light of a petroleum lamp, the smoke stinging their eyes. Then Fausta would tell them stories. *Alice in Wonderland* came up. It didn't surprise the children that the animals talked, since they themselves asked the donkey, the cow, the dogs, even the buds that flower in the pasture for answers. Making yourself bigger or smaller at will by ingesting a minuscule cake with raisins wasn't incomprehensible to them either. Little by little, Modesta, Estela, Chabela, Lucía, Silvestre, Eulogio, Vicente, and Felipe started confiding in her. One of Chabela's classmates had a boyfriend who took her riding on his horse, and they stopped in front of the classroom. All the jealous ones ran to the window to see it. He was Prince Charming.

When Fausta realized that her savings had diminished, she talked with Salustia about the possibility of working.

"Uy, it's hard here." Salustia told her. "There is work for someone like you at the Uriarte's Talavera factory in Puebla. And they say that there's a new observatory in Tonantzintla. One of those where you see the stars. They're looking for secretaries—"

"Observatory?"

"Miss, I see a sparkle in your eyes."

Fausta picked up her things. They gave her apples and a rebozo, and she hugged everyone and promised to return. Salustia walked her to the road to catch a bus to Puebla and another to Tonantzintla, with its church at the foot of the observatory.

The neurasthenic director's bad mood hadn't mattered to her as he looked at her with aversion from behind his glasses. She knew that in the long run she'd win him over. She had crossed the threshold and was inside the sanctum sanctorum, a few steps from the telescope. "He hates hippies," Luis Rivera Terrazas, the assistant director, informed her, extending his hand. "Maybe he mistook you for a Mexican hippie. There are a lot of them around here ever since they established the University of the Americas. They have contaminated the peasants, who now wear necklaces and grow their hair long."

During the first few days, Fausta got a good idea of what Lorenzo Tena's personality was like. She found out that Rivera Terrazas studied the sunspots, and at five in the afternoon he returned to Puebla, like the two secretaries, Graciela and Guillermina González; the librarian; and Braulio Iriarte and Enrique Chavira, the astronomers. The rhythm at the observatory wasn't hard to learn, and when she finished helping Guarneros, she could go into the library and read. At night Enrique Chavira allowed her to accompany him to the Schmidt to observe. She even went alone on Saturdays and Sundays because Chavira had shown her how to work all the instruments. "Listen, this girl is as smart as a whip," Chavira told Terrazas. "She learns faster than I do. At dawn when I close the cupola, she asks disconsolately, 'So soon?' Even my wife has been after me about why I've been getting home so late. Before, I left at twelve at the latest; now it's two in the morning, and it's all because of her. How strange she is. Who could she be?" Without knowing anything about her, they accepted her because her goodwill was obvious.

"She's as light as a feather," Toñita commented. "She offered to change the flowers at the church altar for the sexton, and Don Crispín says she hasn't missed a day."

The passivity at Tonantzintla was conducive to introspection, and Fausta had time to think about what her life had been so far. Her present life filled her with joy. She had found a room in the town. She loved the tolling of the bells, the transparency of the air, market days, the townspeople, whom she greeted religiously. But there wasn't anything she loved as much as accompanying Chavira to the Schmidt.

Luis Rivera Terrazas supported her completely. They had shared tea together on several occasions. Once, Lorenzo heard her burst out laughing in the cafeteria. What could she be telling him? he asked himself. She had also made friends with the González sisters.

Rivera Terrazas casually told him, "I took her to Puebla two weeks ago. She needed shoes. You should have seen hers; there were holes in both soles."

"Did you pick them out for her?" Lorenzo asked sarcastically.

"Almost," said Luis, smiling. "She really needed very heavy boots. It took her entire salary. You should give her a raise. That girl is a genius. It would be good for her to take classes at the University of Puebla. Although they've never heard the word Marxism there, and from what I've seen, she's read Marx."

26

The first time Fausta pronounced the word *bioenergy*, Lorenzo guf-
fawed cruelly, but she didn't acknowledge him. She didn't even
glance in his direction. Fausta was convincing, even he had to admit that. Her enthusiasm went straight to the heart, touching some
chord in her listeners.

"Have you heard her sing her devotional psalms? She's a snake
charmer!" Rivera Terrazas informed him. "She's drunk water from
the Ganges."

"When?"

"Every day."

"Every day?"

"Yes, with millions of pilgrims who wash their grimy scabs, their
stumps, and their loincloths in search of purification. In Benares
she helped burn cadavers with firewood on the shores of the
Ganges, and she collected their ashes with a broom and threw
them into the sacred river that comes down from the Himalayas
and empties into the Indian Ocean. Even today she got up from
her straw mat at four in the morning and practiced hatha yoga.
Lord!" So when he, Lorenzo, was closing the telescope, longing for
the heat of the bed, this senseless fool bathed in the icy waters after meditating?

Fausta entered the library under Lorenzo's inquisitive gaze.
"What are you reading?"

The girl showed him the jacket of *The Magic Mountain* and
went on to say, "Settembrini's long disquisitions bore me, and
sometimes I skip them."

She attended the conferences, sat at the table with the director,
and praised the blue and black corn tortillas Toñita made with her
good hands. "Do you know what Lao Tse says, Doctor? 'To be great

is to extend yourself into space; to extend yourself into space is
to reach far away; to reach far away is to return to the starting
point.' "

"I don't know who Lao Tse is," grumbled Lorenzo.

"Ay, Doctor, lighten up!"

Fausta made him irascible. One afternoon he found her embracing the trunk of a tree, and when he asked her what she was doing,
she responded with another question: Didn't it seem amazing to
him that the origin of a tree whose trunk she couldn't wrap her
arms all the way around was a minuscule seed? When Lorenzo declared, "How banal," Fausta retorted that love could also be contained in an atom.

"And grow to become a leafy tree?" Lorenzo retorted.

"Or drown as birdseed in the mouth of the first bird that comes
along," said Fausta, and she turned and left.

What a rude, impertinent girl. What right did she have to walk
away from him? Until now, he'd always had the last word. No one
said good-bye first. Didn't she realize that she risked being booted
out of the observatory? Kicked out? Well, no. He smiled inside. It
wasn't a matter of physically kicking her, but that wasn't because
he didn't want to. How could that ingrate dare to take away his
calm?

Fausta offered Lorenzo a world he was totally unfamiliar with.
How was it possible that she could have lived so much? Did girls
live on the edge now? Her life involved more risk than that of
any woman of his era, including his sisters, Emilia and Leticia, or
Diego Beristain's sisters—married, mothers of families, housewives.
Fausta, on the other hand, had gone to eat peyote in San Luis Po-
tosi, had met María Sabina, the shaman. She told Lorenzo about
her months in Huautla de Jiménez, living in a hut on the edge of
the abyss—not just the natural one, but her very own, of her mental state. She had memorized the spells, the litanies, the words of
the distributor of hallucinogenic mushrooms.

One day she said to Lorenzo, "I am the Jesus Christ woman, I
am the Jesus Christ woman, I am the Jesus Christ woman," until he
interrupted her angrily.

Once, he declared, "You are not normal, Fausta."

The girl laughed. "Normal like those who eat three meals a day? No. Normal like those who burp with satisfaction? No. Normal like the couples who have nothing to say to each other? No. I have a little bit more imagination, and you would too, Doctor, if you let yourself. If you wanted, you could be a rose."

A rose, me? thought Lorenzo that night on his way to the forty inches.

"That girl is tremendously lucid," commented Rivera Terrazas, "not only with respect to astronomy, but with everything. You should have heard what she said about you. She understands everything there is to know about you."

"Ah, really?" responded Lorenzo angrily. "Then she'll have to hear what I think of her—and my reasons for firing her."

Fausta didn't worry about infringing on the rules of their communal living. She dared to interrupt him one day. "Doctor, you're lying." She didn't even say, Excuse me, Doctor, but I think that you are mistaken. No. Out of the blue, that cockroach dared to challenge him.

"It's her nature," Luis Rivera Terrazas said. "She's like that. You can't change her. Take it or leave it."

Take her? Him, take Fausta, that crazy, irresponsible . . . She was intelligent, yes, but what good was her intelligence? Lorenzo was repelled by anything that had to do with esoteric doctrine, transcendental meditation, gurus, the illuminated, the pious of India. Those who gave up everything to follow a master seemed mentally incompetent to him—at the very least, deluded fools. For him, the only possible India was the India of Chandrasekhar the scientist. The rest was ignorance, misery, evasion, garbage, the delirium of the starving multitude.

Fausta could also read minds. Not only did she delve into them, she also stripped them naked in such a way that, at gatherings, Lorenzo took to following her to witness the moment in which she hurled her judgment.

She gave him vertigo. Throughout his life he'd had little time to think of others, about the noise they make, the laughter they provoke, their movements as they walk. He had seen them from afar. They were an indeterminate mass in space. He had never even asked Norman Lewis about his personal life, and Norman had never questioned him either. They had too much to talk about. He had no desire to know about what was going on with Leticia, Juan, and Santiago, and if anything happened, they would find him to tell him about it and drive him crazy. His buddies, too, moved in a separate orbit. Cut off from Mexico City, his life became infinite. Facing the two volcanoes every morning, he was accustomed to thinking about their existence, and about the sky, like a desert— yes, a desert, but of stars. Then Fausta erupted in it with her intense look.

Was it to make him lose his sanity? "You have to turn everything upside down, Doctor. To question everything, not just sit and contemplate the landscape."

With his heart in his throat, much more alert than before, Lorenzo would wait to ambush her. I'm going to make her fall into a trap, he thought. All his life he had known how to set traps for others; he had watched them pitilessly, waiting for the exact moment when they would stumble. Distrust, and you will succeed.

But Fausta stepped around it and kept challenging him. "The moon, Dr. Tena, is a living organism, not an inert rock surrounded by gases. Selene is our friend. You should greet her seven times each time she appears in her plenitude and ask her to grant you a wish, because she will."

"All I need is for you to give me astronomy lessons. Besides, the moon is the moon, and the Earth is not Gaia."

"No, Doctor. I'm incapable of such irreverence. I'm talking about your relationship with the moon. I think you are categorically wrong. The truth is, you don't know how to treat her."

"Ah, no? And women?"

"Not them either, Doctor, not them either. You need to get with it, I'm telling you."

Had she read Dostoevsky? What did she think of *Crime and Punishment*? When Fausta responded that she gave up reading his works after *The Idiot* and *The Brothers Karamazov* because it seemed unhealthy, Lorenzo went into a convulsion of sarcasm. "Unhealthy? From what I've heard, you're not afraid of any kind of disease."

As with the random occurrences in the atomic universe that the most refined examinations, the most exact measurements and observations, could not clarify, Lorenzo could not find an equation to define Fausta.

That's what she was, random. He couldn't fix or peg her. His high-frequency gamma rays were useless. At least if she would stop intriguing him, he'd be able to rest. What were her measurements? He was incapable of determining her position and her velocity or of stating the rhythm of her movements.

Seeing Fausta on the road to Puebla one day, Lorenzo stopped his car. "Fausta, would you go to Veracruz with me?"

"No way."

"All right, then I'll see you next week."

When he was about to turn the corner of calle Cannon, he saw that the girl was running after him.

"Yes, I'll go with you." And with that, she climbed into the front seat.

"Why did you change your mind?"

"For a cosmic reason you wouldn't be able to understand."

"And you're going just like that, not taking anything?"

"All that I am, I have with me."

"Not even a toothbrush?"

"As long as there are tortillas, I don't need a brush."

Neither spoke again. When the landscape changed and the banana plantations filled their eyes with green, Lorenzo said, "If you want, I'll take you back to where I found you."

"No, Doctor, I want to go, but I don't think we'll make it to Veracruz by nightfall at the pace we're going."

"We could stay in Fortín. Do you like gardenias?"

Fausta kept quiet. Why the hell had she gotten into the director's car? she wondered. Why did she obey impulses that got her into trouble? Right now she could be peacefully at home and not with this incomprehensible man. Rivera Terrazas, with his easygoing ways, was a thousand times better than this mule who didn't stop scrutinizing her! Yet she knew that her relationship with Lorenzo

Tena was more important than the one with Terrazas. Man or woman, bird or chimera, animal or object, planet or comet, no one intrigued her this way, not even her father, who had been the love of her life.

Fausta knew that she could walk away from everything in an instant, without calculating the consequences. She had done it before. But she didn't feel as happy with herself now.

"Do you want to stop and have dinner?"

Fausta felt like responding, Why don't you stop and go fuck your mother, but she didn't. What a coward I am, she thought.

Not in Fortín, or in Veracruz, or in Jalapa, or in Orizaba, or in the restaurant next to the river did they stop viewing each other as strange creatures.

At the hotel, Lorenzo asked for two rooms. Ceremoniously he asked, "What time would you like to have dinner? What about breakfast?" He looked unhappy.

Fausta went for a walk while he sat in the garden, his gaze fixed on the horizon, and she showed up half an hour late for dinner.

He looked at her furiously. "Why are you doing this to me?"

When they returned to the observatory, before entering the gate, Fausta asked angrily, "Why did you invite me?"

"Why did you accept?"

When she got out, Fausta slammed the car door.

Lorenzo went to Mexico City and stayed for almost ten days, and when he returned, Fausta inquired, "How are you doing since our unsuccessful honeymoon?"

Lorenzo had deliberately not come back to Tonantzintla because of this fucking bitch who made him suffer, and now this was how she greeted him, cunningly.

"Let's work this out, Fausta."

"How?"

"I have a cosmic solution. The collision of two planets, immersion in chaos, the circle of the true conical shadow."

Fausta ran her fingers over Lorenzo's lips. "We are ten thousandths of a millimeter from the undulatory phenomenon, and I don't know if a whitish and diffused light is what awaits me. Give my physical matter more time."

Lorenzo took her hand from his lips and kissed it. "It will be as you say, Fausta."

Lorenzo continued exhausting himself with ever more pressing tasks. How much time do I have left? he'd ask himself. At night while he slept, he reviewed everything he hadn't done.

In Tonantzintla, suddenly, he asked Fausta over coffee, "Have you seen me shooting through the sky like a comet?"

When they contemplated Popocatépetl, he would take her arm and say, "My falling in love is volcanic, Fausta." She would hold his hand. "You came and coaxed me with temptation." On another walk he informed her, "I am Goethe's Dr. Faust. I live locked in my laboratory and hear only the tolling of the bells."

"But I'm the one named Fausta, Doctor."

"That's the mystery. Why you and not me? I'm the one who gets sick and tired of men. I'm the one who desires to know the supernatural. You're happy in your skin. I'm a man plagued by doubt."

"Rest, Doctor. You work too much."

"I've always wanted to get out of my skin, but I'm imprisoned."

At first, science had given him a sense of freedom, because his work depended on him. He was finally creative, and he didn't have to deal with anyone. He didn't have to answer to anyone. The fact that they called him "wise fool" protected him and created a singular space for him. He could understand the others—the politicians, the dentists, the administrators—but none of them understood what he did, and that isolated him in his own world. Scientific knowledge wasn't petty; he was certain he was doing something that would benefit others, and that was a pleasing sensation. Most gratifying of all was his relationship with his colleagues throughout the world, which revolved around one theme: research. It connected them, and through it they communicated. But as the years passed, Lorenzo had lost much of his famed energy.

"Science is very demanding," Graef had told him once. "Things change very quickly, and you can't let an advance in your field get away from you, because otherwise you're left out of the game." There had been an anguish in the man's voice that Lorenzo hadn't understood. Now he lived it himself.

27

What disconcerted Lorenzo most was that Fausta propelled him into unknown worlds over which he had no control—as with the computers. With Fausta, each time he ventured outside the perimeter, where his orders as director of the observatory were followed to the letter, Lorenzo revolved in space, not knowing how to behave. Once, at a café, a boy with long hair came up to their table from out of nowhere to ask her to dance. Without even a glance in Lorenzo's direction Fausta got up and followed the boy to the middle of the room.

That afternoon he had invited Fausta for coffee at the only restaurant near Tonantzintla, and she had accepted happily. To his surprise, she asked for a beer. Ten minutes later, when Lorenzo was feeling self-confident, the young woman got up to dance with this disheveled rocker.

"I'm not a rebel without a cause, not a fool out of control," the shrill scream of rock and roll came blaring out of the jukebox. Stupefied, Lorenzo watched her dance—holding the hand of a perfect stranger who spun her, exposing her lovely arm as he lifted it up high. Interrupt them, hit the bum, drag Fausta out, kick the jukebox—all these ideas crossed his mind in a matter of seconds. But he only raised the bottle of Negra Modelo beer to his lips as he watched.

The hippie put one coin after another in the jukebox, and Lorenzo considered walking out on her. Would she be saddened by his absence? No. Would she be afraid? No. He was the one with the fears. Would she ask him tomorrow why he had left? No. Alone with his beer, a frightening sense of abandonment invaded him. I'm an incomplete man, he said to himself, and ordered another beer. With each dance step Fausta trampled his pride and plunged

him into a dark reality. I am obsessed with her, he thought. Far
from giving him satisfaction, that certainty crushed him. Fausta, in
the middle of the room, moved her hips, threw her head back, her
long legs separated, breasts balancing under the blue blouse, delicate arms encircling the man, laughing in his face, an accomplice.
She looked as if she belonged with the sweaty rocker, not with him.
Lorenzo asked for a third Negra Modelo. If he got between them,
could he replace the younger man? He couldn't see himself, Mister
Director, shaking it in the middle of the room; that would be something like the sky dissolving. He had to go to the bathroom, and he
thought about walking out of the café when he returned, but the
uselessness of the gesture stopped him. He didn't want to leave. At
the table, in front of his nth beer, he came to the conclusion that
throughout his life he had paid more attention to his spirit than to
his body, and that he must continue that way or he would fall
apart. The justification of my existence is to work the way I do, he
told himself. Science was his raison d'être. Being an astronomer
was enough to gratify him. He couldn't allow himself the luxury of
feeling dissatisfied, but Fausta made him feel that way. "Fucking
piece of shit that's never done anything in her life!"

At one point he noticed Fausta smiling at him seductively from
the dance floor. That smile alone made him glad he hadn't left. Desire came over him, drowning him like a wave. Yet he still thought
the only thing that could save him was to quash it, return to pure
spirit. The rigor of observing had also given him knowledge of the
secret springs of the souls of others. What would he do when Fausta
returned to the table, if she returned? I'm not going to make the
mistake of acting tragic, he thought. A sudden surge of desire invaded him again, and at the same moment Lorenzo replaced it with
the certainty that Fausta would never love him, or would love him
along with others—even worse, along with other women, and that
was intolerable. The vision of his impulse destined to fail made
him furious with her. Expelling her from his universe would not be
difficult. In fact, there were women to spare.

When the rocker said to him with a grin, "Thanks for letting
me borrow your daughter," he responded, "She looks like me,
doesn't she?"

At that point Fausta put her hand on his arm. "Shall we go?" she asked, taking his hand. Without letting go, they left the restaurant. In the car, instead of sitting near the window, as she usually did, she sat close to him.

Lorenzo became agitated. Why was she doing this to him? Was she crazy or just mean? This whore had gotten the idea that he was incapable of love, yet she came to rub up against him, confusing him with the jerk she'd been dancing with five minutes earlier. Fucking bitches, really. Fucking bitches! Why didn't he just take her to the nearest motel, fuck her, fire her the next day, and be done once and for all with the whole bother?

Iztaccíhuatl appeared in the windshield, in the light fog, and he saw Fausta as if for the first time. All the demons in his heart, all the shame in his spirit gave way before the image, and with a calm voice he said, "I can't change gears."

She jumped away from him.

The perfect summits of Popocatépetl and Iztaccíhuatl, cut out against the deep blue-black of the night, made him recover his place in the landscape. He was the missing piece in the puzzle, a little bit of blue here, a little black there, and that's it. It was finished. The girl, on the other hand, didn't fit, and owing to her very nature, no one knew where to place her. But that was what she wanted—to be different. Hadn't he told her that she was a moon that came out during the day?

He stopped the car in front of the house where she was staying, and Fausta, suggestively, asked him courteously, "Mister Director, would you like to come in?"

"No. I'm going to observe."

"May I accompany you?"

"Tomorrow, my child, tomorrow."

When he arrived home, he felt mortally tired. He took a bottle of sleeping pills out of the medicine chest, swallowed one more than had been prescribed, and fell on the bed that now seemed sad and deep.

Fausta had forced him to return to his adolescence. Also, inevitably, to think about women. They had to be protected, the poor things. So predictable. Reading them as he did took away all the mystery. Bags. About to give birth, they filled up with milk and they emptied of blood and fluids. Soft. Kneeling in the middle of the sheets, they awaited salvation. While the sun tanned him, blackening his body, they swelled up, then prostrated themselves at a man's feet, like a balloon that has been popped. Screw them— a quick ejaculation and let's be on our way. Not getting trapped like Chava in the sweet nectar of Rosita Berain. You had to apply the same formula to women that you did to death: let come what may, get out from between their legs quickly, wash them out of you. Poor creatures. Their time on Earth had still not come.

Fausta defied his parameters; he wasn't the conqueror. This spoiled brat turned him upside down and made him certain of something that he wanted to hide—the fact that he was a weak man. Fausta brought back memories that were deeply buried, and Lorenzo had to reexamine his relationships with those "fucking women." The first, at the Eden movie theater on Sundays. The minute the lights went out, the boys ran, in a stampede that made the floor rumble, to sit next to the girls. Father Chavez Peón would cover the projector lens with his hat when the kisses were pro-longed on the screen, and in row after row of seats the kids yelled, "Kiss, kiss, kiss." Then Chavez Peón, in his black suit, smelling rank, and his Tardán hat pulled down to his ears, got up on the stage to talk about decency. When he got off the stage, the movie would resume until the next kiss, so a thirty-minute episode could last from four to six thirty in the afternoon.

Lorenzo would run and sit next to a girl who was older than he. Socorro Guerra Lira. Her dark hair shone, its lemon fragrance at-tracted him, and she soon responded, letting him hold her hand. He no longer saw the movie, experiencing only his own sensations, which became more compelling as she softened. The desire to kiss her became painful. Socorro pretended not to notice, but when Lorenzo pulled her toward him, she was the one who kissed him first. After that unforgettable day, Sunday after Sunday, Lorenzo was in line in front of the Eden ticket booth, and he ran to the seat that Socorro saved for him, to kiss her at will. He didn't recognize himself, and what he felt scared him. Where would this end? From what he saw, he was the one who imposed limits, because Socorro would put her hand on the fly of his pants, throwing him into unimagined desire. For the first time in his life he knew what ejaculation meant. He returned to the house on Lucerna three hours later, confused and ashamed.

Abdul Haddad had challenged him: "What are you doing with my girlfriend?"

Although Abdul was taller, Lorenzo threw himself on the boy and punched him. The workouts at the Beristains' gym had served him well. The big boy took off, and when he saw Lorenzo coming at him again, he took out a little pistol and shot at his stomach. A great silence fell over the crowd, and the shouts of "Give it to him, Lencho" and "Kill him, Abdul" ceased as in a dream. Before he passed out, Lorenzo had time to wish that Diego had been there. He came to in a white hospital bed. He had a terrible headache and was doubled over with nausea. "It's the anesthesia," Leticia told him, her eyes all watery. Around the bed, she and Aunt Tana were watching over him.

"Young man, we're not going to let you play d'Artagnan anymore."

He recovered at the house on Lucerna. Aunt Tana, Tila, and Leticia took turns at the foot of his bed. "Thank God the bullet didn't hit the intestines, and the wound is superficial. It grazed the sacroiliac; the operation was simple."

He never saw Socorro Guerra Lira again, although the nurse told him that a female voice had telephoned, asking about him between sobs, but she hung up without giving her name. Lorenzo turned red when he heard about the sobbing.

"You're quite a little bull, son," commented the surgeon sympathetically. "You have a strong muscle wall. A few days of rest, and you'll be better than before."

Now Lorenzo was surprised that the memory of Socorro and the Arab sprung up so real and so palpitating from his memory. One afternoon, seated on the edge of his bed, Aunt Tana had unbuttoned his pajama top. "It's too hot, Lencho. Take it off."

Lorenzo felt the same knot in his stomach as he had at the Eden. Doña Cayetana must have perceived it, because she never touched him again. All the heat of Mexico entered through the window of his attic room. "You'll be up and about soon enough. Don't move too much, so it's not so painful."

"Passivity while suffering, Aunt? Never!" On the contrary, the most stimulating of impulses invaded him. "Aunt, I mold my life. I rule myself."

Leticia laughed. "Always such big words."

A prisoner of desire, Lorenzo hadn't recognized himself. He was supposed to be lying in bed because of the pain, but the erections were what tormented him. Tila changed the white-flowered sheets without saying a word, and Lorenzo knew that embarrassment forced them both to keep silent. What happened to him was completely real, and all of them, himself included, pretended not to notice. In this house there are no bodies; no one discusses the tyranny of sex, thought Lorenzo. His frustration had no body either. Only once had Leticia—the only one who he thought was unaware of the duplicity, naïve because of her age—told him, "Aunt Tana told Tila that they must pray a lot for you. See, they do love you."

"What else do they say down there?"

"They say that this happened to you for being horny. Father Chavez Peón came to tell on you."

In the merciless oven of his attic room, Lorenzo was all flesh. Before, he had been all spirit. Now he had to tame his unruly body, hide his impulses under the sheets so that no one would see them, although they surely suspected.

"Your father says that he'll see you when you can come down to the dining room and for you to remember that suffering is purifying," Aunt Tana solemnly communicated.

"If suffering is such a great teacher, why doesn't he suffer and come up to see me?"

"Impertinent boy. Your father in an attic room?"

"Listen, Leti, can you do me a big favor and ask Diego to bring me *The Origin of Species?*"

When Diego came up, they talked not only about Darwin, Abdul Haddad, and Socorro, but about the shooting.

"Show me your wound."

Lorenzo boasted an immense scar.

"How lucky you are, brother! Oh, my God. Does it hurt?"

"It just itches. I want to scratch, but the stitches would come open."

"How many stitches?"

"Thirteen, and they're black thread." Excited, Lorenzo asked his friend if human nature was really the source of freedom.

"I'm not a biologist, Lencho, I don't know."

"You should know, Diego."

"I'm telling you, I don't."

"Okay, ask Dr. Beristain for me."

"Yes, of course. Did I tell you he sends you a hug?"

"Thanks, but ask him about nature."

"Brother, I see that your volcanic nature hasn't changed. I'm sure they're going to let you out soon. Listen, my dad sends you *Facundo* by Sarmiento."

"Couldn't you bring me Victor Hugo's *Les Miserables?*"

"I don't think that's appropriate for convalescence, but it's up to you."

Damn it! If Lorenzo were to go down to the living room right now and tell the de Tenas that owing to the shooting and his having the time to reflect while in bed, another life had been revealed to him, a life that was infinitely better, and it waited for them outside, they surely would have responded that he was the oppressed one, he was the stupid one. Of course they had the best of all possible lives. The de Tenas were considered the cream of society. Great Grandmother Asunción had been a lady-in-waiting to the Empress Carlota. The de Tenas—like the Escandóns, the Rincón Gallardos, the Romero de Terreros, and the Martínez de Ríos—lived up to the motto on their coat of arms, and there were very few families in Mexico with their lineage and honorable family name. They came from Spain, spoke of the king as if he were their property and of Maximilian and Carlota as intimate friends. No, there was no possibility that Lorenzo's discourse would provoke any reaction. On the contrary, only Juan and Leticia would feel it, damn it all.

Lorenzo only went back to the Eden movie theater once. No one had seen Socorrito since the shooting, and Father Chavez

Peón reproached him: "You've ruined her reputation. Who knows if she'll ever be able to marry now?"

His memories provided a respite. The intensity with which he thought about Fausta was making his existence phantasmagorical: Harvard, Tonantzintla—everything was falling apart around him. I have to work, he told himself. It's the only way to forget about Fausta. Love makes me waste time.

"It's already Wednesday?" Lorenzo said. "Oh, my, how time flies."

On hearing him, Fausta replied, "Every day, sometimes twice a day, you lament the loss of time. If no one really knows what time is, what are you worrying about? Pretend that it's very thin air passing by and there's no way to hold on to it, and stop torturing yourself."

Very carefully, through solitary days, Lorenzo made Fausta a participant in his obsession with time. When he spoke to her about Calderón de la Barca's play *Life Is a Dream*, it surprised him that she answered that Góngora and Velázquez were also part of the golden age, along with Calderón de la Barca, born thirty-eight years after Lope de Vega.

"How do you know Calderón de la Barca's work, Fausta?"

"I worked in the theater. I really like the servant's name: Clotaldo, the only one who lived with Segismundo. It's an ugly name and attractive at the same time. Listen, Doctor, as a child, I drew, but since I didn't like my creatures, I gave them ugly names. I remember one was Jedaure. I thought that the day they came out well, I'd call them Rodrigo, Tomás, Andrés, Nicolás, Lucas, Cristóbal, Inés, but I never got to the point where I drew them skillfully, so I never got past Jedaure."

"The search for perfection."

Fausta repeated how Basilio, the king of Poland, locked Prince Segismundo up in a tower because the queen had died in childbirth, and the prophets had assured him that his son would steal his power. "You know, Doctor, no one knows Segismundo except for Clotaldo. When the boy becomes an adult, the king—after consulting with the seers—orders the servant to free his son and take him to the court to test him. Clotaldo gives him a potion, and Segismundo wakes up in the palace. There, because he has never seen a woman, he assaults Rosaura, insults the court, and throws one of the royal attendants off a balcony. Segismundo is a beast. It is impossible for him to be king, and his father sends him back to prison, making him believe it was all a dream.

> *"I dream that I am here*
> *From these prisons carried,*
> *And I dreamt that in another more pleasing state*
> *I appeared. I saw myself.*
> *What is life? Frenzy,*
> *Rapture.*
> *What is life? An illusion,*
> *A shadow, a story,*
> *And the greatest good is small,*
> *All life is a dream. And dreams are dreams.*

"However, Prince Segismundo has fallen in love, and finally the only thing he remembers is his love for his cousin Estrella. Doesn't that story seem cool, Doctor?"

"What?"

Lorenzo and Fausta began to contemplate Segismundo's monologue and to ask themselves why they had less freedom than birds and bears. They recited together " 'and having more soul, do I have less freedom? and I with better instincts, do I have less freedom?' "

Returning to the past was a clear sign of aging, and Lorenzo was afraid. I can cope with my body aging, but not my mind. It must not abandon me. No one can beat me.

28

Each time he returned from Mexico City, Lorenzo's heart contracted at the thought that Fausta might not be at the observatory. She was now part of the Tonantzintla personnel and on the payroll. How old could she be? She gave the impression of having survived many things, maybe too many. How many different bloodlines did she have? Who configured her that way? Lorenzo no longer expected the miracle of self-renewal, yet this woman from hell had given it to him. Fausta used drugs and smoked marijuana. Because she shared her weed and talked like them, the young people felt she was one of them. "What wavelength are you on, My Doc?"

She had approached him, and Lorenzo felt like saying, Don't call me My Doc, but he stopped himself and vengefully asked her, "Do you always wear the same pants?"

"These are different. Look, My Doc, these have pockets on the cheeks; the other ones were on the sides." In turn, she asked him, "Why don't you let your hair grow long?"

"Me?"

"Yes. Like Einstein, long and messy."

On another occasion she became excited when she heard a rock song. "Do you know Janis Joplin? Have you heard her music? What an amazing human being."

A few months after arriving in Tonantzintla, she had shown up with her hair spiked straight up. She had cut her beautiful black braids off. Without disguising his dislike, Lorenzo asked her, "How does it stay up like that?"

"With gel, Doctor, the same kind men use. Look, touch it."

Fausta guided Lorenzo's hand over her skull. It was completely stiff, as sharp as a bed of nails. His hand bounced off. But she still looked attractive with those spikes on top of her head! In time she got bored with it and let her hair grow out.

For Lorenzo, drugs and marijuana implied a sordid world of hippie clubs, discos, rock, abortion doctors, supermarket robberies, promiscuity, and, consequently, a desolate end. He slept with whomever he wanted to, but he was a man. She obviously had gone much further. Nonetheless, she seemed as pure as the T Tauri stars.

Right now, for him, Fausta was the scourge of Tonantzintla, and soon she would be that of the University of Puebla, considering Luis Rivera Terraza's enthusiasm. Luis was very worried about his university, and he would give Lorenzo updates. "At least they're beginning to discuss economic and political problems. Until just recently the only thing that could be considered cultural was the thanksgiving mass."

Lorenzo and Luis spent hours talking about higher education. According to Luis, as you entered the vestibule of the beautiful Carolino building in Puebla, a blackboard announced, LAW STUDENTS ARE INVITED TO THE THANKSGIVING MASS DURING EXAMS. The archbishop visited them frequently, and peregrinations to the Basilica of the Virgin of Guadalupe were counted for credit in the history department. "Where are we living, Lencho?" Luis despaired. "The same happened in the physics department, which had only one textbook. And it was the worst, brother, the worst. It was written by Lerena, a Spaniard who knows as much about physics as I do about dressmaking. And just think, about seventy thousand students buy that book." Luis wrung his hands. "Why don't you teach a class, Lorenzo, just one? Do it for me."

"You know I hate it, Luis. Take pity on my research. I spend too little time on it as it is."

Luis insisted. "I need to find professors who at least don't confuse weight with mass. Imagine, Lencho, I went into a physics class, and I discovered that the teacher didn't know the difference between degrees centigrade and degrees Kelvin."

Terrazas laughed when Lorenzo made fun of his Catholic Communism and his loyalty to Makarenko's "Pedagogical Poem." "At the university another teacher showed me what he calls 'the Mexican race'—an abomination that's a cross between the Virgin of Covadonga and the Virgin of Guadalupe."

Lorenzo laughed. "Man, you even beat Vasconcelos when you talk about the cosmic race. The fifth race, superior to the other four: white, black, yellow, and bronze, all synthesized in the Mexicans. Pinto beans as good as red beans!"

One morning the walls of Tonantzintla were covered with graffiti: "TENA AND TERRAZAS COMMUNISTS"; "ANTI-MEXICANS"; "REDS, GET OUT"; "ENEMIES OF THE VILLAGE"; "DOWN WITH COMMUNISM"; "TRAITORS"; "TENA AND TERRAZAS ARE QUEERS." The anticommunist campaign had reached Tonantzintla. Anyone with new ideas was a threat to rural traditions. Puebla was more conservative than any other state, and a liberal was labeled a Bolshevik, straight out of Moscow.

At the University of Puebla, one hundred twenty students squeezed into classrooms built for sixty. When Terrazas told the instructors, "My friends, it's your duty to stay at the university for eight hours," one of them protested: "I agree, but do you want me to sit under a tree or on a rock?" How could they demand that a full-time professor stay on campus without even a cubicle to call his own? And many students had no space at home to do their homework.

"We can only handle forty students," Terrazas said, "because there are ten tables of four, and here we are, the university with the longest tradition in the Republic."

Lorenzo promised to speak with the Minister of Education, but he and Luis were pessimists by nature. "Poor country! Poor Mexico! What will become of the youth?"

The problems Terrazas struggled with at the University of Puebla reminded Lorenzo of what he had encountered with the founding of the Institutes at the University City and, years later, at the Academy of Scientific Investigation. Alberto Sandoval Landázuri, the director of the Chemical Institute, had knocked down walls himself to enlarge the space on floors 11, 12, and 13 of the Science Tower. "I know the exact specifications for my laboratory—where I want the glass workshop, the warehouse, where the air and vacuum compressors should go." He demanded, mallet in hand, that carbon dioxide extinguishers be installed as well as high-pressure water hoses. He didn't want to take a single risk.

Sandoval had the reputation of being bad-tempered, and he had an extraordinarily energetic voice. Lorenzo had appreciated his directness, thinking, Those are the kind of men I like to deal with. They handled problems the same way. Having tea together in midafternoon became a ritual.

Unlike other men of science, who complained about their wages, for Sandoval Landázuri six hundred pesos a month seemed like a magnificent salary. That total lack of interest in money impressed Lorenzo.

"Something is not right in our Science Tower," Sandoval had indicated. "Since I'm on the top floor, I notice that my colleagues get off the elevator without saying a word. The different disciplines mutually ignore one another. If we haven't been able to awaken the curiosity of the scientists, how are we going to convince the general population? Doesn't it seem like the last straw that our colleagues don't communicate among themselves? You're my buddy, Lorenzo. Help me out here."

And Sandoval Landázuri had laughed when they decided to establish the Academy of Scientific Investigation. "Who will we nominate besides ourselves?" With Lorenzo's support he chose the members. "No, not that one. He's a good-for-nothing." "I can't stand that offensive bitch." "He's a son of a gun; I don't trust him." Like Lorenzo, Sandoval Landázuri felt it was urgent to act rather than to theorize. "We're lagging so far behind, we have neither an infrastructure nor human or economic resources. Our programs are fifty years late. If we aren't able to interest Mexican businessmen, we'll never be able to compete with the scientific development of First World countries. Science is a priority, but as long as those idiot politicians don't understand that, we're screwed, Lorenzo."

Lorenzo had liked presiding over meetings at the brand-new academy. They had first admitted twenty-five members, and then another twenty-five. He insisted on excellence. "First-class people, brother, absolutely top-notch. We have to be strict. No mummies or sacred cows. No solemn asses either." They instituted annual awards for researchers who were under forty years of age. Though they promoted the humanities as well (one of the first to receive an award was a lawyer, Héctor Fix-Zamudio), they gave science priority, and it was a great pleasure for Lorenzo to award one to Marcos Moshinsky, the young physicist.

But Lorenzo's demands had reached unheard-of heights, and some who listened to him were stunned.

"You must have published an article within the last three years. Of course that eliminates Sandoval Vallarta. The older ones who rest on their laurels are not acceptable. Manuel Sandoval Vallarta has not published; therefore he's out."

How could Tena be so dismissive of a leader in the field of science? Sandoval Vallarta had accepted him and recognized him at the Colegio Nacional.

"I think what is important is to prove that you're good in your field," argued Alberto Barajas. "Your requirements eliminate almost all the mathematicians, among them me, and soon Graef himself."

Nabor Carrillo intervened. "It's pure insanity!"

"Marcos Moshinsky, Alberto Sandoval, and I all believe that you must publish continuously to be an active researcher," said Lorenzo.

"No one can publish as frequently as you do," insisted Nabor Carrillo. "Show some moderation, man. We are not going to judge the scientific community based on your parameters. There are not many of us as it is, and if you start eliminating people, you must remember that those who follow could become as merciless with you as you are with the ones who showed us the way."

"If the old ones don't work, they go in the garbage," Lorenzo repeated. "If we demand excellence from the young people, we can't be complacent ourselves."

"You're going to end up all alone."

"I'm willing to take the risk. If we give in now, we'll fail. Science has not integrated itself into the life of the country. They're better off in India and in Africa than we are here. Not even thirty percent of Mexicans make it to elementary school, while in First World countries it's eighty percent. With the exception of the National University and the Polytechnic Institute, our universities shouldn't even be called that. They aren't even at high school level. We don't belong to the elite of research, and you, Barajas, know that better than anyone. If we don't make a titanic effort at all levels of education, we're lost."

"Maybe it isn't how much we publish, but rather how much we know," insisted Barajas. "Publish or perish is a gringo influence."

"Yes, and the only way to become competitive is to contend with the United States."

"Brother, you seem more like Erro every day," Nabor Carrillo said. "You have earned your reputation as an ogre. 'Tena, who fires everyone,' the kids say. They run from you. They complain to me. You claim you're forming a scientific group, and you mistreat them."

"The problem is that you are irresponsible and frivolous, Nabor, just like Walt Disney's three caballeros. Do you remember? 'We are the three caballeros . . .' " Lorenzo executed a few samba steps and added, "All you're interested in is being recognized."

"Since you already are, you don't have that problem. You're going to sink the academy with your intolerance."

"On the contrary, I'm going to sink it if I don't demand the impossible and eliminate the parasites."

For the last four years Tonantzintla had invited scientists from the Soviet Union and the United States to visit the observatory to carry out their own research and to give talks to a small number of guests. Everything would go well until Lorenzo got the guest alone. Involved in laborious discussions, hounded until exhausted, the researcher of the hour would end up shaking his head in agreement.

"This is mysticism, my friend, mysticism and not science!" the director would say. He viewed these diatribes as stimulating for the guest, giving him new ideas for his research.

He did the same with the kids who came to visit from the University of Puebla and the National University. He challenged them for hours on end. During the course of the day, Lorenzo worked out his ideas, wrote them down, and discussed them with Luis, and at night he would throw himself into a discussion with his colleagues. Although he was a fierce polemicist, the next morning Luis would find him discouraged, saying, "I don't know enough about physics." One clear day he shouted that in a few years he wouldn't be able to compete with the young people. "I don't have the academic training, and intuition won't be enough." Nevertheless, his only form of dealing with problems was to view them as a challenge.

"Why do you force Harold Johnson to speak Spanish, Lencho? You make him sweat bullets," protested Rivera Terrazas.

Lorenzo had also corrected Donald Kendall from Texas Instruments, when the visitor said, "I'm an American."

"I'm an American too. You are from North America," the director responded decisively. "In spite of the fact that you covet it, you don't yet have a monopoly on the continent."

"We're in Mexico, and this gringo is going to speak our language," he told Luis.

"We're wasting a lot of time."

"It doesn't matter. I have patience."

"That's what you have the least of."

"The gringo is going to speak Spanish, at whatever cost."

"What's the point? What do you gain with that?"

"Respect, so he knows we're as worthy as he is."

"Lorenzo, the scientific language is English, the Latin of the modern world. Everyone speaks it—the Germans, the Italians, the Swedes, the Dutch."

Tena and Rivera Terrazas both shut themselves up in their offices after that discussion.

In spite of the bad omens, Lorenzo's integrity had strengthened the academy. However, on opening his correspondence one Monday, he found a card from Alberto Sandoval Landázuri: "No way, brother. I haven't published anything in the last three years, and I have to be just as strict with myself. We made the rule and shouldn't break it." Following his own rule, Sandoval Landázuri resigned from the academy.

Lorenzo missed him at the meetings. After instigating the expulsion of Sandoval Vallarta and Santiago Genovés, he felt more alone all the time. He could guess what comments were made as he passed. "He's hateful," he once heard Ignacio González Guzmán say. The other members feared an outburst, but Lorenzo wouldn't let his arm be twisted, although he really missed Sandoval

Landázuri and his keen insight. They even had their pasts in common. Both had worked with Guillermo Jenkins.

"Lencho, put aside your pride, forget your repugnance, and go see Jenkins," suggested Diego Beristain. "He loves Puebla, and if you're diplomatic, he'll probably help you. We're all aware of his fiscal omissions in the sale of alcohol, but he's a businessman—maybe the only one who can understand you."

"Just listen to what you're saying!" said Lorenzo indignantly. "*Fiscal ommissions?* Is that what you call cheating rats now?"

"Rat or not, go see him. I'll do everything in my power to help you, but never, even in my wildest dreams, will I have the resources that Jenkins does."

Owner of half of Puebla, Jenkins had made a huge fortune dishonestly.

The objective closest to Lorenzo's heart was to give scholarships to students. Jenkins's personal secretary called him: "The councilman will see you on Monday at twelve noon."

When Jenkins opened the door to his office and saw Lorenzo, he said, "Ah, the Communist!"

"Ah, the smuggler!"

"So I'm a smuggler? You're mistaken."

Lorenzo turned around to leave, and the powerful hand of the ex-U.S. consul rested on his shoulder. "Doctor, come in."

When Lorenzo finished his exposition, Jenkins said three words: "I'm for it."

"What do you want in exchange for your support?" asked Lorenzo.

"I want you to invite me to see what you've done with the money."

"All right. Maybe you can wash your hands of your sins that way."

As Lorenzo was leaving, a tall, husky man embraced him unexpectedly. "My Lord, are you brave. Jenkins is a great man; he owns the most land in the entire state. Not only is his own fortune colossal, but he's made his followers immensely rich. Are you familiar with his sugar mill in Atencingo, the one that produces alcohol?"

Lorenzo escaped the embrace, but not the hefty man, who said,

"I'm Rivera Terrazas's friend, but I'd like to be your friend as well. Years ago I belonged to the Communist Party. My name is Alonso Martínez Robles, and I'd like you to join me for lunch. Like you and Professor Terrazas, I believe that the revenue is being badly distributed."

The astronomer was on the verge of asking what Robles was doing in the reception area of a capitalist with a shady background, but he stopped himself; Robles could have asked him the same question. Fucking capitalism. Really! What shit it was to have to ask a man like Jenkins for help. Nevertheless, he liked the gringo. Like all executives, he got right to the point. Yes or no. And Jenkins had said yes to him.

Sandoval Landázuri told Lorenzo that when he was very young, he had worked as a chemist at the sugar mill in Atencingo. He had measured the sugar with a saccharimeter and verified the percentages of alcohol—until he realized that Jenkins was bribing the inspectors. Making alcohol with fermented sugarcane juice was prohibited, and in Atencingo it was fermented in large metal vats, to then be distilled. "I hung in there for a month, Lencho, and when I found out about a vacancy in the El Mante mill, I applied for the position."

Like Alberto Sandoval Landázuri, Lorenzo wanted to believe that businessmen would invest in science if you knew the right way to present a project to them. Alberto had had a positive experience with Syntex and Hormona laboratories doing research on steroids. Russell Marker, the chemist, discovered that he could extract saponin from great mullein, a low-growing grass in Oaxaca, and from that he derived sapogenin. With these, they could manufacture male and female hormones using very simple procedures. Somlo, Rosenkranz, and Kaufman, the owners of Syntex and Hormona, became millionaires with the development of the birth control pill.

These discoveries had immediate applications in chemistry and biology, but who invested in astronomy? Lorenzo resented the phrase "You all, you astronomers" because he knew that he was thought of as a lunatic who walked on the roof at night with a paper cone on his head and a cat on his shoulder, ready to take off through the air on his long-distance eyeglass, like a witch. But optics—yes, optics could pique the interest of a businessman because the glass was revenue yielding; it had an immediate relevance. Make our own optic glass to sell more cheaply than imported glass? Could they really compete with Bausch & Lomb? Electronics was also the science of the future, but "we astronomers are lost in the stratosphere, ignorant of world problems."

However, of all the subjects, astronomy was the most romantic, and the students registered for it, especially the girls. The effervescence at the National Autonomous University was contagious, and Lorenzo was pleased by the young, exuberant faces in the elevator that looked at him with curiosity.

"I have more students all the time," Paris Pishmish would tell him with an encouraging smile.

"Good ones?" the director would ask suspiciously.

"I'm not sure yet, but some of them ask brilliant questions. I have to study all night to find the answers."

Graef had faith in the future of science, as did Barajas, who agreed with Graef about everything.

At the university, Rafael Costero informed Lorenzo that young Amanda Silver, a student in the science department, was ranting and raving against him. The director asked to have her come see him.

"They tell me that you're going around calling me a son of a bitch."

"Yes, Doctor," she responded, swallowing hard.

Amanda had read in the newspaper that her teacher Rivera Terrazas, the Communist, who came to the university to teach classes two weeks each month, had been arrested in Puebla. For that she had blamed Lorenzo Tena. What was he doing in Mexico City instead of defending him?

"Ah! Do you believe everything you read in the papers?" Lorenzo picked up the phone, dialed the number for Tonantzintla. Fausta answered, and he asked to speak to Rivera Terrazas. "Luis, I have one of your students here who says you were arrested because of me and that I'm a so-and-so. I'll let you speak to her."

Frightened, the girl took the receiver.

"On the contrary, Amanda," Rivera Terrazas told her. "Tena has always protected me. In 1959, during the railroad strike, he gave me asylum in the observatory. I'm hiding here right now. If you want to come this weekend with your classmates, you're welcome. There is a bungalow where you can stay."

Before heading for the door, Amanda looked at the director out of the corner of her eye. She was embarrassed.

Lorenzo stopped her. "Starting tomorrow, you come to work."

"What about school? I haven't finished yet. And Dr. Pishmish?"

"I want to see you in Tonantzintla in the afternoon starting tomorrow."

How would she progress? His faith in women scientists was limited to Cecilia Payne Gaposchkin. The other ones couldn't even be compared with the men. There was no female Hale or Shapley or Hubble or Hertzprung. Although Erro had named the small road that led up to the observatory after Annie Jump Cannon, to thank her for her enthusiasm about the Tonantzintla project, her contributions didn't even come close to those of Bo, Schwarzschild, Zwicky, Kuiper, or Hoyle.

As for Amanda, her knowledge of physics, math, electronics, and optics would finally be useful. She repeated "I'll be an astronomer" as if it were a revelation.

During her stay in Tonantzintla, it surprised her to see the signs that read TENA AND RIVERA COMMUNISTS.

"Outsiders came and painted that in plain daylight," Toñita informed her while she cleaned the bungalow.

"Let's whitewash it," suggested Amanda.

"Miss Fausta already bought the paint."

"Who?"

"Fausta Rosales. She helps all of us around here."

A flock of kids, guided by Paris Pishmish, crowded around the forty inches at night. Each had his own specific field of observation, and the following morning they compared their plates. In spite of the fact that Lorenzo demanded a great deal of them, they wanted to gain his confidence and, above all, his approval. "They say he's a great literary critic and has read all of Thomas Mann."

Contradicting those who alleged that science was an international activity, impossible to isolate, Lorenzo promoted a science that would serve Mexico. He looked for Mexicans to graduate and compete at the most important universities of Europe and the United States, and although he feared the flight of brainpower, it was a risk he was willing to take, in spite of everything. "Listen, come back. You have a moral obligation to Mexico." But it was impossible to deny that if Mexico isolated itself, it would drown.

Barajas said, "The talent is everywhere. Look at Chandrasekhar—from an aristocratic Hindu family. He traveled to England and stayed in the United States. It's impossible for researchers to return to the Third World. Where are our laboratories? None of our scientists could win the Nobel Prize living in a Third World country."

In Tonantzintla, the kids had little patience. They longed to make a discovery, to find another galaxy and name it after themselves within a month. No humility, none of the slow, laborious toil of bees about which Erro had written. When Lorenzo advised them that the smallest discovery in a hundredth millimeter of the nocturnal dome would be a triumph, they were upset. They burned with their own ambition, the fuel of their youth turning them into shooting stars that were quickly extinguished. They also asked for observation time at Tacubaya, although it was difficult to accomplish much with a refractor telescope that had five meters of focal distance and was thirty-eight centimeters in diameter. They reviewed their plates, and finally, frustrated, they yelled that they would not be observational astronomers but theoretical instead, like Dr. Pishmish.

"Be what you wish, but just work hard," responded the director.

At nightfall, led by the always inquisitive Rafael Costero, some of them dared to knock on the door to Lorenzo's bungalow, and he invited them in for tea. They talked about their own futures and politics, about science in Mexico and politics, about electromagnetism and politics. Many nights Lorenzo ended up inviting them to dinner at El Vasco in Puebla to continue the exchange of ideas. He never imagined that the students would want to know more about him, because for him someone's personal life was of little interest. Was he single or married? Did he have a secret lover? Why

did he like to read so much? What books did he recommend to
them? They feared him, and they deified him. "Doctor, it seems
that you had philosophical training. Were you captivated by Nietzsche? Kant? Sartre? Ortega y Gasset?" Lorenzo spoke to them
about Jaeger's *Paideia*, just as he had with Diego Beristain, for hours
at a time.

With the students, he regained the enthusiasm of his adolescence, but he was tortured by the passage of time and the slow and
difficult advancement of Mexican science. Costero surprised him
by asking, "Why don't you invite Fausta Rosales? She's brilliant!"

"Brilliant?"

"Yes, she has an excellent mind. You can't believe how we enjoy
her. She made friends with Amanda, and they observe together.
She's so conscientious that Amanda is going to give her credit in
her master's thesis."

"Fausta observes?"

"Yes, Doctor. Besides, her life is fascinating."

So Fausta had told them about her life, that devil of a woman.
She hung around with everyone but him.

Curiously, the students made him think about Fausta. Where
did she come from? Why wasn't she more communicative? How
could he get close to her? Had she sold her soul to the devil? If a lot
of kids were lacking a spirit of adventure, he thought to himself,
Fausta had it to spare.

29

"You outrageous Mexican, I hope you can show me your city. I will be staying at the Hotel Majestic," wrote Norman Lewis. He was arriving from Harvard, wishing to spend his vacation with Lorenzo. Wonderful! They'd discuss extremely weak objects, with which Norman was very familiar. Finally, someone to talk astronomy with.

Lorenzo embraced him heartily when they met in the hotel lobby.

"I told you I'd land in Mexico, old chap," Norman said. "It's been ages!"

Seeing Norman, Lorenzo realized how alone he had been, in spite of Diego Beristain's company. Norman hadn't changed. He still had those amazing hands with long, strong fingers, his ambling pace accentuated by his unkempt beard, and his head of unruly golden curls. He's like one of the old gold miners; he filters the universal sand to find nuggets that other civilizations have left behind in the infinity of space, thought Lorenzo.

His face pale from looking at the moon so much, a fragile figure in spite of his almost six feet and his inquisitive eyes, Norman returned Lorenzo's hug.

They shared a passion that united them. They didn't ask each other, how are you, but rather, what are you working on? They dealt with their recent discoveries, and all the rest seemed secondary.

"I want to learn about your art. Let's go to the pyramids tomorrow."

Norman was astonished by Teotihuacán. It was truly the city in which men became gods. He exhausted his friend as they tried to cover the twenty-kilometer expanse. When Lorenzo took him to the Acolman convent, he said that he preferred his hours among the Pyramids of the Sun and the Moon a thousand times over.

After Teotihuacán, Norman wanted to see the rest of the archaeological sites, to examine the codices that recorded celestial phenomena, the measurements, the cycles of villages as big as the ones of ancient Mexico. "Let's go to Chichén Itzá, to Uxmal. Let's go to Mitla, to Tajín, to Monte Albán."

"It looks like your measurements aren't as good as those of the Mexicans, Norman. Haven't you noticed the distance between one site and another?"

Amazed, Norman wasn't even listening to him. "The counting of the years by the Indians is absolutely extraordinary. How is it possible that we don't talk about it at Harvard?"

A guide in a straw hat was explaining that La Calzada de los Muertos, the Road of the Dead, was oriented toward the Pleiades. "Look. Before, you could see them very clearly, but they've moved now. Or maybe they died, because everything in the sky changes."

Norman was surprised that a man on the street would give his interpretation of the solstices and the equinox and would inform him that "the stars disappear from the firmament; they go, like us, to the world of the dead."

At times it seemed to Lorenzo that Norman was delirious.

"Wouldn't your ancestors have had contact with beings from other worlds and acquired their knowledge from them?" he asked. "How would they have had the facility for abstract thinking and mathematics on their own? There must have been an encounter, don't you think? The ability of the ancient Mexicans is out of this world." He asked what noises from space they could have heard and if a peculiar hissing sound had reached them from the Milky Way. Could the stars and the galaxies have sent radio signals?

Norman saw the stars in everything. The first petroglyph in a wall was a map of the sky; three lines represented the constellations. An entire planetarium could be discovered, engraved in a stela. It was enough to connect it with latitudes and longitudes to discover that such a figure appeared tied to the summer solstice.

"Norman, I'm going to show you something else," Lorenzo said. "I'm not going to allow you to leave having seen art only from the preconquest period."

He took him to see Diego Rivera's murals in the patio of the Department of Education. Norman commented, "He knows his job, but it's flat."

Lorenzo explained with much patience that Rivera was rescuing the Indian and repudiating the Conquest.

"I'm not interested in that," Norman answered. "It looks like something you'd find on a pamphlet."

Then, with great anticipation, Lorenzo drove him to San Idelfonso to see Orozco's murals. As if it were his own work, he waited for his friend to be amazed.

In a cold voice Norman let loose: "It's much worse than the other one. This is grotesque."

"What?" shouted Lorenzo, bewildered.

"It's descriptive, like a caricature, stupid, ugly, ugly. It's dreadfully simplistic. I've never seen anything so bad. How is it possible that a village that thought so abstractly could be insulted this way?"

Lorenzo could not contain his fury. "You are the abominable one—who doesn't understand the history of this country."

"His figures are deliberate; the stroke is vulgar and excessive. This is absolutely gruesome," Norman concluded.

"You will listen to me now." Lorenzo was foaming at the mouth. He pulled his friend by the sleeve, forcing him to leave the San Idelfonso patio. As he expanded on his ideas, he calmed down, taking Norman familiarly by the arm and guiding him to the Hotel Cortés.

"Listen, Norman, you son of a bitch. The Indians were ripped to shreds, their structures trampled, their gods and their temples destroyed, their scientific and religious knowledge that you admire so much erased from the face of the earth, first by the Spanish and then by the mestizos. Tell me if anything more tragic could happen to a village. Their smile, their tenderness, their capacity for pleasure, for sharing, for helping, their animal vitality—all were stolen. Imagine what it must have been like for them to lose their gods of fire and water and to see them replaced with a god who not only had no powers but who died like a poor wretch."

"All colonized villages lost their past instantly."

"Shut up, asshole gringo. It's not the same. In our case the wound was fatal. We lost the very meaning of life. We didn't know who we were or where we were going. Until the outbreak of the Revolution, we went from being beaten-down Indians to mestizos suffering from complexes. With the Revolution, beginning with the most defeated—the Indians—we wanted to be born again. Diego Rivera reversed the terms. He exalted the Indians and ridiculed the conquistadores—the ones on the outside and the ones on the inside. Not even the evangelists were spared. Look at them, Norman—syphilitic, drooling degenerates. After that, the Frenchified Mexicans destroyed the work of the muralists with knives."

Lorenzo must not have been very convincing, because his friend stopped him cold: "I can't stand this nonsense anymore. You were more intelligent at Harvard."

"And don't speak to me in English; we're in my country now, you ass!"

In the patio of the Hotel Cortés, they asked for two cups of tea, and Norman assured him, "Listen, your return to Mexico has not agreed with you. You've become an Aztec. You're ready to shove an obsidian knife into my chest. What's wrong with you?"

"You gringos don't understand Mexico."

"I'm more English than gringo, and I didn't come here to rip your heart out to offer it to the gods. I think you left your heart on Lisa's sofa bed."

"Ah, you came here to talk to me about that witch?"

"That witch is perfectly capable of handling her own affairs without my intervention. I came because I'm your friend and because you talked so much about your country that I wanted to learn about it. But if you keep this up, I'll be traveling alone starting tomorrow. You just want to break my face. Do you know what's wrong with you, Lorenzo? You're falling into sentimentalism. If sentimentalism is a liberation, it is also a relaxation of emotions. Our conversations were invigorating at Harvard. You were quite different."

———

"Your driving is ghastly," Norman said on the way to Tonantzintla. "You're going to kill yourself one of these days. Why don't you use the university driver? You'd save an enormous amount of time."

"I don't want to become dependent on anything," responded Lorenzo in an irritated tone. Becoming important hadn't fitted in with his plans. Although giving orders was inherent to his nature, the trappings that went along with the position were repugnant to him.

Norman then told him about Pierre Curie, who had discovered polonium and radium in a wooden shed on rue Lhommond in Paris with his wife Marie. When Curie was nominated for the Legion of Honor, he responded to Paul Appel, "Please be so kind as to give my thanks to the Minister and to inform him that I don't feel the slightest need to be bestowed with honors, but I have a greater need for a laboratory."

"I need two laboratories as well, an optic and an electronic," Lorenzo said.

"Maybe Harvard can help, although I can't promise anything without asking Shapley."

In the days that followed, under Norman's beneficent influence, Lorenzo calmed down. They even played basketball on the old court where he had played with Erro. Norman kept putting the ball in the hoop with a single gesture of his hand. His height gave him the advantage, although Lorenzo's jumping made him exclaim, "You really are a jumping bean!" They laughed a lot, sweated even more, and, finally, went for a long shower.

Norman met Fausta in the library, and they got along immediately. Norman pointed out to Lorenzo that aside from her daily efficiency, Fausta, unasked, took tea to his office, answered calls, made everything easier for him. Lorenzo told him that Fausta would return to the capital with them to put together the *Bulletin* of the Tonantzintla and Tacubaya observatories. "That's great. Your bulletin has achieved global recognition, and there is nothing I'd like better than to go to the printer with you," Norman said enthusiastically.

When he realized that she was an amazing proofreader, in spite of the dry subject matter, the director, who had never before trusted anyone, gave Fausta that responsibility—"the job," as she called it.

They left for Mexico City the night before to be at the printer at seven the next morning, and Fausta corrected the galleys tirelessly. She marked the typos and then read page after page without losing patience as he always did. The typesetter preferred working with her. Fausta was fascinated by the atmosphere at the printer, the long, narrow metal tables where the type was set, the printers, and the sound of the presses, from which Lorenzo immediately grabbed each page to inspect it, carrying them in his arms to the table in a state of extreme anxiety that bordered on hysteria. Making a mistake with mathematical symbols—a plus rather than a minus in an equation—could be catastrophic, the death of a theory. Fausta knew this, and her concerned care touched Lorenzo. She was truly an exceptional proofreader. It was then, with her hair falling in her face, that Lorenzo discovered she had gray hair. "Fausta, your hair is turning white," he told her contentedly, because as she grayed, he was rejuvenated.

At noon they had a sandwich and a bottle of soda with the typesetter and went back to correcting galleys. "The smell of ink is a much stronger drug than any weed," said Fausta, and she smiled to calm the director. "This is a true odyssey, but unlike Penelope, I'm not staying home; I get to correct the sky and its inscrutable designs alongside Ulysses." They finished at one in the morning, and Fausta was punch-drunk. "This lasts longer and takes more care than a night of lovemaking." She laughed so hard that she fell over, exhausted, and Lorenzo said good night to her at the house where she was staying with a friend, saying, "Tomorrow at seven."

The compilation and correction of the *Bulletin* took three to four days, and each day, Lorenzo only became himself again after the last revision. He'd say, "All right, I think that's it . . ." and the printer gave the signal: "Print it."

On the second night they all had dinner in Norman's suite at the Hotel Majestic. Norman and Lorenzo went back to the way things had been before, with one difference—Fausta was with them. They discussed. That's what science was really about—interminable discussion. Neither Norman nor he had the absolute truth, but Lorenzo added his despair about the future of his country to his scientific concerns.

"Shut up, Norman. You all have a future; we don't!" He alleged that the government's total indifference toward science condemned them eternally. "Look at this, we're stagnant. Look at the paralyzed fields in front of us."

"But a president gave you the observatory."

"He did it in deference to Erro. As he would have given a Secretary of Customs a ranch."

"Lorenzo, don't be a pessimist."

"I'm not. That's the way it is in Mexico."

Lorenzo told him that on one occasion he stopped his car on the road to give a peasant a ride. They traveled silently, until he asked the peasant what he dreamed about, to which he responded: "You know, sir, we can't allow ourselves the luxury of dreaming."

Surprisingly, Fausta fiercely backed him up. "Dr. Lewis, do you think that men and women who have been frightened for centuries can really dream? It's not only hunger. What do you know about the sexual poverty of the Mexicans? Where is the freedom over our bodies? Is there any space that isn't controlled by power? Slavery is an example. Those girls you see carrying wood live with daily rape. Millions of women have never known pleasure. Love and marriage will never be part of their lives."

"Rape?" asked Norman.

"Of course, Dr. Lewis. It happens to thousands in my country. Females don't have human rights."

Lorenzo was surprised at Fausta's bitterness as she launched into the topic of sexuality. "The belief that reproduction is the only option for women is one of the reasons why homosexuality is punished; that's why homosexuals are considered perverse, diminished, dirty, incompetent."

Norman intervened. "I thought sexuality was an inviolable and intimate human decision."

Lorenzo, startled by the twist Fausta had given the conversation, affirmed that in Mexico the Catholic Church proclaimed that women should bear the children they had conceived. He added that this particular subject wasn't relevant at the moment. Did she want the three of them to talk about queers?

Norman defended Fausta. No one in the United States maintained the singular idea that sexuality was solely for reproduction. Mexico, a *machista* country, had the reputation of mistreating its women. Thinking of homosexuality as a perversion was a form of discrimination.

Lorenzo interrupted, asking Fausta how freedom could serve these girls if they didn't have water. They had to satisfy their basic needs first. Fausta excitedly reminded him of what he had told her one afternoon in his bungalow—the story that she was going to repeat word for word. At that moment, the actress stood up.

"I'm going to play two roles: that of Galileo and that of Cesare Cremonini." She sat Norman and Lorenzo down, and she greeted them from the next room. "Magnificent Stargazer and Great Master and Lord of Tonantzintla, Cacique of the Valley of Mexico"— she curtsied deeply to Lorenzo. "Illustrious Visitor and Quetzalcoatl of the Twenty-first Century, Observer of Eclipses, Hearer of Radial Sounds, Cybernaut, Discoverer of Electronics." She bowed in front of Norman, and with two leaps, like a minstrel, she continued to act out the play.

Fausta changed her voice and demeanor for each character— Galileo strong, sure of himself; Cremonini trembling and bent over, his voice exhausted. With a quilt as a cape and a towel made into a Venetian cap, she explained, "When Galileo proved with his small telescope that Jupiter had moons and that these moons had motion, he presented himself to the Roman house of Cesare Cremonini, the famous mathematician, and he said, 'Professor, I have proof that Aristotle is wrong. Come see how the moons of Jupiter move.'

" 'Look, Galileo,' responded Cremonini, terrified. 'The science of this world was built on the pillars of Aristotelian knowledge. For the last two thousand years men have lived and died with the belief that the Earth is the center and man is the master of the universe. God made us in His image and likeness. Jesus Christ came down to

Earth and gave us His gift. Christianity, which has gone far beyond Aristotle, was perfected.' "

"Everything we know today, about logic, medicine, botany, astronomy, is Aristotelian," interjected Lorenzo. "For two thousand years the greatest minds have worked in that belief and have made a splendid and perfect unity, but we cannot forget the Jews, the Arabs, the Chinese, and the Hindus, besides the Christians."

Norman stood up, making theatrical gestures. "And the Mesoamerican villages, the ancient Mexicas, the Olmecs, the Maya, and the Incas in South America."

"It's not fair for the spectators to interrupt the show, Dr. Lewis. I'm about to recite Cremonini's answer to Galileo!"

"Pardon me. And what is that answer?"

" 'I have spent my life at the service of Christianity. Its teachings have brought me peace and happiness. Now that I am an old man and have little time left, why do you come to destroy my faith in everything that I love? Why do you want to poison my few remaining years with vacillations and conflict? Don't wound me. I don't want to see Jupiter or its moons.'

" 'But, the truth, Cesare, doesn't it mean anything?'

" 'No. Leave me alone. I need peace.'

" 'How strange. For me peace and happiness have always consisted of looking for the truth and acknowledging it. The world is made up of people like you and me—Cremoninis and Galileos. You want it to stay the way it is; I want to push it ahead. You are afraid to look at the sky, because you may see something that disproves your life's teachings, and I understand that, because our work is difficult. Unfortunately, there are many like you, but only one of us will triumph.'

" 'And if you triumph, Galileo? If you can demonstrate that our Earth is a small, miserable star like thousands of others and that humanity is only a handful of creatures thrown by chance on one of them, what will you have gained? Will you diminish man who is made in God's image? Degrade the Master of the Earth and turn Him into a worm? Is that what Copernicus and Kepler and you want? Is that the true objective of astronomy?'

" 'I never thought of that,' responded Galileo. 'I search for the truth because I'm a mathematician and I believe that whoever accepts the truth is closer to God than those who construct their human dignity on senseless errors.'

" 'Galileo, I'm eighty-three years old. I have based my life on a philosophy and an Aristotelian way of thinking. Let me die in peace.'

"This was the end of Dr. Tena's story," Fausta said, and she closed an invisible curtain before returning to sit between the two men.

"Fausta, what a memory!" said Lorenzo, delighted. "But I don't see how what you just acted out has to do with our discussion."

"Of course it has to do with it. Cremonini's 'let me die in peace' is cowardice. Not wanting to face the truth and wanting to keep thinking in the past, taking refuge in the dogmas of faith in order to find peace. Renewing yourself comes at a price, Dr. Tena. A scientist has to be willing to change criteria as soon as new evidence is proposed. If not, he isn't critical or self-critical."

"I agree with you completely, Fausta," Lorenzo told her. "Science is an evolutionary process, and the young people now know much more than we did, because any contemporary scientist is better prepared than we were. We are the scientists of the thirties and forties."

"Your scientific ideas are progressive, Doctor, but your other ideas are abominable. You just finished telling Norman and me that you didn't want to talk about queers. Many essential topics evade you, or maybe you just don't want to see them. You haven't been able to combine the very big with the very small. Unlike Einstein, you still haven't realized—or don't want to—that everything is relative and that a lesbian on Earth is part of Newton's 1666 law of universal attraction. You're three centuries behind, Doctor. Don't you think it's time you brought yourself up to date? Frankly, I would have expected sounder ideas from you."

When Fausta said goodnight to them that evening, Norman asked admiringly, "Lencho, who is this woman?"

Lorenzo explained that Fausta was a monstrous entity that he had found among the clouds of gas in the Orion nebula, which, as Norman well knew, was a nursery for young stars, located fifteen

hundred light-years away. Of the hundreds of stars that were forming, Fausta had given him a new self-awareness. Thanks to her, he
was now developing the previously unknown ability to take others
into account.

"So she has humanized you?" Norman laughed.

"I think I'm more tolerant," responded Lorenzo seriously. "Although I must confess that it scares me. The stars that have just
been born, like Fausta, cause what surrounds them to explode.
Their torrents of ultraviolet light and their powerful stellar winds
destroy their progenitor. They commit cosmic matricide. What
awaits me? What will become of me in Fausta's spiral arms?"

Lorenzo didn't say it aloud, but for some time the rumors about
her bothered him. Hadn't Braulio Iriarte affirmed that Fausta hung
out with the hippies? For her, all beings were equal—man, woman,
bird, or chimera—each in its own time. Was Braulio joking?
Hadn't he said that Fausta had stripped naked at a get-together—
and that she wasn't all that great, rather skeleton-like, very thin?
What did the motherfuckers who looked at her see? It was true,
Fausta's energy pulled at him. She exercised an inexorable strength
over him, although he couldn't explain it. Her force of gravity held
him captive—it was the oxygen that he breathed, the calcium in
his bones, the iron in his blood, the carbon of his cells. If he ever
came to understand her, maybe he would understand why Florencia
had died.

At the end of three days in Mexico City, Lorenzo noticed that
Norman looked for Fausta's approval. He grasps how intelligent she
is, Lorenzo thought, congratulating himself. Under Lorenzo's loving gaze, Fausta talked about how the politicians were afraid even
of the word *science*. They hid behind the phrase "I was horrible in
math; that's why I'm a philosopher." And Fausta quoted Lorenzo's
response: " 'In that case, you'll never be a good philosopher.' " To
this day the Communications Secretary had not forgiven his arrogance.

At dusk they drove to a place that overlooked the city. Illuminated, Mexico City looked like an immense star fallen onto the
Earth. Lorenzo became indignant at the sight of more houses spi-
raling around the city, widening the misery belts. "What savagery!

They die of hunger in the fields; that's why they come to pile up in those pigsties."

At his side, Fausta drank up his words. She spoke of him respectfully: "Dr. Tena interrupted the president at a public appearance, asking him why the Fishing Ministry is located in the center of the Republic instead of at a port on the Gulf or the Pacific coast. What is Petroleos Mexicanos doing in the Federal District instead of being in Coatzacoalcos or in Poza Rica? At any conference, when he speaks at the Colegio Nacional, Dr. Tena speaks in favor of decentralization. Once, he explained, with perverse irony, how General Heriberto Jara, a hero of the Mexican Revolution, came to occupy a political post and had a shipyard built on the Lomas de Chapultepec and made cement boats."

In Fausta's absence, while sharing their last cup of tea for the night in the Hotel Majestic, Norman asked Lorenzo point-blank, "Why don't you marry her? She's extraordinary."

"She lives inside me. I think of her all the time. The truth is, I haven't had time for a personal life. But I'm going to find time, Norman. As soon as I catch my breath, I'll propose marriage—"

Norman interrupted him. "You're much more conservative than you think, Lorenzo. You're marked by your past. I don't have your set ideas."

"Conservative, me?" Lorenzo was indignant, but that night, when his head was on his pillow, he realized that if he hadn't been so conservative, he would have taken Norman to see Juan. But the very idea made his face burn with shame. Besides, in the shape his brother was in when he saw him last, would Juan have even been able to carry on a conversation with Norman?

The next day the three of them went to the printer, although Norman abandoned them after four hours to go and interview Alfonso Caso. Fausta didn't work with her usual skill. At one point she even stopped correcting, pencil in the air, and Lorenzo asked her, "What are you thinking about, Fausta?"

"About what Norman said—that very soon all of this will be done electronically."

When they met that evening for dinner, Lorenzo continued to harp on the same subject, and Norman tried to calm him down.

"It's more stimulating to live in Mexico than in First World countries."

"Then why haven't you moved here?"

"If you give me a job, I'll come, more so now that I've met your Fausta. I like yours much better than Gide's." Norman laughed. "It would fascinate me to not know what will happen tomorrow. Back in the States, everything is planned well in advance. I've never felt the need to save my country as you do with yours. There I'm lost in anonymity. I'm one of many."

Lorenzo said sarcastically, "Is it great that you lose yourself in the words of Mexican mariachis, pop singers, and soccer? That's all that thrives in this country. The Mexicans are truly alive when they win a match against Jamaica or Bolivia. They dream about scoring goals."

"Great, then score a goal in science."

"I'm going to try."

"I think Dr. Tena already did," Fausta came in, ready to defend him.

"You aren't alone; we'll help you," said Norman, embracing Lorenzo.

"What is happening," said Lorenzo angrily, "is that many who leave the country to get their master's or doctoral degrees choose your country because you offer salaries that we've never seen. But I am going to make sure they come back. So you can help me, but it has to be on my terms."

Norman returned to Harvard, and Lorenzo felt strangely empty. He remembered how at the airport, over the last beer as they were about to say good-bye, Fausta had sung "South of the Border (Down Mexico Way)" to them, her head tilted to one side, with such grace.

Where had she learned English? When? Fausta reached the depths of his soul. He wouldn't mind spinning within her orbit, becoming one of Orion's disks of gas, caring for her. He thought back to when he was very young and had been influenced by Heraclitus' definition of the universe: "This universe, the same for all, is a unit in itself. It wasn't created by any god or any man; it has been, is, and will be an eternal fire that is lit and extinguished according to laws."

Fausta obeyed laws that intrigued him because they were inaccessible.

30

When Carlos Graef informed him that the government was considering the creation of a new National Science Council that would replace the National Academy of Scientific Investigation, which was now overcrowded, and give it a previously unheard of budget, Lorenzo was astonished.

"Guess who the director is going to be and is already making the rounds. And earning a salary neither you nor I have ever dreamed of," said Graef.

"Who?" asked Lorenzo.

"Fabio Arguelles Newman."

"My former student? The philosopher?"

"The very same. He's going to drop in on you one of these days. He's been watching out for us all."

One morning at eleven, Arguelles Newman stopped by to visit Lorenzo. Lorenzo didn't recognize him. He wore a blue Armani suit that would have made Lorenzo's old friend La Pipa Garciadiego green with envy. His hair smoothed down with cream, he was no longer the young existentialist with whom Lorenzo had carried on long conversations six years earlier. Fabio didn't seem to want to remember that meeting. He explained that he had accepted the president's nomination because he wanted to promote science, and now there would be a budget for projects as important as the one in Tonantzintla. Lorenzo had an open invitation for breakfast, lunch, or dinner anytime he wanted, and Fabio would always be available. Here was his private phone number. He lit one cigarette after another, and at one point he lit Lorenzo's with a Hermès lighter. He took out his card and handed it to Lorenzo. FABIO ARGUELLES NEWMAN, PH.D. When he finished his long-winded speech, Lorenzo stood up.

"You are despicable, and I don't want to see you in my office again."

Fabio got up, terrified, and Lorenzo continued, "You were going to be a good astrophysicist, and you've exchanged it for a plate of lentils."

"Doctor, don't insult me. I'm going to continue my research. My position is not permanent. Besides, I'll be able to spend Saturdays and Sundays working on my thesis."

"Really? You haven't even earned your doctoral degree, but you dare to put 'Ph.D.' after your name? It seemed odd to me that you would have finished it in four years. I could denounce you to the University Council, but as my colleagues know and constantly remind me, I don't have my doctorate either. However, my disadvantage is due to unusual circumstances, not self-interest."

"Doctor, this is neither a betrayal nor a reason for you to attack me. When the term is over, I will return to my research. In the meantime I'm going to promote many of my colleagues' scientific projects, and they, unlike you, are pleased with my nomination."

"Fine. There is nothing else to say. Get the hell out of here."

Fabio was so disconcerted that he had to grab the back of the chair to keep from falling. That same expression of insecurity visible all those years ago returned, and made Lorenzo pity him.

"If you're going to faint, sit down."

Fabio collapsed into the chair, drying the sweat from his face, and Lorenzo suddenly felt defeated.

"The worst part, Doctor," Fabio said, "is that you're going to have to work with me on the budget for the institutes that you direct."

"Well"—Lorenzo softened—"don't worry too much about it. I'm an ogre, but I've lost some of my formidable momentum with age."

Lorenzo and Arguelles Newman saw each other again in the Department of Education.

"Doctor, we're going to redo the budgets for your institutions. Besides funding for instruments, you need to pay decent salaries, yours included."

"What are you telling me?"

"We live in different times, and this requires a change in attitude."

"I'm satisfied with my salary, and so are my employees."

"They've complained to me, and I think they're right. Listen, let's go get something to eat, and I'll explain before I give you the paperwork."

"Give me the paperwork now. I'll see what I can do." It was two thirty in the afternoon, and Lorenzo didn't want to go to lunch with Fabio, who left instead with a colleague.

When Fabio returned at five, he found the director of the Astrophysics Institute and the Tonantzintla Observatory in exactly the same place, in the same position, pen in hand, at his side an ashtray overflowing with cigarette butts. He hadn't finished adding salaries.

Fabio went over to look at the list. "Doctor, since there aren't any guidelines, take advantage of this opportunity."

"That's corruption."

"Doctor, please. Follow what the National University does; they already have classifications, increases—not of three hundred or four hundred pesos but three thousand or four thousand. Allow me to convince you to give your people a substantial raise. Look, you have a miserable salary. I've budgeted money not only for salaries, but for the spectrograph, the electronic lab. You have to learn to spend it, and this is the moment. We're going to get rid of the consolidated budget that is adjusted each year."

"You haven't convinced me, Fabio. These are the only increases I am willing to authorize as director."

"Doctor, nobody complains when you give them a raise. It's also a way to avoid problems with the union. If you don't do it, you're going to lose people. How are you going to compete with North American salaries? The first-class researchers are going to leave you. You need to modernize. Do you remember the spectrophotometer worth eleven thousand dollars that you insisted on building ourselves in one of the electronics labs in Tonantzintla rather than spending that much money? We had no idea how to do it, and it ended up costing us twelve thousand dollars. You always insisted that we make our instruments, although we were never trained to do that. However, we obeyed you in the electronic and optic labs, and we had some successes. We received patents in micromachinery and for solar cells, transistors and capacitors, electricity condensers. That made you proud, because Texas Instruments showed an interest in them, but in the end, we were too late. Do you know why we obeyed you, Doctor? Out of fear. In Tonantzintla, everyone except for Rivera Terrazas is afraid of you."

Dizzy from Fabio's criticism, Lorenzo's only answer was to stand up and leave. He refused to allow Fabio to accompany him. He descended the grand staircase, which was surrounded by Diego Rivera's murals, and went out into the street. He hadn't eaten, but he didn't feel hungry. His sadness nourished him. I'm out of touch, he thought. I don't understand anything. It was imperative that he find another location in Mexico to establish a new observatory and install a more powerful telescope. It was no longer possible to observe with the forty inches. The construction of the new observatory would include optic and electronic laboratories. And of course, space for teaching and research. Tonantzintla had been left behind, but not the Tonantzintla and Tacubaya bulletins that had made him famous throughout the world. At least there was that.

Lorenzo's trips abroad were the only things that alleviated the anguish his country caused him. He was invited not only to the observatories at Kitt Peak, Mount Palomar, and Mount Wilson in the United States, but also to the ones in Tololo and Córdoba in the Southern Cone. He now knew Mount Brukkaros in southeast Africa, and Bloemfontein, which he visited with emotion because he had missed becoming director there by the skin of his teeth. The current director greeted him: "So you are the great Dr. Tena!" Specialists from the Smithsonian Astrophysical Observatory, from the American Astronomical Society, and from the International Astronomical Union met periodically at conferences in the great capitals of the world. Exhilarated, Lorenzo would board a plane, remembering the phrase often quoted by astronomers: "The trips are for screwing and getting drunk." And he would drink like a barbarian. He was a different man. He would have thrown his wallet into the first river he came across if a girl had asked him to. The Seine, the Thames, the Danube? You choose. Several times in London he walked through Piccadilly and Downing Street in search of something, but he never did find it, and truth be told, he never even knew what he was looking for. "The heart is a lonely hunter," wrote Carson McCullers, and Lorenzo, well armed and more capable, had shot into the air and the prey had fallen, calling him "Aztec" and begging him to please rip out its heart. Yet now he felt like the poor fawn coming down from mountainous country, as if all the shotguns of the world were aimed at him. He was crippled and badly wounded, full of memories, old, and at the same time like a newborn. His love for Fausta made him vulnerable. How many things he had learned and forgotten in the last few years. He was used to making Claudines and Colettes fall in love with him, telling them he loved them deeply. For all practical purposes, Lorenzo was a desirable bachelor, director of two scientific institutes in an exotic country that Frenchwomen, Russian women, Polish women, Czech women, and Italian women wanted to visit. Nothing seemed as romantic to them as building a life with an astronomer who would awaken them with the birth of the sun to make love, the Milky Way in the center of their bed.

The Mexican entertained them by telling them about the astronomer Tycho Brahe, a favorite of King Frederick II of Denmark in the sixteenth century. Brahe had built Uraniborg, a splendid Gothic castle, on the island of Hven, which had been a gift from the king. He studied the stars from its towers, domes, roofs, and balconies.

Although Lorenzo was much too technical, the women pretended to understand him, because he captivated them with his story. To be in love with an astronomer, to be the mistress of an island, to live in the castle of the stars, what an incredible dream. Each time the Mexican threatened to end his account, they would shout, "Noooooo!" in unison, and Tycho Brahe became as popular as John Wayne. The fact that Tycho Brahe was an accomplished observer was irrelevant compared with what he gave to his lover: the sun, the moon, planets, and comets. Brahe had a fervent disciple named Kepler, who read and reread his fourteen volumes, but Tycho died sad, like all astronomers, on October 24, 1601.

"Why do astronomers die unhappy?" asked Elma Parsamian, a lovely Armenian astronomer.

"Because they cannot see."

Lorenzo admired the Byurakan Observatory in Armenia, which was converted into a magnificent and rich institution, mostly owing to the efforts of Viktor Ambartsumian. When Lorenzo saw it for the first time, in 1956, it was a little smaller that Tonantzintla. Ambartsumian had built it into one of the most prosperous and active observatories in the world. The Mexicans didn't have anything like it in any scientific field. The president of the Academy of Sciences of Armenia had also promoted an impressive chain of scientific, technical, and humanities institutions that were exactly what Lorenzo had dreamed of for Mexico: metallurgy, biology, geology, physics, astronomy, mathematics, petrochemistry, chemistry, mechanics, optics, electronics, history, and philology. All this in a small republic of barely three million inhabitants.

At Byurakan, the things that had once intoxicated Lorenzo no longer had the same meaning. Content with himself—a rare condition—he no longer felt at such a disadvantage with Ambartsumian, for whom his esteem continued to grow. This man had discovered the special distribution of galactic clouds, while also working fourteen and sixteen hours a day on his administrative responsibilities. He attended to a world of problems without considering it a waste of time—unlike Lorenzo, for whom administrative tasks were unbearable.

"What fails the most, Viktor, is the human material," Lorenzo said. "They may or may not be smarter at Byurakan, but at least they never sabotage themselves. In Mexico they wanted to establish a union. I told them that if they worked twenty hours a day, they'd have a right to their stinking union."

"Things go wrong here too, Tena, my friend." Ambartsumian smiled. "You just need to have patience."

"That's exactly what I don't have. Men and women infuriate me. I abhor them, and then I regret it."

"It's useless to regret anything," concluded Ambartsumian.

What a shame there weren't remarkable men like that in Mexico. Thanks to Viktor, Lorenzo's work was known in the Soviet Union, which filled him with humble pride. If he could only accomplish in Mexico a tenth of what Viktor had achieved. Fucking country—and the men who were part of it. Fuck them all. The rhetoric and the lack of vitality forced him to conclude that Mexico was irretrievably lost. " 'We are the wretched of the Earth,' " Diego Beristain had told him, quoting from Frantz Fanon. Lorenzo argued that the most privileged contented themselves with being senators of shit, deans of second-rate universities, leaders of slums, or, worse yet, recipients of worthless awards and fame.

Byurakan, a true Tower of Babel, entertained the Europeans and the North Americans, taking droves of them to Yerevan, to archaeological sites from the fifteenth century B.C. The average income in Armenia was quite high, and the majority of the population worked in agriculture. Lorenzo couldn't help but draw comparisons. If only we Mexicans could hope to be at this point within half a century, he thought. He boiled with rage against Mexico's consolidating demagoguery, the hunger, the lack of education, and he dissolved into criticism of the PRI—the ruling party—and their poor form of governing.

Invited by Ambartsumian, he attended the placement of the first stone of the new institute for scientific instrumental design and construction, in Ashtarak, a town close to Byurakan. Those present were the most noted groups of the region as well as the humblest workers and peasants. It was impossible for Lorenzo to distinguish the peasants from the well to do, something that would never have happened in Mexico.

He spent hours with Jean-Claude Pecker, Evry Schatzman, and Charles Fehrenbach. Drinking Armenian wine that to him seemed sublime and to them contaminated, these French friends were hellbent on collaborating on a project in Baja California. Fehrenbach had invented a comparative spectrum to measure radial velocities. This was one time Lorenzo was sorry he didn't have a better command of French. The language triggered memories of the Marist school and that damned Father Laville! He told them with astonishing fury that he had closed himself off from everything French after the priest had caressed his thighs, saying, "These little West-phalian hams . . ." Lorenzo broke up laughing when he saw the hi-larity his story provoked. "You really are an Aztec, Lorenzo!" They would publish his articles in their entirety whether he spoke French or not. This would be his first publication in Armenian and Russian.

Lorenzo made everyone at Byurakan laugh with his soft growls, exaggerated gestures, and groans. He courageously held his own with only a few words of Armenian. After a meticulous exam-ination of dictionaries and photographs, he was able to clarify is-sues. Exhausted, he tossed and turned at night in bed, trying to explain himself to the men and begging the universe for an expla-nation.

When the discussions ended, when they had each repeated their case two and three times, Lorenzo retired to his hotel room. He awoke at four in the morning and had to wait until eight, when the observatory restaurant opened. It was entertaining to watch him ask the servants, with gestures and faces that made them laugh, for eggs and café con leche. Maybe I chose the wrong voca-tion, he thought. I'm really a fantastic mime. He became one of the most popular visitors. The Armenians stood in line for him to ac-cept their invitations to join them in a breakfast of garlic and vodka.

Having completely lost his sense of time, he had the strange im-pression that he was floating in a void. He didn't know who he was, what the hell he was doing, where he came from. He wasn't sure whether he was his own spectator or the subject of a good or a bad joke. He was neither happy nor disagreeable, just neutral, like a fragment of meteor that moves or is stationary according to laws he was not familiar with. Without a newspaper within reach, he truly believed that nothing was happening in the world, except for Byu-rakan, its scientists, and its silence. The work continued as if part of eternity. Why rush if the universe is infinite and time has only the meaning it is given? He dreamed, floated, remembered Fausta like a distant star with which he could not communicate. Mexico also spoke a strange language; there was no code capable of deci-phering it. Did Mexico really exist? When had he lived there?

What made him Mexican? His was a message without a destination, hurled into infinity just to see if someone would find it. Maybe Fausta?

Maybe he didn't exist. He lived inside his head. His thoughts, asleep or awake, were beautiful at times and at other times torture. How would Fausta see him? Would she remember him? Was he just a venerable old man to her? He had always wanted to abolish the kingdom of feeling. He detested intuition, but now he lived in a sort of hypnotic somnambulism that sometimes made him fear for his sanity. A strong ice-water bath would bring him back to his senses. The rest of the day would be spent floating in a fantastic world that reminded him of Tycho Brahe's dream come true.

Suddenly, in some hotel bed, he would awaken distressed, saying, "Where am I?" As his forehead broke into a cold sweat, it was a struggle to remember. According to the clock, there was a ten-hour difference with Mexico. Therefore, Fausta needed ten hours to reach him. What desperation it was not to be able to make the little clock hands match up. I left Fausta a thousand years ago, he thought. For the first time, he felt as though he were far away, truly very far. He had sent a telegram that was unanswered: LOVE ME, FAUSTA.

When Ambartsumian asked him what was wrong, he responded that he loved Fausta ferociously. "My head is full of stupid, ugly birds," he said. "I tend to forget much of what hurts, encircling myself in a great silence—this magnificent and egotistical silence that we protect ourselves with. All of a sudden the sharp sound of reality erupts and brutally stuns us. How is it possible to live alone so comfortably, so protected, so indifferent?"

Ashamed that he could not conceal his moodiness, he realized that he had reached his limit for staying on in Byurakan. He felt like a donkey on a treadmill, repeating the same argument a thousand times. It's that witch who has put a spell on me. I don't feel good anywhere, thought Lorenzo, annoyed.

Fausta's vitality was aging him. The quickness of her movements was the final blow. When they walked through the Tonantzintla countryside, she, like a pup, got ahead of him, ran back and forth, doubled his distance. She'd take off running in front of him, to return with her cheeks red, her hair blowing, every part of her smiling, even her sex, which he still did not possess.

As they walked, Fausta would break off little branches of rosemary, crush them between her fingers, and put them to her nose. "Smell it, Doctor. How marvelous." She told him about fields of lavender she had bicycled through in France. When? She didn't say. There are women who surround themselves with a halo of mystery, and Fausta was one of them. She walked a lot, frequently going to Cholula on foot.

Lorenzo teased her: "Why don't you train to walk to Puebla and then maybe the Federal District?"

Fausta responded innocently, "Puebla isn't far. I can walk twelve kilometers easily; the tiring part is coming back."

"Your feet must be really tough."

"Oh, yes. Do you want to see?"

Lorenzo did not understand the magic ingredients of her universe.

He looked at her, and her lack of awareness saddened him. "You are like your species, a moral imbecile." He wanted to bleed her, empty her of herself, occupy that space inside her. Ah, how I hate her. Ah, how I love her! Her smallest pore, the tiniest of her down hairs was an object of irritation, of veneration. If he could ever kill anyone, it would be her.

Ever since he started dealing with her, his heart and his head were in a state of torment. Fausta hurt him in the deepest part of his being. Was that love?

At a meeting of university deans, the dean from the University of Puebla addressed Lorenzo, who was not saying a word: "You are an authority, Doctor. We'd like to hear your opinion about higher education."

"I'll speak when the dean of the University of Chilpancingo stops chewing gum."

They looked at him, astonished, and immediately the meeting broke up. On the road back to Tonantzintla, Lorenzo felt bad. Why humiliate the young dean? He didn't measure the significance of his words; he had caused discord on other occasions as well.

Fausta listened to him with the same incredulity when Lorenzo asked her, upon finding her at the observatory, "Fausta, when you saw me, was I walking to the right or to the left?"

"To the right."

"Ah! Then I've already eaten."

His enthusiasm for astronomy equaled his rejection of anything that wasn't directly related to it. The only thing he found time for, besides his research, were the three horses, which had arrived at Tonantzintla as a gift from Domingo Taboada, benefactor of the observatory. "Doctor, you have a lot of space. You can give these noble animals a roof over their heads."

"They're going to wreck my fruit trees."

"Keep them in the lower land where there aren't any."

Lorenzo went out to walk with two apples in the pockets of his jacket, one for Tom Jones. When the horse bit into one, Lorenzo sunk his teeth into the other one with the same exploding sound.

After Tom Jones had come La Muñeca, white and sweet. Domingo Taboada was careful to inform Lorenzo that she was pregnant; otherwise the director would not have accepted her. The day her little colt was born—before Fausta's bewildered eyes—Lorenzo had rolled up his shirtsleeves and put his hands inside the animal. "Bring water," he yelled to the paralyzed woman.

When the colt was standing next to its mother, Fausta asked, "Where did you learn that? I never imagined you as a midwife."

Lorenzo smiled. "It's my secret."

She caressed the soaked animal. "What are we going to name it?"

"El Arete."

What an enigma that Dr. Tena was.

He challenged Fausta. "Let's see if you're skilled enough to ride Tom Jones."

"I don't know how to ride, Doctor. In any case, I'd ride La Muñeca because she's shorter."

"Terrazas said that you can do everything, so I'm waiting."

Fausta resented the director, and he in turn would have liked to split her open, wring her out like a rag, lay her guts out in the sun.

"Doctor, I've often thought that torturers must be just like you."

"Why do you say that?" said Lorenzo, offended.

"Because you always confront those around you. I, on the other hand, believe that people are always better than they seem."

"Really? Well, here in Tonantzintla we have a common goal, but we all compete to achieve it."

Lorenzo assured Fausta that—just as in the sixteenth-century legend that inspired Marlowe for his *Dr. Faustus*—the devil had appeared to him in the form of a dog.

Fausta smiled, but she stopped when she saw him aim his rifle at a black dog that was climbing the slope and shoot it right between the eyes. The animal flipped in the air and fell.

Terrazas had already told her that Tena was an excellent shot, but this alarmed her. "I never thought he could kill a dog. That man scares me," she told him.

"Why?"

"I hate people who hunt."

"Tena is a born hunter. He runs over them on the highway as well."

"Oh, my God."

With infinitely sad eyes, Lorenzo once asked Fausta, "Couldn't you and I go to an isolated country where we wouldn't have to worry about anything?" But in the next instant he attacked her: "You're like Mephistopheles. You've come to tempt me, to make me believe that you have the solution I'm looking for. But of course Mephistopheles is a caricature, a poor devil."

"And I'm a poor devil?"

"Maybe. I'm not saying you aren't."

"I may be a poor devil, but I don't kill defenseless animals."

"Really? What about the cat you hung from the tree?"

"I was a child and not in my right mind."

"How about your big meal of sacred Hosts?"

"That was intentional."

Fausta and Lorenzo were linked by an adolescence that still disturbed them.

Seeing her at a desk in the library, Lorenzo approached with a smile: "Will you give me the rejuvenation potion?" And he left as abruptly as he had entered.

Sometimes Fausta would become impatient. "You, as far as I know, Doctor, have not spent any length of time with a woman. You don't know what it's like to love like crazy."

"Ah, and you do?"

"I have excellent intuition. I know that if you're obsessed with me, it's because you don't have an emotional life."

How many years had it been since Fausta had made herself indispensable at Tonantzintla? It was bliss to see her go up to the observatory on her long, elastic legs. She took young women's strides and exposed her face to the sun. Lorenzo noticed her crow's-feet. "I think she must be around forty," confirmed Terrazas.

Sometimes Fausta disappeared for a month or two. She traveled. Alone? Where did she go?

"To Greece."

"What do you mean to Greece? With what money?"

"With my savings. When you were in Armenia, I went to Greece. I had to see Mycenae."

Lorenzo burned with jealousy and looked for any occasion to punish her. And he always found it, because Fausta gave him cause at every instant. She planted flowers next to the forty inches, and when he saw them, Lorenzo ordered Guarneros to pull them up.

"Why? Miss Fausta planted them."

"If you don't get them out, I will do it." And in a moment of rage, Lorenzo pulled them up, roots and all. Later, on a stroll, he found them again at the far end of the immense garden, planted all together. I'm such a beast! he told himself. He was ashamed when he saw them, because when Fausta asked him what damage the flowers caused, he had responded furiously, "They don't belong alongside an observatory. This is a place of work." I'm a piece-of-shit cretin, he thought later. Fausta brings out the worst in me.

Unlike him, Fausta did not seem to get agitated. If he flew into a rage, she disappeared for a day or two months, and then Lorenzo missed her so much that people at the observatory commented, "Dr. Tena is pretty mad because Fausta left him." She had become his thermometer. She would return, and Lorenzo would go back to normal. Then he fished for clues in her words to calm his fears.

"The only thing that would bother me would be to feel like I'm a foreigner," she said.

That made him conclude, There's no way she would leave again. But Fausta would take another trip, and his unpleasant disposition would return.

When they walked in the evening, after a cup of tea, she said things that calmed him. She pointed to the valley in front of them. "This is the light I'd like to see at my hour of death." She was cruel. She must have been aware that he would die before her, and he, out of shyness, didn't speak to her about death, but was enraptured by her surprising youth.

"Yes, they say I'm like Julio Cortázar," said Fausta. "The Argentine writer who is reenergized each year. A very tall and good man."

"Do you know him?" Lorenzo asked.

"Yes, and he gave me a bottle of his magic elixir, with the condition that I not share it with anyone."

It was impossible to size her up. Maybe someone else could, but he, Lorenzo Tena, was incapable of it. His strength lay in his tenacity, in the logic of his judgment, in his inability to give in. And now he had become obsessed with this woman whom he condemned every time she turned around, and he could not destroy her even when he was alone. "I hate her," he repeated uselessly. What was Fausta? Explain to me, my love, what I don't understand. Tell me who you are; tell me what I can do to stop loving you. Everything about her should have repelled him. Fausta smoked marijuana; she did drugs. The young people felt that she was one of them, although in reality she no longer was. Why had she never gotten drunk with him? "Doctor, sir. See you later, Doctor." My God, how distant. Fausta guarded herself from him. Could he have had her at some moment? Maybe in the beginning, when she first arrived at Tonantzintla—that night when she invited him in after the uninhibited dance with the rock and roller. She had definitely conquered him. It was so easy with other women, but she put up a barrier that he crashed into. Neither through meticulous analysis nor with the constancy of his observation of the T Tauri stars would he be able to understand her source, her consciousness, her evolution. She was the most complex and perturbing object of all those he had observed throughout his long life. By his own choice after the flare stars, he had chosen the blue objects. He never chose Fausta. She had fallen like a meteorite on the cupola of the forty inches, mortally wounding him. Why didn't she stay floating up there? Lorenzo, restless, was now fully aware of his limitations and his predisposition to judge her. Maybe that same lack of mental aperture impeded him from understanding the celestial phenomena.

The recourse of experimentation was denied him; what could he do with her? Dismember her? He had always been a practical observer, and now he was confronting a theoretical problem of extraordinary complexity. Although he put her on plates under a microscope, he didn't understand her. Maybe she was just an insignificant thread, a woman like any other, just a little crazier, whom he had obsessively magnified. But even with that rationalization he could not erase her from his thoughts.

With Fausta he lived the verses of the Song of Songs, which he and Diego had memorized in elementary school: "Love is more potent than death, jealousy is stronger than hell, and its ardor is like the fire of Jehovah's flames . . . Many waters cannot extinguish it, nor the rivers quench it . . . Although one may give his life and his home for love, all he will gain is disdain."

Nothing of consequence had yet happened between him and Fausta, but Lorenzo already experienced her disdain. That's what I have achieved, he repeated to himself. What I am swallowing by the handful—disdain. Fausta knows perfectly well that I love her, and she rejects me for it. Until this very day, once he was possessed, Lorenzo had always been able to throw "the women" very far from his thoughts. But now, at this twilight hour, Fausta possessed him.

With his tendency to idealize, Lorenzo saw everything in absolute terms. He hated or he loved. There was nothing in between. He threw his head back, closed his eyes, and took comfort in thinking about Saul Weiss, a truly unique student. Having this young man in Tonantzintla made up for everything else. Weiss would go far; he would bring glory to Mexico. Seeing him in his cubicle leaning over the desk, Lorenzo was in heaven. The boy's mother sent him clean laundry regularly every Friday, along with some treat that Saul would share. Mrs. Weiss was persistent; every two weeks her sharp voice could be heard on the telephone: "How is Saul doing, Doctor?"

When Weiss began to slack off, Lorenzo called him into his office. "What's wrong, Saul?"

"I'm in love."

He had fallen passionately for one of the secretaries, and one night at eleven he showed up at the forty inches looking for Lorenzo. "Doctor, would you mind giving me a ride to Cholula? I have to call Puebla urgently."

Lorenzo looked at the skinny, big-nosed boy, the goose neck and the incipient balding, the imploring eyes behind the thick glasses. Instead of becoming enraged, he closed the cupola. "Of course, Weiss. Let's go!"

"I can't sleep. I need to talk to my girlfriend."

"Good thing it's not your mother," the director said sarcastically.

Lorenzo was sure that once he was at Caltech studying on a

scholarship, Saul Weiss would forge ahead against adversity, like all boys who struggled with loneliness.

Then he found out that the girlfriend from Puebla had ended the relationship right before the boy left, but everything happened so fast that he never discussed it with Weiss, or Fausta.

"There is something strange about this boy. His mother won't leave him alone," Fausta said.

"He's a genius," protested Lorenzo, "and the rest is irrelevant."

At Caltech, his grades were not as good as expected. There was nothing to distract him; therefore nothing justified the decline in performance. Lorenzo was sure he would bounce back and wrote continuously to encourage him, convinced that the adjustment period had passed and that Weiss was on the right track.

Six months later Lorenzo received a telegram informing him that Saul Weiss had committed suicide, hanging himself in his closet with his belt. "I wouldn't care if I dissolved into nothingness," Weiss had said before he left for California.

Devastated, Lorenzo took to talking obsessively about the suicide. Weiss hadn't even left a note. "Maybe he had a brain tumor."

"No, Doctor. Don't delude yourself. He took his life by choice."

"Don't tell me that, Fausta. It's unacceptable."

"Amanda Silver"—Fausta confided to Lorenzo—"said that you provoke the young people to get the best out of them, but many feel like they are being attacked. Her exact words were, 'He keeps on fucking and fucking and fucking with them, and sometimes it pays off. But he doesn't know when to stop, and as a result, some have developed a terrible lack of self-confidence.' "

"Yes, I recognize that sometimes the results can be counterproductive, but Saul Weiss was a brain, Fausta—a brain."

"Let me tell you what else Amanda told me. She said you got down on your knees in front of Weiss; you wouldn't let him off the pedestal. And you did the same with Graciela Ocejo, an astronomer who has two children. When you asked her how they were doing in school, Graciela answered, 'My son is terribly lazy, and my daughter is very studious.' And when you asked why, she said, 'Because he's bored in school. It doesn't interest him, but he passes.' 'That's serious, Graciela,' you said. "Maybe it's because you don't pay enough attention to him.' Graciela answered, 'Ay, Professor, don't start with that. I already beat myself up. As it is, when I'm here, I feel like I'm a bad mother, and at home I think I'm a bad researcher, so don't hassle me or blame me for my son's behavior. He's old enough to take responsibility for himself.' "

"Amanda," Fausta continued, "says you're inconsistent. According to her, two days later you changed your mind completely, and when Graciela asked you for a letter of recommendation for Mount Stromlo, in Australia, you wrote that she was a good researcher as well as an exemplary mother. Graciela protested, 'Do you know what? I'm not an exemplary mother or an exemplary researcher. Sometimes I do all right. It appears that it's very hard for you to accept people for what they really are.' "

"What does this have to do with Weiss?" asked Lorenzo, exhausted.

"Amanda says that Weiss probably felt that you were raising him up to Orizaba Peak, and if he didn't live up to your expectations, you would drop him into Sumidero Canyon."

"Ah, so you consider me to be responsible for Saul's suicide?" Lorenzo collapsed.

"Of course not. Don't look so tragic."

"Then why are you telling me all this when it's so painful? Don't you see that I'm already upset?"

"I'm telling you because when times are tough, in difficult situations, people speak the truth, and this whole issue with Weiss is a difficult situation. Like Amanda, I too believe that your vehemence can hurt the kids. Saul got good grades, he handed in the homework, and you promoted him like he was a Mexican Einstein. But it seems to me that intelligence doesn't just consist of solving problems; you must also know how to identify problems. Weiss realized that he had to use his brain in a different way at Caltech and that he wasn't the only smart one. It could have thrown him into a depression."

"It's normal. Many get depressed when they first get there, but they adapt and then recover."

"Look, Doctor, a high grade point average is not a guarantee. You yourself didn't have any scientific training. With science you have to know how to invent problems—not only how to do homework, like Weiss did."

Fausta left Lorenzo in a state of total depression. Maybe Amanda Silver is right, he thought. I haven't had to be only an astronomer, but a civil engineer, an administrator, and a healer of souls. Maybe he had been wrong to think that everyone was as relentless as he was.

Lorenzo remembered the first day of the construction of the road to Devil's Peak in Baja California, when he thought he wouldn't have the strength to get off his horse. Pride forced him to keep pace all day with Carlos Palazuelos, the engineer, and his team. Holding on tightly to the animal's back, he pretended it was easy, although the protests from his back and kidneys clouded his vision. He felt certain he was going to fall. Stiffness had turned his legs into two rods; his arms were like iron; his fingers couldn't release the reins. How did he do it? Who knows? Fausta had looked at him uneasily. Either the engineer didn't notice or pretended not to. No one said anything when he sent word that he would not be dining. He simply couldn't stand up.

The pain in his muscles had kept him from sleeping. His temples throbbed all night. I won't be able to go on tomorrow, he thought. In the morning, with superhuman effort, Lorenzo climbed back into the saddle. His pride held him up. He had to set an example. I may die trying, but I won't back down.

In the days that followed, rain let loose, muddying the earth on the mountain and washing it away.

With the water running off his straw hat, the director felt his age. The oilskin poncho he wore covered the horse's haunches as well. Disturbed, the animal continually shook its head. Someone said that the ground would be very slippery; they had to be careful of the mire. Lorenzo took it to be directed at him—the oldest, the city person who was unfamiliar with the terrain.

"The water breaks down the will," commented Palazuelos cheerfully, and Lorenzo felt that he had to prove him wrong.

"Let's start before dawn, Palazuelos."

"No, Doctor. We can't ask them to do that. Besides, there isn't any light."

"We can buy petroleum lamps so we can start digging. It's the only way to defeat the water."

"Where have you seen that done?"

"I give the orders, Palazuelos."

"Yes, Doctor, but it won't work."

There's no question that construction is all about brute strength. We all become beasts of burden, thought Lorenzo. That was what he had to impose—his own strength—and he repeated sarcastically, "The Three Musketeers weren't the same either, twenty years later."

Every day was a confrontation of two forces on the sierra—a fight to the death between nature and the men's will. According to Homer in *The Odyssey*, two enormous wandering rocks, Charybdis and Scylla, had caused the death of the navigators as they crashed into them.

Could this be his odyssey?

Palazuelos and his second-in-command considered dynamiting the side of the mountain to open passage for the road. The dynamiters were waiting to insert the cartridges. But the quarry was too sandy; the mountain would come down.

"We don't need to shake this ground, but rather make it firmer. It's necessary for the terracing," said Lorenzo.

Palazuelos looked at him; this scientist seemed to know about everything. "We're not going to dynamite. We're going to put machinery in. The caterpillar goes in tomorrow," said Palazuelos with respect.

"A trailer will sink into the road here," commented El Hocicón between his teeth. He was the only one who wore a helmet. The rest worked under intolerable conditions. They didn't even have canteens. El Greñas wore a scarf on his head, knotted at each corner, so he could tolerate the rain and the sun.

The adverse conditions, the elevation, the pending forces of nature, and the loose rock made the road construction progress with infuriating slowness. If the terrain had been more consistent, they would have advanced two hundred meters a day, but the gravel

kept rolling down over the cliff. Suddenly, during the night, a five-
or six-meter section would sink to form a pothole that would take
days to fill in. They moved backward at an intolerable snail's pace.
At night, in his sleeping bag, Lorenzo could barely fall asleep,
counting the hours to return to the road. Between the preparations
and the lunch break, the roadworkers lost hours. No one seemed
eager to take up the mallet, the pick, or the shovel.

"It's a myth that roadworkers are laborers," Lorenzo said.

"Fortify yourself with patience, Doctor. That's the only way
we'll come out ahead."

Palazuelos told him that an engineer friend of his had recondi-
tioned a soccer field for the workers during the construction of the
Cuernavaca–Acapulco section of the road.

"That's all we need—to make a field for those idlers so they can
waste their energy."

"A soccer field wouldn't hurt anyone," intervened Fausta.

"If they felt you were sympathetic, Doctor, you'd get more out of
them," insisted Palazuelos.

"I've never heard of such a thing. They're being assholes, and
I'm the one who has to make concessions? It's immoral."

"A soccer field would keep them from spending their pay at the
canteen and visiting prostitutes. It's been tried before, Doctor, and
it improved production. Their camp should also be repaired."

"Our camp is the same as theirs, and we haven't considered
changing it."

"You have a sleeping bag, Doctor. They don't. I'm telling you
this not for humanitarian but for practical reasons. I've seen it myself. The better you treat them, the better they perform. Remember
what happened at the Colorada summit."

Lorenzo looked at Palazuelos with visible irritation. It took superhuman effort not to attack him. Thinking it over, his whole life
was made up of titanic efforts. Calm yourself, beast, calm yourself,
he told himself. The Valium helped, of course. What would he do
without medical science?

He shook with rage at the memory of the stubborn face of José
Vargas. Four years ago Lorenzo had bought a Texas Instruments radiometer to install on the highest peak of La Colorada. The device

cost a ton of money, more than $180,000, but the benefits would make it worthwhile. It practically ran by itself, the only requirement being to "check it"—which even a woman could do going up to the peak two times a week.

Three months later, Fausta had answered the phone in Tonantzintla. With a distraught look on her face, she told him that the radiometer was no longer there; the villagers had thrown the delicate electronic equipment into the gorge. Almost blind with rage, Lorenzo and Fausta took off for La Colorada, arriving at the village of San Fermín like a meteor, and headed straight to the city hall. Lorenzo asked for the names of those responsible. He found himself looking into the face of José Vargas, who avoided his eyes. As he stood there with five men, Vargas related that he had told his companions that if it didn't rain, they could blame the device that "the wise men" had put up there.

"When the engineers came to set it up," Vargas said, "I told you that the people wouldn't allow it, and you laughed at me. Listen, right after we threw it away, it rained for two nights—a continuous rain that got harder at dawn."

The men at city hall listened to José Vargas with respect. Lorenzo exploded and with a commanding voice told them that the radiometer would bring them incalculable benefits and that they had committed a crime against the good of the nation. Each man had a right to be an asshole, but none had the right to voluntarily screw the rest; they had committed a criminal act. "Take me to where you threw it!"

He attempted to rescue some of the pieces from the ravine. He picked up four antennas that were standing erect in the air like hairpins. He located some of the solar panels. How was it possible that this ignorant village hindered his progress? Suddenly he heard Carlos Palazuelos yell from below, "Don't move it. There's something here."

It was the body of a woman in an advanced stage of decomposition.

"No shit. It wouldn't be one of the bad ones," said a peasant. "It must be a girl from around here."

Fausta took Lorenzo's arm.

"Should I pick up the equipment?" asked Palazuelos.

"No. We have to report it. Everything has to be left just as it is."

On the trip back, Lorenzo asked Fausta what in the devil a girl could be doing in La Colorada, almost four thousand meters high.

Tears began to roll down Fausta's face. "Do you think they took her there to throw her off after they assassinated her? Poor woman, I'm sure she wasn't even twenty years old."

What kind of people were they who would throw their dead over a precipice? Who was that girl? Lorenzo went on to call her a child, and by seven that night, when the village began to mourn, he felt her death as if it were a personal loss. Poor child. Damned village! Nothing good could come out of here, not a radiometer or a meteorological station or an observatory. Nothing. They didn't deserve anything. Let them rot. The dead girl among the mangled devices became a symbol of the scientific failure of Mexico. With that, Lorenzo and Fausta put their arms around each other and returned to Tonantzintla.

Now, on this dark night in his bungalow in Tonantzintla, Lorenzo envisioned the girl's cadaver in the ravine, and then he saw Saul Weiss, in whom he had put all his hope. A black butterfly fluttered around his night-light, and Lorenzo thought, It's logical. That's how it should be. Florencia's death waits for me.

Lorenzo found Fausta in front of the computer, where he had left her hours earlier. The shawl had fallen from her shoulders. Her ability to adapt to this new tool, the Internet, surprised him. Without taking her eyes off the screen, she remained, like thousands of men and women all over the planet, in a hypnotic state, mesmerized, waiting for a signal.

Lorenzo still remembered the first computers, gigantic closets crammed full of cables. They were probably rusting in some junkyard, their brains fried by the sun, like the broken-down frames of the automobiles that were once glorious.

As he watched Fausta surrender to the computer, Lorenzo remembered when the first one arrived at Tonantzintla. It was set up in the electronic laboratory, and the González sisters didn't want anything to do with it. "I prefer my Olivetti," Graciela had argued, adding, "It's easier to press a letter of the alphabet that is printed on a black ribbon and leaves its image on the white page than to deal with this incomprehensible novelty." It was impossible for her to adjust. "I hate mice, and chasing one around on the screen is even worse."

Then Fausta had come to Lorenzo's defense. She learned to use it instantly, and her conversation changed. Bits, mobile cells, VHS, Web design, pagers, routers, encryption. Lorenzo protested, "What awful words. You're massacring the Spanish language." Windows. Windows to where? It was only a computer with a hard drive capable of connecting to the entire world in an instant and storing enough information to confuse the library of Babel, as if all the universal wisdom could be condensed in an electronic brain. That was all a computer would be until it could be reconfigured. There was no Quick Restore that could bring it to life.

Maybe Fausta was losing contact with the world because an artificial satellite emitted beeps—beeps that sent her twelve thousand million light-years away instead of bringing her closer. Her programs lasted at least three thousand hours. She ran to eat, if she ate at all, and returned, a cup of coffee in her hand, to cloud her vision, eyes reddened, back bent, inside a visual system designed to capture her and tie her definitively to the fiber optics.

The director baptized the observatory computer "Fausta." It was more of a bore each year, until it became this high density server Altos 1200LP, developed for users who required large processing capacity and needed to maximize space. Science needed to remain on the vanguard of the latest generation of equipment through wireless modems that accelerated the flow of information between the portable devices and the vast contents of the Internet.

Lorenzo claimed that he preferred to dictate to a slave. That's what the women around him were for, to take orders. Even under Fausta's guidance, the director confused the hardware with the Explorer, the bits with the microchips, the software with Microsoft. So much softness was more cutting to him than a knife.

He was missing a tiny connection that would link him to cyberspace. How was it possible that he, a man of science, was rejected by a plastic box? Plastic, no less! Such ignoble material.

The rules of the world of technology were as merciless as he had been years earlier when he insisted at the academy that scientists present new research every three years.

Fausta had never given him the attention that she now lavished on these disturbing boxes.

"You're a computer nerd," he said to her.

"Doctor, this connects me to the men and women of the world."

"Globalization is the new totalitarianism. While you lose yourself inside the computer, I am what I do. That is my identity. I'm a researcher, and I don't go looking around the entire world for a group to join."

Lorenzo once again experienced the frustration he had felt during the fifties, when, his heart accelerated, he had focused the telescope and the Schmidt camera didn't respond. What desperation when the physical means have reached their limit. But he had conquered the Schmidt, and now he was shut out by the two Faustas, both of which were much more complex.

It was cold. Fausta picked up her shawl and arranged it over her shoulders. Was she aware of how much time she spent in front of the computer? Would she exhale her last breath in front of it? "Take that shawl off!" he ordered. "Nothing makes a woman look older than wearing a shawl."

Lorenzo read "mexico.com.mx, servidor unam, search engines." Fausta, that fatal feminine monster, usurped his science and diminished his knowledge. He didn't distinguish between his love for Fausta and his jealousy of the knowledge she hid from him. The accumulation of these tiny signals that shone like stars seemed to say that life in Tonantzintla might revolve around the orders of an intelligent man, but the Hewlett-Packards and the Macintoshes enhanced the human brain, or—even worse—that Fausta the computer had absorbed the Fausta he considered a woman.

"Don't you want to go to the NASA Web page, Doctor? They're transmitting pictures of the solar eclipse live from western Europe," she informed him during one of the moments when she acknowledged his existence.

Years earlier, on July 20, 1969, they had sat together and watched the television as men landed on the moon, and Lorenzo hadn't been ashamed to cry in front of her. She had hugged him and kissed him as never before. He thought that maybe he, like the astronauts, had stepped on the moon and said along with Neil Armstrong, "That's one small step for man; one giant leap for mankind." But after the last kiss, Fausta would not allow him to accompany her home: "I'm really wired, and I have to walk alone for a while."

Now Lorenzo felt rejected by electronics and fell into the world of emotions. Did the computer have a sense of humor? Would it sing until it fell apart and couldn't enunciate the last syllables of the song "Daisy, Daisy," as in *2001: A Space Odyssey?* Although he had never allowed himself to do so before, Lorenzo asked, "Why doesn't the computer say, 'I want you to be very happy'?"

Lorenzo had eliminated Chava Zúñiga from his cenacle of thinkers. "He's not at that level; he's not a credible speaker," he told Diego

Beristain. Diego was the only one worthy of speaking with Arturo Rosenblueth. Norbert Wiener came to the physiology lab at the National Institute of Cardiology to develop a new cybernetic science, and Rosenblueth arranged meetings with him and with Lefschetz and other mathematicians, to which only Rosenblueth's nephew Emilio, José Adem, and Guillermo Haro were invited. Those meetings encouraged Lorenzo almost as much as the two-million-volt Van de Graaff electrostatic generator at the Physics Institute, and the proton and deuteron accelerator that Graef affectionately called "the little ball."

"Of all of humanity's utopias, this is the most perfect and the one that will survive," declared Fausta without taking her eyes off the screen, and she added, doctorally, "Those who lack complete and instant access to the Internet will be left in the dust."

"Fausta," the computer, corrected the page. What a shame Lorenzo's Fausta allowed herself to be contaminated by the Faustian spirit that forced him to participate in a story he didn't understand. Would Fausta know how to convert time, to transcend it? What filters did she possess with all her English terms about megabytes, call centers, and flexible solutions?

"Doctor, why don't you use the virtual library to find references to global astronomical advances?" Fausta had asked him. "Look, Doctor, the Internet is here to stay, and if you don't get into it, you're going to be left out. You know what I mean—out of the real world. Doctor, please, don't be stubborn. You don't need to go to Cholula anymore to buy the newspaper, or make conversation with the owner of the place while you wait for your change, or treat him like a friend so he'll hold it for you. On the contrary, you can read it on the Internet. Save yourself from the real world, and save all the time you waste standing on the corner."

A leap forward in technological communication was a step backward in Lorenzo's ability to communicate with Fausta. As she had said, he felt "left out." Every night, no matter how tired she was, she checked her electronic mail, and captivated, she stayed up until the wee hours navigating through thousands of portals that contained information that could be selected and printed on the Hewlett-Packard laser jet.

Trapped in the invisible space of e-mail, Fausta, previously so obliging, didn't pay attention to anyone. It seemed as if she went from one moment to the next through the monitor. One night after she had told him, exalted, "I have blind faith in cyberspace," Lorenzo asked her whom she was writing to with such speed and emotion.

"To Norman," she responded.

"To Norman?" Lorenzo was surprised.

"To which Norman?"

"To yours, to ours. We've been writing to each other so often that we've become romantically involved through the Internet. We write daily."

Lorenzo turned his back to her.

"Do you want to say something to him, Doctor? I always give him the latest news about you."

"No. When I want to write to him, I'll dictate to my secretary." Lorenzo could hardly speak. He left the lab like a zombie. Surely that bit about them being romantically involved was just Fausta being sarcastic, but you never could tell with her.

Lorenzo slept badly, and when he was finally able to fall asleep, he had a nightmare—Fausta and Norman wrapped around each other, laughing from the horrific blue screen. The next morning, Lorenzo called her to his office.

"About Norman, is it true?"

"Of course it is, Doctor. I've even visited him at Harvard."

"How is it possible that he never said anything to me about it?"

"Maybe he didn't want to hurt you and planned to tell you at some point. I don't know. People in love, Doctor, are alone in the world. They forget about everyone else."

"People in love?"

"Norman and I."

Lorenzo hid his face in his hands, and Fausta repressed an urge to console him.

"That's all, Fausta. You may leave."

On an impulse, he took his briefcase and decided to go to Mexico City. The days that followed were dreadful. Diego, his confidant, wasn't in the city, and Chava would have laughed at him. In any case, it didn't matter. It had also been years since he had purged Juan and Leticia from his life. He hadn't even gone to visit when Leticia was admitted to the hospital on the verge of death. Weighed down by the tasks of the observatory, Lorenzo had let time pass. As he put work before his own health, not to mention his love life, he was letting go of the ties that joined him to others. He had forgotten about Norman, except for the occasional professional letters they exchanged. He, who always found the solution to problems and setbacks, recognized a lost frontier in Fausta. A virus, that's what she was, a virus—the biggest that could attack a computer. And Norman, in his format conversion, was a hacker who was liable for the criminal theft of information, against which Lorenzo would act. Ah, he would act! As soon as he felt able to return to Tonantzintla, he would fill out Fausta's termination papers. She would never again enter the observatory. Second, he would voice his feelings of betrayal to the gringo. Third, he would learn to use the computer, whatever the cost. He would surf the net; he would respond as Fausta had. He would expand and deepen his virtual world; he would sell his soul to the devil. Nothing would defeat him. He could still hear Fausta telling him, "How are you going to differentiate yourself, Doctor, from the new cybernauts with portals born outside of our borders? In the coming era, high-risk investment funds will give preference to the portals that add a comprehensive assortment of peripherals to any computer through a universal-size plug-and-play connection, inherently faster with digitalization. Doctor, the solutions now need to interface with the Web and to be interchangeable and adaptable."

Two weeks later, Lorenzo honked the horn at the door to Tonantzintla and entered with the shining armor of his resolve. He asked Graciela González, as casually as he could, for Miss Fausta.

"She hasn't been here for three days," the secretary said. "She has a virus. Unfortunately, a lot of e-mails have piled up."

The next morning, Lorenzo decided to go down to the village to look for her. She opened the door herself. She was alone in the house. The black circles under her eyes attested to the flu. Seeing her, an immense feeling of compassion invaded him—for her and for himself. He thought of saying, I'm reconfigured, my love, and I ruption. I'm truly crazy! he said to himself. Why haven't I fought as hard for Lorenzo the man as I have for Lorenzo the astronomer? With Fausta, I'm going to stop revolving in this solitary orbit and return to everyday life. This is my last chance.

An uncontrollable emotion caused Lorenzo's hands to tremble. "What am I doing here instead of being down there with her?" he said aloud. Yes, definitely, he wanted to live with her. It wasn't too late to have children, a girl he would name Florencia. Yes. It was impossible to lose Fausta. She was his health, his reason for being. What did reaching completely inaccessible regions matter to him? What were his discoveries of six spectacularly distant objects worth without Fausta? Now he would possess her slowly, give her pleasure; he would wait for her. Now they would love each other. They would finally conclude an act of love postponed for years. Leticia's resplendent figure emerged. He said to himself, For the first time in my life, I'm going to be like you, little sister.

Swiftly, Lorenzo closed the cupola, covered the console, and, with his heart in his throat, ran down the hill to Fausta's house.

Not in his worst nightmares did he ever think that no one would open the door to him, or that Don Crispín, curiously awake at that late hour, would see him and tell him, "I saw her leave a while ago. She looked bad. She took a suitcase. I asked her when she would be back, and she said never."